THE VATICAN CONSPIRACY

PETER HOGENKAMP

THE VATICAN CONSPIRACY

bookouture

Published by Bookouture in 2020

An imprint of Storyfire Ltd.
Carmelite House
50 Victoria Embankment
London EC4Y 0DZ

www.bookouture.com

ISBN: 978-1-83888-843-5
eBook ISBN: 978-1-83888-842-8

Blood alone moves the wheels of history.
Benito Mussolini

War begets war, violence begets violence.
Pope Francis

CHAPTER 1

Father Marco Venetti dabbed the sweat from his beard and fanned the air with his rescinded invitation to the papal mass in St. Peter's Square. It was stifling inside the confessional, and the faithful weren't in a penitent mood this week, giving him nothing to think about other than the appalling heat and his canceled trip to Vatican City. Not that he minded a reprieve from the usual slate of sins—*I have taken His name in vain, I missed mass last week without an excuse*—but it was especially warm this afternoon, and the prevailing breeze had taken an untimely midsummer break.

He heard the shuffle of feet coming from outside his door and sat up in his chair. The door opened, and the kneeler creaked as the penitent—a woman, he guessed, about one hundred and thirty pounds from the groan of the ancient cypress—readied herself to make confession behind the screen. "Bless me, Father …"

Her voice was sultry and familiar, and he still heard it echoing inside his skull late at night when the sea was calm and the waves licked the shore beneath the rectory.

"… for I have sinned. It has been one year since my last confession."

For a second, he couldn't believe it was really her, but her scent was unmistakable, an intoxicating mixture of lavender and Sciacchetrà, the local wine made from aged grapes.

"May the Lord be in your heart to make a good confession."

"I have done something terrible, Marco … I didn't mean to. You must believe me."

He could see only the outline of her head through the opaque shield between them, but his memory painted in the flowing curls of dark hair and the rose color of her full lips—the way she had looked when she had moved away from Monterosso al Mare four years ago, never to return.

"I tried to make a go of fishing. But the Japanese have stolen all the tuna."

He could imagine the splay of her soft hands and the pleading in her brown eyes.

"I need to feed my family. You must understand this."

"What happened, Elena?"

Her breath rushed out, the kneeler scraped against the warped wooden flooring, and she moved out from behind the screen and sat in the chair less than a meter in front of him—nothing between them now other than the warm air and the sacred vows he had sworn. Despite the dim and unflattering light in the confessional, her black hair had lost none of its luster, and her eyes shone as brightly as ever.

"You remember that man I told you about?"

"Antonio?"

"Yes, him."

Antonio was a member of the 'Ndrangheta, the Calabrian crime syndicate that had expanded its reach throughout Liguria and the north of Italy. Marco had done his best to keep Elena away from him; the mobster had been far too interested in her, more, he feared, for the sleek contours of her figure than for the want of her boat. He had envied Antonio, and any other man who could stare at her olive skin, burnt to perfection by the Mediterranean sun, without the constriction of a collar.

"I thought I told you to steer clear of him."

"You did, but I didn't listen. I thought you were just jealous."

"I *was* jealous." A breeze sparked up, carrying with it the odor of salt air and incense. "Isn't jealousy what comes from unrequited love?"

"Your love wasn't unrequited. I loved you just as much as you loved me, perhaps more."

His eyes strayed from her high cheekbones down to the strong line of her jaw, and then even further, to the plunging neckline of her black blouse.

"Then why did you leave?"

"Because you were always going to love God more than you loved me. And I grew tired of sharing you with Him."

A flutter of wings came from above; the pigeon nesting underneath the church eaves had returned to her nest, setting off a chorus of chirping from her squabs.

"I thought things would change, that you just needed more time to see how happy we could be together. But the weeks became months, and the months turned into years, and still you chose God over me."

"What was I supposed to do?"

The chirping of the squabs reached a crescendo, filling the confessional with a shrill warbling.

"You were supposed to leave the priesthood. Choose me over God."

"I couldn't do that, Elena."

"No, damn you, you couldn't."

She leaned in closer, and the neckline of her blouse plunged even further.

"And that's why you still sleep alone every night. You always told me how much you hated the long, lonely nights."

She slid the chair forward, and her foot brushed up against his. The smell of lavender thickened, and a familiar tightness gripped his chest.

"I am a vengeful woman. I had to leave before my resentment could turn into bitterness and hatred."

"Resentment for whom? Me, or God?"

"For both of you."

The pigeon flew away, and the chirping subsided. All Marco could hear was the quick rhythm of Elena's breathing and the mad drumming of his own heart.

"Antonio came to see me a few weeks ago, to ask if I wanted to pick up some refugees. He told me they were looking for work. I didn't want to, Marco, but it was either that or lose my boat."

She paused, waiting for him to say something, but he didn't reply.

"I met them at night, in the Ligurian Sea, just north of Corsica. There were sixteen of them, and I knew straight off they weren't refugees. I tried to get out of the deal, right then and there, but he threatened me."

"Who threatened you? Antonio?"

"No, one of the men I picked up. His name was Mohammed. He told me he would kill Francesca and Gianna if I didn't do as they said."

Gianna was Elena's daughter, a lanky girl with her mother's dark complexion. Francesca was Elena's younger sister.

"How did he know their names?"

"Two of them had already come over. They had been following me around for days. When we got to the drop-off, Gianna and Francesca were waiting for us … Gianna was bound and gagged, and Francesca had been beaten."

Elena stopped speaking for a second and sobbed quietly into her folded hands. Marco was possessed by a powerful impulse to wrap his arms around her.

"When was this?"

"A week ago. I have to get the rest tonight."

"You must go to the police immediately."

"I can't. They are holding my daughter and my sister captive. Two of the men have been staying in my house for the last week. Mohammed told me he would kill my family and me if I tell anyone."

"Go to the police now, Elena."

There was no reply, only the creaking of the chair.

"They are following me. My family would be dead before I reached the police station."

"Listen to me. I want to forgive you. I will forgive you. I know you are sorry. But these men are dangerous."

"I know they are dangerous; he cut Francesca with his knife to scare me."

Marco could see her shaking, and shame overcame him. Elena had come here for absolution, not an inquisition. But there were lives at stake, and it was his duty to convince her to get help.

"You must go to the police."

"You must forgive me, Marco."

The waves slapped against the rocky footings of the church, and the sound of distant laughter floated in through the open windows.

"I will forgive you, but you must go straight to the police."

"He will kill my daughter. Gianna is innocent."

"Elena …"

"I won't do it, Marco."

The quiet conviction in her voice reminded him of her inner strength, the fierce will she had harnessed to raise her daughter by herself, to be a female fishing boat captain in an industry dominated by men. How he had been drawn to that strength, how he had borrowed from it when they were together, absorbing it like a sponge absorbed water.

"Lord Jesus, Son of God, have mercy on me, a sinner."

Marco nodded, exhaling slowly.

"For these and all the sins of my past life, I am truly sorry. O my God, I am heartily sorry for having offended you, and I detest all my sins because of Your just punishments …"

Elena finished the Act of Contrition as the chirping of the pigeon squabs resumed in earnest. Marco raised his right hand, wrapped with the ivory rosary beads his mother had given him on the day he had graduated from the Collegium Canisianum, the Jesuit seminary in Innsbruck, Austria. He had inherited his faith from his mother—his faith, his lean face, and his light blue eyes.

"God the Father of Mercies, through the death and resurrection of His Son … and I absolve you from your sins in the name of the Father, and of the Son, and of the Holy Spirit."

Marco exited the church through the side door, crossed the narrow courtyard overgrown with bougainvillea and potted tomatoes, and entered the rectory. Signora Grecci, his elderly housekeeper, had left a casserole of stuffed peppers warming on the stovetop. A pitcher of iced sangria sweated on the kitchen table. He descended into the cellar on ancient stone steps. Three cardboard boxes were shoved into a damp corner, and he carried the largest of these upstairs.

He retreated to his spartan office overlooking the Ligurian Sea and set the box containing his spearfishing equipment on the wooden desk. A worn wetsuit lay on the top, still soggy from his last dive. He picked it up, folded it, and laid it down on the edge of the desk. The next item was a pair of flippers—a gift from his diving instructor in the navy—and he placed these next to the suit. At the bottom of the box, next to the snorkel mask, were his diving knife and underwater torch. He fitted the torch into a loop on the suit and whetted the edges of the knife against a sharpening stone before slipping it into its sheath on the suit's right leg.

Crossing the tiny office to the closet tucked into the corner near Signora Grecci's room, Marco unlocked the door and examined the rack of spearguns fixed to the wall. There were three in total—the Father, the Son, and the Holy Ghost. He selected the Holy Ghost because he could never recall missing a shot with it, and fitted a titanium spear to it. It wasn't the Beretta 9mm he had used in his naval career—the gun that had saved his life and those of his salvage unit in Somalia on that fateful day—but he was going to need a weapon if he wanted to save Elena's life.

He closed the box and returned it to the cellar. On the way back to his office, he detoured through the kitchen to pour a glass of sangria, then reclined in his chair with his rosary beads wrapped around his hands, beseeching the Savior for courage.

Marco said evening mass with a fervor he hadn't had since his ordination and nibbled on the stuffed peppers in the rectory's small kitchen afterward. *Peperoni imbottiti* was his favorite dish, but there was enough garlic in it to awaken the dead, and his appetite was poor. Returning to his office after dinner, he killed time by working his rosary, but even the smoothness of the worn beads couldn't put an end to the disquiet in his soul. He walked over to the window and watched the water darken as the light died. He had stood there many times, mesmerized by the splashes of bright color in the harbor—the pink and orange buildings squeezed against the gray sandstone, and the blue and yellow rowboats littered along the winding path to the water—letting the words to a sermon drop into his head.

Elena had loved the view from the window as well, from her first meeting with Marco to register Gianna for catechism classes until that sunny afternoon with the sea breeze buffeting her hair when she had told him she was leaving. Many times, he had watched her standing in front of that window overlooking the bay, staring at the contrast of her shapely silhouette against the azure sky.

He returned to the desk, wrapped the rosary beads around his hands again—as his mother had taught him—and prayed for strength.

As soon as it was dark, Marco crossed himself and descended to the rocky beach below the rectory. A small boat with an outboard engine was tied there. He got in and motored out to sea. He ran quiet and blind, keeping his small searchlight switched off. It wasn't as if he needed to see anyway; he had made the trip hundreds of times before, and he could trim the rudder by the slap of the waves against the keel.

He cut the engine and used the oars to guide the craft into a small cove, well hidden from the Sentiero Azzurro, the clifftop walkway that connected the five villages of the Cinque Terre. He had been here many times before, casting his net for anchovies and listening to the arguing of the gulls. He secured the boat, stripped down to his wetsuit, and stuffed his clothes and speargun into a waterproof satchel. Looping the bag over his shoulders, he slipped his fins on and dove in, swimming away from the shore with powerful strokes. The currents in this cove were dangerous, and he knew no one else would be using this area to escape the heat.

He reached deeper waters and turned to the south, swimming parallel to the shoreline. Taking advantage of his long frame and a lifetime in the sea, he reached his destination in a half-hour and circled the boat, trying to determine if there was anyone on board. When he was satisfied there wasn't, he hoisted himself over the gunwales using the anchor chain and looked around.

The *Bel Amica* was just as he remembered it: a small diesel-powered fishing trawler in a horrific state of disrepair. There were countless such boats in these parts, probing the dying Mediter-ranean for the fruits of the sea. He grabbed his torch, adjusted the beam to a soft glow, and did a quick circuit of the boat. He found the storage closet right away, in the back corner of the wheelhouse. It should have contained cleaning supplies and equipment, but he had guessed it would be empty. He pushed aside an old mop, the sole occupant, and sat on the floor. Then he closed the door, which was warped from decades of exposure, and settled in to wait. The closet was cramped and warm and smelled of rat urine, but it was home for the time being.

He reached into his satchel, groping instinctively for his rosary beads before remembering that he had left them in his desk, where they wouldn't be a party to what was coming. His fingers closed over the plastic handle of the speargun. He placed it on his lap and closed his eyes, listening to the sounds of the sea: the scraping of the anchor chain, the popping of the hull as it bobbed in the swell, and the whine of the wind against the superstructure. The briny smell made him think of his father, who had been the captain of a destroyer in the Italian navy. That Marco might have chosen a different path had been out of the question, ever since his father had given him a radio-controlled boat when he was five; both he and his older brother Claudio had entered the navy directly after graduating from secondary school in Trieste.

The dull thud of oars against boat announced that he had company. He rested his palm against his weapon, but there was no need; there was no mistaking Elena's voice, uttering curses in low tones as she went around the boat in preparation for setting sail.

The engines rumbled, and the anchor chain clanked. It was a calm night close to shore, and the *Bel Amica* rocked gently with the swell, guided by Elena's practiced hand. Farther out to sea, the northerly gusts of the *tramontana* picked up, and Marco felt the laboring of the twin diesels beneath him as they tried to maintain speed against the headwind. Despite the lateness of the hour, he had no interest in sleep, and so he passed the time trying to imagine the men they were picking up—the men he planned to kill to save Elena's life.

CHAPTER 2

Corsica neared, announcing itself by blunting the *tramontana* and filling the air with the unmistakable scent of the Corsican *maquis*, the dense underbrush that smelled like rosemary and thyme. The fishing boat slowed to a crawl, and Elena thrust the port screw into reverse to maintain course in the chop. The thud of a gangplank signaled the arrival of passengers, and Marco sat up straight and put his hand on his speargun, listening to the shouts.

Someone entered the wheelhouse and began conversing with Elena in Arabic. A few other people boarded, and Marco committed their voices to memory. There was a high-pitched, almost effeminate voice, two guttural snarls, and a murmur with sepulchral undertones—this would be the one to watch. Marco had listened to enough disembodied voices to guess the whisperer had killed before, perhaps many times, and would relish doing so again.

It was the suffocating heat, the smell of diesel fumes, and the shouts of the men on board that broke open the vault in which he had buried the memory of the day, many years ago, when he had killed three men, Somali pirates all, but still children of the same God they all worshiped in one way or another. There had been eight altogether, six riding shotgun on either side of a skiff that had materialized on the starboard side of the *Anteo*, and two others on a second skiff on the lee side—a skiff he hadn't seen emerge out of the early dawn.

He had been on watch that morning, walking the length of the salvage vessel more to stay awake than for any other reason. Trying

to scare them off, he fired two rounds over their heads as the first
skiff came alongside, succeeding only in engendering a murderous
round of return fire from the pirates, all armed with a variety of
assault weapons, mostly AK-47s and AKMs. But he had chosen
his firing position well, tucked behind the boom of the crane that
lifted the submersible, and the bullets had only clanked off the
sturdy metal. And he would have continued to avoid deadly force
if it hadn't been for the RPG-7 one of the pirates had attempted
to bring to bear against the *Anteo*. A trio of bullets in the man's
chest had put a stop to the grenade attack; another man fell to a
head shot before the skiff sped away, disappearing into the murk
from which it had come.

It was over as quickly as that, or so he had thought, not realizing
that a second skiff had pulled up alongships on the lee side. One
pirate had already boarded by the time Marco had crossed the vessel
with some vague premonition that all was not well. He wouldn't
be alive to relive the moment again and again, during a thousand
restless nights, if the man's AK-47 hadn't snagged on a hanging
piece of pipe, giving Marco the chance to take him down to the
deck with a head-first dive. The pirate was a small man and wiry
thin, but Marco would remember to this day his feral strength,
the raw power in his frame that wasn't extinguished until he had
buried the hilt of his diving knife in the man's chest.

The engines throttled up, dispelling the unwanted memory. The
screws thrashed, rattling the floorboards. The *Bel Amica* started
a wide swing to starboard, making for home. Marco checked the
luminous dial of his diving watch and made some rough calcula-
tions. They were three hours from shore; Elena was still safe. He
guessed the men wouldn't kill the captain yet, needing safe passage
through unfamiliar waters. No, the danger zone was close to shore,
possibly within sight of the drop-off area.

He spent the next two hours listening to the enemy, gauging
their position and strength. After a time, he could identify the men

by the slap of their boots on the deck and the sound of their voices. The high-pitched one belonged to a small man named Amad. The snarlers were large, heavy men called Asim and Tariq, and the menacing voice belonged to Karim. There was no doubt Karim was in charge. Marco could tell by the way the others addressed him and the fear in Elena's voice when she spoke to the man.

With time, the men's voices moved off to other parts of the boat, leaving Marco and Elena alone in the wheelhouse. The minutes passed, marked by the creaking of the deck and the pit in his stomach that deepened with their inexorable advance toward shore.

At last a door swung open, and Tariq trod into the wheelhouse, barking a command at Elena. Elena said nothing. He repeated his command, which launched her into a tirade of Arabic that Marco was pretty sure hadn't been taken from the Koran. He squeezed the grip of the gun, knowing the hour was at hand. There was a loud crash, and the boat veered to port. He heard grunts of pain from the wheelhouse and the sounds of bodies rolling on the deck. He sprang up and thrust through the door.

In the dim light of the cabin, he saw Tariq kneeling over Elena, attempting to drive a knife into her chest. The man looked up in surprise as a new foe appeared out of nowhere and grabbed for the sidearm holstered on his waist. Marco raised the speargun and shot Tariq in the neck, keeping his streak with the Holy Ghost intact. Blood gushed from the jagged wound, staining the planking red.

Feet pounded on the stairwell leading up from the cabin beneath: Karim coming to his comrade's aid. Marco grabbed the handgun from Tariq and shot Karim three times as soon as he cleared the bulkhead. His rifle clattered to the floor, and he fell against the stairs and slid out of sight.

Elena pushed Tariq's lifeless body to the side and muttered something to Marco, but her words were drowned out by the angry shouts coming from outside the wheelhouse and the rush of more feet toward them. Marco would have been cut down if not for Elena. She dove at him, and they tumbled to the floor, falling down the stairs beneath a murderous hail of bullets. He landed against Karim and fired a volley into the wheelhouse, stopping the enemy's advance for the time being.

Elena thrust Karim's rifle into his hands. "Keep shooting."

Marco jammed the stock against his shoulder and squeezed the trigger, raking the cabin with a short burst as Elena struggled with a panel in the rear wall. She wrestled it free with a thump, revealing a crawl space into the bowels of the boat, and slithered inside head-first, with her arms pressed against her sides. He fired another salvo as she disappeared, not aiming at anything in particular, just trying to keep the men in the wheelhouse pinned down. Elena had something in mind, some gambit, and he needed to give her enough time to play it.

The clip was empty, and he discarded the rifle in favor of Tariq's handgun, firing every time he heard a movement. In between salvos, he rolled Karim over and searched him, but Elena had taken his sidearm; the only thing he was carrying was a folded piece of paper in the breast pocket of his shirt, which Marco slid into the waterproof compartment sewn onto the thigh of his wetsuit.

The murmuring above him increased, and he fired another shot, only to hear the hollow click of the firing pin. The men in the wheelhouse heard the noise as well, and Marco soon heard the slap of feet on the deck. He pulled his diving knife from its sheath, glad he'd had the forethought to sharpen it, and pushed against the wall abutting the stair, ready to ambush the pair as they stepped over Karim.

Two shots exploded above him, and then two more, followed by the thud of bodies against the floor. He let go of the wall and ascended into the wheelhouse. Elena was at the wheel; if there hadn't been enough dead bodies on the floor to fill a small morgue, he might have been able to convince himself the whole thing had never happened.

"Hello, Marco."

"Hello, Elena."

He moved forward to stand close to her. She didn't move away when his arm brushed against hers. Darkness filled the windshield, save for the stray wash of moonlight reflecting off a breaker. The smell of diesel fumes and blood stained the air.

"Where are we going, Elena?"

"Riomaggiore. Mohammed and another man are holding Gianna and Francesca in my house there."

"You moved to Riomaggiore?"

Riomaggiore nestled into the slopes above a rocky cove at the southernmost end of the Cinque Terre, less than ten miles away, but over an hour's drive, due to the twisting and precipitous roads, from Marco's rectory in Monterosso.

"Where did you think I went?"

Marco didn't say, which didn't mean he hadn't given it plenty of thought. At times, Elena's whereabouts had been the only thing to occupy his mind—that and the unmistakable feel of her, soft and warm, a feel that still tingled in his fingers more than he cared to admit.

"Where were you taking these men?"

"Castello di Giordano. Do you remember our time together there?"

He would never forget Castello di Giordano. It was a large medieval castle built on a rugged island off the coast near Fegina. He had gone there on retreat every year during the week after Easter, walking the paths in solitude, until the diocese had leased it out three years ago to cover costs.

"Of course I do."

His last week there had been a memorable one. The other participants had canceled at the last minute, leaving him alone on the island—until Elena had shown up midweek on the pretense that she needed to deliver supplies to the dock below the servants' quarters.

The servants' quarters were perched on top of a rocky bluff on the backside of the island. Marco had been assigned to them since he was a novitiate. On that starry April night four years ago, lying on the four-poster bed that dominated the bedroom overlooking the Ligurian Sea, he had glimpsed the fires of Gehenna—and had no desire to go back.

"Do you ever think about what happened, Marco?"

There were times—mostly late at night, as sleep eluded him—when he thought of nothing else. He would never be able to purge from his brain the sight of her naked form silhouetted against the starlight filtering down from the heavens. The warmth of her bare skin against his never strayed far from his mind, and the sweet scent of lavender tortured him to this day. He had broken his vow of celibacy that night, and even though it had never happened again—much to Elena's ire—it remained broken, shattered in a thousand pieces on the floor like an expensive vase fallen from a table.

"I think about it all the time."

The diesels coughed, and the hull creaked as the *Bel Amica* plowed through another medium-sized roller.

"Did you really think you could have us both? Did it ever occur to you that I might have wanted more than the barren future you promised?"

"Yes, it occurred to me."

"And yet you steered me away from any man who so much as looked in my direction, so that you could have me all to yourself."

"I was trying to keep you safe."

"Safe from what? A real relationship? Intimacy? Happiness?"

In the dark watches of a hundred sleepless nights, Marco had asked this same question of himself. The answer had always been the same. He had been trying to save Elena from herself, from her penchant for bad choices and self-destruction. Or perhaps he just told himself that, in a meager effort to justify behavior unbecoming of a priest.

"I was being selfish. I'm sorry, Elena."

She acknowledged his apology by shoving the throttles forward; the engine responded with a throaty roar. La Spezia glowed on the horizon, a smudge of light on the starboard side of the windshield, and she adjusted course, spinning the wheel to port with the deft touch of a thousand prior journeys.

"You're damn right you were being selfish. You're the one who swore the vows, not me."

He scooped up the Holy Ghost from the floor, then crossed to where Tariq was lying prone on the deck and yanked out the spear. The tip was covered with clots of blood and clumps of fat. He wiped it on Tariq's fatigues, then pulled the man's eyelids shut as he said a prayer. He repeated the process for each of the slain men.

The boat crashed through another wave as he rejoined Elena at the wheel. "I just wanted someone to share my life with, Marco. Was that too much to ask?"

"It was too much to ask of me."

He knelt down and examined the men Elena had killed. Ignoring their wounds—she had shot both of them in the back, opening two holes in each man's chest—he scavenged a pair of silenced pistols.

"Who are these men?"

"I don't know. I swear to you, I have no idea."

He handed Elena one of the pistols. "Since when have you been so good with a gun?"

"Since Mohammed put a knife to Gianna's throat and threatened to kill her. That's when."

The *Bel Amica* plowed through another roller, and the coastline stared at them with weak yellow eyes. Elena throttled the engines back and swung the wheel hard to port. "We're south of La Spezia now. Riomaggiore is just northwest of here."

Marco nodded. Being the son of a naval captain, he had spent a good deal of his time at sea, and he knew navigation as well as the Psalms—maybe better.

Closer to Riomaggiore, Elena throttled the engines back and flipped off all the lights. The cirrus clouds had thickened considerably, and the meager light from the crescent moon was heavily filtered. It was a small miracle she could pilot the boat in such circumstances. They sliced through another roller, throwing a sparkling curtain of spray high into the air.

"I want you to know I am sorry too, Marco."

"Sorry for what?"

"About the way things turned out. I was a single mother with no prospect of a job or anything else. I needed someone. You were there for me, without judgment or condescension, and I repaid your kindness by walking out the door and never returning."

"Why did you come back?"

"I didn't know what to do ... I had made such a mess of things."

She stopped speaking and switched on the wipers to clear the wind-driven spray from the screen.

"I couldn't just let them kill Gianna. I knew you would know what to do. You always did."

She had always placed too much trust in him. What if he had washed his hands of her this time? He couldn't bear to think of her alone or dead. That had always been his problem.

"You knew I was on board, didn't you?"

She nodded without taking her eyes off the windshield.

"How did you know?"

"Look at the bottom of the closet door."

Marco bent down and switched on his flashlight. Elena had taped a strand of her hair—now broken into two pieces—across the gap between the door and the frame.

"I used you, Marco, but there was no other way to save Gianna."

"We haven't saved her yet."

"At least she has a chance. She is an innocent girl. She shouldn't have to die for the sins of her mother."

The silhouette of the coastline, dark and menacing, appeared in the windshield. He knew it was time to confess his own sins, before time washed his desperation away, and he carried them to his grave. "I want you to know something, Elena. When you came into my life, I was struggling with everything: my priesthood, my happiness, even my faith. You changed all that for me. Maybe that's not how it's supposed to be for a priest, but that's how it was for me. You may not have realized it, but I needed you as much as you needed me."

Elena cut the engines to a throaty murmur, and the *Bel Amica* slowed. "I wanted to hear that four years ago. Why are you telling me now?"

She spun the wheel to starboard and increased the engines just enough to afford steerage in the rough seas. The specter of Riomaggiore, gauzy and vague, appeared in the windshield.

"I should have told you a long time ago, but for whatever reason, I didn't. I just wanted you to know."

She reached out and pulled him close, and they stood in the darkened wheelhouse, pressed together in a tight embrace. For a minute, Marco forgot about the dead men at his feet and enjoyed the warmth of her body and the brush of her hair on his neck.

It would all come back soon enough—the smell of gunpowder, the gush of blood, the sound of men struggling to take their last breaths—but for now, he just held her close and prayed for time to stand still, a prayer he knew could never be answered.

CHAPTER 3

It was nearing 3 a.m. when they approached the harbor. Elena cut the engine, and the *Bel Amica* slowed, drifting into the small inlet set off by stony piers on either side. She floated past a motley collection of blue-and-white rowboats and a pair of sleek skiffs powered by huge outboard motors, coming to rest twenty feet from the shore.

Marco dropped the anchor, and Elena jumped out of the boat, splashing to shore with her gun held above her head. She scurried down the quay as Marco doubled his pace to catch up with her, and they entered the old harbor square, still empty at this hour. Making their way past the café where Marco had once had a latte with Padre DiPietro, an older priest from La Spezia who had been chosen to be his mentor, they started up the hill at the top of the square, skirting around the ice cream stand, which was famous for its *gelato limone*.

They ran up the cobbled street, footfalls echoing in the darkness. At the top, Elena turned left onto the Via Gasperti, and they continued on, their progress only slightly slowed by the steep gradient. There were fewer houses this far up the slope, just the occasional dwelling, bigger than the ones below, though with the same rectangular shape, adobe construction, and bright colors. At the top of the cobbles, a small side street sliced into the steep hill, a narrow gravel road lined with large garbage cans that spilled over with fetid contents, fouling the air with the stink of rotting vegetables, curdled cream, and used coffee grounds. As soon as they were past the parade of garbage, Elena stopped to catch her breath, sinking to her knees to draw whoops of air into her lungs.

Once their breathing had quieted, they made their way along the street, keeping close to the wall that ran along the right-hand side. There were no street lamps, and a layer of thin cirrus cloud covered the half-moon, which radiated a meager light. Elena stopped behind an old Fiat parked on the side of the road, kneeling down in its shadow. She pointed straight ahead, toward the hazy silhouette of a small house built into the steep hillside. A single light burned on the ground floor; the rest of the house was dark, not surprising considering the price of electricity in the Cinque Terre.

"That's Francesca's room, with the light on."

Marco nodded as a now familiar tightness gripped his chest.

"I'm going to go up and around, and enter the house from the third floor." Elena indicated a narrow flight of steps that cut through the high wall to their right. "This path leads to the next street above, which circles behind my house. I can get in from there. Give me five minutes, and then come in through the front door."

She reached into the pocket of her jeans and produced a single key, handing it to him. "The latch sticks. You have to pull the door as you are turning the key."

They looked at each other in the pale moonlight. Her brown eyes were fearful but determined, and her full lips that tasted like ripe strawberries were pressed into a line.

"Five minutes. You understand?"

He marked the time on his diving watch, which glowed weakly in the darkness. "Yes, I understand."

She leaned in and kissed him lightly on the cheek, then disappeared from view. He knelt there watching the inexorable progress of the second hand on his watch, thinking about the people waiting inside the house, the people he planned to kill. He thought about the Holy Ghost—the speargun, not the third person of the Holy Trinity—and wished he'd had the forethought to bring it along, but he hadn't, and he would have to make do with the handgun, which, though not as familiar, was a good deal more practical. He removed the clip, confirmed there were plenty of 9mm rounds left, and snapped it back into place. He'd already done this several times on the boat; it was more of a way to kill time than anything else—kill time and avoid thinking about the previous hour, filled with the harsh reports of gunshots and the screams of dying men, and the next hour that promised more of the same.

Elena opened the gate that let out onto the road above and slipped through, closing it quietly, avoiding the place where it scraped noisily against the stone. She jogged up the road, spurred on by a profound disquiet. She just wanted to see her daughter sleeping in her bed and listen to her breathing. She had made many bad choices in her life, and she was deeply afraid that her daughter and her sister were about to pay for them. It had never occurred to her to be ashamed of the person she'd become, but she understood how shame felt at this moment, as the breeze blew through the untended vineyards above her, and the waves roared against the rocks below.

She stopped in front of a makeshift gangplank between the road and a small rooftop porch. Taking her gun out, she snapped off the safety and stuffed it in her waistband, then walked across the gangplank and let herself in. She slipped off her shoes and tiptoed down the circular stairs that descended from the landing.

The door to her daughter's bedroom was ajar, and she nudged it open and went in. Even in the dark, she knew Gianna wasn't there; there was no smell of the lavender shampoo with which her daughter washed her hair, and she couldn't hear the sounds of her small chest heaving.

But she wasn't panicked yet. Her sister slept in the downstairs bedroom, and Gianna usually slept with her when Elena was out at sea. She pulled the gun from her waist and went down the main stairs, feeling her way. How often had she done this after coming home from work in the dark, guiding her way by feel so as to not wake her sleeping family?

The men who had been keeping her family captive had been staying in the living room; she lifted her gun, ready—hoping—to kill them both as they slept on the couches, but the room was empty. She started toward the bedroom, but the slight squeak of a chair on the kitchen tile stopped her. Perhaps her sister was waiting up for her to come home safe. She walked into the kitchen, arm behind her back so as not to frighten whoever was there. She need not have bothered. There was no way her daughter, gagged and bound to a kitchen chair, could be more frightened than she already was. Her brown eyes were wide with terror, and an ugly bruise covered her right temple.

Something hard smashed into Elena's head, and she crumpled to the floor. She tried to get up, but she felt a sharp pain in her ribs, and the breath left her. Strong hands wrenched the gun from her grasp and sat her up against the wall.

"Mohammed warned you, Elena." The man's voice was pregnant with malice. "But you ignored him."

He walked over to the kitchen table and sat down behind Gianna. He produced a knife and held it to her neck. The blade bit into her skin, and blood streamed down, staining her white blouse with splotches of crimson.

"He is not the sort of man you should ignore."

Elena made a move to get up, but he lifted his gun, and she sank back against the wall.

"I have very little time, so I will make this short. I will give you two minutes to tell me what happened. If you tell me the truth, I will kill you and spare your daughter." He ran his fingers through Gianna's dark hair. "If you refuse, I will make this cut on her neck deeper until you talk."

To illustrate his point, he put the knife back against Gianna's neck and pressed harder, causing the dribble of blood down her neck to become a small stream.

The sea breeze whistled with unusual vigor for this time of year, almost December-like in its strength. As a consequence, the breakers crashed with ferocity, creating a din loud enough to drown out the staccato hammering of his heart as Marco watched the last seconds tick away. When the appointed time came, he switched off the safety on his gun and ran along the wall until he reached the house. Crouching down, he made his way along the front of the building, passing beneath the windows that looked out onto the quiet street, the village beneath it, and the sea below that. He stood up once he had passed the last window, extracting the key from his pocket. Before he inserted it, he put his ear to the door and listened, but all he could hear was the hiss of his own breath as it drew in and issued forth.

He inserted the key and pulled the handle as he twisted; the latch released, and he opened the door wide enough for him to walk through. Elena's voice spilled out from the kitchen to his left. He tried to discern the words, but even if she had been speaking Italian—which she wasn't—her rushed cadence would have thwarted his efforts. But he didn't need to understand the words to appreciate what had happened: she had been captured, and now she was trying to cover the sound of his entry with a breathless monologue.

He slipped through the open door and slid across the wood flooring in the direction of the kitchen. Elena's voice, ripe with terror, was clearly audible as he crossed the living room, trying to get a better angle. He took two more steps and stopped; in the dim light afforded by a small lamp, he saw exactly what he'd feared seeing.

Elena's daughter was tied to a kitchen chair. A gag obscured her pale face, and her eyes were large with fear. A man stood behind her, holding a knife to her throat. Blood seeped from a wound in her neck. Marco stepped back quickly lest the man see him, but his gaze was focused straight across the kitchen, likely centered on Elena, who was out of view. Elena had mentioned that there were two men, but there was no sign either of the other man or of Francesca. Marco craned his neck around, searching the interior of the house, but saw no one else.

The seconds ticked away, bearing witness to his growing paralysis. He needed to act, but action eluded him. Then inertia grabbed him and flattened him against the wall. There were two people on the other side of the plasterboard whose lives depended on him, and they were all going to die if he didn't do something. He closed his eyes, trying to conjure up an image to motivate him, but all he could see was the lifeless form of Karim lying on the floor of the *Bel Amica*, oozing blood from multiple gunshot wounds.

Basim watched the seconds wind down on the silver dial of his watch. Elena was still speaking, spewing drivel in clear, firm Arabic about a priest killing Karim and Tariq and the others. He couldn't believe the woman wasn't telling the truth; perhaps she realized he was going to kill them both anyway.

"You have ten seconds, Elena. Tell me what really happened, or say goodbye to your daughter."

"I have told you what happened."

He found her conviction profoundly disquieting. In the course of his bloody and brutal career, Basim had extracted many confessions. One particular interrogation came to mind as Elena reiterated her fantastic tale for the third time without changing so much as a single detail. He had been in Palestine, in the small kitchen of an Israeli informant who had betrayed him. The woman had held stubbornly to her story until Basim had choked the life out of her child in front of her, at which point the truth had spilled out of her mouth like a raging torrent.

The final seconds dissolved, and he set down his knife and wrapped his thick fingers around the girl's neck. Elena stared at him with a silent fury that excited him on some primeval level.

"Tell me the truth now, or I will kill her."

Marco understood the man's threat clearly, despite his ignorance of Arabic, causing a fresh layer of sweat to dampen his brow. There was an undertone to the words that needed no translation. He had to act now.

He tiptoed across the living room floor, gripping the handgun with both hands, envisioning himself wedged between two rocks, darting out to snap a shot at a passing fish. He spun around the corner, leveling the weapon as he wheeled. His eyes searched for the target, ignoring everything else. He saw a patch of brown skin below a well-trimmed beard and squeezed the trigger. He heard the dull thud of the suppressor and felt the recoil of the gun against his sweaty palm.

The man tried to cry out, but the bullet had eviscerated his trachea; his windpipe filled up with blood, and the shout became a gurgle. His hands went limp and slid off the girl's neck, and he slumped to the floor. He tried to get up, but Marco held him down with his foot until he lay still.

Elena tore at the gag binding Gianna's mouth. Marco switched on the light and ran into the living room to look for the other man, but all he found was a collection of custom-made furniture and a pair of expensive watercolors. Climbing the stairs, he searched the bedrooms, which were clear as well. When he returned downstairs, Elena had freed her daughter from her bonds. They were standing in the center of the kitchen, hanging onto each other for dear life, sobbing into each other's shoulders.

"Where is Francesca?"

Elena looked at him with widening eyes and mumbled something to Gianna, who responded with a gush of words in the Ligurian dialect.

"The other man left with her a few hours ago."

"Where did they go?"

Gianna shook her head, her large brown eyes brimming with tears. Elena sat down on the chair, pulling her daughter onto her lap. It was at once a tragic and heart-warming scene, but one that couldn't continue indefinitely.

Marco bent over the felled man and examined him in the feeble light of the lamp on top of the kitchen counter. He was medium-sized, with a lean face that might have been viewed as handsome if the blood weren't drained from it, and a long, almost feminine neck marred by the gunshot wound. He carried no cell phone, wallet, or identification; he had nothing on his person other than a holstered sidearm and a bloodstained jambiya in its sheath.

"Elena."

Her eyes opened as if against a great weight. Marco could see in them many things, among them relief, understanding, and anger. The anger was more prominent than the other emotions. She knew where they had to go—to the Castello di Giordano, where she had been told to take the men—and she knew what they had to do when they got there.

"I can't leave her."

"We can't bring her with us."

Gianna's sobs increased in volume; Marco could feel them resonating in the floor, which shook slightly beneath his feet.

"I have a friend on the Via Gasperti; I will ask her to watch Gianna."

"It's three in the morning."

Elena shrugged, reaching for the phone. It was answered swiftly. She delivered a barrage of Ligurian dialect and hung up without waiting for an answer.

"Let's go."

Marco pointed to the dead man, who was oozing a steady stream of blood over the kitchen tiles. "What about him?"

"He's not going anywhere."

"What if someone finds him? We may not get back for a while."

"My neighbors all think I work for the 'Ndrangheta. No one comes near this place."

Elena retrieved her gun from where it lay on the marble tiles and motioned for Marco and Gianna to follow her out the front door. Her friend was waiting for them on the porch of a narrow row house at the top of the Via Gasperti. If she was put off by Marco's presence, she didn't show it, wrapping her short arms around Gianna and ushering her into the house without looking back.

Elena stood watching Gianna until she disappeared, then followed Marco, who was already running down the street. They reached the harbor without seeing anything other than a lone cat skulking across the road in front of them, and splashed into the water. The twin diesels coughed to a start, Marco raised the anchor, and Elena piloted the *Bel Amica* out into open water.

"There is a stone jetty underneath the cliff upon which the guest house was built," she said.

Marco nodded, remembering it vaguely from his days as a retreatant. "Can you bring us there without lights?"

"Yes, but they will hear us."

"Not at high tide. The sound of the waves crashing against the rocks is deafening. And then what?"

"There is a flight of steps hewn into the rock."

Marco remembered the time he had taken Elena and Gianna for a picnic lunch on a bluff overlooking Vernazza. Elena had not ventured within twenty meters of the cliff's edge.

"Can you climb it?"

"I would climb to the gates of hell if it meant saving my daughter."

"Good, because that's where we're going."

CHAPTER 4

The cliff was steeper than Marco had remembered it, and higher as well, the steps zigzagging over one hundred meters in steep ascent before they ended on the back porch of the castle's guest quarters. The handrail escorting them up the precipice was largely gone, rising only a few meters before it disappeared. Elena went first, and Marco followed close behind, using one hand to probe the rock for handholds and the other to lock around her waist. Their progress was slow; at times, fear stiffened her legs, and Marco was forced to wrap both his arms around her—*how good it felt to wrap his arms around her*—and push her up the steep incline.

They rested midway up the cliff in a natural alcove formed by a fissure in the sandstone. He had spent many hours in this spot, trying to hear God's voice in the roar of the breakers. How many times had he gotten down on his knees and asked if he had made the right choice? The howl of the wind had been the only response, which he was left to interpret as best he could.

"You are sure the key is still there? It was four years ago."

"Nothing changes in Liguria, Elena. That's why I like it here."

A pair of cawing gulls swooped by, which Marco took as encouragement to go on. He turned to nudge Elena, but she was already standing in front of him. Her eyes were wide with fear, but her teeth were clenched, and Marco detected a faint glimmer of hope in the erect bearing of her spine.

"She is alive, Marco. I can see her face in my mind."

"Keep watching her."

Up they went, marching to the drumbeat of the breakers and the vocal accompaniment of the gulls. They rested one last time near the top, just underneath the steepest stretch, and Marco used the pause to make sure the safety catch on his speargun was off. He prayed he wouldn't have to use it, but it was a half-hearted prayer, without conviction. The men he was about to face were men of guns and steel, and he would have to fight them in kind.

The wind whined against the cliff and rose like a thermal, in swirling currents of warm air. A curtain of gray appeared above the black rock, and they ascended the last flight of steps in a crouch and peered over the rim.

The guest quarters were in front of them, a low stone building situated on the edge of the cliff. The castle itself, a huge geometric figure in the murky light, was perched at the tip of the island, at least a kilometer to the south. All they needed to do was cross the short distance to the back door of the guest house, retrieve the old skeleton key from under the clay pot, and they were in. The problem was the sentry pacing back and forth along the narrow strip where Marco used to sit and enjoy the view.

Elena stood up as soon as the guard turned away from them, and shot him in the neck. He dropped to the ground without a sound, and she kicked him over the side and watched him slide down the polished sandstone face with the self-satisfied look of a woman who had just brought a bag of rank trash to the curb.

A scream emanated from his left. He thought at first it was Elena—the voice was identical—but Elena was still standing in front of him.

"Francesca!"

He bolted across the porch, pushed the clay pot out of the way, and snatched up the key. Turning back to the door, he saw Elena's back already filling the open frame and heard the *thump thump* of the muffled handgun. He followed her inside, jumped over the body lying on the floor, and made for the bedroom. The massive four-poster bed was still there, but the decorative draping had been slashed down and pulled to the floor. Elena was ahead of him, pointing her pistol at a man wearing a white uniform, who was holding Francesca fast against him, his gun pressed into her temple. They exchanged words in Arabic, which—other than the name Mohammed—Marco couldn't understand, and glared at each other murderously, which he understood well.

Mohammed demanded something, likely wanting Elena to drop her gun. Elena didn't reply, but her pistol didn't waver from its mark. Mohammed repeated his demand, punctuating his words by pressing the barrel of his gun into Francesca's temple, creating a bruise that blossomed like a red flower on her olive skin. Marco stepped into the room, watching the stalemate in front of him: neither person spoke; neither person moved.

The strike of the gun against the floorboards sounded as loud as a shot in the silence. Elena stared at the weapon for a second and then kicked it toward Mohammed, giving Marco no choice. He aimed and fired; the spear struck Mohammed in the arm, just below the shoulder, releasing his gun from his grasp. He shoved his hostage out of the way and dove for Elena's gun with his unscathed arm outstretched.

Marco yanked the handgun out of his belt and fired three times. Mohammed hit the floor and rolled over once before coming to rest, lying supine with half of his face gone.

Marco would never forget the next five minutes, nor would he ever clearly remember them; they were just a collage of sights and sounds stuffed into a recess of his brain.

Elena grabbed his arm. "We need to go."

It was a sentiment with which he concurred, but he knew there would be no true escape, only a change of venue with the same bloody wallpaper. Francesca appeared in front of him, and

Elena ushered them toward the front door before returning to the man lying face down on the floor. She rummaged through his pockets, relieved him of his cell phone and a set of keys, and followed Marco and Francesca out.

The guest quarters were positioned at the back of the island. A maze of footpaths cut through the forest of Aleppo pines and cork oaks, connecting the castle, the guest quarters, and the garage complex. Elena led them to a wooded spot near the garage, which was built on a swath of flat land near where the causeway provided the only escape from the island.

"There is a sentry, Marco."

"Where?"

"Inside the garage."

"There is only one? Are you sure?"

"Mohammed made me do errands for them. There was always someone inside the garage. I never saw anyone else." She tossed him the keys she had taken from the dead man. "These are the keys to his van."

"Which one is his?"

"I'm not sure. Try the one nearest the door. We will wait for you to come out of the garage and join you just before you get to the causeway."

Marco left them standing there and followed the path behind the garage, trying his best not to kick any loose stones. He peered through the circular window, smeared with decades of sandstone dust. The garage was dimly lit; only a naked bulb of low wattage illuminated the large bay. There was a small door near where he was standing. He remembered seeing the groundskeeper standing in its open frame, smoking Tuscan cigars and spitting on the gravel walk that led inside. He switched the gun to his left hand and tried the handle; it turned with a creak.

There were two passenger vans inside the garage, long Fiat Ducatos equipped to transport a dozen men each. A movement caught his eye, and he shrank back against the wall. Footsteps echoed, and sweat beaded underneath his beard. A head poked out of the door, seeking the cause of the noise.

Marco reversed the gun in his hand and slammed the grip down on the man's skull, crumpling him to the gravel. He took a second to make sure the man wasn't going anywhere—and to make sure he hadn't killed him, which, thankfully, he hadn't—and passed into the garage. A quick circuit of the bay confirmed he was alone, but there were no windows at the front, so he had no idea if there was a sentry there. He went out again through the back door, stepping over the prone form of the man he had just knocked unconscious, and circled around, finding no one.

Returning to the garage bay, he jumped into the van Elena had suggested. Mohammed's key fit the ignition. He activated the door opener, waited for the door to glide open, and started the engine. Leaving the lights off—it was just light enough to see without them—he pulled out of the garage and stopped in front of the causeway. Elena got into the passenger seat; Francesca climbed into the back.

The causeway had been in poor condition four years ago, and the passage of time had done nothing to improve things. The asphalt roadway was rutted and full of potholes—some opening up to the water below—and the guardrail was flimsy at best and missing in spots. Halfway across, they drove over the drawbridge used to allow boats to pass through the channel, and Marco stopped beyond the control booth on the far side. He got out and motioned for Elena to follow, leading her to the side of the causeway, where he pointed to a length of white pipe bolted to the supports.

"The phone cable runs inside that pipe."

She nodded, and he ran back to the control booth. Most of the boats sailing in these waters used cell phones to trigger the drawbridge, but there was a manual mode as well. He toggled one of the levers, triggering a set of flashing lights and lowering the car barrier. When the gate was in place, he pulled the second control, and the hydraulics whirred, lifting the metal grate he had just driven over. When the drawbridge was fully vertical, he sliced all the hydraulic lines with his diving knife and used the butt of his gun to destroy the control mechanism.

Elena was in the driver's seat when he returned to the van. He jumped into the passenger seat, and she pulled away. At the end of the causeway, she turned onto the main road, which ascended the steep ridge that had kept the Cinque Terre isolated for generations. Olive groves and vineyards glowed in the first light of dawn. Sheep grazed on the narrow terraces of grass cut into the hillside. When they crested the top of the ridge, Elena pulled in to an overlook on the side of the road and hopped out. Marco joined her, and they gazed back the way they had come.

The light had gathered enough to see the island sitting like a sentinel off the shoreline. It was still too dark to make out more than the outline of the castle and the guest quarters, but the garage was visible in the headlights of the van that had pulled out. They watched in silence as it jolted over the causeway and stopped in front of the barrier. Marco imagined he heard shouting, but it might only have been the whine of the breeze or the crash of the waves.

"You didn't happen to grab the boat keys, did you?"

Elena shook her head. "No, but the main tank is almost empty, and I started pumping the auxiliary tank into the water before we got off. It will be empty by now, though the register is stuck on full. They will run out of gas twenty miles out to sea."

With these comforting thoughts in mind, they got back into the van and drove away. Elena followed the ridge road for a kilometer and turned onto the local highway heading inland. Marco stared at the lemon groves and listened to Francesca's breathing as she slept on the middle seat. After a time, they pulled into a rutted track leading through a stand of beech trees and stopped in front of a one-story stucco house. A battered Opel hatchback was parked there, keeping watch over a flock of straggly chickens.

"Wait here."

Marco had never been to Elena's father's house, but she had talked about it so often he felt like he had. Her father was an Iraqi surgeon who had fled Saddam Hussein's reign of terror and come to Italy looking for opportunity. But the Italian government had refused to grant him a medical license, and so he waited tables at a local restaurant at night and ran a free clinic during the day. His Italian wife had died during Francesca's birth, and he had raised his daughters as best he could under the circumstances.

Elena helped her sister out of the van, and they disappeared into the darkened house. She came out ten minutes later alone, with a basket of bread and oranges hanging from the crook of her arm, and got back into the driver's seat.

"How are they?"

"My father picked up Gianna and gave her a sedative. She is sleeping."

"What about Francesca?"

"He is tending to her now."

"Did you call the police?"

Her dark eyes narrowed, and her brow furrowed. Her full lips compressed into a line.

"Why not?"

"Because I don't want to spend the rest of my life in prison."

In an effort to cut down on the rising tide of illegal immigration into Italy, the Italian parliament had passed several strict laws discouraging human trafficking.

"But you can explain what happened, how they duped you …"

Her only reply was a slow shake of her head. He remembered the same look from a time long ago. The circumstances had been different—she had demanded he choose between her and Him; he had wanted, begged, really, to keep them both—but the conviction and the finality were the same. *No.*

"But the *Bel Amica* is on the island; it will lead them to you."

"My boat was stolen."

"Did you report it stolen?"

"I wasn't aware. I've been away."

"But Francesca and Gianna …"

"*They* would never sell me out."

She let the sentence hang in the air that tasted of oranges and lemons. *But how about you, Marco, will you sell me out?*

"There might be another way," he said.

Her breath let out, slowly and almost too softly to hear, but there was no mistaking its aroma, fruity and pungent.

"Those men. They came here for a reason."

Her head lifted, and her shoulders drew back, accentuating the curvature of her chest.

"If we can find out what they came here to do …"

She turned her head toward him, locking him in her dark gaze.

"But I don't know who they are. I told you that."

"You heard nothing?"

"No. They knew I spoke Arabic, so they were careful not to say anything around me."

After Elena's mother had died, her father had stopped speaking Italian around the house. Both Elena and Francesca had grown up bilingual.

"You must have heard something. You were with them for a week."

"No, I didn't. I swear it."

They sat in silence watching a feral cat stalk across the road in front of them. Liguria had been overrun with feral cats, which the residents liked much better than the rats they had been brought in to kill.

Something licked at the corner of Marco's mind, but with the exhaustion, the hunger, and the bloodshed, the smell of which still hung in his nose, he couldn't grasp it. He opened the glove box and searched through it, but other than the owner's manual, the rental agreement, and the registration, it was empty. He got out and inspected the back of the van, which only revealed the spare tire and a road emergency kit. And then he remembered the sheet of paper he'd taken from Karim. He fished it out, climbed back into the van, and flipped on the map light.

"What's that?"

"I don't know. It was in Karim's pocket."

He unfolded the sheet of paper and held it up in the light. One line of script had been scratched across a sheet of graph paper, but not in any language Marco could decipher.

Elena snatched the paper from him and examined it. "It's Arabic."

"What does it say?"

"It doesn't say anything; it's a street address."

"Where?"

Elena didn't reply. She fired up the ignition, waited for the navigation system to activate, and punched in the address.

"It's in Orvieto, a commercial area south of the city."

Marco had spent two years at the Pontifical Gregorian University in Rome, during which time he had taken the train to Orvieto to attend mass at the cathedral and stroll through the narrow alleys of the old city, but he didn't know the surrounding area well.

"I've delivered things near there before," Elena said.

He didn't ask what those things were. Elena had been involved with Antonio even before she had abruptly departed from Marco's life. He had feared their break-up would lead to more involvement with the 'Ndrangheta, but she had demanded he choose, and he had chosen Him. This involvement also explained the lavish furnishings and expensive artwork in her house, which were well above her pay grade.

"How far away is it?"

"I can make it there in three hours."

"And then what?"

"I don't know, but if we find something, we can call the police then."

Not waiting for Marco's consent, she shifted the van into gear and started winding her way up and over the steep ridge upon which Liguria had been built. Within ten minutes, time that Marco had spent with his eyes closed, silently asking the Savior for guidance and courage, as well as forgiveness, the entrance to the A10 loomed ahead in the dim light. Elena merged into the light traffic heading southwest.

Orvieto—and whatever fate had in store for them there—was three hours away.

CHAPTER 5

Giampaolo Benedetto pulled the brim of his Andalusian hat down low and adjusted the knot of his matching scarf. It was summer in Italy, and the heat was horrifying, even at this early hour, but Giampaolo had spent years cultivating a certain look, and he wasn't about to let a few degrees Celsius get in the way. It was Sunday, and the traffic on the outskirts of Orvieto was light; only the occasional lorry rumbled past, breaking the quiet of the morning with the heavy drone of its engine and the vibration of its tires on the tarmac.

Giampaolo completed a circle surrounding his destination, stopping every now and again to tighten the laces of his Testoni Oxfords, using the opportunity to steal a glance behind him to make sure no one was following him. He saw nothing other than the outline of the old city rising into the Umbrian sky, and a handful of anonymous vehicles, one of which was the Opel sedan he had rented, parked along the street. It had pained him to leave his silver Mercedes-Maybach sedan in the driveway of his villa in Monti, but there were consequences to the decision he had made a year ago, and his beloved car would not be the only thing he would be forced to abandon.

Checking his Rolex—a gift from the previous pope, a sainted man who had only lasted a year before succumbing to a stroke—he walked across the street and used a key to open the gate; in front of him, a crumbling cement sidewalk led to a dilapidated warehouse. He surveyed the street behind him as he closed the gate; it was empty, but that did nothing to dispel the unease that hung in the air as heavily as the odor of wet clay from the kilns next door. He scanned the warehouse, confirming that nothing had changed from the last time he saw it: the windows were all barred with wrought iron; the adobe exterior was chipped in many places and covered with graffiti in others; and a flight of pigeons lined the edge of the terracotta roof, filling the morning with their cooing.

With a last look behind him, he crossed the rutted sidewalk and used the same key to gain entry to the back of the warehouse, where the office was located. Stacks of old ledgers gathered dust in featureless cubicles; an adding machine lay overturned on the garbage-covered floor. A wood-paneled wall dotted with pin-ups separated the area from the rest of the warehouse. One of the pin-ups, depicting a voluptuous blonde in black lace panties and nothing else, reminded him of one of his girlfriends, and he stared at it for a minute, considering taking it with him as a memento. Deciding against it—he was, after all, leaving her, and several others as well, behind—he walked across the room and stopped in front of a door, knocking twice and then twice more as per the prearranged signal. The door swung open from the inside, and Giampaolo passed through into the wide, rectangular room that abutted the office. A row of lockers was cut into the far wall, each containing a complete uniform, including riot helmet, ballistic shield, and black combat boots.

"You are late."

Giampaolo turned around to face the man who had addressed him. He was of average size, with dark hair and dark skin, dressed in a pair of gray slacks and a gray pullover. Giampaolo had met him several times before, the first time shortly after the last papal enclave; he hadn't enjoyed any of the meetings.

"You have the keycards and the permits?"

"You have the money?"

The man nodded. "As soon as you hand them over, I'll transfer the cash."

Giampaolo's face flushed; a bead of sweat trickled down his face and seeped into his silk scarf.

"That wasn't the arrangement we made."

"Arrangements change."

"Not with me they don't."

They glared at each other as an overhead fan whirred, creating an anemic breeze that only made the heat worse.

"Perhaps I can convince you to cooperate." A silenced handgun appeared in the man's hand, and a smile replaced the scowl.

Giampaolo laughed. "You'll have to try harder than that."

The gun—some kind of Eastern European semi-automatic, he thought, perhaps a Makarov—didn't waver, but the cocksure smile did, albeit only momentarily.

"Give me the keycards and the permits, or I will kill you and take them myself."

"I wouldn't recommend that."

"No? Why not?"

"Let me show you."

Giampaolo lowered his hands slowly and removed an envelope from the breast pocket of his blazer, handing it to the man pointing the gun at him.

"Open the envelope, please."

The man ripped it open, revealing five white keycards.

"Notice the passcodes are not there."

The deal they had made had specified that the five keycards be accompanied by the passcodes that corresponded to them. But the labels on the cards were blank.

"That wasn't our arrangement, *Signor* Benedetto."

"As you said, arrangements change."

Something scrabbled overhead, a rat most likely—the damn place was overrun with them—and the wail of a distant ambulance seeped in through a broken window. Neither man moved.

"Put the gun on the floor, kick it away, transfer the funds, and I'll give you the passcodes."

It was the other man's turn to sweat, which he did profusely, darkening the collar of his gray pullover. A foul odor emanated from him, which Giampaolo was at a loss to decipher. A mixture of garlic, onions, and coffee, perhaps, he couldn't be sure, but he was doubly glad he had applied a second dab of his scent, which had been created especially for him by a *parfumerie* a few blocks from Vatican City.

"Put the gun down and kick it away."

The man made no move to comply.

"I am going to leave in three seconds, unless you do as I say."

The sweat continued to pour off the man, but the gun didn't flinch.

"One …"

The gun—it was definitely a Makarov, he was sure of that now—started to shake.

"Two …"

The man's finger whitened on the trigger.

"Three …"

The gun dropped to the floor, coming to rest between them. Giampaolo gave it a nudge with the toe of his shoe, sending it spinning to the other side of the room.

"Now transfer the funds."

The man produced a tablet from his pocket and started tapping away. A minute later, Giampaolo's cell phone vibrated in his pocket. He fished it out and confirmed that five million euros had been transferred into his bank account in Bern.

"Give me the codes," the man said.

Giampaolo reached inside his blazer and extracted his Beretta. It was a lovely gun, a pearl-handled model 92 that had been given to him by Cardinal Lucci, the Vatican's Secretary of State, on the occasion of Giampaolo's tenth anniversary as the Inspector General of the Vatican Security Office. It had been intended for decorative use—he had displayed it above his desk in a glass frame—but that did not mean it didn't fire. He had made sure of that several nights ago, in the pistol range in the basement of the office's headquarters on the Via del Pellegrino.

He waited for the man to get about ten steps away—not to be sporting, but to avoid blood spatter on his suit—and shot him twice in the back. The man fell against one of the lockers; his head came to rest on top of a pair of boots. Giampaolo realized it was unnecessary—and probably a mistake—to kill the man, but he had been fantasizing about doing it for so long, he couldn't help himself. And anyway, the guy was a terrorist, wasn't he? Killing him was doing the world a favor, worth the trouble of having to drag him out of sight before the others turned up.

He picked up the fallen envelope and walked into the warehouse, which was empty save for five vans parked in single file. He strode over the floor, his leather soles loud against the concrete, and pulled up in front of the lead van. It was a Mercedes Sprinter, painted all white, with tinted windows and the iconic blue shield symbol of the Prima Security firm.

He went around to the passenger door and climbed inside the van. Taking out one of the keycards, he used a Sharpie to write a six-digit code on the label, before depositing the card and a signed permit in an envelope and placing it in the glove box. He did the same for the van behind and continued down the line. When all the vans were prepped and authorized to enter the Vatican, he retraced his steps and went back to the office. Grabbing the man by his feet, he dragged him into the next room, depositing him in a closet, which was empty other than several boxes of blank paper that were already spattered with enough blood to look like some kind of modern art exhibit. He closed the door, pushed an empty desk against it, and went to the break room, where a pile of old towels had been dumped on the floor. He used them to wipe up the blood, then exited the warehouse, throwing the bloody towels in a rusty dumpster on the edge of the property, where they would be found eventually, but only long after he was gone.

CHAPTER 6

The Umbrian sun had just cleared the horizon as Elena pulled off the E35 west of Orvieto. In the distance, the multiple spires of the Duomo ascended into an azure sky atop the volcanic bluff upon which it—and the entire city—had been built. Marco had been to the cathedral many times and would have loved nothing more than to ride the funicular up to the top of the hill, attend mass, and have lunch afterward at the Ristorante Maurizio across the street, which served a lovely vintage of Orvieto produced from the grapes that grew on the western flank of the bluff. But Elena turned away from the city center, in the direction of the low hills that stretched to the south of the town, breaking the momentary spell under which he had been lingering.

She turned again, onto a rutted track that went southeast, and drove past lemon groves and wheat fields waving in the morning breeze. At a T intersection, she went right, following a secondary road flanked by Italian cypresses. She slowed down as they crested a small hill, pointing ahead and to the left.

"This is the place."

Their destination was a low-slung warehouse that looked like it hadn't seen a new coat of paint—much less a renovation—in years. The terracotta roof was missing as many tiles as it had retained, and graffiti marred the walls. Elena pulled into the driveway and stopped in front of the lone garage bay, which was closed by an automatic door. Marco grabbed the handguns from the glove box and handed one to Elena, who placed it on her lap, then activated the remote opener.

The door lifted at a crawl. As it rose, his curiosity about who would be waiting for them sank, replaced by a growing sense of dread. By the time it was midway open, he had no further inclination to find out what was going on and who was behind the door; instead, he wished he was back at St. John the Baptist, kneeling in the first pew, looking out the window at the Ligurian Sea as it lifted out of the dawn. If Elena felt the same, there was no way to tell by reading her face, which remained impassive and relaxed, without tension. Her brown eyes stared forward; her brow did not furrow with concern. The Lord had put her together well, he couldn't help but think, even as the door lifted to reveal his uncertain future; she was as hard on the inside as she was soft on the outside.

The door finished its ascent, revealing a line of white vans parked fender to fender along the long axis of the otherwise empty building. Elena put the van in park, stuffed her gun into her waistband, and pulled her blouse out to cover it.

"Are you ready?" she asked.

Marco was not ready, but there was no putting it off. Fate fell heavily upon him, as if he were wearing a yoke attached to a large load. Elena got out of the car, and he followed, his own gun jammed into his belt in the small of his back. No one was there to greet them as they walked into the bay. Marco opened the door to the lead van, and it too was empty.

They searched the interior for the next ten minutes; save for the five vans, there was nothing there. The warehouse looked like it hadn't been used for some time. The only signs of life were the rodent droppings scattered over the cement floor like confetti in the wake of a parade.

Elena was gazing at the lead van, which, like all the rest, was a white Mercedes Sprinter. Emblazoned on its side was the blue shield of Prima Security. Having lived in Vatican City for two years, Marco was familiar with the company, which was the only one ever called upon to assist the Gendarmerie inside Vatican City.

"Prima Security?" Elena said. "I've never heard of them."

"They're based in Rome. I used to see them around when I was in the seminary at the Pontifical Gregorian University in Vatican City. They come in to help with crowd control for large events."

"What are the vans doing here?"

"I have no idea."

Marco walked around the van and hopped into the passenger seat. The console between him and the driver's seat was empty, and there was nothing on the dashboard. He tried the glove box, but it was locked. Elena came up next to him as he tried to force the latch on the compartment.

"Try the keys."

She pointed to the keys dangling from the ignition. He reached over, grabbed them, and opened the glove box. Inside, on top of the usual items, was an envelope marked with the emblem of the crossed silver and gold keys, the official insignia of the Holy See. He slit it open with his finger, revealing a single sheet of paper and a keycard with a magnetic stripe on one side; on the other side, six numbers had been written on a white label.

He unfolded the sheet of paper. It was a permit allowing access to St. Peter's Square, signed by the Inspector General of the Vatican Security Office.

"Is it dated?"

He searched the document, finding what he was looking for in small print just above the signature.

"It's dated today."

"Today? What's going on today?"

Marco looked at his diving watch. "This morning at nine a.m., Pope John Paul III is saying mass outside in St. Peter's Square. The entire Catholic Bishops Conference of Nigeria is co-celebrating with him."

"How do you know this?"

"I was selected to be part of the congregation, but the Gendarmerie scaled the number of invitees back because of security concerns."

"I heard Mohammed speak about some kind of protest."

Marco nodded. "Boko Haram is organizing it."

"Who is Boko Haram?"

"It's an Islamic jihadist group based in Nigeria."

"What do they have against the pope?"

"When John Paul III was a cardinal in Nigeria, he was an outspoken critic of sharia law, which Boko Haram was trying to inflict on the country. They have been making death threats against him ever since he was elected."

He stared at Elena as if trying to find the key to the puzzle in the depths of her dark chocolate eyes and the curve of her caramel skin as it stretched over her cheekbones. But the answer wasn't there—only more questions—and he left the van for another look in the warehouse.

"Where are you going?"

"There must an office of some kind. Maybe there's something in there."

He jogged over to the far wall, into which a number of doors had been cut at irregular intervals. The first one led to a small storeroom, which was filled with piles of broken pots and smelled of urine. The next door opened into a bathroom, which Marco, having not used one in quite some time, put to good use. Elena was waiting for him when he returned to the bay, gesturing for him to follow her.

"Come and look. I found something."

She ran to the end of the bay, her footfalls echoing against the opposite wall of the garage. She passed several doors and turned in to the second to last, leaving it open wide for Marco. A long rectangular room lay in front of them, in which twenty lockers had been constructed, ten against either wall.

"Take a look at this."

She was standing in front of a locker, holding up a long shield. It was painted blue and bore the shield insignia on the front.

"It's a riot control shield."

"I know that." She stepped toward him, holding it out. "Take it. Feel how heavy it is."

Marco grabbed the shield. He had expected it to be heavy—it needed to be to deflect hurled stones and swung clubs—but it was far heavier than it needed to be, even for that. He set it down on the ground and flipped it over to reveal the back. A thin cover made of hard plastic had been fitted, creating a hidden compartment. Using the tip of his diving knife, he pried the cover off. An assault rifle, several extra clips of ammunition, and a block of what looked like putty were clipped in place.

Elena pointed to the putty, which had been wrapped in cellophane. "What is that stuff?"

"It's Semtex, a plastic explosive."

"How do you know that?"

"I used it all the time when I was in the navy. It has a lot of applications for marine salvage."

He used his knife to pry open several of the other shields. All were the same as the first. He put the knife away and sat down on the bench in front of the lockers.

"How do you put all this together, Elena?"

She counted the lockers, pointing at each one with her index finger as she added them up. Walking over to the nearest, she took out a black leather combat boot, turning it over in her hands. She set it down and grabbed a riot helmet, donning it and lowering the dark glass visor, obscuring her face.

"I picked up twenty men between the two trips. We have to assume that those men were meant to fill these uniforms."

Marco nodded. "Yes, but for what purpose?"

She lifted the assault rifle from its cradle inside the shield, holding it deftly in her arms. "There's only one purpose for a gun like this." She lifted the gun into shooting position and placed her eye behind the telescopic sight. "To kill people. This Boko Haram hates the pope, you say. Maybe they want to do more than protest against him."

"Do you think we just stopped an attack against the pope?"

She set the gun down against the locker and picked up the brick of Semtex, inspecting it carefully. "Not only against the pope, but against the basilica as well."

Marco nodded, but a shroud of disquiet remained over him. He looked at the permit and keycard again, staring at them with unseeing eyes.

"Clever really. They organize a protest, knowing that Prima will be asked to help with crowd control, and substitute their men—all armed to the teeth—for the real security officers. Once the pope and the Nigerian bishops process into the square, they whip off the covers, and it's all over."

"How do the vans gain entry into St. Peter's Square?"

Marco held up the keycard. "There's an unmanned gate on the Via Paolo VI. The keycard has to be swiped, and the passcode entered after that."

"Why the permit, then?"

"There's a second checkpoint manned with officers from the Vatican Security Office. All vehicles are inspected before they are allowed to enter the square."

Elena leaned over and grabbed the shield from the next locker. Inspecting the back for a moment, she found a latch underneath the carrying handle, which released the cover easily. It dropped to the ground, clanging against the cement floor. "These shields won't pass inspection. Do you know what that means?"

Marco didn't reply, instead getting up to walk up and down the line of lockers. Finding what he was looking for in the last locker on the far side, he sat down and started taking off his shoes.

"Did you hear me? I asked if you knew what this means."

He tried on one of the boots from the locker. It fit. "It means that the officers at that checkpoint are in on the job, and that there might be others as well."

He checked his watch. It was just after 7 a.m.

"Rome is ninety minutes away; if we get going straight away, we could be there in time."

"In time to do what?"

He took off his shirt and donned the black jersey and padded vest hanging on the hook. "That's the part I haven't figured out yet."

CHAPTER 7

Andreas Bruckentaler stood tall and straight, his halberd pointing skyward, his gaze centered out and over the congregation seated in front of him. He guessed that any stray glances falling upon him would see the picture he was trying to project: a calm lieutenant of the Swiss Guard protecting the pope as members of his order had done for over five hundred years. But it was a lie; outward appearances aside, he was nervous.

Standing with his back against the podium upon which mass would be celebrated in less than thirty minutes' time, looking east toward the Piazza Pius XI, he could see the growing unrest among the Gendarmerie forming a boundary between the Vatican and the protesters. The line was several hundred meters away, but even from that distance he could make out the tense posture of the defenders and the anxious pacing of captains waiting impatiently for reinforcements to arrive.

He could also hear the fear; although he had the veneer of a medieval warrior, he was very much a modern soldier underneath. In addition to his Kevlar armor, he had a miniature earpiece fitted inside his ear canal, which was crackling with nervous chatter. In past papacies, he would also have carried a SIG Sauer P220 semi-automatic pistol, but Pope John Paul III had issued a papal decree forbidding the Swiss Guard from being armed in the absence of 'credible and clear danger to the pope.'

Despite what had been hailed as solid intelligence from the Security Office, the protest was not a medium-sized affair. The report had predicted several hundred in attendance, mostly bored and disaffected youth. But several thousand had turned out, including dozens of known troublemakers. Worse still, only half of the Prima riot-control officers requested by the Security Office had shown up. The Inspector General of the Security Office was supposedly working furiously on it, but there was no sign of the badly needed men.

Oberst Jaecks, the commander of the Swiss Guard, had begged the pontiff to divert the mass to the basilica, but the Holy Father wouldn't hear of it. Ongoing renovations had closed much of the seating, meaning that more than half the guests would need to be turned away, and the congregation had already been reduced because of the demonstration. 'There have been protests for two thousand years,' the pope had responded. 'We will have mass as scheduled.'

Bruckentaler peered sideways, checking his men. There were eight guardsmen in full regalia positioned around the massive wooden structure upon which the temporary altar had been positioned. In the event of an emergency, he had the responsibility of bringing the pope to safety, by whatever means. In this case, the escape route lay to the north. On that side of the square, very close to Maderno's fountain, there was a well-hidden set of trapdoors that led down into the catacombs, guarded by an armed officer from the Security Office. Bruckentaler needed only to cover the hundred meters to the entrance and get the pope below. The trapdoors were made from a titanium alloy capable of deflecting a tank shell. Once underneath, the pope would be safe.

All he had to do was get there.

Giampaolo parked the Opel sedan at the base of the hill and looked at a map of the neighborhood. Above him, perched on a peak of the Alban Hills, the Palazzo Apostolico loomed like an eyrie in the sky. He oriented himself to the map, which depicted Castel Gandolfo from the west, the opposite side from where he normally ascended to the castle. Lago Albano and all the tourists there to see its shimmering waters lay to the east. He fixed the directions in his head, shifted the car into gear, and drove on up the slope.

Halfway up the hill, he reached a private villa. As he inched forward, the massive gate guarding the villa opened in front of him, then closed after him, sealing him from the view of anyone outside. There was no one inside the grounds to witness his presence either. He grabbed his attaché case from the passenger seat and took a last look around. Hedges of laurel and cypress arced away from his position, date palms speared into the sky, and the sweet scent of roses drifted on a soft breeze.

The door next to the massive garage bay was open; he turned the handle and passed inside. Ignoring the collection of expensive sedans parked there—never something he was inclined to do—he proceeded to the back, where another door led to a passageway bored into the rock. His footfalls echoed as he made his way down the tunnel, the beam of his flashlight bobbing up and down with his strides. The air smelled of mildew and pine pitch, with which the passage had been lit for years.

The passageway ended at a T, and he turned left, mounting a steep stairway hewn from the rock. He paused to breathe at the midway point, taking advantage of a stone bench to rest his legs and consult the map again. When his breathing had normalized, he resumed his assault on the staircase, his rested legs taking the steps two at a time.

The growing light told him he was nearing the top; he turned a corner, and the brightness grew. Coming after the blackness of the trip through the mountain, the ambient light hit him like a tangible wave, knocking him back a step. He stopped to don a pair of sunglasses—not his signature pair of Ray-Ban Aviators, but a cheap pair of obviously fake Wayfarers he wouldn't have been caught dead in a week ago. Between the glasses and the cheap straw fedora he had bought at the same tourist shop in the south end of Rome, his own wife wouldn't have recognized him, not that she had done much more than glance in his direction in the past few years.

He was on a parapet overlooking the sprawling expanse of papal gardens below him. It was rumored that Pope John Paul III's favorite pastime was strolling through them early in the dawn of each day, which made Giampaolo despise them all the more. Two doors led away from him. He chose the one on the right; its lock yielded to one of the keys on the ring he produced from his pocket. The narrow corridor twisted and turned in front of him, leading—at least according to the map—into the heart of the *appartamento pontificio*. There wasn't a sound to be heard; the air was redolent of sandalwood, which the pope burned to remind him of his homeland.

One more turn, and he was there. He put his ear to the door; hearing nothing, he unlocked it and went inside. The pope's private apartment sprawled in front of him. Unlike the rest of the palace, which was all marble and baroque architecture, John Paul III had redone his residence in a style that—Giampaolo concluded—said much about the man and his fitness to be pope. Simple wooden furniture and braided rugs clashed with the murals painted on the walls.

Walking to the back of the residence, he put on a pair of nitrile gloves and opened the door to the pope's private study. Against the far wall, stacked high with an eclectic mix of books, including sacred texts on loan from the Vatican Pontifical Archive, primers on Italian grammar and vocabulary, and American crime fiction, of which the pope was said to be fond, was the pontiff's massive mahogany desk. Setting the attaché case down on its surface, Giampaolo removed a bag of cocaine, depositing it in the central drawer. He considered stashing some away for his personal use, but he didn't want to prolong his time in the study, with the ominous feel of the pope's presence and the reek of sandalwood hanging in the air.

A pile of papers littered the back of the desk. Giampaolo extracted a sheet of parchment from the attaché case. The heavy paper was covered with flowing script; Pope John Paul III's name adorned the top. At the bottom, a lead seal stamped with the Ring of the Fisherman confirmed that it was a papal bull—except that Pope John Paul III hadn't written it, and had in fact never even laid eyes on it. He placed the fake document on top of the stack and dumped a bag full of pornographic magazines into one of the side drawers, where they wouldn't be too obvious.

And that was that; he closed the attaché case and left as quickly as he'd come, making his way back to the villa in less than ten minutes. He turned around and took one last look at the palace on the hill above him, before getting into his Opel and driving away.

The drive to the Tyrrhenian town of Anzio was a pleasant one. The sky was blue, the air that rolled in through the open window of the Opel was warm and smelled of pine, and the radio blasted a succession of songs by Dave Matthews, whom Giampaolo adored. He parked the car at a trattoria, left the keys under the seat as per the arrangement he had made with the man he had paid to bring it to Rome, and wandered down to the harbor. It was a beautiful Sunday morning, and the streets were bustling with the usual traffic: fishmongers selling the fruits of the Tyrrhenian Sea, fruit growers hawking produce from the Lazian countryside, and immigrants from Africa peddling selfie-sticks.

He walked past the beach, which was already lined with royal-blue umbrellas, thinking about the evening he had spent at the beachside restaurant here several years ago with his wife and her parents; the monkfish had been superb. After climbing the steps to the quay, he turned around, closed his eyes, and took in Italy for the last time: the soft whisper of the morning breeze, the smell of garlic and anchovies, the taste of sea salt on his tongue. And then the moment passed, and he walked the length of the pier and located the man who was picking him up, standing in a blue and white boat at the end of the dock. Without another look, he grabbed the ladder leading down to the water and descended as quickly as he could. The man on the boat helped him aboard, and they shoved off, motoring slowly at first, and then faster as they exited the harbor and entered deeper waters. Neither man spoke; there was nothing to say, and it was better this way, with only the whine of the outboard and the whistle of the wind to fill their ears.

CHAPTER 8

Rome had a well-earned reputation for being one of the most snarled-up and congested cities in the world, a reputation it was living up to as Elena turned off the outer ring onto the Viale dello Stadio Olimpico. Marco glanced again at his diving watch, which reminded him that the mass would be starting in less than fifteen minutes. Elena, who had always had a knack for understanding what he was thinking, jerked the steering wheel, guiding the van into the breakdown lane. They drove past a long line of stopped cars and swerved back into the right lane as the traffic cleared ahead, setting off a medley of horn blasts and yelling.

"I hear the Vatican is nice this time of year."

"What was that?" For a minute, he didn't realize she was trying to distract him, to take his mind off what lay ahead, not to mention the difficulty of getting there.

"The Vatican. I hear it's nice this time of year."

Marco didn't agree. The heat was appalling, the crowds were thick and noisy, and what little breeze there was smelled faintly of garbage.

"Really? I much prefer January."

And he did. The cold drizzle kept the tourists away, and only the winter wind could be heard in St. Peter's Square, whipping the cold spray from Maderno's fountain toward the small line of faithful waiting to pass through the metal detectors.

"Personally, I don't like the Vatican at any time of year."

"No? Why is that?"

Elena changed lanes and continued down the Piazzale Maresciallo Giardino, which ran parallel to the River Tiber as it flowed out toward the Tyrrhenian Sea to the south and west.

"The man I loved chose the Church over me."

"Why does that make you hate the Vatican?"

"It's the embodiment of the Church. Why wouldn't I hate it?"

He had always hoped her bitterness wouldn't endanger her faith, but he had been hoping against hope, and he was not surprised to hear that her loyalty—to the Roman Catholic Church, at least—had been shaken, if not destroyed. He brooded about this as she wove her way through traffic and turned onto the Via Leone, the road named for Pope Leo IV, who had saved the Vatican from the Saracens by building the Leonine Wall around Vatican Hill.

"Then why are you helping me?"

"I'm not helping you, Marco, or the pope, or the Roman Catholic Church. I'm helping myself. I'm making sure I don't spend the rest of my life in prison."

Elena turned off the Lungotevere dei Mellini and stopped at a light on the Piazza dei Tribunali. Neither of them had spoken much in the last five minutes, as if neither had wanted to break the fragile truce that had been established between them. Sweat beaded underneath Marco's beard and dripped onto the collar of his freshly starched Prima uniform as she swung left onto the Via Paolo VI, and the unmanned security gate materialized in front of them, positioned—as Marco remembered—at the beginning of the Via Tunica. He handed her the magnetic keycard; she swiped it through without even a tinge of expression on her face, just visible beneath the bulletproof visor of the riot helmet, which she wore tilted open. If Marco didn't know better, she might be parking her car on her way to another monotonous night of work patrolling the Vatican Museum. The woman was constructed of stainless steel and titanium; small wonder that a man like him, made of mere flesh and bone, had been drawn to her.

The display asked for their six-digit authorization code; Elena typed it in, and the barrier ascended. The Via Tunica skirted the back of the colonnades—which obscured their view of the square to their right—and ended at the Petriano entrance, the main gateway into St. Peter's Square from the south. Marco twisted to get a better view, but all he could see was the massive granite pillars that comprised the entrance, and the back of the large screen that had been set up to simulcast the celebration. Elena slowed as two unarmed Gendarmerie officers waved them down and pulled to a stop.

She lowered her tinted window, holding out the permit Marco had taken from the glove box. One of the officers inspected it briefly and mumbled a few words into his radio.

"You're late."

Elena shrugged her shoulders.

"Pull over there." He pointed to a spot thirty meters ahead, across from a guard booth on the left-hand side of the road. "Don't enter the square until the security officers have searched the vehicle."

Elena nodded and parked the van by the curb as the officers went back to their post. Marco looked over at the guard booth without turning his head; a darkened window stared at him, but the adjacent door didn't budge.

"What's keeping them?" she asked.

"They're expecting five vans."

"How long will they wait?"

"It's possible we became separated in the traffic … two or three minutes at the most."

Marco lowered his window and stuck his head out, getting his bearings. He could hear *Missa Papae Marcelli*, the customary music to precede a papal mass, being played in the square to his right, but the Petriano entrance and several banks of loudspeakers still blocked his view. Three hundred meters behind him, to the west, he heard the distant sounds of the protest bubbling up from the Piazza Pius XI: the faint thunder of hundreds of stomping feet, along with angry shouts amplified by bullhorns.

Inside the guard hut, Ahmed Mansouri snatched up a cell phone from the top of the makeshift desk, dialing the number for Bandar al-Nashwan, the man he had paid to organize the protest in the Piazza Pius XI. "Are you ready on your end?"

Al-Nashwan didn't answer right away. Then, "Yes, why?"

"We have to move up the timetable."

"Is something the matter?"

Mansouri didn't reply. He peered out the tinted windows and contemplated the van. From the outside, it appeared as expected. But he knew there was something wrong—not that he was going to tell al-Nashwan that. The vans were supposed to arrive together, in a tight formation of five in a line. If they had become separated in traffic, they would have re-formed on the Via Tunica before proceeding through the gate.

"We are ready, Ahmed. Say the word, and I will overrun the square."

Mansouri could hear the angry crowd over the phone. Uncertainty gripped him; he wanted to call for instructions, but Mohammed eschewed cell phones. He was on his own.

He stared at the single van waiting patiently at the curb, looking for a hint of what to do. But there was none. He would have to rely on his gut, and his gut told him something had gone very wrong.

He kneaded his forehead as he made up his mind. "Send them into the square."

He set the phone down and looked at the other man in the room, a young Saudi he had himself recruited to the cause. They exchanged no words; both knew they would not realize their dream of bringing the hated basilica to the ground. But all was not lost—they could still kill the pope who presided over it.

Mansouri picked up the phone again and called the man in position to make that happen: Sowsan bin Nawwaf, his oldest friend, who was waiting by the trapdoors in front of the obelisk with a rifle in his hands.

"Only one van made it, Sowsan."

"I am sorry to hear that, Ahmed."

"I have ordered the protesters to storm the square. You are ready on your end?"

Mansouri heard the sound of a weapon being cocked.

"I am ready."

Al-Nashwan put away his cell phone and pushed his way to the head of the Piazza Pius XI, where dozens of excited teenagers were hurling curses and the occasional stone at the police officers barring their entrance into Piazza San Pietro. He stopped some way behind the front ranks of the protesters and sidled up to a group of three dozen people, older than the others and less animated. They stood there, hands in pockets as if bored, saying nothing. He looked them over; they were ill-dressed, unshaven, and unkempt. But al-Nashwan didn't care; the rougher the better, especially considering the job they had to do. He grabbed one by the shoulder and pulled him close.

"It is time to earn your money."

The man was short and stout and resembled a Neapolitan mastiff, especially in his face, which was wide and full of wrinkles. He looked around at his companions, and then at al-Nashwan.

"We want more money."

"Why?"

The man nodded toward the large number of police awaiting them. "That's why."

Al-Nashwan rubbed his chin. He had guessed already that the ruffians would demand more, which was why he had offered a lesser amount to begin with.

"That wasn't the arrangement."

"Arrangements change."

"How much?"

"Five thousand."

For the kind of beating these men were going to take, he thought, it was more than fair. And it wasn't his money.

"Done."

Mastiff smiled, revealing a mouth with many missing teeth. Judging by the scars on his face, he'd earned his lack of dentition the hard way. He turned around and gathered his comrades, mumbling something that was lost in the yells of the crowd and the music coming from the large speakers on the edge of the grounds.

Al-Nashwan shouted for the way to be cleared, and the three dozen men bolted forward. They hurdled the barriers that had been erected to contain them and sprinted across the no-man's-land between them and the Gendarmerie. The police officers barely had a chance to raise their batons, the only weapons they had, before the thugs were upon them.

Al-Nashwan jumped on top of a concrete barrier to get a better view. The melee was on. Bodies were everywhere: fists flew, legs kicked, and batons flashed. The sound of it was appalling: grunts of pain, the snap of breaking bones, and the sharp crack of batons hitting skulls. He watched for a minute, mesmerized by the sheer volume of the violence, before he realized his side was losing.

His mercenaries were fighting tenaciously, but they were outnumbered. He had been sure the mob would follow the initial assault, but they hadn't. In fact, the beating the vanguard was taking was having the opposite effect. With every head that thudded against the tarmac, the throng receded.

He jumped down from his perch and grabbed a fistful of M-80s from his pocket. He ran deep into the crowd, lighting and dropping the firecrackers on the ground as he moved forward. By the time he reached the front, the first set of explosives had detonated. The back of the mob panicked, pushing forward to get away from the new threat. The second wave of explosions ignited the crowd further, and the last salvo catapulted them headlong into the line of Gendarmerie, who were screaming into their radios for reinforcements. The police swung their batons in a futile effort to resist, but they were too few. The mob poured forward en masse and swept aside the defenders. It breached the line and flowed into the square, bloodthirsty and riled. Behind it, the imams still bellowed into their bullhorns, further inciting the riot.

The throng followed the beat of the war drums, the urging of its masters. It was a single being now, a collective beast beyond the control of the individuals of which it was made. It invaded the square, moving in all directions at the same time, but mainly forward, in a direct line toward the pope.

CHAPTER 9

Andreas Bruckentaler's mouth was dry as he witnessed the crowd spilling into the square. But he recovered quickly, shouting instructions into his microphone as he ran up the front stairs toward the pope. To his amazement, the pontiff was still standing behind the pulpit, delivering his homily, ignoring the angry mob descending upon him.

"Holiness!" Bruckentaler called out as he approached the marble lectern.

The pope stopped speaking and looked up, his large brown eyes taking in the situation in the square. Bruckentaler didn't wait for orders. He grabbed the pontiff by the arm and started toward the north end of the platform. The rest of his team converged around them, and they ploughed through the stunned bishops in tight formation, two men to a side, forming a square around the pope.

When they reached the end of the platform, Bruckentaler risked a look to his right. The congregation, five thousand strong, had finally sensed the approaching throng, and were in the process of evacuating their seats—as quickly as possible and in any conceivable direction. To say it was chaos was to woefully understate the disorder. He looked away; the plight of the mass-goers was not his responsibility. His only concern was the safety of the pope, whose nearly eighty-year-old legs were having a difficult time keeping pace.

The problems began at the foot of the stairs. Whereas the hundred or so cardinals, bishops, monsignors, priests, and deacons on the crowded altar platform had moved aside to let the phalanx pass through, the panic-stricken crowd on the floor of the square did not. People were everywhere; they bounced off, scrambled around, and trampled over one another as they attempted to get away from the mob, which had already penetrated deep into the formerly empty space at the eastern end of the square.

Bruckentaler yelled more instructions, and the pope's body-guards changed position. Four remained in place around the pontiff, forming a tight diamond, with Bruckentaler taking point, employing his tall, wide frame like a shield. The other four marched in advance in V formation, using their halberds to clear the way. It was tough going, but they forged ahead, leaving behind a wake of bruises and injuries.

They were still several hundred feet from the trapdoors when the first platoon of protesters spotted them. He heard them before he saw them, twisting and flailing to fight through the crowd, shouting in Arabic and brandishing stolen batons, chair legs, and fistfuls of stones and broken bricks.

But the defenders had protected popes for over five hundred years, against far more formidable foes than these. Two of the lead guardsmen broke ranks and ran straight at the attackers, ignoring the hail of rocks being hurled in their direction. The bulk of the stone-throwers fell back, all but the pair up front. These two waved their batons with fierce determination and rushed straight at the men guarding their target.

Their attack was in vain. The guardsmen swung their halberds sideways, felling the attackers easily. Both dropped to the ground, hemorrhaging blood from chest wounds. One attempted to get up; he received a severe kick to the ribs for his efforts and didn't move again. But the commotion did not go unnoticed, attracting the attention of a larger group of protesters, including several of the agitators who had led the attack on the Gendarmerie. Bruckentaler screamed into his microphone, begging for reinforcements, as he watched the horde advance pell-mell toward them.

*

Marco sat in the passenger seat and waited for his hour to come. His mouth was dry and his skin damp from sweat. He turned up the AC, which was already almost maxed. The heat was appalling, even at this hour. He offered a silent prayer, not even exactly sure for whom he was praying. He just wanted to pray; it helped him endure the wait.

He thought about his former life. He remembered the small stone church overlooking the ocean, felt the salty breeze on his face, and smelled the aroma of frying anchovies. Why was it, he wondered, that he had always taken these simple pleasures for granted, as if they weren't the divine blessings he now saw them to be?

The door of the guard hut opened, and two men stepped out, advancing upon the van in a purposeful fashion. They were wearing dark blue uniforms with the white badge of the Security Office in plain view. He reached underneath the seat to collect his gun, hoping to God he was right about them being impostors.

"Let them get in the van."

The lead officer circled around to the passenger side, leaving his subordinate in position on the driver's side. Elena punched a button on the console, and the back door opened on hydraulic power. The security officer got into the rear of the van, reaching inside his coat as he sat down. Marco realized he was going for his gun and twisted in his seat, whipping his own gun around. The barrel raked across the man's face, spattering blood on the windows. The man's head snapped back against the seat, but his gun hand continued to swivel in Marco's direction.

Marco saw it coming, in a rapid series of still frames, microseconds apart. He tried to knock the gun away with his own weapon, but his arm was on the wrong side of the man's body. It was the end, he thought, still seeing the sequential snapshots of the gun barrel, aperture pointing almost straight at him. And then he heard two blasts from behind him, followed by the thud of the man's head against the window. Two holes had opened up in his chest, belching blood like Vesuvius, and the handgun tumbled uselessly to the floor.

Elena's gun went off twice more, blowing out the driver's window, and Marco screwed his eyes shut against the showering fragments. When he opened them again, the second officer was no longer standing next to the van. He swiveled around, looking out the rear of the van, to where the Gendarmerie had been holding station, but he didn't see them. From the cacophony of wailing sirens, screams, and bullhorns audible through the blown-out window, he was pretty sure he knew why they had left their post.

He grabbed his shield and exited the van, grabbing a radio from the fallen officer, who was lying on the cobblestones with his face missing. Elena came up behind him and they ran into the square. The mob had broken through the line, and was surging forward like the tide. Here and there a remnant of the defense inserted itself in front of it, but the throng was too large and too angry to be stopped. It crashed over the defenders like a wave, breaking them with its relentless force and sucking them beneath the undertow.

St. Peter's Square was gone, replaced by a roiling ocean of humanity. People were everywhere; waves of them flooded the empty spaces, running in any direction but toward the onrushing protesters. Eddies formed where large groups of fleeing mass-goers ran into one another, causing swirling currents of terrified people. There were simply too many of them trying to get away at once, and the result was pandemonium, a churning, panic-stricken bedlam.

"Marco, they are evacuating the pope."

Elena pointed in the direction of the basilica. A huge altar had been erected at that end of the square, on which the pope had been co-celebrating mass with the Nigerian bishops. But all attempts at saying mass had been abandoned, and the holy men were streaming from the podium like ants from a burning hill.

Marco could see the pope, surrounded by his phalanx of Swiss Guards, literally being dragged through the fleeing congregation.

The radio crackled to life as the Swiss Guard officer commanding the platoon of guardsmen around the pope screamed for any and all listeners to help. But it was clear that the Gendarmerie and the Prima riot-control officers—the legitimate ones who had showed up—were still trying to hold the line in front of the Piazza Pius XI in an effort to prevent the rest of the protesters from entering the Piazza San Pietro, while the other Swiss Guard platoons, though fighting furiously to get to the pope, were on the wrong side of the massive altar.

"Elena, let's go."

With that, Marco secured his shield on his arm and jumped into the fray, not bothering to look behind him to see if she was following.

Sowsan bin Nawwaf watched the chaos swirling around him in every direction. He stood over the trapdoor leading down to the catacombs; four portable wooden barriers formed a square around him, and a second set of barriers formed another square around those. Between the barriers and his Heckler & Koch MP5 submachine gun, none of the fleeing congregation had sought refuge next to him. According to the official plan, he was supposed to keep this space clear until the pope was in close range, at which point he would move one of the barriers and raise the trapdoor, keeping it raised until the pope and his accompanying guardsmen had passed below. Once they were safely inside, he would close the door and not allow anyone else to follow.

But the plan set out by Mohammed Sadir was completely different, and Sowsan had no intention of allowing the pope to slink away to safety. The minute he was in range, he would shoot any of the guardsmen in his way and kill the pope before throwing down his weapon, shedding his uniform, and disappearing into the crowd.

CHAPTER 10

Bruckentaler barked orders into his microphone, directing four of the guardsmen to stay to protect their flank. They broke off immediately, forming a line to hold the perimeter against over a hundred angry protesters. The remaining four pressed on, the screams of the oncoming mob lending haste to their endeavors. They were close; Bruckentaler could smell the finish line. The destination loomed ahead, a small cordoned-off area in a churning sea of bodies. He had instructed the man from the Vatican Security Office to unlock the doors but leave them closed, lest the panicked crowd try to find refuge in the tunnel.

They plowed through the last wave of people, and they were there: a twenty-five-square-meter rectangle of open space created by heavy wooden barriers. Inside the outer barrier, a second set of barriers was set up around the trapdoors; inside the inner square, a very serious-looking man brandishing a Heckler & Koch MP5 stood at the ready. Bruckentaler radioed to him to open the door and push aside one of the barriers, but the officer ignored him. Bruckentaler spoke a short command into his microphone, and the lead guardsman moved one of the outer barriers and strode forward with purpose.

He didn't get far. The security officer leveled his weapon and fired a burst into the guardsman's torso, throwing him back out of the way. The guardsman next in line reacted quickly, hurling his halberd like a spear. But the assassin dodged the missile easily and felled the man with a well-placed shot. The third guardsman rushed forward, holding his halberd like a lance in front of him. The gunman fired on him, but his Kevlar absorbed the bullets, and on he went, though slower than before, getting within five feet of the gunman before a second burst knocked him down.

Bruckentaler saw the third guardsman fall and knew what it meant. He was the only thing between the gunman and his mark. The thought had barely entered his brain when the assassin's Heckler & Koch swiveled and fired. Bruckentaler's chest exploded with pain, even with the Kevlar armor on, and he began to list. He tried to keep on his feet, but his legs wouldn't obey the command to stand, and he toppled over, leaving nothing between the gun and the pope but twenty feet of air.

Marco ran across the cobbled piazza, Elena behind him, using the riot shield to batter his way through the swirling throng. He shoved another trio of spectators out of his way and forged on, a growing feeling of hopelessness in his belly. It was just too far, and the going too slow. He let his angst fuel his tired legs as he angled across the growing swell of refugees toward the Bronze Doors. He reached the lee of the massive altar structure, and his pace quickened, as the crush of fleeing guests was much thinner behind it. He traversed the fifty-meter width of the altar quickly, and for the first time his hopes rose that they might actually reach the pope. As to what would transpire when they got there, he had no idea; he was taking one step at a time.

But his hopes were dashed as he waded back into the heavy swell on the far side of the altar. He and Elena were trying to go north; the traffic flowed west toward the relative safety of the basilica. It was like swimming against the tide; they had to struggle just to keep their position, much less make any progress toward their destination.

They got a break when several of the rioters happened past, parting the crowd like the Red Sea. The two of them streaked across the empty space, making up seconds of priceless time, only to come face to face with more of the rabble. There were five of them, and for some reason—he forgot for a minute how they were dressed—the angry youngsters appeared to have it in for them. As soon as they saw Elena, they made straight for her. Marco would have loved to avoid a confrontation, but he didn't have time to run around in circles trying to dodge his pursuers.

He was still considering his options when Elena yanked her pistol out of her belt and shot the first one in the thigh. The wounded boy screamed bloody murder, and his comrades parted to the four winds, opening up another lane in the crowd. Marco took advantage and ran another thirty meters unimpeded, until the next wave of fleeing guests brought him to a standstill. He was pushed to the ground by the surge and barely avoided being trampled to death. When he got to his feet, he had lost his bearings, and a pit opened up in his stomach.

Suddenly he heard a burst of weapons fire, close, over to his right. He looked around for Elena, but she was lost in the churning horde, and he crashed straight into the surge of people fleeing from the gunshots, hammering people out of the way with his shield. He vaulted over a downed spectator and saw the gunman, ahead and to his right, his gun pointed at the pope. It was point-blank range, but there was still a lone guardsman standing in front of the Holy Father. Marco raised his own weapon, but there were people in the way, and he couldn't get a clear shot.

The gunman fired, and the pope's defender tottered. Marco took another long stride and jumped, extending his arms in front of him. The guardsman fell, and the gunman fired again, the report deafening. But the bullets clanged against Marco's shield, whining away into the distance. The force of the shots slammed the shield against him and dislodged his helmet, which tumbled lazily to the ground. His momentum carried him past the pope, and his head smacked against the cobbles, clouding his vision. He skittered into one of the fallen guardsmen, coming to rest.

The last thing he heard before the darkness swallowed him was the sound of Elena's pistol—*boom, boom, boom*—and the thud of a body hitting the stony ground.

CHAPTER 11

Marco opened his eyes, and a thin gauze of consciousness ebbed in. Or perhaps it wasn't consciousness; maybe he'd died and was in purgatory awaiting his final judgment. Or was this hell? He had a feeling he'd met the admission criteria, but the cool breeze wafting over his head told him otherwise; hell couldn't have a breeze like this. His pupils dilated, and the meager light fell upon his retinas. He was lying on a large bed in a spacious room. Starlight filtered in from floor-to-ceiling windows in the opposite wall. Purple velvet curtains fluttered in the wind swirling in from the night.

He pulled off the sheets and sat up in bed. He was wearing a pair of dark cotton pajamas, long enough in the leg but much too wide in the waist. His shoulder ached slightly where a ricochet had grazed him, and his forehead felt tight, as if gripped by an overly zealous headband, but otherwise he felt fine. There was a pitcher of water sweating on the table, and he filled a glass and took a swallow, trying to moisten his arid mouth.

He heard a noise to his left and turned to watch the door open from the outside. A man walked in and shut it, then sat down in an oversized leather armchair. He was a large man, tall and broad-shouldered, with a chest that reminded Marco of the barrels his grandfather used to age grappa. His skin was the color of the night sky, and he had brown eyes that sparkled even in the dim light. He was wearing a black robe with a purple scarf that would have looked ridiculous on most men, but Pope John Paul III pulled it off quite easily.

"How are you feeling, Father Venetti?"

"Well, Your Holiness."

Marco had seen the pope before, in a small audience shortly after his election. It had been a landmark moment in his life, but it hadn't prepared him for the experience of sitting alone with the Supreme Pontiff of the Roman Catholic Church. Or perhaps his uneasiness stemmed from the fact that John Paul III was the 217th successor to St. Peter, while he himself was a priest with enough blood on his hands to fill a large baptismal font.

He got up from the bed and crossed to the window, trying to walk away from his disquiet. Several lights burned in the distance, easily several hundred meters below his position.

"This isn't Vatican City. Where are we, Holiness?"

"Castel Gandolfo."

The Palazzo Apostolico di Castel Gandolfo had been the summer residence and vacation retreat of popes since the 1929 signing of the Lateran Treaty, which relinquished the former estate of the Emperor Domitian to the Holy See. Marco had heard a rumor that Pope John Paul III was especially fond of the pastoral setting that Gandolfo afforded him and had to be dragged back to "that other place in Rome" when his visits were over.

"What are we doing here?"

"Enjoying the beautiful breeze. It's fearfully hot in Rome."

The pontiff spoke Italian fluently—not bad for someone who'd grown up in the watery slums of Makoko—with only a trace of an accent. Marco wanted to pin it down, but couldn't; it was the mellifluous accent of a man who spoke many languages and dialects.

"Cardinal Lucci also thought it wise to get you out of Vatican City. The Polizia di Stato were buzzing around like angry hornets. This seemed like a more proper place to recover."

"How did I get here?"

"The Swiss Guard wanted me to leave the Vatican immediately after the assassination attempt. I insisted we go together."

"Thank you, Holiness."

The pope smiled, displaying teeth that dazzled brightly against his dark brown skin. "You saved my life. It seemed like the least I could do."

And then it came back to him: the sound of gunfire and the screams of the crowd; the frenzied swirling of the throng and the grim visage of the man trying to kill the pope; the smell of fear hanging in the air like a fog; the taste of vomit, acidic and bilious, lapping into his throat.

Prior to this morning, he had been the pastor of an eight-hundred-year-old parish overlooking the Ligurian Sea. His worst offenses were the curses he uttered whenever AC Milan was scored against—which had been quite frequent of late. Now his conscience was so overloaded he'd be saying the Our Father until the end of time.

"What happened to Elena?"

"She's fine. A remarkable woman. Neither the shooting nor the six-hour inquisition at the hands of the Vatican Security Office seemed to faze her."

"Shooting?"

"Elena killed the man who tried to assassinate me."

Marco vaguely remembered hearing the report of her pistol before he lost consciousness. "Where is she?"

"Still at the Vatican."

"What about her sister and her daughter?"

"They were flown down to join her. They are all together now."

"And the terrorists on Castello di Giordano?"

"They attempted to flee the island on Elena's boat and ran out of fuel in the Ligurian Sea. A fishing vessel spotted them, and the Guardia Costiera dispatched a frigate to investigate."

The pope stopped speaking and came to join Marco at the window overlooking Lake Albano, whose waters shimmered like a mirror in the moonlight.

"The terrorists opened fire on the frigate, and the captain had no choice but to return fire, sinking the *Bel Amica* and killing all the men on board."

More death and destruction, Marco thought. Was there no end to it?

"How are you feeling?"

It was a difficult question. *Empty* was the only word he could think of, but it seemed to match the hollow feeling in his innards, the vacuum in his chest.

"I'm fine."

"Oberst Jaecks, the commandant of the Swiss Guard, is very keen on speaking to you, but I will tell him you're not up to it yet."

In truth, Marco *wasn't* up to it yet; he wasn't sure he was ever going to be. But if it needed to be done, he might as well get it over with. "Perhaps after a meal?"

The pope picked up a telephone and held a brief conversation. "Veal and peppers in twenty minutes."

"Will Oberst Jaecks be coming?"

John Paul III shook his head. "Cardinal Lucci is joining us for dinner. He wishes to speak with you."

Cardinal Lucci arrived as dinner was being served. He was a small man with dark hair and light blue eyes the color of sapphires. He greeted Marco warmly and joined them at the table on the porch overlooking Lake Albano. A priest brought out a serving tray loaded with heaped dishes and a bottle of Chianti. Lucci poured three glasses and raised his own in a toast.

"To a speedy recovery, Father Venetti."

Marco swallowed the wine, savoring the cool feel of fluid in his arid mouth. They ate in silence for a while, enjoying the food and the cool night air.

He guessed the Cardinal Secretary hadn't come all the way from the Vatican just for dinner, and he was correct; after a polite period, Lucci asked him to tell his story. Marco did as he was asked, regurgitating the entire episode, from Elena's confession to the events in St. Peter's Square with which they were both familiar.

"I am sorry you were given this cross to bear, Marco."

Marco was sorry also. He'd used the washroom prior to dinner and had barely recognized himself in the mirror. There were dark smudges underneath his light blue eyes, and his normally tanned skin was pale.

"On the other hand, I am happy the Lord chose you for the job. If it wasn't for you, I would be dead, buried beneath the rubble of the basilica."

"Was I chosen, Holiness?"

"Elena could have decided to seek absolution at a different parish. But she didn't. The Holy Spirit guided her to you."

"Why do you think it was the Holy Spirit?"

"Let me ask you a different question. Why do you think it wasn't?"

The breeze picked up, carrying with it the earthy smell of truffles and the tinkling of sheep's bells from the pastures below.

"There is something you should know. I was in love with Elena at one time."

The pope contemplated this without comment. Cardinal Lucci set down the piece of Brie he was eating.

"When was this?"

"Four years ago."

"Elena never said anything about it when I spoke to her yesterday."

"No, I am sure she didn't, Eminence."

"You said this was four years ago. What happened?"

Marco shrugged. "She realized I was never going to leave the priesthood, and I didn't see her again."

"Until three days ago, that is, when the door of your confessional opened."

"She was terrified and desperate for absolution."

"And yet she didn't confess to the priest at San Sebastiano Martire, the parish she has attended for the past four years."

"San Sebastiano? She was going there?"

"Yes, she told me yesterday, and I confirmed it with Father DiPietro, the pastor of the parish. She had been attending mass on a fairly regular basis, and her daughter made her First Holy Communion there two years ago."

A dog barked below them, and Marco saw a Maremma sheepdog chasing a pair of sheep that had strayed from the flock. When it had herded them back to the group clustered underneath a large acacia tree, it returned to its spot on a knoll just above the animals entrusted to its charge. How many times, Marco thought, had this same scene played out in this dusty theater above the waters of Lake Albano?

"Tell me something, Marco. Are you still in love with Elena?"

A bead of sweat moistened his brow, and his mouth was parched. "I thought I was, Holiness, still, after all this time. But I don't think I am now—maybe I never was."

"Don't be ashamed of it. A man without love is nothing more than a resounding gong or a clashing cymbal, which explains the orchestra that plays continually inside the walls of the Vatican. No, what we need—what this world needs—is more love, not less of it."

The priest acting as their waiter reappeared and cleared the table, returning with a silver coffee service. Marco poured three cups of espresso and passed them out. He sipped at his, relishing the strong bite in the back of his throat and the churn of acid in his stomach.

"I am sure it wasn't easy to kill those men, Father Venetti, especially since you are a priest. But you were stopping terrorists, not robbing a bank. Imagine the carnage in St. Peter's Square; there were five thousand people there this morning. You prevented a massacre. I agree with His Holiness. The Holy Spirit knew what It was doing when It chose you for the job. And let us all thank God for that."

CHAPTER 12

Cardinal Lucci returned to the porch after seeing Father Venetti back to his room and leaned against the railing, turning his back on the world that had been conspiring against them. "Our enemies gather at the gate, Holiness."

"And yet the gates still stand, Eminence."

"But for how much longer? We are fortunate to be alive."

"We are fortunate to have a breeze like this on an otherwise oppressive night. We are alive for an entirely different reason."

"Which is?"

"Father Venetti delivered us from this evil."

Lucci lifted his demitasse cup in appreciation. "Amen." He leaned over and selected a piece of mango from a tray of fruit that had been set on the table. "And the next time?"

"If and when the next time comes, we will again survive, as we have survived for over two thousand years. Who knows, perhaps *you* will be pontiff by then."

"I wish I shared your faith. Perhaps if you better understood the threats we face, you might—"

"I might what? Be as pessimistic as you? You should spend less time inside the Vatican Security Office and let them do their job."

"There's little chance of that."

"Can I ask you something, Vincenzo?"

Here it comes, Lucci thought. It was rare for the pontiff to address him by his given name, and it always portended a subject he didn't want to discuss.

"For all your micro-management of the Security Office, what good has come of it?"

"None that I can see."

"That's what I thought."

The pope poured two glasses of an Alsatian Riesling the priest had left to wash down dessert. Lucci accepted one and swirled it in the moonlight, creating sticky legs that crawled down the glass.

"Holiness, there's something you should know."

The pope gazed at him but said nothing.

"Do you know Giampaolo Benedetto?"

"The Inspector General of the Security Office?"

Lucci nodded.

"Yes, of course."

"How well?"

"Well enough, I suppose. What about him?"

"He's missing. No one has seen him since yesterday."

The pope considered this news in silence for a minute. From the pursing of his wide mouth and the deep furrow in his dark brow, Lucci could see he wasn't happy about it.

"I suppose that means you think he was involved in the attack?"

"You suppose correctly."

"Do you have any evidence to support your supposition?"

"Unfortunately, yes. The terrorists had three men inside the Security Office. Benedetto hired all three within the past year. Normally, each would have had an independent background check, but he signed off on their hiring papers without one."

"Why was this allowed?"

"I could blame staffing issues in the research department, but the truth is, Benedetto is the Inspector General of the Security Office. His family has worked for the Vatican for years. His grandfather was the chief of the Gendarmerie for two decades."

The pope acknowledged this with a small sip of wine.

"He also issued all the documents giving the terrorists entry into St. Peter's Square."

They were quiet for a minute, with only the drone of the cicadas to distract their thoughts.

"Why did he do it, Eminence?"

"For the same reason Judas handed Jesus over to the chief priests."

"Thirty pieces of silver?"

"Adjusted heavily for two thousand years of inflation, yes."

"It's reassuring to see that human nature hasn't changed much in two millennia."

Lucci didn't comment—or mention that the Security Office had heard rumors that Benedetto was a racist as well—and turned to gaze at the distant waters of Lake Albano, shimmering in the weak moonlight.

"Is it true about the Nigerians being involved?"

"Boko Haram has claimed responsibility for the attack, but I would hardly call them Nigerians. They are jihadist militants who happen to be based in Nigeria."

"They are Nigerians, just like I am. Why would my countrymen take up arms against me?"

"Several of the other men involved are known Saudi terrorists; remember that. We have no idea who was really behind this attack."

"What do the Saudis have against me?"

"I'm not sure really; they weren't even on my list."

A camp of Mediterranean horseshoe bats whirled in the night air above them, occasionally getting close enough for Lucci to feel the rush of air as they flew past on the hunt for mosquitoes.

"Your list?"

"The list of people who want your papacy to end as soon as possible."

"Ah, that list … Who *is* on it?"

"The Chinese, of course. You will remember I was dead set against your condemnation of their labor policies and human rights abuses."

"Am I supposed to just sit quietly and let these things happen?"

A bat fluttered past Lucci's head, close enough to mess up his hair, which was still mainly black, with only a few streaks of gray. He smoothed it straight back and placed his red zucchetto on top of his head in an effort to ward off further incursions.

"The Indian government was not pleased with your criticism of their environmental policies."

"The earth was here before us and was given to us. Never have we so hurt and mistreated our common home as we have in the last two hundred years."

Lucci had heard him say this many times before, and though he couldn't agree more with him on this one issue—just about the only one—it made keeping him safe a much more difficult proposition. It also made for more mosquitoes, because the pope had forbidden the use of insecticides on all properties belonging to the Holy See. To combat the subsequent plague of the tiny blood-suckers, he had sanctioned the construction of scores of bat houses, and bats had become as ubiquitous as mosquitoes.

"And then there are the Russians, Holiness."

"I knew you would be bringing them up."

"Yes, well, I did warn you not to announce your desire to seek unification."

"Is Christ divided? Did he ask St. Peter to be the rock upon which he would build eight different churches?"

"I don't think he did, no, but the Russians don't really care about that, frankly. What they do care about is nipping any chance of renewed religious fervor in the bud. The powers-that-be in Russia have spent a lot of time and energy castrating the Russian Orthodox Church, to the point that Patriarch Alexy III never says anything even remotely political. Perhaps you should take a page from his book?"

The pope dismissed this idea with a grimace and a wave of his fingers, which were thick and strong. It was rumored that the Vatican's goldsmith had had to greatly expand the previous pope's Ring of the Fisherman in order to get it to fit Pope John Paul III's massive finger.

"There will always be an angry captain to sound the war horn, Eminence. But why did these men heed its call? There's a deeper evil at play. And if we want the basilica to stand for another two millennia, we had better discover what it is."

"Men have been killing each other for thousands of years, Holiness. It has been the method of choice for conflict resolution since Cain slew Abel."

"Sounds like you're advocating for it."

Lucci shook his head. "Just observing it. As an Italian, I can't help but be a student of history."

"And what do your studies tell you?"

"That armed conflict is as inevitable as death."

"A strange thing for a cardinal of the Roman Catholic Church to say."

"With all due respect, Pope Leo IX led his own army into battle against the Normans."

"And his army was decimated at Civitate. You need to be careful with history, Vincenzo. It is a dangerous thing. Despots throughout the ages have tweaked history to justify their actions. Great evils have been perpetrated under its banner."

"The same thing could be said for religion."

"For once we agree."

Lucci reached for the Riesling but changed his mind; excellent though the vintage was, the combination of alcohol, caffeine, and the pope's rebuttals was having an unsettling effect on his stomach. Less than a year into his papacy, John Paul III had already achieved legendary status, simply by virtue of being the first black pope in over two millennia. But there was far more to him than the color of his skin. He was a truly spiritual man—rare for a pope—and an intellectual as well. Many a cardinal had skulked away from a discussion with him with his tail down like a beaten dog.

"I hate to change the subject, Holiness, but there is something we need to discuss."

The pope didn't reply. He pushed his chair back, springing up easily for a man of his great size and long years, and joined Lucci at the railing.

"We need to issue a statement, the sooner the better. Today's press release will buy us time, but the world will want to hear from you."

Lucci had crafted a brief story that had aired that morning. The short audio segment had credited an officer of the Gendarmerie with saving the pope's life.

"Have you given it any thought?"

"Much. I am thinking about making an address in St. Peter's Square tomorrow."

"Perhaps a more subtle response is in order. Why don't we let the press office read your statement?"

The pope shook his head. "We have an opportunity here."

Acid licked at Lucci's throat, and he reached reflexively for the foil of Brioschi in his side pocket. He ripped open the packet, dumped the contents into a glass of water, and watched the bubbles rise to the surface. The pope was right, he thought. There was an opportunity here: an opportunity to castrate the Church forever. "An opportunity to do what?"

"Emulate Christ. That's what defines us as Christians."

If there was one thing Lucci hated, it was getting a catechism lecture from the pope. He took a long swallow of the antacid, but it was too late; he could already feel the sting in his esophagus.

"When St. Peter cut off the ear of the High Priest's slave, Christ placed it back on. We will do the same. We will fight hatred with love, prejudice with tolerance. There is no other way to respond."

"And how do you think that message will be perceived by the perpetrators of this mission?"

"I have a different question. Suppose we track down and kill everyone responsible for the atrocity. What then?"

Lucci said nothing.

"Ten more terrorists rise from the ashes of each one killed. You can't stop violence with more violence. You only beget more."

"You may not believe this, Holiness, but I agree with you on a philosophical level. But terrorism isn't a philosophical problem. It's real, and it requires a real solution."

"Such as?"

"Such as holding the perpetrators responsible so they don't try again. I don't think building a Muslim community center in Rome is an effective deterrent."

The pope laughed, easing the building tension. "How did you guess?"

Lucci almost choked on a mouthful of his Brioschi. "I was being sarcastic."

"Sarcasm doesn't become you."

"Nor does naïvety become you. It is a grave mistake to forgive the perpetrators before they are brought to justice."

"Justice? To whose justice are you referring? Man's, or God's?"

"I have no authority to speak for God." Lucci bit his tongue so that the words *unlike you* didn't roll off it. "So I have to settle for whatever justice man can dispense. They will be watching, Holiness, the people who did this. And they will be listening to the tone of your message. If they don't hear what they want to hear, they will set the dogs on us once again."

"Tell me what they want to hear."

"That you understand the social injustice that spawns the violence, that you apologize for the poverty of the Muslim world that creates the unrest, that you abhor the West's lack of interest in addressing any of the real issues underlying the spread of terrorism."

"Well said. I may need to borrow some of your phrasing."

"If you want to destroy the Church, be my guest."

"These statements are not true?"

"Of course they are true. But that doesn't mean they should be uttered aloud, by you, in this situation."

"And here I was thinking the truth would set us free."

"Not in this case, Holiness."

Not in this case.

CHAPTER 13

Abayd al-Subail was not an intelligent man, but he had survived this long in a difficult business for one reason: he relied solely on his instincts, and his instincts were good. He sat at his desk now, in the large office on the second floor of the six-stall garage located behind Haus Adler, peering sightlessly at the huge bank of flat-screen TVs displaying the continuous feed from all the CCTV cameras monitoring Prince Kamal el-Rayad's property on the Untersberg, the monstrous peak towering over Salzburg. There was something wrong—something way beyond the failed attempt to kill the pope—and he knew it. His instincts told him so, and they were never wrong.

He had told the prince as much months ago, but his boss had dismissed his concerns—for only the first time since he had been his bodyguard. And Abayd had been the prince's bodyguard for a long time, ever since el-Rayad had assigned him the job on the playground sands of their elementary school. The prince's father had decided not to send him to England like his older brothers, enrolling him instead at the local public school. In his father's vision, he was to become a great man of the people, a leader grounded in the lives of ordinary citizens. In reality, the prince had been a pariah from the outset; the only grounding he'd received usually followed a well-aimed kick or punch from one of his classmates.

It had all stopped, of course, as soon as the prince had had the good sense to bring Abayd on board, for a share of el-Rayad's handsome weekly allowance. Forty-plus years later, he was still doing the same job, albeit for a considerably higher wage. The whole time he had relied on his instincts. They hadn't failed him in forty years, and they weren't failing him now: something smelled. Worse still, he had been unable to convince his boss there was a problem; the man was too obsessed with destroying the Vatican to listen to reason.

Abayd crossed to the window as the sun dipped below the Gaisberg, the small mountain on Salzburg's western flank. He hated it here, he realized, no matter how picturesque the old city was. For starters, security was a nightmare, especially with the prince out and about every day. But it was more than that; he hated everything about Austria. The wine was too sweet, the food too heavy, and the air too light.

As this was to be their last Mozart Festival for some time— Abayd suspected forever—the prince was planning to paint the town red, because it would not be long before the Vatican Security Office and Europol concluded that Prince el-Rayad of Saudi Arabia had planned and financed the attempted assassination of the pope.

Not very long at all.

The Vatican possessed nearly unlimited financial resources and had allegiances in every corner of the world, particularly Europe. When the trail led the pursuers to the prince—and Abayd was sure, despite all Mohammed's reassurances, that it would—they needed to be safely back in Riyadh.

The shuffling of feet from behind him distracted his attention, and he turned to see Jibril entering his office. Jibril was Abayd's first cousin and his most trusted aide. He was also a genius with computers and electronics, a talent that endeared him further to Abayd, who was not.

"We need to talk."

Abayd nodded and led his cousin down the stairs into the back of the garage that lay beneath. There were currently four vehicles inside: a Lamborghini Murciélago, two black Mercedes sedans, and an armored Bentley limousine. They slipped out the back door, and walked along the edge of the cliff upon which the garage was perched. When they had gone fifty meters from the building, Abayd stopped in the middle of a grassy plateau and turned toward his cousin.

"So, what do we have to talk about?"

"Did you know there was a problem with KiKi's phone?"

"Yes, I'm the one who sent him to you. Why, *is* there a problem with it?"

"You could say that."

"Are you going to tell me what it is?"

Jibril fished his Marlboro cigarettes out of his pants pocket, lit one, and consumed half of it in one long drag. "The prince was complaining he had no memory space. I immediately thought he'd used it up storing his porn collection, but it wasn't that. There was plenty of space remaining, but his phone just couldn't access it."

"Why not?"

"I thought at first it was a glitch, but I plugged it in to my computer and ran a diagnostic."

"And?"

Jibril blew a long stream of smoke. "The phone checked out."

"So what's the problem? Virus?"

"Something like that. The prince downloaded a program onto the hard drive."

"What kind of program?"

"A very large one. Normally, a massive program like that would be obvious, but this one wasn't. I wouldn't have found it without some powerful software I recently acquired, and even then, I was lucky."

"What does this program do?"

"That's just it, cousin; I'm not sure. I'm working on it, but I didn't want to wait to tell you."

"How much longer will it take?"

"I don't know. A few hours at best, maybe never."

"Never?"

"Possibly. The whole program is encrypted. I can't read a word of it."

"But you have software to get around encryption codes, Jibril; I authorized payment for it. You did buy it, didn't you?"

The prince had deep pockets, and it was not unheard of for his staff to reach inside them to line their own wallets. Abayd knew this well, because he was the worst offender, easily doubling his salary by embezzling money from the security budget.

"Yes, I have the software, but it didn't work."

"How could that be?"

"I'm not sure. It would help if we asked KiKi. If we knew where he got the program, I might be able to think of a way to read it. Or I could tell him I found the problem and see if he wants to delete the program."

"How do you know KiKi downloaded it?"

"Nobody else has access to the phone, except for you and me. I didn't do it, and the possibility of a caveman like you doing it is zero. That leaves him."

"It doesn't make any sense. Why would he download a program that hides from him? He already knows it's there."

"Why don't we ask him?"

"No. Can you tell me the date and time it was installed?"

"Probably, with some work. Why?"

"I have a hunch, that's why."

"Want to tell me about it?"

"No, and don't mention a word of this to anyone other than me."

"You're a secretive bastard, Abayd."

"That's why I'm still alive, cousin."

CHAPTER 14

The Roman Catholic Church had acquired its fair share of enemies over the course of its two-thousand-year history, making the job of the Vatican Security Office an undertaking of some magnitude. The *raison d'être* of the office was to know the identity and divine the intent of every foe. It was a difficult task, and the improbability of doing it successfully kept Vincenzo Lucci up till all hours most nights. Although Cardinal Lucci was not part of the office, as Secretary of State he was in charge of the overall security of Vatican City, and he was not the kind of man to let others do his work.

He lived in a spacious apartment in the Apostolic Palace, not far from the pontiff, an irony that was a mainstay of Curial gossip. In truth, he had been greatly disappointed by John Paul III's election. The British bookmaker Paddy Power had listed Lucci himself as one of the favorites prior to the conclave; his odds had risen all the way to three to one a few days before the white smoke had drifted from the Sistine Chapel. After the election, he had almost considered turning down John Paul III's request that he serve as Secretary of State, even though it was a job for which he was well suited.

But in the end, he had come to be very happy managing the affairs of state for the world's only religious oligarchy; or at least he had been happy until now. Now, he sat moodily behind the large mahogany desk in his study, silently seething about the catastrophe that had almost befallen the Church.

On his watch, of all times.

The appearance of Cardinal Scarletti, the Under Secretary of State, who had served for the last three papacies, gave him some relief from his self-inquisition. "He has arrived, Eminence."

"Send him in, Giuseppe."

The heavy oak door opened, and a lone man entered and sank into the brown leather armchair in front of the desk. He was well shy of average height and sat in a slumped posture, making him look even shorter. He was dressed in a gray suit and a striped necktie, and his face wore a dour expression, as if he was an attendee at the funeral of a poorly cherished family member.

"Why so glum, Mr. Foster?"

"It comes with the territory, Eminence."

Lucci didn't doubt it; Foster was CIA.

"Things could have been a lot worse, don't you think?"

"Wrong verb."

Lucci lifted a neatly trimmed eyebrow. "What do you mean?"

"They *should* have been a lot worse."

"And yet they are not. Perhaps God isn't dead quite yet."

"I don't believe God had anything to do with it, and neither should you."

"You do realize I am a cardinal?"

"No, you're not; you're the leader of the second most despised country in the world. And if you think God averted that attack, you're going to sit on your hands and rely on him to stop the next one."

Foster got up and walked over to a dark cherry wood hutch, reaching inside to produce a bottle of Buffalo Trace bourbon and a pair of glasses. He set the glasses down on Lucci's desk and filled them both.

"No thanks."

He ignored Lucci and handed over the glass. "Trust me, you're going to need it, and the next one will be stiffer."

"I take it the news isn't good."

"That all depends upon your point of view. I'm sure you won't be thrilled, but I can hardly contain myself."

Lucci swallowed his bourbon; his throat welcomed the scorch of the alcohol. "Why are you so excited?"

"I kind of like Rome. It sure beats Prague, where they sent me last. At least you can get a decent meal from time to time."

"You'll be staying, then?"

"You've got enough enemies to keep me here until the end of my career."

"You don't have to be so cheerful about it. Let's hear it, Mr. Foster."

"Already? I haven't even finished my first whiskey."

"Drink up, then."

Foster complied. "Have you ever heard of a Saudi prince named Kamal el-Rayad?"

"No. Should I have?"

"Maybe. He's one of the richest men in the world—and consequently, one of the most dangerous. His ancestral lands sit on top of the largest known oil field."

"I do remember hearing something about him recently, now that you mention it."

Lucci reached into his desk and extracted two cigars from the box tucked away in the back. He knew he shouldn't—his doctor frequently reminded him that the cigars exacerbated his heartburn—but he had a strong feeling he was going to get a severe case of indigestion anyway.

"He was in the news a few months ago. He had gotten into trouble with the House of Saud, which isn't surprising, because the House of Saud has hated the House of Rayad since the end of the nineteenth century."

"This history lesson has a point?"

"Yes, and I'm getting to it. You got someplace to go?"

Foster lit up his Maduro cigar and blew a thick stream of the honey-flavored smoke into the air, where it formed a cloud around the chandelier.

"Al Saud ultimately defeated the Rayadi, who lost all their power by the 1920s."

"But not all their land?"

"No, they retained a huge swath of land in Nagd, outside Riyadh. And they have been quietly pumping oil and making billions of American dollars by selling it exclusively to us. Everything was hunky-dory between the two houses for years, until just recently."

"What happened?"

Foster shrugged. "Kamal el-Rayad happened. The treaty that ended the war between the two families specifically stated that although the Rayadi were to be allowed to keep the majority of their ancestral lands, they had to stop using their royal titles, a stipulation with which they happily complied for almost a century, until a few years ago, when Kamal el-Rayad starting calling himself an emir. The House of Saud ignored it for a while, which el-Rayad took as a sign that they didn't have the will to oppose him on the issue."

"But they did oppose him?"

Foster got up and started pacing back and forth, stopping every so often to take a sip of his whiskey and make sure he still had Lucci's attention.

"You bet your reverential ass they did, so hard that the CIA analysts in the Mideast section thought el-Rayad was going to lose all his land. But someone intervened, and the whole thing was swept under the rug. El-Rayad even got to keep using his title." Foster punctuated this point by flicking the ash from his cigar in the general direction of the ashtray that Cardinal Scarletti had placed there in anticipation of his visit.

"Who intervened?"

"Don't know. Somebody with very big balls, I can tell you that."

Foster sank back into the chair, as if the pacing had exhausted his capacity for exertion.

"Why are you telling me this?"

"We strongly suspect that el-Rayad is a major supporter of Islamic extremists."

"Suspect? Does that mean you don't have any evidence?"

"None whatsoever. But when has that ever stopped us?"

Lucci got up and took his turn pacing, his black robe swishing behind him. "And you think this el-Rayad had something to do with the attack on the pope?"

Foster nodded. His face remained unexpressive, and his small gray eyes betrayed nothing other than their irritation from the cigar smoke, which had grown heavy. "I'm pretty sure of it."

"And why would he want to do that?"

"Because he's pitching a tent for you guys that a herd of camels could hide under."

"I have no idea what you're talking about."

"Sure you do, Eminence. But let me spell it out for you anyway. El-Rayad wants to level Vatican City and rollerblade through the rubble."

"Why?"

Foster shrugged. "Next time he stops by, I'll ask him. What difference does it make?"

"I would like to know."

He laughed, sending droplets of saliva and whiskey high into the air. "Why? 'Cause you're going to change his mind?"

Lucci's face reddened, matching his sash. "Why didn't you tell me about this before?"

"There aren't enough hours in the day to tell you about every wingnut that hates the Church. And until a few hours ago, that's all we had him figured for."

"What happened a few hours ago?"

"I had a visit from a friend of mine in the CIA's Directorate of Operations. El-Rayad can't pick his nose without them knowing about it."

Foster stubbed out his Maduro and extracted a different cigar from his breast pocket. Lucci gave him a disapproving look, but the American ignored him and stuffed the cigar between his thin, bloodless lips, then lit up, filling the air with more smoke.

"What did your friend in the directorate tell you?"

"I was getting to that, Eminence. They have an informant in the prince's network. They knew something was afoot, but they had no idea what. Until the day before yesterday, of course."

"They should have warned us."

Foster laughed, causing him to choke on a wisp of cigar smoke. "No, they shouldn't have."

Lucci drained his glass. "Why not?"

"If they blow the whistle and warn you, el-Rayad knows he has a leak, and the source is gone. Simple as that."

"So why say something now?"

"I was getting to that. For starters, the attack has already happened, so there's no worries about blowing the source. Secondly, and this is the bad news which I was referring to, we haven't heard the last from the prince."

"No?"

Lucci's pacing stopped. He stood in front of a window overlooking St. Peter's Square, which was still cordoned off with yellow tape. A large company of Sampietrini, the men and women who were charged with maintaining Vatican City, had taken over the square, endeavoring to restore it to its former luster. With time, the tape would be removed, and the faithful would return to find that little had changed, other than the erection of a small stone memorial to the score of people—including four Swiss Guardsmen—who had died in the attack.

Just another bloodbath in the two-thousand-year history of the Church.

"The informant reported in again this morning."

Lucci rubbed his narrow forehead. He felt a headache coming on, which was scarcely surprising given his lack of sleep, alcohol intake, and the noxious smoke. "I can hardly wait."

Foster took a long puff of his rapidly shrinking cigar. "There's going to be another attack."

Lucci refilled his glass and took another swallow of whiskey.

"However, there is some good news, Eminence."

"Yes?"

"My friend … he wants to meet with you."

"What does he want?"

"He didn't say, but I suspect he's going to offer to help you."

"There will be strings attached, I suspect?"

"Is the pope Catholic?"

"That is the same question I ask myself every day, Mr. Foster." Lucci paused so that the CIA man could appreciate his cleverness. "Your president has spoken to me much about increased cooperation between the Vatican and the United States." He stopped walking and faced Foster. "Can't you make this problem go away for us?"

"Allow me to give you a lesson on international politics. Let's forget for a moment that Prince el-Rayad is from Saudi Arabia, our staunchest ally in the Mideast. Let's assume we have incontrovertible proof that he funded the attempted assassination of the pope. We don't, but let's assume we do for the sake of argument. What are we going to do about it?"

The throbbing in Lucci's temples picked up; it felt like someone was stabbing his forehead with an ice pick.

"Nothing, and I will tell you why. This prick supplies us with ten billion barrels of oil every year. If he even suspects we're out to get him, he'll turn off the spigot, the price of gas will go to six dollars a gallon, and we'll have a national crisis on our hands. No administration is going to take that risk."

"What about the Italians?"

Foster showed his teeth. "You're killing me tonight. The Italians! The prime minister is so embroiled in controversy he can't take a leak without consulting his lawyers. And you want them to take on a Saudi prince with more money than God and his own private army!"

"I don't know why I like you, Mr. Foster."

"I'm likeable, and I tell you the truth, unlike those yes men you surround yourself with. The unadulterated truth."

"Okay, so tell me the unadulterated truth. What should I do?"

"Meet with my friend."

"I thought you said you couldn't help us."

Foster smiled the kind of smile a teacher might give to his best student after he incorrectly answered a difficult question.

"No, I said we couldn't take care of the problem for you. But we can give you information, and in the end, information is more important than anything else."

"How do we do this? I assume he isn't just going to stroll into my office."

"You assume correctly. I already took the liberty of making preliminary arrangements. I will meet you at our embassy in Rome tomorrow night at nine p.m. Have your driver park in the garage below the basement. Stay in the car until I come for you."

Lucci nodded. "See you tomorrow night."

"We're not done quite yet."

"We're not?"

"No. You haven't told me what really happened in St. Peter's Square."

"Actually, I did."

"The thing about God not being dead?"

Lucci nodded.

"Care to elaborate?"

"I want your word that the following conversation will never be repeated, in any form. This is between you and me. Agreed?"

Foster had been appointed by President Patrick Shanahan to help the Vatican deal with the multiple threats to its security. As a presidential appointee, he had the highest-level security clearance and the authority to share any information he deemed pertinent. More importantly, he reported only to three people: the director of the CIA, the Secretary of Homeland Security, and the President of the United States.

"As long as what you tell me doesn't concern our security, I agree."

"It has nothing to do with your security."

Foster nodded.

Lucci returned to his desk, poured another whiskey, and retold Father Venetti's story. Foster, a thirty-five-year veteran of the CIA, listened without interruption until the end.

"If you made that tale up, you're a lot cleverer than I gave you credit for, and if you didn't, you're a lot luckier."

"How much of Venetti's story can you corroborate?"

Foster considered this as he flicked his cigar, showering ash over the burgundy carpet. "Most of it, actually, although I don't know jack about this assassin priest of yours."

"Father Venetti is a Jesuit priest, Mr. Foster, not an assassin."

"Anyone who kills four Islamic extremists is an assassin in my book—and one I'd like to meet." Foster got up from his chair and walked around the room, smoke trailing from his cigar like a locomotive in dire need of repair. "You got a dossier on him?"

Lucci nodded and pointed to a thin manila folder on his desk. "I had it brought by courier from La Spezia last night." He opened the folder and began to paraphrase. "He was born in Messina … His father was a captain in the Italian navy … His mother is a teacher in a local Catholic school … Educated at Istituto S. Ignazio, a Jesuit secondary school in Messina … Spent eighteen months in the navy, as a lieutenant in the Gruppo Operativo Subacquei, the sub-branch responsible for underwater salvage and repair … Discharged ten years ago …"

"Did he receive any commendations, reprimands, weapons training?"

"He received the Gold Medal of Military Valor, the highest award given by the Italian navy, for saving the life of the other sailors in his unit when they were attacked by pirates off the coast of Somalia."

Foster stared at him. "Are you shitting me?"

Lucci shook his head. "Eight Somali pirates tried to hijack his salvage unit in the Gulf of Boosaaso; Father Venetti killed three of them, wounded one, and drove off the other four."

Foster whistled. "And they discharged him afterward?"

"At his request. He entered the seminary shortly thereafter at the Collegium Canisianum in Innsbruck, Austria."

"Wait, he kills three men and then goes into the priesthood?"

"Father Venetti is a very complex man, Mr. Foster. His father comes from a martial family, navy men the whole lot of them. His mother is from a religious family from the South Tyrol. Father Venetti is a man of both worlds, with a strong sense of duty and an equally strong conscience. Even in the line of duty, killing three men could not have been easy to accept. Perhaps entering the seminary was his way of seeking absolution. I don't know—I didn't ask him—but I wonder.

"Anyway, he was ordained after seven years in the seminary and spent the first four years as an associate pastor in the diocese of La Spezia. Five years ago, he was made pastor of San Giovanni Battista in Monterosso."

"Any slip-ups? One-night stands? Brief flings? Accusations?"

"You really are a depraved man."

Foster shrugged. "It's a depraved world."

"I do see a notation at the bottom here." Lucci pointed to the last page of the dossier.

"Yes?"

"One of the other priests in his deanery, a Father DiPietro, did mention something to the bishop."

"About what?"

"About rumors he had heard concerning the amount of attention Father Venetti was paying to a young woman in his parish."

"I'll bet you that's Elena."

"It doesn't say, but I agree. In any event, the bishop looked into the matter and saw no grounds for an investigation, and that was the end of it."

Foster stubbed out his cigar on the marble bookend atop Lucci's desk, and sat down again, slumping worse than ever. "So, let me sum this up. A Jesuit priest from Monterosso with nothing more than a speargun killed four highly trained terrorists, including Mohammed Sadir, a man on the most wanted list of every Western country from Israel to the United States. Additionally, he personally saved the Holy Father's life during an event that was being covered by international television."

"That about sums it up, Mr. Foster."

"Maybe you were right after all."

"Right about what?"

Foster raised his glass; what little of the bourbon remained sloshed around in his unsteady hand.

"About God not being dead yet."

Lucci clinked Foster's glass with his own. "I'll drink to that."

CHAPTER 15

Marco awoke early, dressed in the black robe that had been laid out for him, and moved out to the porch. A gray dawn was breaking over the old city. A flight of stone steps curled away from his perch, and he started down, descending into a labyrinth of foliage and fragrant blooms. He wandered around in the early-morning gloom, following a winding footpath of crushed stone. A bench presented itself, and he sat down, listening to the bickering of the sparrows. The light collected, and he made out another bench to his right, wedged in between two azalea bushes. A large figure sat in the middle of the bench, hunched over a wooden staff.

"Is that you, Father Venetti?"

"Yes, Holiness."

"I thought so. Come join me."

Marco sat down next to a brown ceramic mug of coffee belching steam into the air.

"Did you not sleep well?"

"I have been sleeping for three days. What about you?"

"I like the early morning. There are no cardinals around to bother me. Only sparrows. I like the sparrows better."

Marco assumed that by cardinals, the pope meant men, not birds.

"Coffee?"

He nodded.

The pope stood up and vanished into the gloom. Several minutes later he reappeared, accompanied by a black priest carrying a tray loaded with coffee and supplies. They sipped their drinks and listened to the muffled sounds of the early morning: the distant bark of an excited dog, the low rumble of a truck climbing the steep gradient to the castle, and the incessant chatter of the sparrows.

"Do you know what John Paul II did after he was shot four times by Mehmet Ali Ağca?"

Marco nodded, but said nothing. It was common knowledge that the pope had issued a statement saying he had forgiven the Bulgarian.

"Do you know why he forgave him?"

Marco had his theories, but he kept them to himself. The Holy Father had a point to make; Marco wanted to let him make it.

"Because there was no other choice. All other roads would have led to more hatred and further violence. The Pole understood that; he was an inspired man."

The pope drooped a long arm down and shoveled a handful of bird food from the pail at the foot of the bench. He tossed it in front of him, creating a maelstrom of feathers and small darting bodies.

"In Nigeria, my people don't have enough to eat, and in Italy, even the sparrows grow fat. That is why they hate us. Remember that."

The priest returned, and the pontiff whispered a few words in what Marco assumed was his native tongue. He disappeared again, long black robe swishing, and came back soon after with a platter of fruit. He set it down on the tray, smiled widely at Marco, and melted away.

"How will you respond?"

"I don't know. That's why I am here. The quiet resounds with wisdom."

"Perhaps I should leave."

The pope shook his head. "There is no need."

Marco nodded and remained seated, glad to have company. He had woken up to the endless replay of his misadventures and had grown tired of them as one grows tired of a movie seen too many times. He had succeeded in putting the horror show of sights and sounds and smells to the back of his mind, but he could still feel it there, like Pandora's box waiting to be opened.

"What would you do?"

"Why do you ask?"

"The Cardinal Secretary and I have a difference of opinion on the matter."

"Aren't you the pope?"

"Yes, I am. But it isn't that easy. Cardinal Lucci is a perceptive man. He has counseled me wisely many times. I would be a fool not to consider his opinion."

Marco selected a slice of cantaloupe and cut a wedge of cheese; he was famished.

"What does Cardinal Lucci say?"

"He is concerned that taking the same approach as John Paul II would invite more attacks. He believes the jihadists would see forgiveness as weakness, an unwillingness to fight back."

"I think he has a point."

"Unfortunately, so do I."

They lapsed into silence, bearing witness to the gathering of the light.

"On the other hand, perpetuating the cycle of violence is unthinkable. I would just as soon raze the basilica myself."

"Is there not a difference between punishing the perpetrators of terrorism and perpetuating the cycle of violence? John Paul II forgave his assailant, Holiness, but he didn't release him."

"But the situations are not comparable. The Bulgarian acted alone, at least if you ignore the report of the Mitrokhin Commission. This most recent attack was a highly organized and coordinated event, requiring significant amounts of time, money, and people. The response has to be larger in keeping with the nature of the crime."

"Now you sound like Cardinal Lucci."

"I don't think so, Marco. I certainly hope not, anyway, no disrespect to His Eminence. By larger I mean more comprehensive, not necessarily more violent. But an effort at destroying us such as this has to be addressed, at every level. It is my nature to seek out the more fundamental causes of the problem; it is Cardinal Lucci's to look for the more immediate."

The pope threw more seed into the air, creating another flurry of birds.

"Cardinal Lucci wants to punish the responsible parties, and you want to correct the underlying conditions that drove the parties to terrorism in the first place."

The pontiff nodded.

"I'd say it's a lot easier Lucci's way."

"And that is why nothing ever gets solved, Marco. The real problems are difficult to understand, much less solve. But I think we are obligated by our humanity to try."

"Is it possible to do both? Or does one choice obviate the other?"

A black cat, hidden until this point behind a large echinacea plant, made a sudden lunge at the sparrows and succeeded in snaring one. It walked away with its prize hanging limply in its mouth. A moment later, the rest of the flock returned to the path, pecking at the remaining food as if nothing had happened.

"I think you can't do both. How can you win the battle for the hearts and minds of the Muslim world when you simultaneously slaughter their leaders?"

"The jihadists are not the leaders of the Muslim world."

"Perhaps not, but sympathy for their cause runs very deep among Muslims. The more we press the attack, the deeper the sympathy runs."

"So we lie down every time they attack us, just so we don't risk making them hate us more? You can't turn the other cheek when the enemy has Russian-made plastic explosives."

"The tenets of Christianity don't lose relevance with the advance of technology. On the contrary, they become more critical as the destructive power of modern weaponry increases. The price of war becomes impossibly steep with thermonuclear weapons and only God knows what else. The pursuit of peace is the only answer."

"But they aren't playing by the same rules, Holiness. Christian principles mean nothing to them."

"But they should mean everything to us. It is *our* response to this atrocity that will determine if and when the next attack will come. If they provoke us, and we respond in kind, the cause is lost."

"I agree with everything you have said, Holiness, I do. But one fact remains: the only reason you are sitting here talking to me is because I did not do as you said."

The pope nodded. "I realize that, and it gives me great pause." He stopped speaking, true to his word, and contemplated the flock of sparrows. "Great pause."

Abayd sat behind his desk and stared at his laptop, a rare smile on his round, dark face. His cousin had just texted him the date and time when the mysterious computer program had been installed, confirming that he wasn't paranoid—not that he ever gave that theory much credence.

As the head of the prince's bodyguard, Abayd kept a detailed record of KiKi's daily schedule, and he kept it forever. As a consequence, he knew for certain that KiKi had not downloaded the program, because at the precise moment of its installation, he had been under sedation during a routine colonoscopy. Abayd also knew that only one other person had been allowed in the room: his personal physician.

He allowed himself to bask in a short moment of personal satisfaction, and then permitted the angst to settle in his brain. As his instincts had told him, they were in big trouble. Dr. al-Sharim had not risked his life to install a program on KiKi's phone to monitor his health. He also had not done it alone; Abayd stood ready to bet his pension he was working with a foreign intelligence agency, most likely the CIA.

He was sure it had started with the doctor's trip to Monaco several years ago. He had ordered full-time surveillance, but his watchers must have missed the contact. Not that this surprised him; his men were good, but the CIA was better.

The fucking CIA.

Small wonder Jibril had been defeated by the encryption. The NSA was second to none in this sort of thing. He picked up the phone and texted his cousin to meet him on the knoll. He waited twenty minutes, and then went out and walked up to the rendezvous.

"Where have you been?"

"Never mind that." He told Jibril about what he'd discovered.

"How do you know it's the CIA?"

"Feminine intuition."

"I hope you're wrong."

"I'm not."

"The fucking CIA, Abayd!"

"We need to know what's in that program."

Jibril reached inside his black nylon jacket for his Marlboros; he was a nervous man who liked to smoke cigarettes to calm his nerves. Apparently, it didn't work very well, because he lit one after another. Abayd waited for him to clear his mind with a deep inhalation, looking him over as he waited. Jibril was not your typical bodyguard. He was small and slight, with a narrow, hairless face and thin, wispy hair.

"There might be a way."

"I'm listening."

"It's going to be expensive."

Abayd was sure he could hear the cash register sounding in his cousin's brain. The man was as much of an opportunist as he was—which was saying something. "Go on."

"If you're right about the CIA, there are certain products available if you know where to look."

"What kind of products?"

"Code-breaking software."

"Will it work?"

"I'm not sure. I've never tried anything like this before."

"How much is it?"

Jibril considered this question during a long drag. Abayd could see him punching the calculator buttons in his head, adjusting the price to include his personal fee.

"Fifty thousand dollars."

"Get it. I don't care about the damn cost. I need to know what's in that program, and I need to know very soon."

"I need a few days."

"A few days? Can't you just download the fucking thing and get on with it?"

A smile crossed Jibril's face. "If it were that easy, cousin, even a Neanderthal like you could do it."

Abayd ignored the barb. "Get going right away. Give me KiKi's phone and find him a spare to use in the meantime."

"What am I supposed to tell him?"

"I have no idea, but you're a sneaky bastard; you'll think of something. And Jibril, I don't care if you are my cousin; if you breathe a word of this to anyone else, I will kill you myself."

CHAPTER 16

Cardinal Lucci had never been in a CIA safe flat before, so he had no idea what to expect. Even so, he couldn't help but feel disappointed. It was nondescript to a fault and smelled like an old smoking jacket. He wrinkled his nose and looked around. Molded plastic chairs and battered sofas littered the interior; the walls were bare and scored with tack marks; the unpolished wooden floor bore a thousand scuffs. A small kitchenette lay off the living room; an old coffee pot and a battered refrigerator were its only occupants.

In stark contrast, he was likely to remember the man sitting across from him for all eternity. He was tall and lean, with neatly combed dark hair. His navy suit was tailored to perfection, and a red-striped tie was knotted neatly around his long neck. When he shook Lucci's hand, it was with the correct amount of firmness, and his words were chosen precisely, as if he'd had many hours to prepare his remarks.

"So, Eminence, we have a few things to discuss."

"We do, Mr. Blair. Or is it Director Blair? Agent Blair, perhaps? You didn't mention your title."

"No, I didn't."

"You have me at a disadvantage then."

"Yes, I do." Blair poured coffee into a pair of well-used mugs. "Our mutual friend, Mr. Foster, spoke with you already?"

Lucci nodded.

"Good. Then let us proceed to the crux of the matter. We share a powerful enemy. Prince Kamal el-Rayad believes it is his legacy to be the man who destroys Vatican City."

"That is what Mr. Foster has said, Mr. Blair, but the question is why. Why does the prince believe this to be his legacy?"

Blair breached the distance between them and handed Lucci one of the mugs before retreating to his previous position across the room.

"I guessed that you would want to know this, so I took the liberty of doing some research." Blair consulted the sleek watch adorning his wrist. "You are familiar with the Battle of Ostia?"

Lucci nodded. In 849, a Christian armada commissioned by Pope Leo IV defeated the Saracens who had attacked Rome and destroyed St. Peter's Basilica. "Raphael's painting of the battle hangs in the Apostolic Palace where I live, a constant reminder of the Church's embattled history."

"Good, then I will get right to the point. Prince el-Rayad traces his lineage back to Asad ibn al-Furat, the Saracen commander who was defeated in Ostia. Asad tried three times to sack Vatican City and was unsuccessful each time. El-Rayad has vowed to finish the job for him.

"That is where we come in, Eminence. As Mr. Foster made you aware, we have developed a source inside el-Rayad's camp. This source contacted us recently with some disturbing news. I am sorry to tell you the prince plans to strike again—soon. And when he does, it will be with a violence neither of us dares comprehend."

"If you are trying to get my attention, you had me at 'destroys Vatican City.'"

"We would very much like to help you avoid such a fate. To this end, we have critical information to share with you."

"I'm all ears."

Blair grinned with slight embarrassment, as if he were a salesman forced into explaining a hidden charge of great magnitude.

"I wish that it were so easy, but things don't quite work that way."

"You want something from us in return?"

Another smile, but this time the embarrassment was gone, replaced by the expression of a teacher hearing his student grasp a difficult concept for the first time.

"You have been very critical of several Latin American leaders."

"If you are referring to the presidents of Brazil, Argentina, and Chile, you are using the word 'leader' rather loosely, don't you think?"

"You see, this is what I am talking about. The Vatican has great influence in that part of the world. This type of rhetoric coming from the Holy See has been very detrimental to these men."

"These men are butchers."

Blair winced at Lucci's word choice. "We have been wanting to discuss this subject with you for some time, but we have been waiting for the right moment." He permitted himself a slight smile. "But in tragedy, opportunity looms."

"What is it you want me to do?"

"There is an election coming up in Brazil. The left-wing candidate you support must not win the presidency. He is as close to a communist as they come; his election would destabilize South America."

"If you are asking me to denounce him, you're wasting your breath."

"We are not asking you to do anything that drastic."

"What *are* you asking me to do, then?"

Blair extracted an envelope from the breast pocket of his suit and handed it to Lucci, who opened it, took out the contents, and began reading. When he was finished, he folded the single piece of paper, returned it to the envelope, and gave the envelope back to Blair.

"I can't sign that."

"It's not a condemnation; it's just a statement of neutrality."

"I know what it is, Mr. Blair. I may not speak seven languages fluently like the Holy Father, but my English is excellent. Yes, I understand it's a statement of neutrality … The thing is, I'm not neutral."

"Perhaps if you better understood the threats you face …"

Lucci almost choked on a sip of coffee, but not because it tasted like a mixture of sewage and battery acid. He had said almost the exact same thing to the pope three days ago.

Perhaps if you better understood the threats we face …

"I did not want to come to you so soon," Blair said. "It would have been much better for you to come to us. But after I spoke to my source, I did not feel it could wait."

"What did your source tell you?"

"I will tell you what he said; I will tell you a great many things that you should know … no, not *should* know … that you *need* to know for your nation's continued existence in this troubled world."

Blair smiled; Lucci imagined a crocodile luring a thirsty antelope into the waterhole where it lurked.

"Do we have a deal?"

"Yes, we have a deal."

Lucci crossed the room, his loafers slapping against the pine floor, and shook hands with Blair.

"Your source, who is it?"

"His name is Khalid al-Sharim. He is el-Rayad's personal physician, a job he has held since the mid-nineties. Several years ago, suspecting that his patient wasn't the benevolent person he claimed to be, al-Sharim tried to quietly tender his resignation, but el-Rayad sent several of his bodyguards over to his house to persuade him otherwise. Realizing that he would never be allowed to leave the prince's employ—alive, that is—he spent the next six months gathering information about el-Rayad's activities before approaching us for a trade: everything he knew about the prince in exchange for extracting him and giving him a new identity and a new home."

"And ten million dollars, I suppose?"

Blair shook his head. "No, he was clear about that. He wasn't after money."

"That's refreshing."

Blair smiled again, this time the socially awkward smile of a man forced to admit something embarrassing.

"Actually, it isn't. We have always preferred to pay our informers. It gives us a certain amount of leverage."

He waited for Lucci to interject, which he did not, and so he went on.

"The extraction was supposed to have taken place at Haus Adler, el-Rayad's residence outside Salzburg, where he vacations every year in August. In light of the detailed information that al-Sharim had given us about the location, we decided to turn the extraction into an assassination and extraction. Or at least we wanted to; President Shanahan refused to sanction the assassination."

"Why?"

Blair smiled again, this time a polite smile; combined with the half-lidded look past Lucci's shoulder and the dismissive wave of his well-manicured hand, Lucci got the message that it was none of his business.

"What about the extraction?"

"I could lie to you …" Blair licked his lips unconsciously. "But I will not. We have been postponing the extraction to keep the information coming, and it's a very good thing for you that we did."

He paused to remove a gray MacBook from his attaché case and turned it so Lucci could see it. The screen was filled with a picture of two men standing on the deck of a large yacht. Blue-green waters shimmered in the background. "This picture was taken by MI6 two months ago. Do you recognize either of these men?"

Lucci shook his head.

Blair pointed to one of them. He was tall and lean and possessed the wiry musculature of a tennis player. He had dark hair and a matching beard, trimmed to perfection. His eyes were large and black and penetrating. "El-Rayad."

"The other man?"

"Is Rodovan Pavlović. There is a long and sordid story behind him."

"I would like to hear it."

"Perhaps another time, but suffice it to say that he is a Serbian arms dealer of some notoriety."

"His notoriety … it's well earned?"

Blair nodded, just a slight drop of his head and a brief flutter of his eyelids. "Very well, I should say. We believe that he is the only arms dealer to have ever acquired nuclear weapons."

Lucci gulped his coffee down in an effort to ease the dryness in his mouth, which had taken on the arid condition of Death Valley, a place he had seen last year on a visit with a brother who lived in California.

"It all started in northwest China, in one of the most remote places on earth. The Chinese military has a large facility there, including a biological research laboratory and a nuclear weapons storage complex, in a mountainous region north of Urumqi. In 2015, a fire ravaged the facility, releasing a lethal virus."

"How do you know this?"

"An NSA satellite discovered it during a routine pass shortly afterward. Every man, woman, and child within two hundred kilometers was dead. Livestock lay bloated in the fields. The lifeless bodies of dogs and cats fouled the landscape. When the People's Army finally got back in, they found that two DH-10 nuclear warheads were missing."

Lucci took a second look at the man on the screen. He was short and squat, with the powerful build of a weightlifter and the bulbous nose and ruddy complexion of a man who drank vodka as if it were the only thing able to quench his thirst.

"Are we sure that Pavlović has the weapons?"

"No, we are not. But some associates of mine ran a sting operation last year, creating a fictional African warlord who was shopping the international black market for nuclear weapons. A person believed to be Pavlović responded, and we almost nabbed him, but he smelled a rat late in the game and bailed."

The rapid beating of his own heart filled Lucci's ears. He tried to tell himself it was just the coffee, but it was a lie; he was afraid. He could smell the fear, acrid and bitter, rising in his nostrils.

"Please don't tell me that Pavlović plans to sell the nuclear weapons to el-Rayad."

"I am afraid I must, Eminence. Al-Sharim confirmed it this morning."

His heart accelerated; the pulse of his blood pounded in his ears. He forced himself to take a deep breath, exhaling the air slowly through his nose.

"The DH-10 is a small weapon, in the range of one kiloton, but enough, I should think."

"Enough?"

"Enough to wipe Vatican City off the face of the earth."

The blare of a car horn and the whine of a motor scooter floated up from the street below.

"Pavlović plans to deliver the weapons to el-Rayad's mountain chalet outside Salzburg sometime in August. Do you know what will happen if el-Rayad takes possession of those warheads on Austrian soil?"

Lucci knew. Since border stations had been eliminated to enhance trade across the continent, all that lay between Salzburg and Rome was six hundred kilometers of highway without so much as a sobriety checkpoint.

"El-Rayad has to be stopped before he obtains the weapons. Otherwise, Eminence, Vatican City will be nothing more than a burn mark on the canvas of history."

Lucci crossed to the window and peered behind the curtains. A faceless tenement building stared back. The smell of rotten fish permeated the panes; the Tiber couldn't be far away.

"Perhaps you would consider a more active role, Mr. Blair?"

Blair lifted an eyebrow. "A more active role? How do you mean?"

"Resurrect the operation that was canceled a few years ago. Extract Dr. al-Sharim and assassinate el-Rayad."

Yet another smile appeared on Blair's polished face. This one conveyed apology and regret. "There is nothing I would like to do more. But I am afraid that would be impossible."

"Impossible? Why?"

Blair set the computer down on a small table, creating space by stacking the ashtrays covering the marred wooden surface.

"Because el-Rayad is a very rich man, and he has wisely chosen to be extremely generous to a number of United States senators who happen to sit on the Intelligence Committee that provides oversight of my agency."

He started pacing back and forth across the room, three steps in one direction, a neat pivot on the heel of his custom-made wingtips that produced just the slightest squeak, and then three steps in the other.

"But in the event of you declaring your neutrality in the Brazilian election—and emphasizing this with the Latin American Bishops Council when you meet next month—I can extend you a token of our appreciation."

The oldest of thirteen children born to a prominent Sicilian banker and his wife, who was a direct descendant of Prince Alberto of Sicily, Lucci had spent a lifetime granting favors as opposed to begging for them, and his election as Archbishop of Palermo had done nothing to lessen his distaste for asking for help. But Vatican City had never before been threatened with a nuclear holocaust—at least that he was aware of—and desperate times called for desperate measures.

"We would be greatly indebted to you for any additional assistance you can provide."

Blair extracted a sealed manila envelope from his attaché case. "These are the plans for the mission that was scrubbed three years ago. There is no point in reinventing the wheel, and time is of the essence."

He walked over to Lucci's position by the window, holding the envelope against his chest. "It goes against every fiber of my being to share these plans with you, but I am equally opposed to a communist overthrow of Brazil."

He handed Lucci the plans as if he were surrendering the deed to lands that had been in his family for generations.

"Haus Adler is a secure fortress guarded by a private army of mercenaries, all former Saudi Royal Army Green Berets. But it does have a weakness."

He fetched his computer, clicked a few buttons, and a massive mountain chalet appeared, perched on the end of a peninsula of rock that jutted out from the face of a cliff.

"This is Haus Adler. It was originally built by the Habsburgs as a mountain getaway. Due to the number of enemies the Habsburgs had engendered, Haus Adler was situated on this bluff so that it could be approached from only one direction: from the east, along this narrow corridor flanked by a two-hundred-meter drop on either side."

He closed the computer and set it back on the table, knocking off one of the ashtrays in the process, which clanged against the floor and spilled its ashy residue over the pine boards.

"Several members of our team were world-class free climbers. By the time the operation was aborted, they had already scaled the cliff face. Unfortunately, they removed all the pitons when they evacuated, but their approach is documented in the information I gave you.

"All the security cameras and guard patrols are on the other side of the grounds. Once your assault team reaches the top of the cliff, killing the prince should be no more difficult than shooting fish in a barrel."

CHAPTER 17

It was far too early in the morning when a soft knock at his door woke Abayd from a restless sleep. He got out of bed and opened the door, and Jibril walked into the room, reeking of cigarettes. He started to open his mouth excitedly, but Abayd clamped a large palm over it before he could speak.

"Not here."

He got dressed and led Jibril back outside. This time, they stopped on the edge of the precipice, where they had an excellent view of the sheer drop. Dawn had broken, but it was still cool and damp; their footsteps were plainly visible in the dew-covered grass.

"Where have you been?" he asked.

"I told you it was going to take time."

"Four days?"

Jibril shrugged and reached for his cigarettes.

"The news is good?"

"Yes and no."

"I am in no mood for games, Jibril. Just give it to me."

Jibril's narrow face grew even more pinched. "Okay, cousin, have it your way. The good news is, I was finally able to decrypt that program."

"What's the bad news?"

"There's a lot of bad news. First off, you were right about its origin: no question it's NSA."

"How can you tell?"

"The stars and stripes insignia—they put it on everything."

Abayd didn't like levity of any kind, much less at his expense, but he let it go.

"What does the program do?"

Jibril lit a cigarette. "Its primary mission is to copy every document, file, and program on the hard drive, compress them, and send them out piggybacked on top of a phone call."

"Why does it go to all that trouble?"

"Because that way, the outgoing transmission never shows up on the calls summary."

"Clever."

"You haven't heard anything yet. In a similar vein, it poaches emails, text messages, and phone calls."

"Phone calls?"

"Every call KiKi has made since this program was inserted into his phone has been recorded, compressed, and sent. I hope he hasn't made any off-color jokes."

He had made many, Abayd guessed, given his penchant for all things perverse and pornographic, but that was the least of their worries. Although the prince was very careful about saying anything incriminating on his cell phone, the Americans now knew many of the players in his network. It was an excellent starting point, of which Abayd was certain they were taking full advantage.

Jibril took a long drag on his Marlboro and crushed it with his sneaker, in the attitude of a funeral attendee throwing dirt on the grave of a loved one. "You haven't heard the really bad news yet."

Abayd turned his head and spat on the ground. He could feel it now, the familiar tightening in his forehead. He massaged his temples, rubbing the muscles with his powerful fingers, but he knew there were some pains for which there was no cure.

"One week ago, someone activated a sub-program."

"Why didn't they just have it running from the beginning?"

"Too risky. The sub-program is vast, hundreds of thousands of lines of code. To run a program of this size in a cell phone is dicey;

the processor just isn't that powerful. So they waited to activate it. I'm guessing they were frustrated with the yield from the phone call recordings and decided to chance it."

"What does it do?"

"The sub-program activates the microphone, leaving it on at all times, even when the phone is off."

Abayd reached into his pocket for the foil of Tylenol that was always there, waiting for a headache to start. Tearing it open, he swallowed the tablets without water, throwing the waste over the edge of the cliff, where it fluttered out of sight.

"You're telling me this thing is a listening device?"

Jibril nodded. "And it's always listening, unless the battery is removed."

"KiKi carries that damn thing with him all the time, Jibril."

Abayd had never been an anxious person, always confident in his ability to deal with whatever was thrown at him. But for the first time, the cold hand of anxiety touched him, wrapping its icy fingers around his throat, rubbing his chest with its frigid palm.

They were out there; he could feel it. Having studied covert tactics, he suspected they were close, probably even in line of sight. He stepped closer to the precipice and looked down. There were a dozen or so homes on the lower slopes below the cliff upon which the Haus Adler was perched. Several of them were vacation rentals, available to large groups of people—such as a CIA hit squad.

"What do you think they are planning, Abayd?"

"They are going to swarm over us like a hive of hornets and kill every last one of us."

Jibril's small eyes grew wide. Fear was written all over his shrew-like face. He lit another Marlboro and took a massive drag as if it might be his last. "What are you planning to do about it?"

Abayd grabbed his cousin's cigarette and threw it over the cliff. They watched it as it fluttered in the early-morning breeze.

"We're going to kill them all first."

CHAPTER 18

Vincenzo Lucci climbed up the last flight of steps, cresting the summit of the Janiculum Hill, which the locals called the eighth hill of Rome. Morning had not yet given way to afternoon and its oppressive heat, and Gianicolo Park always had a nice breeze, which currently whistled through the umbrella-shaped penumbras of the stone pines for which the area was famous. Lucci found a bench under the shade of a trio of three such pines, gazing down at the Altare della Patria, the huge monument built in honor of Victor Emmanuel, the first king of a unified Italy. Ten minutes later, he heard Foster approaching, huffing and puffing as if he had climbed Mount Etna.

"For Christ's sake, why don't we meet on the Matterhorn next time?"

Foster sat down heavily for such a small man, cursing under his breath until his breathing resumed its normal pace.

"This had better be good."

Lucci laughed. A dark humor had overcome him ever since the failed assassination attempt.

"Maybe you should walk a bit more and drink whiskey and smoke cigars a bit less."

"Now you're my doctor? It's bad enough that I have to listen to my wife nagging me …"

As a peace offering, Lucci handed him one of the two bottles of water he had bought from the concession stand adjacent to the Acqua Paola fountain. Foster drank half of it in one swig and wiped his sweat-beaded brow with a handkerchief he produced from the pocket of his gray suit, which was the only thing Lucci had ever seen him wear.

"All right, I'll quit bitching. How'd the meeting go with Mr. Blair?"

Lucci looked around to make sure that they were out of earshot—they were; Gianicolo was almost always quiet, which was why he loved it—and filled Foster in on his meeting with the CIA agent.

"Honestly, that's about as good a deal as you're going to get with that guy. He's as slippery as they come."

"And the information he gave me—you have no reason to doubt it?"

"None at all. Don't get me wrong, Blair would lie straight to his mother's face if it benefited him, but it doesn't benefit him to lie in this circumstance. As long as it suits him to tell the truth, that's what you'll get, which is why you always have to understand his motivation, capeesh?"

Lucci nodded. He was well familiar with this tactic from his frequent dealings with the Roman Curia, whose cardinals generally employed the same strategy.

"I tried to get him to do the job for me."

"Let me guess: he told you the CIA can't move on el-Rayad because he has several senators on the Intelligence Oversight Committee in his pocket?"

Lucci nodded. "Is that not true?"

Foster just shrugged and drank from his water bottle. Lucci stood up abruptly, wiping the pine needles from his black cassock. "Come on, I want to show you something."

"What? I just got here."

But Lucci wasn't listening, already heading up the cobbled road. Foster caught up with him on the Passeggiata del Gianicolo as it let out onto the Piazza Garibaldi. Lucci pointed to the massive statue of the Father of the Fatherland sitting on his horse.

"Do you know who this is?"

"I don't really give a shit."

"His name is Giuseppe Garibaldi; he is one of the most famous generals of all time. Certainly he is the most famous Italian general."

"So what?"

"Garibaldi was intensely anti-Catholic and vehemently opposed to the papacy; in 1862, he gathered an army of thousands to march on Rome, shouting 'Rome or Death!'"

"What happened to him?"

"He got neither; he ended up in prison in La Spezia, a stone's throw from where Marco lives in Monterosso al Mare."

A tour bus crawled past their position, belching black smoke, coming to a stop on the other side of the circular area around the statue. The front door opened, discharging a phalanx of Japanese tourists armed with cameras.

"I assume there is a reason you brought me up here?"

"A very good one. I needed a break from the Vatican, and the café across the way serves the best espresso in Rome."

Lucci started across the square, and Foster reluctantly followed, dodging between a pair of the inevitable Vespas, their motors whining in fury. At Bar Stuzzichi, they settled into a standing table on the terrace underneath a massive cork oak, sipping espressos and watching the rubberneckers gather for the firing of the Cannone del Gianicolo, which had detonated every day at noon since 1847, when Pope Pius IX ordered it to be set off at this time to synchronize the ringing of all the bells in Rome.

"There is a famous story about the Garibaldi statue. Do you know it?"

"No. Do tell."

Lucci laughed at Foster's sarcastic tone and finished his espresso.

"When the Lateran Treaty was signed in 1929, establishing Vatican City as a sovereign nation, the statue was turned around so that the horse's backside faced the Vatican. Romans who don't like the Catholic Church—and there are plenty of those, I'm afraid—love to say that Garibaldi's horse is farting on the pope."

They left the café and started down the hill in the direction of Trastevere, walking beneath a canopy of plane trees and towering beeches.

"I have the plans Blair formulated three years ago for the assassination of Prince el-Rayad and the extraction of Dr. al-Sharim, the Americans' source inside Rayad's camp."

Lucci gave Foster a brief summary of the plans developed by Blair's team.

"They seem to be in order. All I need are some soldiers to carry them out."

He stopped next to a massive beech trunk scarred by generations of initial-carvers.

"This is where you tell me that you have changed your mind about the CIA doing the job for us."

Foster chortled his reply. Lucci wasn't sure if he was laughing or choking on his saliva, but he was sure of one thing. The answer was still no.

"I thought as much. Fortunately, I have something else in mind."

"Oh yeah, want to enlighten me?"

"Have you heard of the Corsican Guard?"

Foster rolled his small gray eyes.

"I'll take that as a no."

They continued their descent down the east side of Janiculum Hill, stopping at a bench overlooking the Japanese Botanical Gardens. Azalea bushes and red maples dotted the hillside around them; the sour stench of rotting gingko leaves hung faintly in the air.

"La Guardia Corsica was formed by Pope Julius II, mostly as a way to get a large number of Corsican immigrants off the streets of Rome, where they were notorious for getting into fights and stealing. Their tenacious nature made them excellent soldiers, and their numbers and influence grew quickly, especially given that the Swiss Guard had not yet been created."

"Why have I never heard of them?"

"Do they not have history books where you come from?"

"You may find this hard to believe, but the rest of the world could give two shits about what happened in Rome two hundred years ago."

"It was five hundred years ago, and here we are now, discussing it. That implies relevance, does it not?"

"Pretend I have a short attention span, Eminence."

"That shouldn't be difficult."

Lucci waited as a pug led an elderly couple in their direction. When it finished marking a small bamboo plant with its urine, it trotted off, dragging the couple behind it.

"The Corsican Guard was disbanded in 1664, when Pope Alexander VII signed the Treaty of Pisa, in reaction to a fight between the guardsmen and French troops stationed in Rome. However, there is a little-known clause in the treaty"—Lucci permitted himself a satisfied grin—"that allows the Secretary of State of the Vatican to reinstate the Guard in the event of imminent danger to the pope. I should think impending nuclear annihilation is imminent danger enough, wouldn't you?"

"Where are you going to get the bodies? You can't round up a bunch of saps just off the boat from Corsica and hand them spears."

"Leave that to me, my friend. There is something I wanted to ask you about, though."

Foster regarded Lucci from the other end of the bench. His small face was scrunched up, making him look like the pug that had just peed on the bamboo.

"I had an inspiration."

"Oh God …"

"You don't like inspirations, Agent Foster?"

"Anything that starts with an inspiration ends badly. Period."

"Is this CIA doctrine?"

"No, Foster's hard-earned rules of engagement."

The American buried his face in his hands, rubbing his forehead with short fingers that hadn't seen a manicure this century. His stubby fingernails were cracked, pitted, and in general need of attention.

"Okay, spit it out."

"I want Father Venetti to be a part of the team that goes to Austria."

"I was actually going to suggest something like that myself."

"Something like that?"

"Yes. Don't include him with the main team. Use him as part of a second team, positioned above the target with a sniper to provide covering fire."

"That's interesting, because the American plans call for exactly the same thing."

"Great minds think alike."

"Or perhaps Mr. Blair may have mentioned the plans to you?"

Foster shrugged and lapsed into silence as a group of schoolchildren and their chaperone walked past on their way to the entrance of the gardens.

"He might have."

"Is there anything else he might have mentioned?"

"Not that I can think of."

Lucci looked askance at him, but let the issue drop.

"As it turns out, I had the same thing in mind. But I need a sniper. Any ideas about where I can find one on such short notice?"

"Fortunately for you, Eminence, I do."

"Oh?"

"Her name is Sarah Messier. She's American, actually. Ex-CIA."

"Ex-CIA?"

"She left the agency when Obama made it almost impossible for the CIA to kill anyone." Foster splayed his hands, regarding Lucci with an imploring look. "What's the use of a sniper if you can't kill people?"

"What's she been doing in the meantime?"

"Freelancing." He paused. "Off the record …"

"All our conversations are off the record, Mr. Foster."

"… the CIA has used her a time or two."

"You're sure she's available?"

Foster nodded. "She's got an independent streak a mile wide, which didn't sit well with her last employer. It's going to be a while before her phone rings again."

Now it was Lucci's turn to massage his temples, which he did with enough force to leave red marks on his patrician forehead.

"Independent streak? Would you care to elaborate on that?"

"She bailed out on her last job a few hours before the hit."

"Bailed out?"

"It was a suicide mission dressed up as just another day of work. She figured it out a few hours before the mark arrived and headed for the exit."

"Please tell me why I should be hiring a sniper who doesn't complete the job?"

"For the best reason there is. You don't have a whole lot of choice."

CHAPTER 19

When Cardinal Lucci arrived, Marco was sitting in his room, trying to pray and succeeding only in staring into space. The cardinal was dressed in a long black cassock with a scarlet sash and wore a matching silk skullcap atop his thick head of black hair. Marco went to stand, but Lucci waved him off and sat down next to him.

Marco could see there was something on his mind; the perpetual furrows on his forehead were a little deeper, and his eyes were lit pale blue like the morning sky over the castle.

"Can we talk?"

Marco nodded. He had grown fond of Lucci over the past ten days. He was a man of paradoxes, a human oxymoron. He was a thoughtful, pensive man, but quick to make judgments. He was generally considerate, but given to occasional bouts of rudeness for which he was unapologetic. His outlook was mostly positive, except for the stray flurry of pessimism. And he was right-to-the-point, but vague when it suited his purposes.

"What's on your mind, Eminence?"

"You, Marco."

"Me?"

"Your future, I mean."

So here it comes, Marco thought. He had been waiting for this, the killers-aren't-fit-to-be-priests talk. He doubted Lucci had one canned and ready to go, but he was a clever man, savvy enough to make one up on the fly.

"I assumed I would be returning to my parish."

"Is that what you want?"

Marco wasn't sure what he wanted. He loved it here, on the hill overlooking Lake Albano. Glancing across the fields and small villages below was like visiting the Louvre to view an Impressionist watercolor. The soft breeze always carried the scent of lavender, and the chapel next to the papal apartments where he celebrated mass every morning infused him with a peace and tranquility he'd thought he would never find again. But he knew he couldn't stay here forever: Monterosso beckoned, especially at night, when he longed for the slap of the waves against the rocky shore.

"Yes, Eminence."

"Then I will make a deal with you, Father Venetti. I need someone for a special assignment for a couple of weeks. When the job is complete, you may return to your parish."

"What's the job?"

"It has to do with the assassination attempt on the Holy Father."

"A pontifical commission?"

"No, nothing like that. Something out of the box, actually."

The hollow feeling returned to Marco's guts. "How far out of the box?"

"Way, way out."

Lucci pulled an envelope from the depths of his cassock. "Inside you will find a summary of everything I have learned about the origin of the terrorist attack. I wrote it myself; no one else has seen it."

Marco extracted two sheets of paper from the unsealed envelope and began reading. When he was finished, he returned the pages to the envelope and handed it back to Lucci.

"Where did you get all this information?"

"The CIA contacted me through back channels."

"What's their interest in the Vatican?"

"They don't have one; in exchange for their help in this matter, I need to convince the Latin American bishops to remain neutral in the upcoming Brazilian presidential election."

Lucci walked over to the window, pulling the drapes open. Sunlight streamed in; dust floated in the diagonals of light. Marco suspected the guest room in which he was staying had been vacant for a good long time. As further evidence of this, several cobwebs dangled from the ceiling, out of range of the nun, wizened and bent, who came in every day to tidy up.

"I'll need to bribe them, but I should be able to manage."

"Bribe them? How?"

"I'll promise them that the next cardinal the pope names will come from Latin America. It's something they want badly. For that price, they'll go along with it."

"But will the pope agree?"

Lucci nodded, a slight grin cracking his narrow face. "It's his idea, actually. And there's an opening in the Curia; I have been trying to get him to choose an Italian bishop to fill it, but he won't hear of it. The only reason he hasn't already named a Latin American bishop is because of my staunch opposition. If I relent on the matter, it will be a done deal. And that is well and good, because I don't plan to sit on my hands and wait for Prince el-Rayad to incinerate Vatican City."

Lucci drew another document from the interior of his cassock like a magician producing a bouquet of roses from thin air.

"These are blueprints for a mission to kill Prince el-Rayad and extract a CIA source from within his camp. The Americans developed them three years ago, but the recently elected President Shanahan refused to sign off, and the mission was shelved."

"They are taking it off the shelf?"

"No, they are not. I am. Actually, we are."

"We?"

"Yes, you and I, Marco."

"I'm not following you."

Lucci summarized the plans the Americans had given him. Marco wasn't sure he had heard him right. Had the Secretary of

State of Vatican City really asked him to take part in an assassination?

"What do you want me to do?"

"I want you to be on the second team."

"With the sniper?"

"Yes. You'll go in as a team of two, separate from the primary team, and establish a shooting position on a hill above the prince's compound. Your job will be to coordinate with the primary team and act as a spotter for the sniper. It's the primary team's job to kill the prince; the second team is there to cover their withdrawal … and as a fail-safe."

"Why me? Why not someone from the Security Office?"

"It will be many moons before I trust anyone from that office."

"The Swiss Guard?"

"Out of the question; not in the charter."

Marco's mouth felt arid, as if he had just taken a long walk without water in a hot, dry place. "But I'm not qualified. I am a priest, that's all."

"You'll be going as an observer, not an assassin."

Marco was not wild about the idea; he had slept well last night for the first time since the beginning of this hellish series of events, and his appetite had returned with the morning dew.

"There's another issue, as well."

"Which is?"

"The pope."

"You haven't told him about your plan?"

"Of course I haven't. We don't see eye to eye on how we should respond. I am certain he would be dead set against the idea."

Marco was certain of this as well—making him feel worse about violating the pontiff's trust by going behind his back.

"I need you, Marco. I need you to make sure we are no longer under threat of nuclear annihilation. And once this is done, I need you to tell the pope what happened."

"Can't you do that?"

The glimmer in Lucci's eyes dimmed a little, and his face darkened. Marco thought perhaps his body had shifted so that the sunlight wasn't striking his face at the same angle.

"The pope doesn't trust me. I could tell him, but he won't believe me. But if it comes from you, that is a different story. The Holy Father believes you were brought to us by the Holy Spirit."

"What do you believe, Eminence?"

"We both know the pope is infallible when it comes to these matters."

"This is a matter of faith or morals?"

"This is a matter of our continued existence on the face of the earth, Father Venetti." Lucci's face took on the color of his sash. "And we have no further time to debate."

He had never really had any choice in the matter, Marco realized. And for some reason, this realization made him feel better.

"When do I go?"

"Soon. I have made arrangements for your training."

"Training? You said I was to be an observer, Eminence. How much training does an observer need?"

"Quite a bit, I should think. The proceedings will place you directly in harm's way; I want you to be prepared."

"Prepared for what?"

Lucci started pacing up and down the length of the room, with his fingers steepled together and head bent, as if he were processing behind the Eucharist during the feast of Corpus Christi.

"I'll be frank. The other member of your team …"

"The sniper?"

"Her name is Sarah Messier. She's American, ex-CIA. She came highly recommended. She insists that every member of her team—meaning you—is fully committed."

"Fully committed?"

"It means exactly what you think it means."

Machine-gun fire reverberated inside his skull; his hands vibrated from the recoil of his weapon; the satiny smell of blood engulfed his nostrils. He wasn't sure if he was reliving the horrors of Somalia, the nightmare on the *Bel Amica*, or the torment on the island, but he was sure of one thing: he didn't want to go back.

"The two of you will be traveling together, posing as a married couple on vacation in Austria. It's August in Salzburg, the Mozart Festival is in full swing, and the city will be crawling with tourists. No one will pay any attention to you."

Marco nodded, but in truth he had only half heard Lucci; dying men wailed in his ears.

"We have no intention of giving you a more active role, but things don't often proceed as planned. In the event that they don't, your orders are clear. Make sure the prince does not buy those weapons. By whatever means necessary."

CHAPTER 20

Lucci sat in the back seat of the Mercedes sedan that had picked him up at Falcone Borsellino airport, staring at the rocky coastline of Palermo as the vehicle climbed the switchbacks of Monte Gallo. It was a steep pitch, and even the big engine of the Mercedes had to strain, its roar loud enough to cover up the pounding of the surf against the shore. Leaving the window open despite the oppressive heat, Lucci stuck his head out of the gap and took in the land of his birth. Vincenzo Lucci was Sicilian first, Italian second.

The whining of the engine faded as the sedan crested the top of the hill and pulled to a stop in front of a massive gate that looked better suited to a military base than a residence, waiting for the sheet of steel to slide open on silent hydraulic power. When the way was no longer barred, the car moved forward, climbing again, raising clouds of red Saharan dust dumped there by the sirocco blowing in from Libya. They weaved up the slopes covered with the pink blossoms of bougainvillea and oleander, and parked in front of a sprawling villa.

Lucci let himself out of the car and passed underneath a stone archway into a grass courtyard filled with lemon trees, Italian cypresses, and red palms. Having been to his sister's house many times before, he navigated expertly past the long rows of white-flowered pomelia, inhaling their vanilla aroma, and entered the kitchen through the back door.

Maria was standing at the stove, white apron covering her peach sundress, frying sardines in a cast-iron skillet. The oily scent of the fish evoked a hundred memories; every one of them involved his sister, head bent over the pan, long black hair falling around her face.

"You'll be staying for dinner?"

"Of course."

She made no move to turn around; her only movement was a slight flick of her right wrist, expertly stirring the sardines with a wooden spoon.

"Pasta with sardines."

"Yes, I can smell them."

A staple of his youth, pasta and sardines was his favorite.

"You'll be seeing Pietro?"

"I brought him communion."

A nod of her head was her only response. Something brushed against his leg; Romulus had arrived. He scooped up the cat, stroking the fur behind its ears.

"There's something I want to tell you."

"Eduardo is waiting for you …"

"Maria, we need to talk."

She walked over to the pantry without so much as glancing in his direction, her peach sundress billowing in the wind, returning with a handful of spices.

"We'll eat in twenty minutes."

"Maria …"

"He's on the porch."

Lucci remained where he was.

"Don't bring the cat. Eduardo hates him."

Lucci set Romulus down and exited the kitchen into the pool area, around which the villa had been centered. A pair of chaise longues awaited occupants; a table with an emerald green sun umbrella beckoned. The porch was on the north end of the property, with excellent views of the Monte Gallo massif to the west and the Gulf of Palermo to the east. In strictly technical terms, the villa was situated on property belonging to the Riserva Naturale di Capo Gallo, but a man like Eduardo Ferraro had never been limited by such things as strictly technical terms.

Ferraro was standing against the railing, dressed in white cotton pants and a light blue short-sleeved shirt open at the neck. A creature of habit, he stood there every evening, smoking the same type of cigars that he gave to Lucci for his birthday every year, sipping a glass of Minella Bianca from the vineyard he controlled on the southern slopes of Mount Etna. Now he pointed to a second glass, resting on top of the railing not far from where he stood.

"You had a good trip, Vincenzo?"

"Yes, thank you."

"It was good of you to come. Maria appreciates it. I poured a glass of wine for you. Try it; it's quite good."

Lucci didn't feel like trying the wine; he had come here for a reason, and that reason was not wine tasting. But a man like Ferraro was impossible to refuse. He sipped the straw-colored wine, letting the taste of mineral and fruit linger on his tongue. He would have preferred to get straight down to business, but pleasantries were obligatory at the Villa Ferraro. They discussed the suffocating heat—it had been hot even by Sicilian standards—the poor play of the Azzurri, the Italian national football team, and the scourge of weevils laying waste to the island's precious red palms. Ferraro had gone so far as to hire an extra gardener to pick the weevils from the more than two hundred palms on the estate.

"So, Vincenzo, you did not come all the way to Palermo to hear about my pest problems."

"*Sì*, Eduardo, it turns out I have pest problems of my own."

"Pests, in the Vatican?"

"We're inundated with them."

Ferraro set his wine down and used his hand to smooth his thinning hair.

"And you're looking for some advice on how to eradicate them?"

"Not just advice. We're looking for eradicators as well."

Despite having left school before the sixth grade to work in the sulfur mines of the island's interior, Ferraro was one of the brightest people Lucci had ever met, and certainly the most ruthless.

"Eradicators?" He sipped his wine. "I might know where to get some."

"Good, because that is why I came to see you."

"They are going to cost you."

"I wouldn't have come if I weren't willing to pay the price."

"You know what I want?"

Lucci nodded. "I've already made the arrangements."

Ferraro's face remained impassive; he rubbed his wide brow with fingers that had grown thick carrying baskets of sulfur crystals inside the narrow shafts of Tallarita, the infamous sulfur mine in Riesi.

"You wouldn't fuck with an old man, Vincenzo?"

"No, never about something like this. But I warn you, there will be a price to pay."

"Have I not paid enough of a price already?"

"Isn't Pietro the one paying?"

"*Sì, sì*, but his father as well. There is a part of me incarcerated there with him."

Pietro Ferraro, the oldest of Eduardo Ferraro's three children and his only son, had—despite Lucci's stringent objections—joined the family business after his honorable discharge from the 4th Alpini Paratroopers, a specialized mountain combat regiment in service since World War I. Three years after that, the former military hero—who also happened to be Lucci's godson—passed from fame to notoriety and disgrace after murdering magistrate Roberto Caruso. Convicted to life imprisonment, he was serving his sentence not more than fifteen kilometers away, in the ill-famed Casa Circondariale Pagliarelli outside of Palermo.

"That judge, you know he was in the Corleones' pocket?"

"That doesn't change anything, Eduardo."

"No, maybe not for you, but to me it makes all the difference."

Ferraro walked over to the fridge built into the back of the house, trailing cigar smoke that hinted of honey, grabbed a new bottle of wine, and filled up both glasses.

"How did you do it?"

"The governor of the prison is an old friend. I asked him for a favor."

"And he just granted it?"

"I am the Archbishop of Palermo, Eduardo. The governor comes from a pious family. I knew he would accommodate my request."

Ferraro's wide face curled into a snarl; his dark eyes smoldered like the molten lava flowing from the slopes of Mount Etna two hundred kilometers to the southeast.

"Your sister asked you to obtain her son's freedom two years ago, and you refused. But now you want something in return, and you just snap your fingers, and Pietro is free?"

"Pietro isn't free, Eduardo; he will never be free. He killed a magistrate; no one, not even the prime minister, would ever consider pardoning him."

"I don't understand. You said it was arranged."

"I did. But I didn't say *what* had been arranged."

Lucci sipped his wine, letting his point sink in like the winter rains into the volcanic soil.

"The Corleone family has been trying to kill Pietro in retribution for murdering Roberto Caruso, who, as you pointed out, was on their payroll. A door gets left open … a knife is carelessly misplaced … and Pietro is dead. These things happen in Pagliarelli with regularity. Except that it won't be Pietro who is killed."

"The medical examiner …"

"Is a friend of mine. Have the body cremated and scatter the ashes over Monte Gallo."

Down below, in the Gulf of Palermo, a knot of sailboats took advantage of the stiff breeze; a ferry steamed north toward Naples; hundreds of beachgoers walked the white sands of Mondello beach, looking at this distance like a line of marching ants.

"And now I will tell you why the governor agreed to do this." Lucci stared at Eduardo, refusing to shrink from his surly gaze. "He didn't do it so that Pietro could return to the family business."

"Then why?"

"He did it because his godfather needs him; the Church needs him."

"What are you talking about?"

"I'm going to tell you a story, Eduardo. I hope I don't need to tell you never to repeat it."

Ferraro looked injured; his right hand fell over his heart.

"You know I can be trusted."

Ferraro might be duplicitous, dishonest, and deceitful, but he could keep a secret. Lucci told him about the plot to kill the pope and destroy Vatican City, omitting only the smallest of details.

"I can see why you want Pietro for such a mission."

"He is a world-class climber and a decorated paratrooper; he is the perfect man for the job."

Pietro had learned to climb in grade school on the precipitous slopes of Monte Gallo, which was literally in his backyard, and had graduated to the steep inclines of Mount Etna by the time he had finished high school. Prior to enlisting in the Italian army at age twenty-two, he had summitted eight of the top ten highest peaks in the world.

"There are hundreds of climbers good enough for the job. That's not why you want him." Ferraro raised his index finger, wagging it back and forth as he stared at his brother-in-law. "You want him because you know it will mean that the men I provide for your Corsican Guard will be the best I have, because my son's life depends on them. This is very clever of you, Vincenzo, and exactly what I would have done in your position."

"And what else would you do in my position?"

"Use fewer men. Twelve is too many. They will only be tripping over one another."

A bell clanged in the kitchen. Eduardo grabbed his glass in one hand and the bottle in the other, and led Lucci back through the pool area into the dining room, which was situated under a low-hanging terracotta roof. The table had been set with blue and white Minton china, silver flatware, and Waterford crystal; large vases of roses adorned the center. Ferraro sat at the head of the table, Lucci next to him. Maria brought out the food but didn't sit with them.

They ate in a silence only occasionally broken by the *hoop-hoop* of a Eurasian hoopoe looking for a mate. When they had finished, Maria cleared the dishes, depositing bowls of panna cotta with raspberry sauce and cups of espresso.

"What arrangements have you made?" Ferraro asked.

Lucci shrugged. "Other than for Pietro, none."

"Good, leave them to me. I have only one request."

There were few things Lucci enjoyed more than his sister's panna cotta. He finished it before Ferraro could continue, lest his words spoil the taste of cream and raspberries.

"I want to see him before he leaves for Austria."

It was a reasonable request, one that Lucci had been expecting. "He can't come here; people will be watching for him."

"No. I agree. He'll know where to meet me."

They drank their espressos; the male hoopoe cried out for company. *Hoop-hoop. Hoop-hoop.* The ceiling fan whirred, dispersing the scent of the roses, which swirled in the air like the vapor of honey.

"And afterward, what will become of him?"

"That will be up to him. I will see that he gets a new identity, but even with that, I don't think it would be wise for him to return to Sicily."

"Not for a while, certainly."

"Not ever. There are too many people who would recognize him."

"He is Sicilian. He belongs here."

"Then let him stay at Pagliarelli."

"Perhaps America, then."

"So he can expand the family business across the Atlantic? I don't think so."

A green and brown Italian wall lizard appeared on the tabletop. It ran across the linen cloth and stopped beneath one of the large vases, feasting on a beetle that had fallen off the roses.

"Where, then?"

"Leave that to me."

Maria came to clear the table, shooing the lizard away with her hand. Lucci waited until she had been gone for a minute, then nodded to Ferraro, and passed into the kitchen. His sister was standing in front of the sink, with her back still toward him, washing the china by hand as the dishwasher stood idle next to her.

"Thank you for dinner, Maria."

She nodded.

"It was delicious."

She rinsed the water glasses and dried them meticulously with a dish towel. Her pace was always the same, deliberate and methodical, never hurried.

"I know what you are thinking."

Lucci said nothing. Maria moved on to the plates, which were the same pattern of Minton china that their mother had used.

"You are thinking that I must regret marrying Eduardo against your advice."

"I try not to, but I can't help feeling you would have avoided a lot of heartache if you hadn't married him."

"I don't regret it, Vincenzo. Not one little bit. He is a good man … you don't know him like I do."

When the plates were washed and dried, she turned around and handed them to him, never once letting him see her face. Lucci opened the cupboard next to him and put them away.

"Will you absolve Pietro?"

"If he asks for absolution, of course, but he has never done so."

"He is sorry for what he did."

"Is he?"

"Yes, he told me so."

Romulus returned, jumping up on the counter against which Lucci was leaning. He could feel the cat rubbing its spine against his back.

"What will you give him for a penance?"

"I'll think of something."

CHAPTER 21

Marco glanced at his watch, confirming that Elena was late, not that he expected anything else. In all the time he had known her, he couldn't recall a single event to which she had arrived on time. Nor did he mind particularly; the bench on which he sat and waited was only a few meters from Lago Albano. The waters lapped onto the sandy beach with such placidity he thought he might be lulled to sleep. A flock of white clouds had flown in on the westerly breeze, shading him from the evening sun, and the smell of grilled sardines wafted over from a beachside café just a few hundred meters down the shoreline. He nodded off.

Elena was sitting next to him when he awoke. She was dressed all in black—he couldn't remember the last time she wasn't—and her dark hair flowed down over her shoulders in long ringlets.

"Enjoy your nap, Marco?"

He had. It was the first time in the last week he had awoken not having been deeply entrenched in a nightmare.

"Yes, thank you."

They made small talk for a while—*you look good, Elena … so do you*—as they watched the brightly colored kayaks glide over the lake, the beachgoers stroll around on the sandy shore, which had been imported from the nearby coast, and the clouds float past the dome of the church on the hill above the lake.

"Let's take a walk."

He got up, and she followed him down the path that encircled the lake. When they were clear of the beach, he waited for her to catch up, and they meandered down the track.

"Are you and your family still in Rome?"

"Yes, but we're leaving this afternoon."

"Where are you going?"

"I don't know. Cardinal Lucci has made all the arrangements."

They stopped under the shade of a grove of oaks and allowed a runner to flit past. The man had so many water bottles strapped to him, Marco almost asked him for a drink.

"Your sister and daughter … they are well?"

"Well enough."

"They have been through a lot."

"I worry most about Gianna …"

Marco bent down and picked up an acorn, of which there were dozens scattered on the grassy ground, providing sustenance for the squirrels that dodged about in the underbrush.

"Gianna is her mother's daughter, with her mother's strength. She just needs time."

"It will be good to get out of the Vatican. It's beautiful, and everyone has been so nice, but I am beginning to climb the walls."

"I know what you mean. There's an old joke that gets retold in the Vatican all the time, that Pope Leo IV didn't build the wall around Vatican Hill to keep the Saracens out … but to keep the Curia in."

She laughed easily, and they continued on, following the now cobbled path as it ascended a cliff that rose straight up out of the lake. At the top, the path merged onto a narrow road bordered by an adobe wall topped with flowerpots. A store on the other side of the road sold overpriced artwork; as Elena window-shopped, Marco sat on the wall and watched a scull race across the water. Ever since Lago Albano had hosted the rowing events for the 1960 Rome Olympic Games, it had become home to a number of rowing clubs, which still used the original buoy system put in place for the Olympiad.

The path diverged from the road on the other side of the cliff and descended back to the lake, where it ran beneath a cluster of carob trees. A young family was enjoying a picnic dinner on the bank of a stream that flowed fast and noisy down the steep incline.

"I'm glad you came. I've asked Cardinal Lucci about you, but he hasn't said too much."

"Actually, I've been asking to come since the day after St. Peter's Square. I was so worried about you."

She reached out and grasped his hand; her palm felt like velvet.

"I'm fine, really."

"Sure you are."

"Okay, so I'm not, but tell me something, Elena. How am I supposed to be? I killed four men. It isn't the easiest thing to live with."

"That's why I came, Marco … to apologize."

"Apologize? For what?"

She blushed slightly, staining her face pink, which contrasted nicely with her dark blouse.

"For what? Look at yourself! It looks like you haven't eaten or slept in weeks."

"I thought you said I looked good."

"I didn't mean it."

"I'm fine."

She squeezed his hand. "I am sorry. Please forgive me."

"There's nothing to forgive. I already told you that."

"I want you to know I am a very different woman now; I am just sorry you had to be the one to pay the price."

They enjoyed a glass of local wine at a café situated next to the trail and started back as twilight overcame the lake valley.

"I need to talk to you about something," Marco said.

"What is it?"

"I'm not going back to Monterosso, at least not immediately."

Elena didn't reply.

"Cardinal Lucci has an assignment for me."

"Oh?"

He stopped and looked around. They were on a secluded section of the path, well away from the closest people, in a grove of massive plane trees. The rays of fading light and the ambient sound—the clunk of oars moving in their locks, the cries of the gulls—were absorbed by the dense canopy of trees; it was dark and quiet.

"He wants me to go to Austria."

"Austria? What for?"

He told her about el-Rayad and the nuclear weapons, and the prince's intent to deploy them inside the Vatican.

"What does he expect you to do about it?"

"He's assembled some kind of assault team to kill the prince before he takes possession of the warheads. I'm to be part of a second team that provides reconnaissance and cover fire for the first."

She stared at him, narrowing her eyes.

"What does he need you to do that for? Can't he get someone else?"

"No."

Her eyes narrowed even further. Her full lips disappeared into a line. "No? Why not?"

"Because according to him, the pope trusts me. Lucci wants me there so I can report to His Holiness when I get back."

"Why can't he do it himself?"

It was the same question Marco had asked himself many times since Lucci had requested he take part. Or had it been a demand rather than a request? He wanted to think it had been, to ease the burden on his conscience, which was already starting to bubble over like a witch's cauldron.

"He says the pope wouldn't believe him."

A pair of young lovers ambled past, not giving them even a glance. They were so intertwined that it made for difficult locomotion, and it took them a minute to move out of earshot.

"Are you going?"

This is a matter of our continued existence on the face of the earth, Father Venetti. And we have no further time to debate.

"I told him I would, but I am having second thoughts."

"Why?"

"I'm a priest. I should be saying mass, anointing the sick ..."

She shrugged. "You can—and will—do those things for the rest of your life. This is your chance to serve the Church in other ways."

"I hadn't expected you to be on Lucci's side."

"I'm not on Lucci's side. I'm just practical. Lucci is a powerful man. Saying no to him is a bad career move. On the other hand, if you do what he wants, you'll be writing your own ticket."

"I didn't become a priest to spend my time sucking up so I can make bishop."

She shrugged. "What's the harm in going? He wants you there so you can tell the pope what happened."

It was the same thing he had told his conscience during its nightly interrogations of his soul.

"I suppose you're right."

"I am right, Marco. Go to Austria. Make Lucci happy. And then you can go back to Monterosso and watch time stand still."

Elena watched Marco head up the hill toward the Papal Palace, making short work of the steep gradient with his long strides. When he had disappeared behind a row of Italian cypresses that looked like they had been trimmed by a surgeon with a scalpel and a pair of magnifying loupes, she walked back to the waiting sedan and got in the back.

She took her new cell phone out of her pocket as the driver—unseen and unheard on the other side of the darkened glass barrier that separated her from the front of the vehicle—engaged the transmission and merged onto the road, which was bereft of wheeled traffic. There had been no incoming calls. She turned the ringer on and left the phone on her lap, watching the lake disappear as the driver rounded the back of the hill, heading for the motorway and Rome.

The phone rang after the car had reached the outskirts of the city. She answered it on the third ring.

"How did your conversation with Father Venetti go?"

"He's still having second thoughts about going to Austria."

"Still? I thought that's why I agreed to let you say goodbye to him. So that you could dispel his second thoughts."

She continued to stare out the window at the faceless suburbs.

"You don't know Marco very well, Eminence. He'll always have second thoughts; it's just his nature."

"Does that mean he won't be going to Austria?"

"No, of course not. I convinced him to go."

She imagined the slight trace of a smile appearing on Cardinal Lucci's face. She heard—or thought she heard, anyway—the faint whisper of an exhale that might accompany that smile.

"Excellent."

"Can my family and I get out of the Vatican now?"

"In a few days, once Marco leaves for Austria. I want you around in case he loses his nerve again. You seem to have a good effect on him."

"Where are we going?"

"Don't worry about it. I'll find a good home for you."

"I want to go back to Riomaggiore."

"Where the police found a dead terrorist in your kitchen? Where you are under investigation for smuggling and involvement with organized crime?"

"I thought you told me you were going to smooth those things over?"

The car passed under a street lamp, and the reflection of her face developed on the glass like a quadrangle of film in a bath of silver nitrate. The image was dark and grainy; the countenance that stared back at her seemed troubled.

"I will make sure the Gendarmerie forgets they ever happened. But this will take time. If you go back now, there will be many questions that neither one of us wants you to answer. For the time being, it would be best if you and your family just keep a low profile and stay out of Riomaggiore."

The line went dead, and she was left alone with her reflection. After a time, she grew tired of its company and closed her eyes, dozing off for the rest of the trip.

CHAPTER 22

The interrogation room of the Pagliarelli prison was exactly as Lucci remembered it from the last time he had come to visit his godson, six months previously: cramped, faceless, and redolent of sweat and desperation. Pietro Ferraro was exactly as he remembered him as well—short in height, with a wiry muscularity, also redolent of sweat and desperation. Lucci examined him in the gloom. Pietro was his mother's son, with the same lean face and expressive eyes, which had grown dull and lifeless with the boredom of incarceration, and the same black hair with a tendency to curl.

"Hello, Pietro."

Pietro nodded.

"How have you been?"

Like his mother, Pietro was a person of few words. He shrugged.

"I want to talk to you about something."

A glimpse of expression returned to his dark eyes, but it faded as quickly as it had appeared.

"I need your help."

If Pietro was curious about how he could help his godfather, it didn't show in the slumped attitude of his shoulders and the downward lean of his head.

"Anything, Eminence."

"I hope you mean that."

"I do, but how am I supposed to help you inside a prison?"

The heat burned like a furnace in the tiny confines of the room. A bead of sweat dripped down from Lucci's face, soaking into his collar.

"If you are willing to help me, I can get you out of here."

"For how long?"

"Forever."

Lucci dabbed his brow with a scarlet kerchief that matched his zucchetto.

"I'm going to tell you what I have in mind for you. If you agree to go along with it, tonight will be your last night in this hellhole."

"I would do anything to get out of this place."

"Let me tell you first, and then you can make your decision."

Lucci repeated the same story he had told Pietro's father.

"What do you think?"

It was a superfluous question, but one his conscience demanded he ask. Pietro's answer was merely a nod of his head, but it spoke louder than a shout.

"You understand what I am asking? You are not going to Austria for the fine mountain air. You are going to kill a Saudi Arabian prince hunkered down in a fortress, guarded by his own private army."

"What is the worst that can happen?"

"I am glad you asked that." Lucci cleared his throat, selecting his words with the utmost care. "The worst thing that could happen is being captured by the police and identified as your true self. That would be catastrophic. I think you understand my meaning?"

Pietro nodded. Already Lucci could begin to see his nephew emerging from the hollow shadow of himself he had been a mere ten minutes ago: his shoulders had risen; his spine had become more erect.

"Yes, I understand perfectly."

"And you wish to proceed?"

Pietro looked around, taking in the walls of unpainted cinder blocks, the cheap laminate of the tabletop, the decades of grime coating the window separating the two men.

"Immediately."

"Good."

"I have only one condition."

Lucci paused; he had expected conditions from Eduardo, but not from Pietro, who had everything to gain by agreeing to his terms.

"What is it?"

"I want absolution."

Lucci wasn't sure if Pietro could hear his sigh of relief.

"Go ahead."

Pietro said the act of contrition, pausing often when he couldn't remember the words, continuing once Lucci had spoken them for him.

"I murdered a man. I slit his throat as he slept in bed next to his wife." The words came out sharply, like the edge of a well-honed knife. "I knew it was wrong. But I did it anyway."

His voice faded into a stifled silence. Lucci felt the sobs coming before he heard them, shaking the desk at which he was sitting. He reached out to comfort his godson, but his hand rebounded off the divider, leaving him nothing to do other than sit and wait for the sobbing to end.

"My father wanted him dead, but he hadn't ordered it. I was just trying to win his approval."

The sobbing resumed. Lucci slipped the kerchief underneath the glass. Pietro ignored it for a second and then reached for it as if he were picking up something he didn't want.

"The only thing he said when I told him was that I should have killed the wife as well."

He wiped the tears away, but the sobs continued, the great heaving of his shoulders and spine, the whoops of air rushing into his chest.

"I just couldn't do it. She'd done nothing wrong."

Lucci sat patiently. From his long experience as a confessor, he knew that all sobbing stopped eventually. After a while, Pietro wiped his face one final time and pushed the now sodden kerchief back underneath the divider.

"Caruso was one thing; his wife was another."

"Are you sorry you killed Caruso?"

"Yes, I am."

"Then I absolve you in the name of the Father, the Son, and the Holy Ghost. Go forth and sin no more."

Pietro crossed himself in synchrony with Lucci.

"When I say 'Go forth and sin no more,' do you understand what I mean?"

"I think so."

"Let me clarify, then, because I want there to be no ambiguity. It means that your involvement with the family business is at an end."

"Did you tell my father this?"

Lucci nodded. "I did, but it will only mean something when you tell him yourself."

"When will I see him?"

"Very soon. But don't tell him about our agreement until after you return from Austria."

Pietro didn't respond, staring sightlessly into the glass.

"Did you hear me?"

"What will I do?"

"I am sure I can find you something, but let's not get ahead of ourselves."

Lucci looked his godson in the eye.

"Before we proceed any further, I want your word that you will never join the family business again."

Pietro said nothing; Lucci watched the slow bobbing of his Adam's apple.

"Do I have your word?"

A nod.

"I need to hear you say it, Pietro."

Silence.

"You have my word."

CHAPTER 23

Abayd and Jibril sat behind the stainless-steel desk in the prince's massive office and waited for him to appear. The office was on the top floor of Haus Adler, where it shared the space with the prince's equally massive bedroom. It was very fitting, Abayd thought, as he waited for his boss to show up: the prince's two favorite pursuits—making money and making his concubines earn theirs—all on one floor. At least it made for easier security.

The door leading from the bedroom opened, and KiKi stepped into the room, a mug of coffee in his hand. He was a tall, wiry man with a neatly trimmed beard covering a lean face the color of the desert sand at dusk. He sat behind his desk and rubbed his eyes, deepening the dark circles underneath, then glanced at his diamond-encrusted Rolex.

"This had better be good, Abayd."

"It isn't good at all, KiKi."

El-Rayad eyed his chief bodyguard suspiciously. "All right, old friend, let's hear the bad news."

Abayd nodded at Jibril, and his cousin started speaking. El-Rayad listened quietly, without expression, as he drank his coffee, which he took strong and scalding hot. When Jibril had finished delivering the bad news, the prince walked over to the window, swept aside the curtain, and stared out into the morning sunshine.

"Where is my phone now?"

"On Jibril's desk."

"I assume you left the battery out."

"I put it back in, actually."

"Why?"

"Because I'd wager my pension there is a CIA hit team poised and ready, just sitting around with their fingers on their triggers, waiting for the word to come up here and slaughter all of us. They will get suspicious if the battery remains out for too long."

"What do you propose?"

"We leave immediately. The faster we get back to Riyadh, the better. The CIA can't touch us there; here, we are sitting ducks. The Americans stomp around Europe like it's their own fucking country. They wouldn't think twice about killing every last one of us."

"Leaving right now is not an option. What other actions do you suggest?"

Abayd nodded to Jibril, who beat a path to the door.

"The Gulfstream is at the airport. I've taken the liberty of putting the crew on standby. The helicopter is also ready. We could be gone by noon."

"I'm not going anywhere. I am not afraid of the Americans."

"You should be, no matter how many senators you have in your back pocket."

"You think they are here already?"

Abayd got up, walked over to where KiKi was standing, and looked out. Salzburg stretched in front of them like the web of a gigantic spider. He could see the main runway of the airport, tantalizingly close, and the racing shadow of a passenger jet as it made its approach.

"The insertion of that program on your phone is the culmination of years of work and planning, which means the Americans have dedicated a team to bringing you down. I am sure they suspected you were funding terrorism and hoped the listening device in your phone would provide evidence of your involvement. Even the CIA would need approval from higher up, and they aren't going to get it without some kind of proof. So my question is, did you give it to them?"

"I have that phone with me at all times, Abayd. If it has been recording my conversations, we have to assume the CIA knows the Vatican was our doing."

"Then we should be leaving."

"We can't leave right now. We are due to receive a delivery in a few weeks. I am not going anywhere until I have my hands on the package."

Abayd assumed the prince had taken leave of his senses; surely he couldn't have heard him say he planned on going through with the purchase of the nuclear weapons. It wasn't possible for anyone—not even KiKi—to be dumb enough to stay here with the Americans right on top of him. It just wasn't possible.

"Surely you're not intending to continue with this fool's errand?"

"You disappoint me, Abayd. I didn't think you would quit so easily."

"It's not my game. It's never been my game."

"You're wrong, old friend. If it is my game, that makes it your game as well."

"You do realize the Americans aren't going to just watch you walk away with—"

"No, they aren't. That's why you're going to get rid of them for me."

Abayd sighed with resignation, but not surprise; he had known this was coming. "I will need to move as soon as possible, to make sure we strike before they do. You understand what this means?"

The prince nodded, his dark eyes resolute. "We will need to pick up the packages immediately after we dispose of the Americans."

"Very good. Inform the supplier."

"He will not be happy."

"He's a greedy bastard. Throw in another fifty million. That will cheer him up."

"Fifty million?"

Abayd shrugged; it wasn't his money.

"When?"

Abayd had already been considering this question. He needed to find the Americans, survey their position, create an attack plan, and then execute it. The task was formidable, but not impossible, and he had several things in his favor. He had plenty of men already in place and enough firepower to engage a battalion. In addition, he had a good idea as to how he could locate his adversaries. All he required was a bit of luck.

"Seven days. We pick up the package in seven days."

Kamal el-Rayad opened the balcony door of his bedroom and stepped out under the steep eaves of Haus Adler, which slanted down sharply above him. It was early, and the morning air had a chill to it despite the calendar's claims that it was August. The barometric pressure was high, the sky clear, and the conditions for viewing were excellent; even without the Zeiss binoculars that hung from a peg on the railing, he could make out the Festung Hohensalzburg looming ominously above the skyline of the old city. He stared at the scene until every aspect of it was ingrained in his mind, until he could close his eyes and see the Gaisberg—the low, rounded mountain on the other side of the city—as well with his eyes shut as with them open. Inhaling the floral aroma of the red geraniums that grew in the flower boxes hooked to the railing, he memorized the smell as well, burning it deep into the storage spaces of his brain.

The reason he loved Salzburg was that it was the antithesis of Riyadh, where he lived the other eleven months of the year. Riyadh was flat, Austria as curvaceous as the most well-endowed of his concubines; Riyadh was modern and sterile, Austria was ancient and vibrant; Riyadh glowed brown in the light of the Arabian sun, Austria flushed green and verdant against the Alpine sky.

And he was never going to see it again.

After a time, and with great effort, he disengaged from the railing and went back inside, sitting down at his desk. He turned his iMac on, verified his identity with both a facial scan and thumbprint, and activated the Skype application. A drop-down box appeared, and he typed in a series of passwords. As soon as the last of them was accepted, the screen came to life, featuring the face of a middle-aged Caucasian male with a large bald head, unencouraging expression, and unsmiling eyes.

"Hello, KiKi."

El-Rayad nodded.

"I trust everything is well in Austria?"

"No, Anatoly, everything in Austria is not well."

"I'm sorry to hear that."

"Me too."

El-Rayad repeated what Abayd had told him. The man on the screen listened, his expression becoming more and more dour with every word out of the prince's mouth.

"This is bad news, my friend. How did you handle it?"

"Abayd wants to leave immediately; I told him that wouldn't be possible. He is concerned that the Americans intend to attack imminently; I ordered him to find and kill them before they can strike. In fact, I plan to leave as soon as I can, certainly by the end of the day. Both the Gulfstream and my personal helicopter are already on standby. I should be back in Riyadh in time for evening prayers."

"I am afraid you are going to have to cancel that plan."

El-Rayad stared at the screen, thinking he hadn't heard properly. A headache germinated in his forehead.

"I'm sorry? I don't think I understood you."

"You understood me just fine. I said you are going to have to cancel your plans. You and your entourage are staying right there."

"You dare speak to me like that?"

"I will speak to you any way I want."

El-Rayad slammed his palm against the massive oak desk, which caused the photograph of his harem standing beneath the imposing peak of the Untersberg to fall off and clatter against the tile floor.

"It seems His Royal Highness is forgetting about what happened with his cousins from the House of Saud, isn't he?"

"That has nothing to do with this."

"That has everything to do with this. You see, if it hadn't been for me and my friends, the Saudis would have taken everything you have, including your precious oil-soaked sands and your beloved title. But we intervened, didn't we?"

El-Rayad's headache tripled in intensity, threatening to blow his head apart. He grabbed his water bottle and drank greedily, but the throbbing in his temples only worsened.

"Yes, and I appreciate your help, but I lived up to my part of the deal."

"Oh really? How is that exactly?"

"The pope—"

"Is still alive, isn't he? How is that living up to your part of the deal?"

El-Rayad tried to object, but all he could do was stammer something about doing his best. Reaching inside his desk, he extracted his flask of Johnnie Walker Blue Label, drinking it straight from the container.

"When you asked us to intervene on your behalf with the House of Saud, we didn't say we would do our best, we said we would take care of it for you. Didn't we?"

El-Rayad nodded and drank from the flask again. The Scotch burned like fire in his esophagus.

"What do you want me to do?"

"Nothing. Abayd is a competent man. Let him deal with the Americans or whoever is gunning for you."

"You don't think it is the Americans? But the computer virus … Abayd is certain it's NSA."

"It may be, but that doesn't mean anything. I would worry more about the person you just tried to kill."

"What's the pope going to do about it?"

Anatoly closed his eyes for a minute, looking very much like a teacher trying to keep his patience as his student blurted out one incorrect answer after another.

"The pope isn't going to do anything about it, but he isn't alone in Vatican City. There are many others there, including several hard-liners who would like nothing better than to bring back the Crusades."

Anatoly stopped speaking, and el-Rayad used the pause to drink more Scotch and light a cigarette.

"The supplier? Did he agree to move up the delivery?"

"Yes, of course. One week from now."

"Good. I will come to Salzburg personally to supervise."

The throbbing in the prince's temples returned; he finished the last of the Scotch.

"There is no need for you to do that. I can handle it."

"The mountain air will do me good. I'll be there in a few days. In the meantime, keep Dr. al-Sharim busy and out of the way."

"I was going to throw him off the cliff."

"That's because you are a fool. Keep him busy until I get there."

"And what will happen if I am not here when you arrive?"

"You don't want to entertain such an idea."

"I already am."

"Then you should also entertain the idea of losing your title, your ancestral lands, and, quite possibly, your freedom. How does that sound?"

El-Rayad didn't reply. The flask quivered in his right hand, but he made no move to refill it—at least not yet, with Anatoly watching.

"That's what I thought. Stick to the plan. I will be there in three days."

CHAPTER 24

The gun was a Beretta 92, chambered with 9mm Parabellum, the same semi-automatic Marco had used in the navy; he lunged for it as the target closed in on him with frightening speed. Grabbing it, he slipped off the safety and found the trigger with his finger. He leveled the gun, aiming for center mass, but he couldn't see the target clearly in the low light of the shooting range. His finger whitened on the trigger, but didn't apply the requisite three pounds of pressure. The target barreled forward, quietly propelled by the hydraulic apparatus underneath. At the last second, Marco could see it distinctly; it was Mohammed, or rather, a credible likeness of him before Marco had shot most of his face off. It reached the end of the rail; a buzzer sounded, creating obnoxious echoes in the closed space that masked the report of the Beretta as it fired twice.

The reverberations of the gunshots faded, absorbed into the soundproofing that lined the cellar. Marco switched on the safety and scrambled to his feet. Inspecting the silhouette target, he noted the two holes in the middle of the chest, grouped together nicely.

"Don't be too smug, Marco. You were late with your shots."

Pietro stepped from behind the control panel; his pale face betrayed no expression.

"I couldn't ID the target; I shot as soon as I confirmed it was Mohammed."

Marco's trainer shook his head. He had short dark hair with a slight curl, and expressive dark eyes; at the moment, they were expressing frustration and impatience. Even after spending nearly the whole day with him, Marco knew little about him other than his name and that he had been a paratrooper with an Italian army regiment in Afghanistan. "No. You had a split second of opportunity. You hesitated."

Marco thought about arguing, but he held his tongue. There was no point; Pietro would make him do it again and again until he was satisfied. It had certainly been that way all morning, on the rifle range in the shadow of a nearby hill. Before Marco had even been allowed to shoot, Pietro had insisted he field-strip and reassemble the M4 assault rifle again and again until he could do it without hesitating. The shooting drills had been even more exacting: he hadn't let Marco move on until he had grouped three consecutive bullets inside the standard sixty-centimeter target at three hundred meters. At least the weather had cooperated, with sunny conditions and no sign of the Chinook winds that often gusted, hot and dry, down the leeward slopes of the Anti-Appeninni.

"Let's do it again."

Pietro's speech was like everything else about him: efficient and straight to the point. He moved in a similar fashion, propelling himself with a compact, effortless gait. He didn't expend energy on anything he didn't have to—superfluous words, gesticulations, or even facial expressions.

"Get in position."

Marco set the gun on the ground and took two paces back. "Now."

Pietro activated the hydraulics, this time sending several targets down the course on their way toward Marco, who had grabbed the gun and assumed a supine shooting position with his elbows propped on the ground, holding the Beretta in front of him with both hands as Pietro had instructed him. The targets bobbed in and out of cover, moving too fast to identify much less fire upon.

"Breathe."

Marco let his breath in and out, trying to control the pace of his respirations. A target popped out from behind a wall; it was Elena. She hung in space for an exaggerated amount of time; his finger eased off the trigger. Another target appeared, moving laterally across an alley. By the time he recognized one of the men from Boko Haram, the target was safely behind a car. He squeezed the trigger anyway; the bullets thudded into the heavy plywood mock-up, sending splinters flying.

"You just gave your position away. Don't pull the trigger unless you have a clean shot."

A target reversed, flying backwards. He thought he glimpsed a familiar face, but it was moving too fast. It emerged from behind a dumpster, giving him a clear shot. He pulled the trigger twice, wounding Pope John Paul III in the shoulder.

"Don't fire until you have identified the target."

The whir of the hydraulics increased; sweat moistened his palms. A terrorist cut-out popped up out of nowhere; Marco's finger was late to the trigger. Both shots went wide, deflecting off a wall into the deceleration trap, where they rotated at high speed until they lost kinetic energy and fell to the floor.

"Focus."

A target popped up from below ground. Marco recognized the man who had killed three of the Swiss Guardsmen. He fired; the first bullet punctured the target's face, the second clipped his ear.

"Center mass only. No head shots."

And so it went. Time marched on, marked only by the whine of ricocheting bullets, Pietro's clipped shouts, and the growl of Marco's stomach—Pietro had not allowed him to eat. They took a short break to load more fifteen-round magazines, but not to use the bathroom.

"Simulate battlefield conditions at all times. How often is your enemy going to give you a break to eat and relieve yourself?"

By the time the training session ended, Marco had qualified as a marksman on the pistol range, passed the hand-to-hand combat test, and aced the rifle accuracy examination. But he had yet to master the moving silhouette targets; time simply ran out. They collected their gear and vacated the premises of the shooting club, which was situated on a rare patch of flat ground in between two rugged hills northeast of Poli, an hour's drive from Rome. They wound their way back down to the city in Pietro's car, a tan Renault sedan that, like Pietro himself, had many miles under its belt despite its relative youth.

Marco tried to make small talk, but Pietro was a man of few words. 'Where are you from?' was answered by 'Italy.' To 'Who do you work for?' Pietro replied, 'The Vatican,' and the query 'What do you like to do on your days off?' netted no response other than a rush of air through Pietro's window.

"How many people have you killed?"

The question startled Marco, who had been watching the sun sink below the low hills to the west, leaving a crimson stain on the white clouds above.

"I'm sorry?"

"You heard me the first time."

"Why do you ask?"

"You excel at target shooting, but as soon as you aim at a silhouette, you hesitate. It's as if there is a debate going on in your head."

"I wouldn't say debate. It's more like an old motion picture, except in color, accompanied by a soundtrack of gunshots and screams."

"It doesn't matter what it is. It's going to get you killed. And that might get *me* killed."

"You? How?"

"I'll be leading the assault on Haus Adler. If it's going to be successful—and it is going to be successful—I need someone on top of that hill who isn't going to hesitate."

They rounded a corner and descended a steep hill. Olive groves glistened like silver in the fading light, stretching away as far as Marco could see.

"Any suggestions?"

"Slow your breathing, stay in the moment."

"And if that doesn't work?"

Pietro thought about this as Marco rolled his own window down, letting in the hot air that smelled faintly of sulfur vapors from the nearby springs.

"I once knew a great trauma surgeon. I met him in the Hindu Kush when I was fighting in Afghanistan with the 4th Alpini Paratroopers. We were clearing a valley of Taliban fighters and thought we had driven them all out. One day, they ambushed my patrol; three of my men were seriously wounded. We got them down to the battalion aid station barely alive. This surgeon from the U.S. Army saved all three of them. Never have I seen someone so calm in the face of so much chaos. Men screaming in pain, blood spurting from wounds, nurses shouting out orders."

He drifted into silence for a minute at the recollection. The only sounds were the low purr of the motor as the car descended the hill and the rush of air through Marco's window.

"I went back to see him a few weeks later to ask him how he stayed so calm in such a stressful situation."

"What did he say?"

"All bleeding stops."

"All bleeding stops?"

"One way or the other."

"Why does that help?"

The car slowed as it went through a small village, a cluster of red-roofed adobe buildings stacked on top of a rocky bluff overlooking a valley of orange trees.

"Because focusing on the outcome of the process heightens nervousness and worsens the results. Understanding that all bleeding stops one way or the other helped him focus on the process, rather than the outcome, which in turn made the outcome better."

They turned a corner, and the village was lost to sight, but the fragrant smell of oranges lingered.

"Focus on the moment, on what you are doing … ignore what might happen and what has happened. See only what you are doing in the present moment."

Pietro lifted his gaze from the road for a moment, fixing Marco with his watchful brown eyes.

"All bleeding stops."

CHAPTER 25

Lucci paused in front of the door to the papal apartments and took a moment to compose himself. If there was one thing he hated, it was being summoned to a meeting when he had many other things to do. To make things worse, it was summer, and John Paul III was at Castel Gandolfo, a half-hour drive through the snarled streets of Rome. But Lucci hadn't risen to his current position without the ability to navigate through the treacherous waters of the Vatican's hierarchy; regardless of their differences, John Paul III was still the Supreme Pontiff of the Roman Catholic Church, and Lucci would pay him his due.

He knocked twice and pushed the door open; there was no one in the apartment. He walked past the bookshelves and desk crowded with texts, magazines, and manuscripts, making his way toward the porch overlooking Lake Albano. The pope was an organizational nightmare, he thought, as he took a detour around a five-hundred-year-old table weighed down by a sloppy pile of ancient books, but there was no denying his brilliance. Lucci had made the mistake of underestimating the pontiff on one occasion, and he would never do it again.

John Paul III was sitting on a wicker chair on the porch. There was a second chair on the other side of a small table, and the pope waved for him to sit down. A small pitcher of white wine sweated in the heat, and Lucci could see his glass was already filled. He could tell it was going to be more than just a quick conversation, and his thoughts strayed to the mountain of paperwork on his desk.

"Holiness."

"Good evening, Eminence. Thanks for joining me."

Lucci sipped his wine, and his spirits perked up. At least the pope had had the good sense to serve a decent vintage for a change—a white from the steep slopes of Mount Etna in Lucci's home island. "Did I have a choice?"

The pope laughed. "You always have a choice. Remember that when I am gone. You always have a choice, even when you are certain you don't."

"Are you going somewhere?"

The pope refilled his wine glass, nodding. "I leave in two days' time."

"Where?"

"Nigeria."

In the current times, a papal visit to a foreign country required a monumental effort; everything from the obvious security issues to subtle political concerns had to be weighed and balanced. It was impossible for an undertaking of this magnitude not to have come to Lucci's attention, yet he had heard nothing.

"I wasn't aware."

"I asked Oberst Jaecks to keep the arrangements quiet. This is not an official visit."

"Vacation?"

The pope shrugged. "Let's call it that. I had already scheduled several weeks off; I am simply changing the venue."

"I didn't realize Nigeria was a vacation destination."

"We both know it isn't."

Lucci considered this with a mouthful of wine, which overflowed with the minerals spewed from the earth with the frequent eruptions of Mount Etna. "If you're looking for the root cause of the attempted assassination, you should be flying to Riyadh, Holiness."

"I have decided to leave the Saudi problem to you. You are the Secretary of State, after all."

A wise decision, Lucci thought. "Then why are you going to Nigeria?"

The pope didn't reply, but Lucci knew the answer anyway.

"The Nigerians weren't the problem. The Saudis were just using them to get at you."

"So you say. But the fact remains that antipathy for me grows like a weed in the northern half of the country. If I don't get my hands dirty in the soil in which the weeds grow, they will choke the life out of my homeland."

"You will remember that I warned you against coming out so strongly against sharia law."

"You did at that. But sometimes silence is not an option."

"I didn't say you had to be silent. I counseled you not to make an issue of it. There is a difference."

"Muttering to myself about women being stoned to death for committing adultery doesn't solve anything."

"Whereas issuing a papal decree condemning it very nearly got you killed."

The pope laughed and took a sip of his wine.

"Go to Nigeria, Holiness. I will hold down the fort in your absence."

In point of fact, Lucci thought the trip was a complete waste of time and resources, but it wasn't his place to say. Moreover, it would leave him free to deal with the Saudis as he saw fit, without any interference whatsoever. By the time the pope returned from Nigeria, Father Venetti would be returned from Austria with the prince's death certificate in his hand, and no one would be any the wiser.

"I plan to take Father Venetti with me."

A cold chill overcame Lucci, as if a dark cloud had just settled in front of the sun.

"Out of the question. He's still recovering from his concussion."

"Exactly, that's why I already cleared it with his physician."

"There are other considerations as well."

The pope raised a dark bushy eyebrow. "Such as?"

"I have given Father Venetti an assignment."

The pope regarded him curiously. "Of what nature?"

"You told me you would leave the Saudis to me. This is a significant undertaking, for which my office is not sufficiently staffed. Father Venetti is a capable man, and I fear he is growing a little bored. Asking him to help me with this issue solved two problems at the same time."

The pope said nothing at first, and Lucci thought the moment had passed.

"Very clever of you, Vincenzo. Just make sure your solution doesn't create any new problems."

A dozen replies buzzed through Lucci's head, but he thought the best course was to remain silent.

"Father Venetti is a talented man, Eminence; on that, we agree. But his wounds run a lot deeper than the scratch on his shoulder."

For a moment, Lucci was sure the pope had read between his carefully selected words and interpreted his intent correctly, but then he shook himself, embarrassed about his flight of insecurity. There was something about John Paul III that did peculiar things to him, which was one of the reasons he avoided him whenever possible.

"I will bear that in mind, Holiness."

"Do you know where Father Venetti is? I haven't seen him all day."

Lucci responded that he hadn't seen the priest either. No small wonder, he thought, since he was off in Umbria getting a crash course in fieldwork from Pietro. Since getting his nephew out of prison less than a week ago, Lucci had been putting him to work, which was a good thing, because it had cost him dearly to do it. Despite what he had told his brother-in-law, the prison governor had wanted far more than just Lucci's request, and he had likewise had to pay off the medical examiner as well.

"Do you know if he will be here tomorrow?"

Lucci shrugged. "Can I relay a message?"

"Tell him I will be back in two weeks, and until then he is welcome to stay here."

Lucci nodded and waited for the pope to make another comment. When none was offered, he bowed slightly at the waist and started his escape.

"Eminence."

"Yes?"

"I'm not making a mistake leaving Father Venetti in your care, am I?"

"I certainly hope not."

Lucci reached the door and passed through before the pope could say anything more, then paused for a minute on the other side.

I certainly hope not.

CHAPTER 26

The soft, almost intimate knock came at 8 p.m., exactly when he had been told it would come. Marco pushed himself off the sofa and shuffled across the dingy hotel room to let her in. He peered through the spyhole before he opened the door—more out of curiosity than anything else—and saw her standing there in the drab third-floor hallway of the Hotel EuroStar. Her image was distorted by the layers of grime caked on the glass, but he could still see it was the woman whose photograph Lucci had shown him.

He opened the door, and she walked in, toting brown paper shopping bags in both hands and pecking him on the cheek as she brushed past. He shut the door and followed her across the worn burgundy carpet. She set her shopping bags down on the chest of drawers and stuck out her hand. He shook it automatically, without taking his eyes off her face. She had large green eyes, high rounded cheekbones, and a wide mouth bordered by full lips painted the color of a cardinal's sash.

"Hello. My name is Sarah."

Her accent reminded him of Magdalena, the American woman he'd dated during his time in the navy. Her cream-colored sundress did as well, although Magdalena hadn't had the same deep bronze skin or the lean, muscular arms that swung in step with her shapely legs.

"I'm Marco."

She moved over to the small table—Marco watched her walk and forgot about Elena for a moment—and sat down on a plastic chair. "Come, sit."

He grabbed a couple of Peronis from the refrigerator and joined her. They made small talk for a little while as the TV blared in the corner, unwatched. Marco got up to turn it off—the Azzurri were losing anyway—but Sarah asked him to leave it on.

"Are you a football fan?"

She laughed easily, denying it. "I just like the noise. It makes it hard to eavesdrop."

And then Marco remembered who she was and why she was there. It had all been pushed out of his head by the flash of her teeth as she smiled and the scent of jasmine that followed her wherever she went. But it came tumbling back with this realization, never to leave again. She was an American sniper. He was traveling with her to Austria to observe the assassination of a Saudi prince before he could acquire two nuclear warheads.

"You don't look like an assassin."

"The good ones never do."

Her laugh made him want to say more clever things. "More like a lawyer or a doctor."

She excused herself into the washroom, and he phoned for room service. They ate spaghetti bolognese at the small table, washing it down with a bottle of red wine. They conversed easily as they ate, speaking in English.

"You sound like an American," she said.

"I dated a girl from Maryland."

"What happened to her?"

"We broke up years ago … lost touch. I got a Christmas card from her a few years ago. She was living in Boston … some sort of biotech engineer."

"What other languages do you speak?"

"German, with a distinct Tyrolean accent, and Italian, obviously."

"Obviously." She removed any offense with a prize-winning smile that caused his stomach to turn over.

"And Latin, of course."

She gave him a curious look, and Marco remembered she didn't know he was a priest. "Latin?"

"My Greek isn't bad either."

She smiled the kind of smile a beautiful woman always smiles when men brag about themselves in order to impress her. Marco, slightly embarrassed by the departure from his modest nature, cleared the table and brought the dishes into the hall. When he returned, Sarah had retreated to the bathroom; most likely, he thought, to avoid hearing him drone on about his abilities as a linguist. He sat down and picked up the remote, trying to distract his disquieted mind.

The door opened, and she appeared, dressed in a pair of black Spandex pants and a white cotton shirt. She moved over to the bed and pulled up the covers on the right-hand side.

"Mind if I take this side?"

"Take the whole bed, Sarah. I'll sleep on the couch."

"Better sleep in the bed with me." She patted an anemic-looking pillow. "We're supposed to be married; wouldn't look good if we have separate beds."

Marco had no idea who was going to notice, but he didn't argue; she had the look of a woman who lost few arguments. She got into bed and sat with her legs extended, a pillow covering her lap.

"Tell me about yourself."

Marco rarely felt comfortable talking about himself, but it was easier to talk about the other Marco, the Marco that Lucci had invented, the faithful servant of the Vatican who traveled the world in pursuit of security for the Holy See. Her interest in the narrative only increased his enthusiasm for telling it, forcing him to cut himself off by retrieving another pair of Peronis from the mini fridge.

"What about you?" he asked.

"What do you know about me already?"

"You're American. That's about it."

"That pretty much sums it up."

He opened the beers and extended his arm to pass her one while remaining sitting on the couch.

"Where are you from?"

"You've never heard of it."

"I've been to the States twice. Try me."

"Rochester, Vermont."

"Never heard of it."

"It's a small town in the mountains. Nothing ever happens there."

"Sounds perfect."

And it did, to the thirty-six-year-old priest from Monterosso, another place where time blurred, one day of azure sky and aquamarine ocean indistinguishable from the day that preceded it and the day that followed.

"Not when you're eighteen. I got out of there as quickly as I could, joined the service."

Marco had, of course, done the same thing at the same age, if for a completely different reason, which in his case was the absolute expectation that he would follow his older brother, his father, and every other male relative in his father's family into the navy.

"Which service?"

"The U.S. Air Force. I wanted to be a sniper; they wanted me to be an electrician. When they saw my scores on the rifle range, they sent me to sniper school."

"Where did you learn to shoot so well?"

"In my backyard, when I was five."

"Five years of age?"

She nodded. "My mother decided she wasn't keen on child-rearing when I was two and hit the road. My father figured he could raise me any way he wanted, since there wasn't anyone else around to tell him otherwise. And so I had a gun in my hand before I went to kindergarten."

His thoughts strayed to Elena, who had also been raised by her father without the benefit of a mother in her life. Marco had always presumed that she had derived much of her strength from being forced to do for herself so many of the things other children had done for them. Perhaps Sarah had benefited in a similar fashion.

"My first job was to keep the rabbits out of the vegetable patch. My father used to pay me a dollar bounty for every rabbit I shot."

"The neighbors didn't object?"

She laughed quietly at this. "Neighbors? In the backwoods of Vermont? Our closest neighbors lived two miles down the road."

Marco tried to imagine a land so vast that the people next door lived out of rifle range; growing up in a suburb of Trieste, where one house was right on top of the next, he couldn't.

"How often do you get back to Vermont?"

"There isn't much for me there, so not often. But I did go a few years ago … just showed up one day."

She lapsed into silence at the recollection. Marco was curious as to what she had found, but he had enough difficult memories of going home to his own father's house—it was always referred to in this way, as if his mother didn't also live in it—to be patient.

"This woman answered the door. She told me my father had gone to Alaska for the summer … asked her to keep an eye on the place until he got back."

"He went to Alaska for the whole summer?"

She nodded. "My father … he's a different breed."

Marco's father was a different breed as well. When Marco had told him—shortly after he had been awarded the Gold Medal of Military Valor—that he was leaving the navy to enter the priesthood, a chasm had opened up between them that, despite many attempts, he had never been able to cross.

"I think I'm going to turn in."

"Okay, I'm just going to watch TV for a while."

He lowered the volume and began to flick through the channels. After ten minutes of fruitless surfing, he gave up the effort and made ready for bed. She was still awake when he lay down, although her breathing was slow and deep, indicating Morpheus was not far away. His thoughts strayed back across time, slicing through the years like a scalpel, and settled on the first night he'd lain in bed with a woman.

Sarah reminded him of Magdalena, or maybe she didn't resemble her at all and his impish mind was trying to torture him. It had been in Rome, coincidentally; he had been a lieutenant in the navy, on leave from his salvage ship. It was a complex memory, crammed full of a variety of emotions—sheer joy, horrible guilt, and, of course, confusion—but one that came to mind often, almost always at night, when the dark and the quiet encouraged him to delve into the recesses of his brain.

Sarah rolled over and pulled the sheet down. The light from outside streaked in through a crack in the cheap curtains and fell on her face, illuminating her dark skin with its soft glow. My God, he thought, how beautiful she was, even with her green eyes closed and no hint of her wide smile. He wondered how such a person had ended up as a sniper. It was hard to think of her like that, even with the barrel of her semi-automatic peeking out from under her pillow.

Not that he was in any position to throw stones.

As he drifted off to sleep, a succession of images floated through his mind's eye: Mohammed's disfigured face etched into the communion wafer; Tariq's bulging eyes and lizard tongue protruding from the faces of the faithful kneeling to receive; and, the most disturbing of them all, the lifeless form of Pope John Paul III lying in the burned-out wreck of St. Peter's Basilica.

CHAPTER 27

Pietro Ferraro got out of the van and surveyed his home for the near future. It was a typical Austrian farmhouse, with three stories built of darkly stained pine covered by a steeply angled roof. He had stayed in something similar a dozen times in his youth, in the hills above Innsbruck, where his mother's distant cousins lived in alpine meadows dotted with brown cows.

It was unimaginable that they'd rented it on such short notice in the height of summer—and in Festival season no less—but nothing was unimaginable for his father, who had proved time and again that money and the credible threat of violence could get him anything he wanted.

He climbed the steps leading to the porch that wrapped around the second floor of the house and entered the main living space through a glass slider. The Corsican Guard was there, all ten of them sitting on the chairs and sofas that surrounded the massive stone hearth built into the opposite wall. They were a surly lot, but he was familiar with all of them, having worked with them prior to being incarcerated. He nodded to them; they nodded back as they sat there drinking small glasses of grappa and smoking foul-smelling Sicilian cigarettes. It was a diverse group by age and region—there were three Siracusans and a couple of Nisseni; the rest were Palermitani—but with a common thread: they were all killers.

Pietro moved to stand next to one of the Palermitani, a short, stocky man with a thin veneer of black hair combed straight back over his squat head.

"Luca."

The man grunted a hello and went back to sipping his grappa. One of the Nisseni, a man named Custanti, who was good with a switchblade, tried to raise the bottle of grappa to pour a glass for Pietro, but Luca held his hand down with a forearm the size of the average man's thigh.

"No grappa yet. Talk first."

"I didn't know you were giving the orders now, Luca," Pietro said.

Luca shrugged. "Some of us have been working while you were on vacation."

The hair on Pietro's neck bristled, but he remained calm. "What would you like to talk about?"

"What the hell are we doing here?" Luca spoke slowly, carefully, as if he had measured each word and decided it was exactly the right one.

"We're here to do a job. That's all, just like any other day at work."

"Just like any other day … is that right?" Luca snorted his derision. "Then why are there a dozen assault rifles in the basement?"

A murmur arose from the Siracusans seated on one of the couches. All three of them were short, powerfully built, and as dark as the ash from Mount Etna, which smoldered upwind of their homes.

"We're taking somebody out, nothing that any of us hasn't done before. That somebody just happens to be a prince with an armed bodyguard, so we're packing a little heavier than usual."

The hubbub died down for a second, and Pietro seized the opportunity to flip open his laptop, type in the password, and open a file. The computer was already connected to the large flat screen on the wall underneath the mounted head of a huge red stag, and now a picture of Haus Adler appeared, looking minuscule sitting atop the massive rock upon which it was built.

"This is Haus Adler." He used a laser pointer to circle the chalet. "It is Prince Kamal el-Rayad's home for the month of August." The red dot dropped down over the cliff face in front of the residence. "This is our way in."

A curse was muttered. Someone belched, filling the air with the aroma of anchovies and grappa.

"There's no other way?" This was from the other Nisseno, the man sitting next to Custanti on the near sofa. His name was Carlo, and he had recently killed a man with a gardening trowel.

Pietro hit a few keys on the computer, and the view changed; Haus Adler was still visible, but now from above. A lengthy driveway ran along the edge of the precipice, leading to a large garage.

"This is the other way in. It's barricaded, patrolled twenty-four hours a day, and monitored by over three hundred closed-circuit television cameras."

He switched back to the view of the cliff face. "Over the next few nights, I am going to climb this face. The base is only a few clicks up the road from here." He pointed through the window toward the dirt road that wound into the dense grove of pines surrounding them. "I'm leaving pitons in place and stashing ropes. Once all the pitons are in, all I have to do is climb up ahead of the rest of you and fix the ropes, and we should be able to reach the top in three or four hours."

He paused to look around the room and was greeted by grim stares, surly faces, and a collective lack of enthusiasm. Only Custanti, a man he had climbed with on several occasions, looked on with interest.

"You were all selected because you have climbing experience. It will be a walk in the park once the ropes are up."

"What happens when we all get to the top?"

"Only six of us are going up. Two will stay at the top, in case we need cover fire on the way out." Pietro used the laser pointer to highlight the flat patch of ground between the cliff and Haus

Adler itself. "Four of us will cross this space; two will take up positions here at the base of the house, one on either side. Luca and I will be the only ones to enter the building. Surprise and stealth are the keys here, not firepower."

The screen changed, showing a close-up of the massive four-story alpine residence. Pietro used the pointer to indicate the top floor.

"Prince el-Rayad lives on the fourth floor. No one else is allowed up there, not even his wives."

"How do we get up there?" Luca seemed a little happier now that he knew he would have a chance to slit the prince's throat as he slept.

Pietro highlighted a tree that had been espaliered against the south side of the house, in the traditional way of the local farmers.

"By climbing this pear tree to reach the porch around the second floor." He enlarged the picture of that side of the house. "This is a staircase that runs between the second and fourth floors. It will take us straight up to the prince's bedroom."

"Security system?"

One of the Palermitani had asked the question; it was one for which Pietro had been prepared.

"Haus Adler was built in the early 1800s, so it doesn't lend itself to retrofitting a sophisticated security system. According to the latest information from the CIA, only the fourth floor has any security, and that is just an easily defeated contact alarm on the sliding door."

"The latest information? Are we going in on three-year-old intel?"

More flak from the Palermitani. He knew them better than the rest and had expected them to give him little trouble.

"It's what we have. I wish it were more recent, but it's not. So, I am going to check out the house the night before we go in. I'll be up there anyway putting the last of the pitons in. If they have added more security, we'll have a whole day to adjust the plan."

A bottle thumped down on the table as the Palermitani refilled their grappa glasses. The fire crackled in the hearth, and the flames danced, casting moving shadows against the far wall.

"If you're being honest with us."

"Why wouldn't I be?"

The man who had been asking the questions shrugged. He was bigger than the others, very large by Sicilian standards, with a narrow head, sallow skin, and bright blue eyes that seemed incongruous with the rest of his face. His name was Alessandro; Pietro didn't know him well, but he was familiar with his reputation as a stern man with a mercurial temper and a penchant for excessive violence.

"This whole job stinks like a bad fish. We have no business here."

"We do have business here."

"*Sì, sì*, bad business. This isn't what we do. We shouldn't be here … we *wouldn't* be here if your father hadn't made a deal he had no right to make."

"What deal is that, Alessandro?"

Alessandro drank his grappa in one swallow. Pietro walked over to where he was sitting, hunched over the table, clutching the glass with both hands.

"If you have something to say, say it now."

The tall Sicilian stood up, towering over him.

"All right, I will. Your father has wanted to get you free since you were sentenced. And here you are, suddenly out of prison like magic, telling us we have to take out someone from Saudi Arabia that none of us have ever heard of, and that we don't care about."

The two men glared at one another as a low murmur flooded the room. Glasses thudded against the table.

"That's the deal I'm talking about."

"I don't meddle in my father's business." Pietro paused for a second, letting the implication that Alessandro *was* meddling in his father's business sink in. "I'm here following orders, just like I have always done. Just like we have all always done. Just like *you* have always done."

The murmuring died down a bit.

"Tell me, Alessandro, is that going to change? Or are you still going to follow orders?"

The room went quiet, other than the hiss of the flames and the occasional crackle of a sap ball igniting; the only movement was the play of the shadows on the wall.

"No, it's not going to change. I don't like it … but I'm still following orders. For now."

CHAPTER 28

Marco woke early and went for a walk to clear his head. He stopped halfway at a small church to pray and check for tails. Finding none, he walked back to the hotel. Sarah was showering when he returned, and so he rang room service for a continental breakfast.

She emerged wearing a large towel and smiled a greeting, then snagged a piece of melon and a cup of coffee and retreated back to the bathroom. When she came out ten minutes later, she was wearing a dark silk suit and a white blouse, and her hair was pulled back in a ponytail.

She twirled around in front of him. "What do you think? I picked it up yesterday."

"I think you're going to cost me a lot of money. Mr. Romano doesn't like to part with his money."

Their passports listed them as Marco and Sarah Romano of Utica, New York. They were Americans of Italian descent, making their first trip to Europe.

"That explains this third-rate hotel, which Mrs. Romano doesn't like."

He finished eating and took a quick shower, trying to avoid conjuring a mental image of the shower's most recent occupant. But it was a difficult task, and he cut his time short for fear of failing. He dressed in black slacks and a dark gray cotton shirt, feeling confident he looked like an American on holiday in Rome. They packed their few things quickly and left via the back staircase.

In the garage beneath the hotel, Sarah led him to a silver Volvo sedan and threw him the keys.

"You drive."

It was still early, and traffic was light, at least by Roman standards. Marco took the A1 and headed north, thinking about the time, several weeks and a different lifetime earlier, that he had driven south on his way to stop Boko Haram from assassinating the pope and razing St. Peter's Basilica.

"What's our plan?"

"We're driving to Salzburg." He checked the rear-view mirror, as Pietro had instructed him, seeing nothing other than the outskirts of Rome slowly fading away. "We'll check in to a hotel in the old city. Tomorrow we'll hike the Untersberg and scope out the shooting position above Haus Adler."

It didn't seem like much of a plan to him, but what did he know? He was a Jesuit priest from Monterosso, and the sooner this was over, the quicker he could return there, to his quiet parish overlooking the Ligurian Sea.

They stopped north of Bologna to refuel and eat lunch at a café next to the gas station. Sarah drove after the break; Marco tried to take a nap—he hadn't slept well—but his mind was active, and he couldn't rest. He thought about the woman in the car with him. Who was she, really? How had it come to be her livelihood to kill other people, like a fireman put out fires or a janitor mopped up mud from a dirty floor? And, the most disquieting question of them all, why did he feel himself drawn to her, like a moth to a porch light?

She was beautiful, yes, but Italy was full of beautiful women, and he had always—with the glaring exception of Elena—been able to keep himself in check. No, there was something more about her, something he couldn't name, that beckoned him like the Sirens of mythology beckoned the Greek sailors on their way home from war.

They stopped at the rest area overlooking the Brenner Pass and got out to stretch their legs. Marco had been here several times in his life, but the severity of the landscape never failed to impress him. He marveled at the steepness of the slopes and the narrowness of the grassy valleys pinched between the sharply angled hillsides.

They returned to the A10, heading north to Innsbruck, taking in a pasture full of brown cows and small hay barns. It was good to be back in Austria, he thought, even if it was to witness an execution.

"How long have you worked for the Vatican Security Office?" Sarah asked.

"I'm not really with the Security Office. I'm only on loan to them."

"From whom? If you don't mind my asking."

He did mind, but he didn't say as much. There was something about the soft fragrance in the car and the exposed patch of skin at the nape of her neck that weakened his resistance. What kind of priest was he? But he knew the answer: the regular kind, with all the human frailties one would expect.

"The Secretariat."

"I didn't realize the Secretariat had an enforcement arm."

"We like to keep a low profile."

"So do I, Marco. So do I."

"Are you married?"

She stopped staring out the window at the Hochkönig, a massive pile of rocks rising into a cloud-specked sky, and turned to look at him. "Of course I'm married."

He was surprised by her answer, not judging her profession to be well suited for married life. And a little disappointed?

"I'm married to you, darling, and have been for ten wonderful years."

"I meant in real life."

"So did I, Marco. Right now, this is my real life, and it's yours too." She punctuated her message by placing her hand on his bare forearm. It felt like warm silk. "Haven't you been happy?"

"Yes. Very."

CHAPTER 29

Abayd snapped his cell phone shut, slipped it into the pocket of his black blazer, and stuffed his Glock in his chest harness. He knew he shouldn't carry it—there were strict federal laws against gun possession in Austria—but he didn't feel dressed without it. He took the back stairs down to the garage, hopped into a black Mercedes sedan, and backed out.

He drove quickly along the two-kilometer track that wound next to the edge of the cliff, his mind on other things. At the end of the driveway, he headed down the mountain toward Salzburg. Turning right on Glanegg Road, he skirted along the eastern slope of the huge mountain, reflexively checking his mirrors for a tail. He drove past the Moosstrasse, the main artery to the center of the city, and turned right on the road to Berchtesgaden, following it up the winding valley in the opposite direction from the stream raging along the side of the road. He turned off the main road onto a steep track between farm pastures, passing a small church in a clearing and continuing up, following the road as it ascended a narrow valley between two ridges.

The track ended at a trailhead, and he parked the car behind a large beech tree and started up the path, which led to a ledge overlooking a waterfall. He spent a few seconds watching the water cascade down the rocky face, then peered over the edge. A dozen boulders greeted his gaze, pounded smooth by centuries of falling water. He gauged the drop to be about fifty meters, plenty for his purposes.

He spent the next ten minutes poking around, making sure no one was in the area, then returned to the clearing above the waterfall. He didn't have long to wait; several minutes later, he heard the scrape of a boot on rock, and a head appeared, floating above the trail. A moment later, the rest of the man came into view, and Abayd breathed a sigh of relief. He had come alone as instructed.

They shook hands, and Abayd faked a warm greeting. He had met the man three years ago when KiKi—against his advice—had flown his entire harem of wives and children over for the August holiday. As big as Haus Adler was, it could not accommodate everyone, and he had been forced to find alternative housing for the security detail. He had needed an agent who could be discreet, someone who knew how to take a five-hundred euro note and tuck it into his wallet. It had been a long and frustrating search—Austria was not a country full of people on the take—but he had ultimately netted the man currently shaking his hand.

"You look well," Abayd said.

"You too."

"You have the information?"

The man nodded, his brow furrowed slightly. "You have the payment?"

Abayd patted his jacket, feeling the hard bulk of the pistol beneath his blazer. "I have it right here. And if the information is accurate, I will pay you twice what we discussed."

The man pulled a folded sheet of paper from the back pocket of his black jeans. "You wanted me to find a property that was rented recently, perhaps as recently as one or two weeks ago. You were looking for a fairly large group, at least ten and possibly as many as twenty. A private location was a high priority, correct?"

Abayd blinked.

"I found eight rentals that met these criteria." The man handed over the folded sheet.

Abayd glanced at it quickly. It was a list of the properties, the address of each, and the name of the renter.

"You will see that three of the properties are within a four-kilometer radius." The man handed him another sheet of paper. This one contained additional information on each of the places on the narrowed-down list, including small black-and-white pictures of the exteriors.

Abayd glanced over the listings. One property had been rented by a family of music lovers from Australia, another by a group of French hikers. The third rental piqued his interest immediately. It was a large farmhouse situated on a dead-end road, rented only three days ago by a producer of documentary films, who had paid the entire sum, including a hefty security deposit, up front.

The man tapped the third entry with a finger as thick as a stuffed grape leaf, something of which Abayd was quite fond. "I thought this one might be of particular interest to you. It is only a few kilometers down the mountain from Haus Adler."

This was the place, Abayd was sure of it. The Americans were right under his nose. "And you didn't discuss this with anyone else?"

The man seemed offended. "You offered to pay for discretion, so I was discreet."

Abayd took one last look around. He didn't see anyone, so he fished out a stack of hundred-euro notes from his pocket and held them out. The man reached for them, unable to keep a look of sheer joy from stealing over his face.

Abayd dropped the bills before the man's fingers could close over them, grabbed his wrist, and twisted it violently. His victim yelped in pain and went limp, falling into Abayd's grasp. He thrust forward with his squat, powerful frame, carrying his prey to the brink, then sent him downward with a shove. He braked sharply—lest he follow the poor sap in—and watched him plummet to his death, tumbling end over end as he did. His body smashed against the rocks with a thud and slid into the water racing through the narrow flow-off, lost to sight.

Abayd picked up the bills and shoved them into his pocket, where they would remain. He had already expensed the cash; there would be no point in returning it. He shot a last look around and started down the trail, hoping never to see this place again.

CHAPTER 30

Marco and Sarah arrived in Salzburg as the sun sank beneath the Mönchsberg, the small mountain that pinned the old city against the rushing green waters of the River Salzach. Marco parked the car in a garage underneath the mountain, and they exited onto the street via a tunnel blown out of the rock. He led the way around the corner onto the Getreidegasse, the signature street of the old city, and stopped underneath a gold sign announcing the Hotel Goldener Hirsch.

They passed inside and checked in as Mr. and Mrs. Romano. Marco paid for the room with cash and left an imprint of a credit card he'd been given by Lucci to cover any incidental charges. The concierge led them to a rear-facing room on the fourth floor, with a porch overlooking the Universitätsplatz.

"It's a little touristy, but we'll blend in nicely," Marco said apologetically.

"What now?"

He shrugged. There were some experiences—like staying in a hotel room with a beautiful woman—for which he had little preparation.

"I'm famished. Want to pick up some takeout?"

Marco wasn't hungry, but he wanted some air. "Sure. Chinese?"

"Surprise me."

He went back downstairs. The bar was crowded, and he made his way through the throng milling inside the antler-adorned walls. He turned left on the Getreidegasse and walked past the Nordsee and the Eduscho coffee shop. The cobblestone street was still thick with pedestrians, so he cut through a narrow passageway leading to a parallel street.

It was years since he had been to Salzburg, and he didn't have a good idea where he was going, but he had been in the car—with her—all day; he needed a chance to think and stretch his legs. Turning left, he headed toward the Salzach. He found the footbridge leading over the river and started across.

Dusk had fallen over the city, but the August heat held on stubbornly. He lingered on the bridge, watching the green waters flow underneath, like the uncomplicated days of his former life. They were gone forever, he supposed, despite Cardinal Lucci's promise that he could go back when it was all over. There was no going back, really.

The woman in the hotel room was a perfect example of his dilemma. He had almost run out of the room to get away from her, not because she was rude or unattractive, but rather because she was charming and beautiful and he couldn't keep his eyes off her. Elena was one thing—he could handle her—but Sarah was another. When she smiled, he couldn't remember where he was or what he had been thinking about. Perhaps temptation would make him a better priest. If so, he was soon going to make bishop—which despite what he'd told Elena, he did aspire to.

He left the bridge and walked through the Mirabell Gardens, the air heavy with the scent of roses. He found a Thai restaurant on the Linzer Gasse and placed an order for two lemon-grass chickens. While he was waiting, he veered left into an alley that ran along the base of the Kapuzinerberg, the nipple of rock that thrust up from the eastern bank of the Salzach. He found what he was looking for after a few hundred meters: a small chute cut into the wall between a pair of stone benches adorned by gargoyles. A narrow stairway led up from there, and he followed it up, passing several Stations of the Cross chiseled into the stone in baroque fashion.

When he reached the top of the steps, the city was gone, and the forest stood in its stead. A well-worn path cut through the trees, and he took it, ending up in the yard of the Capuchin monastery perched atop an outcrop of rock overlooking the old city. He had been here years ago, prior to becoming a priest, to listen to the monks sing vespers. From the low chanting emanating from a grilled window, he could hear that they still did so, and he walked around to the back of the abbey and pulled open the large wooden door, passing inside. There was a small knot of people gathered there, in the vestibule of the abbey's chapel, listening to the two rows of monks garbed in brown cloaks.

O God, come to my aid.
O Lord, make haste to help me.
Glory be to the Father and to the Son and to the Holy Spirit,
as it was in the beginning, is now, and ever shall be,
world without end.
Amen. Alleluia.

The evensong continued, enveloping Marco in a cocoon of peace and tranquility, but one that didn't last. A gust of wind blew the heavy door, which banged against the jamb with a loud crack similar to the report of the gun Marco had used to kill Mohammed. The cocoon of calmness and harmony dissolved, replaced by the familiar soundtrack of Francesca's screaming and the whine of bullets. He tried to bring it back, but the best he could manage was a static-filled buzzing that wafted in and out of his auditory cortex like a fading radio signal. Eventually, he stumbled out in defeat, shutting the doors behind him. He didn't belong there anyway; the friars were men of God who had dedicated their entire lives to prayer, and he was a sorry excuse for a priest with blood on his hands and lust in his heart.

CHAPTER 31

Elena found Lucci in the garden, watching a cluster of clouds slip in between the jagged peaks of the Tofane Gruppo to the west. She finished descending the stone staircase that led down from the villa, and stood next to him, gazing at the village of Cortina d'Ampezzo tucked into a narrow valley five hundred meters beneath them. Neither spoke for a moment, but Elena had no delusions that the Cardinal Secretary of State had come all the way from Rome just to admire the view.

Cardinal Lucci looked much like he had the first time she had seen him, sitting across from her in the bowels of the Vatican, listening quietly as officers from the Security Office had asked her the same questions again and again.

'I already answered that question.'

'Why don't you answer it again?'

'Why don't you look at your notes? That's the reason you're taking them, isn't it?'

He reached inside the depths of his black cassock and produced a manila envelope sealed with wax. "I have something for you."

"What is it?"

"Open it up and see."

Elena made no move to take the envelope from his outstretched hand. "I'm not in the mood for playing games, Eminence."

Lucci adjusted his zucchetto, the red skullcap he was rumored to wear at all times, and stuffed the envelope back inside his robes. "It is an acceptance letter for your daughter."

"Acceptance to what?"

"The Scuola per Ragazze in Rome."

"I wasn't aware she had applied."

"I took the liberty of doing it for her."

"I could never afford it."

"She's been awarded a full scholarship."

One of the larger clouds, its underbelly stained pink with the setting sun, bounced off the Tofana di Dentro and settled over the Tofana di Mezzo, obscuring its rocky summit from view.

"I thought it might be nice for her to be near her grandfather."

"Her grandfather lives in Liguria."

"The pope wants to open a medical clinic in Rome to serve the burgeoning Arabic population. Your father is being considered for the position of medical director."

"Considered?"

"Strongly considered."

"He doesn't have a medical license."

Lucci produced another document, and this time Elena accepted it, holding it up to catch the fading rays of the sun. It was a medical license, complete with the stamp of the Ministry of Health.

"His application was turned down twenty years ago. Were you aware of that?"

"Yes."

"Does he know?"

Lucci shook his head. "I thought I would let you give it to him."

"I suppose you have arranged something for Francesca as well?"

"The medical clinic is going to be part of a large community center for Muslim immigrants, run by Caritas, a prominent Catholic charity. Francesca would be an ideal person to work there, don't you think?"

"Ideal? She can barely write in Italian, and her speech isn't much better."

"Which will make her a natural liaison to the people we are trying to reach. And her Arabic is excellent."

"Where will she live?"

"I have leased a large apartment in Trastevere."

Elena had been to Trastevere before, once, in a different lifetime a thousand years ago, and had fallen in love with the winding cobbled streets and the sidewalk cafés bustling with patrons.

"Trastevere is too expensive."

"The landlord has generously agreed to waive the rent."

"And what if I say no?"

"Say no to what?"

Elena pointed at the Tyrolean villa where she and her family had been staying since leaving Rome. "To this." She waved her father's newly minted medical license through the air. "And this."

"You paid for these things already, by saving the pontiff's life. Consider them thank-you gifts."

"And my sister's position at the community center? My father's application for medical director of the clinic?"

"These things are under consideration. As I mentioned, very serious consideration."

"I may not be the perfect Catholic girl, but nor am I a fool. You want something from me. Please tell me what it is."

Lucci's weather-beaten face stifled a grin. "Yes, I do. I want you to go to Salzburg, to keep an eye on Marco."

"Why?"

"I'm concerned about him."

"Concerned about him how?"

The sound of a local music festival drifted up from the town square. The constant hum of strings had been a nice change when it had started the week before, but after a few days, she had found herself looking forward to the return of the whisper of Il Maestrale through the pines and the constant cacophony of the jays.

"I'll be frank. I'm concerned he is going to let his conscience get in the way of doing his job."

"Maybe you should just let him walk away."

"I can't do that, Elena, as much as I would like to. Marco is the only person the pope trusts. He *has* to be there."

There was another rustle of Lucci's robes, and another document appeared in front of her. This one was a contract offering the Rapido Securita firm forty thousand euros per month to serve as a consultant to the Holy See.

"Rapido Securita is a shell corporation. All incomes garnered are funneled through a series of offshore accounts into the bank account I just opened in your name at the Banca dei Paschi di Siena. There is a branch on the Via del Corso, not far from your apartment."

"I see you have thought of everything."

"Most things, yes."

Elena looked at the contract again.

"I get a hundred thousand euros just for signing?"

Lucci nodded.

"How do I earn that kind of money?"

"The hard way, I suspect." Lucci waved a hand at the village below. "There is a car waiting for you, a black Alfa Romeo sedan parked outside the Grand Hotel Savoia. After you sign that contract, you will drive the car to Salzburg and wait for Marco inside the Salzburger Dom. I'm not sure when he will go to the Dom—perhaps as early as tomorrow, or a few days after—but I want you to be there when he does."

"Is he expecting me?"

"He's expecting someone; I didn't tell him who."

A murder of ravens floated down on the breeze and settled onto the row of pines that flanked the steep ravine leading up from the village, cawing at the bright yellow Fiat 500 laboring up the serpentine driveway.

"What then?"

"I have no idea, but you're a resourceful woman. You'll figure it out."

"Do you know what I hate about the Catholic Church?"

"No, I don't, but please tell me."

Elena ignored his sarcasm, something Lucci used frequently.

"You're expecting me to be a good Catholic girl and do what you tell me without questioning why. But I'm not Marco. The accommodations are great, sure, and I really need the money you're offering, but I still want to know what the hell is going on."

"No, you're certainly not Marco, although I can see why he is drawn to you."

The wind freshened, bringing in a line of dark clouds from the west, and the air turned damp; a storm was in the offing.

"Okay, you want frankness, so I'll be frank. Vatican City is on the brink of extinction. If Prince el-Rayad gets those nuclear weapons, my country will cease to exist. Marco needs to be there so he can report the all-clear to the pope, and you need to be there to ensure Marco doesn't just get up and leave. He is a different person when you are around. He draws strength from you.

"There is another reason as well. I meant it when I said you are a resourceful woman. You were in a very tight spot, Elena, and yet you saved yourself, your family, and the pope in the process."

"What if I say no?"

"You aren't going to say no."

"Is that what you said to Marco?"

He shook his head. "Marco wanted to return to his parish in Monterosso; I implied that his return was contingent upon him going to Austria. You have no such dilemma."

He pointed at the chalet above them.

"This estate belongs to the family of my Under Secretary, Cardinal Scarletti. He has made it known that you can remain here as long as you want."

"We have no income, Eminence. How are we supposed to pay for it?"

Lucci chuckled; it was the closest attempt at a laugh Elena had ever seen him make. "Have you not heard of the Scarletti family, Elena? They are one of the richest and most powerful families in Italy. Some say as rich and as powerful as the Medici family once was; they are just a lot quieter about it."

The bells rang in the tower of Santi Filippo e Giacomo, the eighteenth-century church in the heart of the old town. Elena had gone there several times over the past few weeks, mostly as an excuse to accompany the charismatic Cardinal Scarletti on his daily pilgrimage.

"I have two conditions."

"What are they?"

"You say nothing to my family about it. I will tell them I am going back to Liguria to pack up."

"And the other condition?"

"My daughter gets the money if I don't come back."

He produced the contract again, pointing to the last paragraph, which she read carefully; he had already made provisions for such a contingency. She took the proffered pen and signed at the bottom.

"Everything you need is in the trunk of the car, except for this." He handed over a fabric envelope.

She undid the thread clasp and removed the contents: a silenced automatic and two spare clips. It was the same gun she had taken off Karim in the cabin of the *Bel Amica*—the gun she had used to kill five of the terrorists.

"You've had good luck with that gun, Elena. I pray that it continues."

CHAPTER 32

The food was still warm when Marco returned to the Goldener Hirsch. He deposited the crumpled white bag on the desk and walked around behind Sarah, who was examining a large paper map, which she had spread out over the king-size bed, holding down the corners with blue and white checkered pillows. He looked over the chestnut brown hair spilling over her shoulders; the object of her study was the square meter of paper. One half of the area was given to a satellite photograph of a mountainside; the other half exhibited a topographical map of the same real estate.

She smiled a hello and went back to her scrutiny of the map. The Untersberg was a huge mountain, soaring over two thousand meters into the alpine sky, which straddled the border between Austria and Germany. Marco had climbed it on several occasions as a boy and remembered it well. It was a severe mountain, with steeply angled faces and imposing cliffs, which erupted from the flat ground surrounding the western flank of Salzburg.

"I've climbed it before. The *Gasthof* on the summit serves an excellent *Wienerschnitzel.*"

He pointed to a high-resolution photo of a large dwelling, built in the typical alpine style, with a steep roof and long overhanging eaves. Boxes of red geraniums hung beneath the many windows, and fruit trees were trained along the white stucco walls.

"Haus Adler. It was the mountain retreat of the Habsburgs, who ruled Austria for a century. It was taken over by the federal government in 1918 and served as an Alpine hut for eighty years. One of el-Rayad's subsidiary companies bought it from the Austrian government ten years ago. He drags his entourage here several times a year."

They leaned in and studied the map more closely. Haus Adler was situated on a peninsula of rock that jutted out from the face of a cliff like the point of a knife. Marco suspected the building was positioned there to maximize the view, but it made for excellent defense as well. It could only be approached from one direction, a narrow strip of rock connecting to the bulk of the mountain behind.

He retreated to the desk and opened the white paper bag. Sarah sat down next to him, and they ate; the food was over-seasoned. Afterward, they sat on the balcony and watched the crowds on the Universitätsstrasse slowly ebb, washing down their dinner with a bottle of white wine Marco had procured from the bar. He decided she was the kind of person he could be friends with, despite the fact that he was a Jesuit priest, and she was an American sniper. It seemed to him, right then, that such small details didn't matter much, with the night air cool on his neck, the Veltliner crisp on his palate, and the smell of her perfume barely detectable over the aroma of sausages wafting up from the *Bosna* stand in the passageway below.

His thoughts strayed, despite his efforts to keep them at home. Elena was sitting across from him, looking away. He couldn't tell where they were, but it didn't matter. They had been fighting, throwing around the usual jabs. She was jealous; he was just tired and desperate for sleep.

His focus returned to the moment, and he studied Sarah's profile in the soft glow of the light emanating from the room. Her large eyes were almond-shaped, and her high facial arches hinted of Slavic blood. He imagined that her full lips could easily form a pout. He decided she didn't really resemble any woman he knew, but a familiarity lingered like the scent of a candle after the flame had been snuffed out.

She rose and went back inside, and he watched her through a crack in the curtain, noting how she picked her way carefully through the room like a woman with a secret, afraid of jostling into something lest it spill out in the collision. Or maybe she was just a precise person; he supposed that a sniper would be.

She passed into the bathroom and reappeared a short time later dressed in the black Spandex running pants, glued onto her lower half, and a loose-fitting cotton T-shirt. It seemed to him a strange outfit for bed, but then he had never needed to run for his life upon awakening; perhaps she had. She lifted the covers and settled into bed, pulling the comforter up tight to her neck.

Marco sat back in his chair, poured the last of the wine into his glass, and took a large swallow. With any luck, she'd be sound asleep by the time he made it to bed.

CHAPTER 33

Marco woke early the next day and joined Sarah for breakfast in the dining room. He filled up on thick slices of brown bread smothered with butter and a large bowl of yogurt with strawberries. Sarah picked at a slice of Swiss cheese and drank several cups of coffee. After eating, they wandered down the Getreidegasse and stopped in a sporting goods store, where they bought hiking clothes and backpacks. In the open-air market on the Universitätsplatz, they traded some of Marco's large stack of euros for the makings of a fine picnic lunch: a French baguette, two large wedges of cheese, two half-liter bottles of Stiegl, the local beer, and a couple of Milka bars. In a hat shop on the Marktplatz, Sarah picked out a traditional Austrian felt hat for Marco.

"I look like a German tourist."

"Yes, you do." She handed over a two-hundred-euro note to the shopkeeper. "Although I think you're adorable in it."

Marco didn't want to be adorable, but he left the hat on. They returned to the hotel and changed. Sarah put on a pair of chino hiking shorts, which she had the legs for, and a tight-fitting polypropylene top. Marco donned khaki shorts and a navy shirt. He packed the lunch in his backpack, filled their water bottles, and stowed away a pair of Gore-Tex anoraks in case the weather changed. Sarah tucked a trail map inside her pocket and looped a pair of binoculars around her neck, and they started off.

They went by foot to Ferdinand-Hanusch-Platz and waited in the morning sunshine for the 25 bus, surrounded by a company of Japanese tourists. They boarded the bus and sat behind a stocky hausfrau, arms filled with overflowing grocery baskets. The bus weaved out of the old city and took a direct course toward the Untersberg, which they could see straight ahead, rising into the sky as if it had been thrust upward from below and held there by a subterranean being of mythical proportions—which, according to local legend, it had been.

The bus deposited them at a *Gasthaus* at the base of the mountain, and they started up the Dopplersteig, a narrow flight of steps cut into the steep rock face. The air was light and cool, but the going was severe; they hiked in silence, saving their wind for breathing. Sarah led the way. She wasn't long in the leg, but her gait was steady, and she was sure of foot. Marco followed, one eye on the trail and the other on the ever-enlarging view.

They made good progress despite the gradient, and by midday, a thousand meters were beneath them. After a short break, they began ascending a vertical face four hundred meters high, into which the trail was hewn. They held onto iron stanchions bolted into the rock as they climbed, lest a misstep send them plummeting into the abyss that opened up on their immediate right.

They passed by a number of markers as they went, commemorating fallen climbers. Marco crossed himself as he went by each one, mouthing a silent prayer that he wouldn't be the next one to drop over the edge. They crested the shoulder of the mountain as the sun rose directly overhead, warming the air even at this elevation, and stopped for lunch in the shade of a rocky outcrop, enjoying the vista and the chance to rest.

Marco tore off a chunk of the bread, jammed a large piece of cheese inside, and handed it to Sarah.

"*Mahlzeit.*"

They ate without hurry, savoring the simple fare. Marco found himself wondering what his life might be like had he chosen a different path. A lot like this, he decided, and then tried to change the subject in his head, because it was a dangerous line of thinking for a priest.

He looked at Sarah, and his peril took shape. Her blue shirt had darkened with sweat and clung to the swell of her breasts with a tenacity that left little to the imagination. She was leaning against a rocky spur, head lifted to catch the rays of sunshine that poured over the ledge above. Her eyes were shut, and her mouth had fallen open, making Marco think she was napping. She had her legs propped up, and her shorts had slid back, exposing the toned muscles of her thighs. He tried to avert his gaze, not wanting to add voyeurism to the growing list of his sins, but his eyes refused to change direction.

After a long while, her breathing deepened, her legs relaxed, and her shorts fell—mercifully—back over her knees, allowing Marco to look away. In need of a diversion, he dug through his pack and unearthed the trail map, which he spread out on his lap. He located their position and traced a path with his finger to the target, which was at the same elevation, but three kilometers to the north as the crow flew. The problem was a ravine cutting a deep gash in their path, giving them no alternative but to go all the way to the top and descend via another trail that took a more northerly route. It would be a long hike, but they had made good time thus far, and the day was still young.

He roused Sarah from sleep with a carefully placed hand on her shoulder, and they resumed their hike. A wind sparked as they climbed, carrying in a line of high cirrus clouds. Marco didn't think they looked too ominous, but you could never be sure, and he was glad he had brought the anoraks. It was cooler anyway, with the wind and the filtering of the sun, but Marco welcomed it; if Sarah's shirt got any clingier, he was going to miss a step on the trail and fall a very long way.

They reached the summit early in the afternoon and joined a stream of tourists coming out of the cable car station positioned on a shelf of rock just underneath the peak. They walked past the cable car station and started down the Weitwanderweg, a less precipitous trail that meandered down and around the mountain on a northeasterly track. The trail passed the Alpenverein, the clubhouse of the Alpine Club, and they stopped to watch a hang-glider pilot assemble her craft, lug it over to the runway, and soar into the blue heavens on a thermal.

After an hour's descent, they turned onto a spur trail that led north, skirting along a rocky ridge with excellent views to the west. They stopped in midafternoon on a knoll covered with latschen bushes, the straggly evergreens that grew at higher elevations, an area that included most of Austria. The breeze had freshened, but the thin layer of clouds had given way to an azure sky, and the combination of wind and sun had yielded a very pleasant day.

The conditions were perfect for hiking, and with most of Europe on holiday, the mountain-goers were out in full force. They spotted a group of schoolchildren from Vienna, chatted with a gaggle of spelunkers hiking up to a cathedral-sized cave cut into the slope several kilometers above, and joined an elderly couple from Glanegg, a small town at the base of the mountain, having lunch on the knoll. They ate more of the food, and drank the beer, in the warm afternoon sunshine, and listened as their new companions filled them in on the local lore.

It was the mixture of the alcohol and the sun, Marco guessed, with a measure of endorphins from the exertion, that gave him a feeling of contentedness bordering on mild euphoria. The wind slacked off, the sun burned brighter, and sluggishness gripped him. He tried to fight it—it was bad form to sleep on the job—but resistance was futile. He closed his eyes and dozed off into a restful unconsciousness.

CHAPTER 34

The Roman sun burned in an azure sky; only a slight breeze made it bearable. Lucci sat down on the stone wall enclosing the Fontana dell'Aquilone in the center of the Vatican Gardens, glad that the guided tours were done for the day. He leaned forward, cupped a handful of water, and splashed it on his forehead. The water spilled down his neck and soaked into the T-shirt he wore underneath his cassock, giving him a little relief from the oppressive heat.

There was also relief from the oppressive *agita* that burdened him; he chewed a few more antacids, calming the sour lick at his throat. But he knew the reprieve—like that from the heat—would only be temporary.

"Only a Sicilian like you would want to meet outside in the middle of the afternoon in August."

Lucci turned to see Cardinal Scarletti, who had taken a seat next to him on the wall.

"I'm afraid forty degrees is too hot even for me. But at least we have the place to ourselves." He looked around to confirm his supposition: the normally crowded Eagle Fountain was deserted other than the two cardinals.

"I can't tell if you are enlightened or just paranoid."

"I don't think they're mutually exclusive, do you, Giuseppe?"

They laughed quietly and lapsed into silence, listening to the splash of the water as it cascaded down the falls.

"Thanks for coming, Giuseppe."

Scarletti smiled, which had the effect of softening his patrician features. "As I serve at your discretion, Vincenzo, it would have been foolish of me to do otherwise."

"At my discretion?" Lucci raised a very well-groomed eyebrow. "I don't think so. We both serve at the pope's discretion. For better, or for worse …"

He stopped for a moment, and both men looked over their shoulders. Still there was no one in sight; even the birds had the good sense to roost in the dense shade of the cedars that had been imported centuries ago from Lebanon.

"Everything is okay in Cortina?"

"It was, until Elena left to … er … pack her belongings."

Lucci hadn't said anything to Scarletti about the reason for her abrupt departure. "I'm sure she won't be gone long. You'll make sure her family is comfortable while she is away?"

Scarletti nodded, taking the time to adjust his scarlet zucchetto, the same shade that Lucci wore. The two men were about the same age and height, and had the same color hair—black streaked with gray—making them virtually indistinguishable from behind. The similarity had spawned the moniker "the twins," a nickname in which the other cardinals took great delight but never used in their presence.

"So, Giuseppe, the pontiff called last night …"

"Oh? What about?"

"Giampaolo Benedetto."

"And?"

"The pope thinks he had help from inside the Vatican."

Scarletti nodded. "I wouldn't doubt it."

"I'm glad to hear you say that, because I want you to be in charge of finding out who."

If Scarletti was happy to hear about his assignment, it didn't show on his narrow countenance.

"Me? Why not someone from the Security Office?"

"They are already looking into it, not that I expect them to get very far. But I am referring to help from within the ecclesiastical body. You are better positioned than anyone else to look inside the Curia."

Scarletti removed his rectangular glasses and rubbed his forehead with his well-manicured fingers. The Under Secretary of State always had the newest spectacles, courtesy of his brother, who controlled a large Italian eyewear conglomerate.

"What do you want me to find?"

"Nothing."

"Nothing?"

"Of course. This whole mess is bad enough if it is just Benedetto; it becomes ten times worse if someone in the Curia is involved. The pope wants us to beat the bushes until we find someone, but I don't think that's a wise idea."

"But if we don't find the responsible party, aren't we inviting another attack?"

"I'm not saying not to poke around, but it's a matter of how you do it. A careful enquiry is one thing, but we don't need another Spanish Inquisition. Understand?"

"Yes, I think I do."

"I know many clerics who don't like Il Riformatore, but that doesn't mean they want to see him killed. No one disagrees with the pontiff more than that bastard Garcia, but he doesn't have the balls to do something like this. Frankly, I don't think any of them do."

Cardinal Garcia was the executive of the Congregation for the Doctrine of the Faith, which residents of Vatican City referred to as the Holy Office, and had been appointed by the previous pope to a five-year term. A theological conservative, he was frequently at odds with Pope John Paul III, who was not.

"Does that mean you don't agree with the pope's contention?"

"It's common knowledge that I don't agree with the pope on almost anything; his hypothesis on Curial involvement is just another unfounded conspiracy theory in my opinion. But that doesn't mean you shouldn't look into it—if for nothing else, just to say we did."

A trio of nuns marched past, heads bowed more out of deference to gravity and time than respect, on their way to the Mater Ecclesiae Monastery fifty meters distant.

"If I didn't know better, I'd say you're afraid of something."

"I'm afraid of a great many things, primary among them the press catching wind of a possible Curial conspiracy. We need to get back to the basics, like shepherding our dwindling flock; heaven knows we've been doing a poor enough job of that lately. If we get any further distracted, there may not be any Catholics left to shepherd when we're done sorting it all out."

"Are there any ground rules for the investigation?"

"Please don't call it an investigation. Giving something a name or a title makes it seem … real."

"It's not real?"

"Between us? Yes, it's real. Beyond us, it's just a figment of the pope's imagination."

"I see."

"I thought you might. That's why I handpicked you for this task. It calls for discretion … you're discreet."

The breeze picked up, swaying the fronds of the palm trees. The smell of roses drifted down from the garden on the hill above them.

"Who do I report to?"

"Me. I suspect the pope is going to want to touch base with you personally once he gets back from Nigeria, but for now, me."

"How often?"

"You're making it a thing, Giuseppe. Don't do that. Do you know what happens to 'things' in this city? They grow. No 'thing' ever goes away here."

"It is the Eternal City."

"Please don't remind me!"

Lucci splashed more water on his face. The smell of chlorine engulfed his nostrils; his eyes teared from the acidic sting of the chemical.

"There are two questions unanswered." He held up his index finger, adorned with the cardinal ring designed by and given to him by Pope Benedict. "One, did Benedetto have help inside the Vatican, and if so, who? The second question is more pressing: where is Benedetto now? When you find something out, you tell me, and only me. Right away, no matter what the time. Are we clear?"

"Very."

A group of Jesuit priests walked past them, heading to Radio Vaticana just up the hill from them. From where he stood, Lucci could see the tall antenna on the top of its administration building cutting into the sky like a lance. The Jesuit order had run Vatican Radio since Marconi had set it up in 1931, only to be put under the authority of the Roman Curia by Pope John Paul III, ending eighty-five years of independent operation.

Scarletti got to his feet, rubbed the dust from his black cassock, and waved his goodbye. "It's always a pleasure, Vincenzo."

"Likewise, Giuseppe."

Lucci splashed himself one more time with the water and watched as Cardinal Scarletti walked toward the basilica, whose bells were tolling loud and clear in the hot, dry air.

CHAPTER 35

Marco woke with a shiver; the sun had disappeared behind a bank of pewter-colored clouds, and the breeze blew with a new zeal. Sarah was sitting next to him, looking over at something to the southwest with the Zeiss binoculars. He followed her line of sight and saw Haus Adler in the distance. It was several hundred meters below their position and at least three kilometers away in the linear plane. He rummaged through the backpack, found his anorak, and donned it. He grabbed Sarah's and tossed it on her lap. A group of teenagers were clumped on the knoll behind them; a straggly-haired youth was strumming on a guitar, belting out a surprisingly good rendition of Bruce Springsteen's "Thunder Road." Sarah handed the binoculars to Marco and slipped into her anorak.

Marco raised the glasses and looked over Haus Adler, which was a large rectangular building with murals of alpine scenes overlaid on the stucco. He dropped the power down and surveyed the real estate. Haus Adler was situated in the center of a large appendage of rock, several acres in area, jutting out from a long ledge running in a north–south orientation. From his vantage point with a tree-covered promontory in the foreground and nothing but air behind it, it looked like it was suspended on an island of rock in the sky. A long drive wound along the bluff from the south, terminating in a large garage that lay behind the main building, wedged in between the edge of the bluff and the down-slope of the promontory.

Sarah tapped him on the shoulder, and he lowered the glasses. She had the trail map spread out on her lap and was indicating a point that corresponded to the promontory. "We need to get here."

It was the ideal spot to reconnoiter the target. They would have the high ground, a non-obstructed view, and only three hundred meters of distance. There was only one problem: it was too close. They would be spotted. He shared his concerns.

"We'll have to go tonight."

Marco glanced up; the clouds were thickening and showed no signs of breaking up.

"There won't be any moon tonight; we won't be able to see anything."

"I brought night-vision equipment."

They consulted the map. The spur trail continued north from their current position. They would need to leave it after another kilometer, bushwhack down a rocky slope, and then climb the nearside of the promontory. It would be an easy task in daylight, but much more difficult at night.

Marco traced the route with his finger, and Sarah checked it out with the glasses. "Think we can manage it?" she asked.

"Yes."

"So do I." She took the glasses away from her face and looked at Marco. "Let's hike back to the *Gasthof* at the summit, have some dinner, and come back after it gets dark."

"Why don't we just have dinner here? There's plenty of food left."

"Because I have a terrible craving for *Wienerschnitzel*."

It was around eleven by the time they reached the top of the promontory overlooking Haus Adler. They had started off at nine, having eaten a heavy meal, in the gathering dusk after sunset. A local church group had occupied half the tables at dinner, and they had followed them out after dessert—a thick piece of *Apfelstrudel* smothered with whipped cream—and slipped past the tram station as they climbed into the last car of the night. They had made it back to their lunch spot in the gloom, Marco leading the way, with Sarah holding onto his hand like a caboose in tow. They had used the night-vision goggles for the remainder of the trip, turning the darkness into an eerie green glow.

The ascent of the promontory proved easier than expected. There was a game trail leading up, carved by generations of chamois, the dog-sized goats that inhabited the mountain slopes. They followed it to the top and settled in on a flat spot between two latschen bushes.

Haus Adler was right underneath them, or at least it appeared that way from their vantage point. It looked even bigger from close up, especially with the lights burning from almost every window. A pair of headlights appeared from the left, and they watched them sweep around a distant corner and then straighten, cutting through the blackness. As the vehicle approached the house, the grounds took form under the illumination of the lamps. Marco noted it all: the rows of firewood stacked neatly against the south wall of the garden shed, the vegetable garden beyond the garage, the swimming pool immediately behind the main house, and the tangle of berry bushes positioned on the extreme southern end of the estate. By the time the car stopped and the lights were extinguished, he would have bet his modest pension he could navigate around the property with his eyes closed.

Sarah brushed against him, and he looked over. She had assembled a rifle and was fitting a telescopic sight on top.

"What are you doing?"

She screwed the barrel into the receiver. "Practicing."

"Why?"

"Because it makes perfect."

She installed the sight, which had the girth of a soup can, folded down a bipod from the end of the black composite stock, and checked her watch.

"How long?"

"Just over a minute."

"Not bad."

"It's not good, either."

They remained there for several hours, until Marco grew so stiff from not moving he had to get up. By that time, he knew every square centimeter of the grounds from sweeping over them again and again with the binoculars. He knew the timing of the sentries; he could distinguish one from the other by their gaits, the heat signature of their bodies on the infrared wavelength, and how they held a cigarette. He knew the schedule of the car used to patrol the long drive that evacuated the property: it departed from the garage at eight minutes past the hour and returned twenty-three minutes later.

It seemed silly to him to keep such a rigid schedule, but what did he know? He was a Jesuit priest from Monterosso, and only the One with infinite wisdom knew what he was doing here, lying prone on a rocky butte, wedged in between the hard, cold boughs of an evergreen and the warm, soft limbs of an American sniper. Three weeks ago, he was absolving his parishioners from their transgressions and advising them to avoid the near occasions of sin; now he was plotting to kill a Saudi prince before he incinerated the Vatican in a nuclear firestorm.

It was too improbable to fill him with guilt. It was like waking from a hazy dream during which he had broken his vows, only to drift back to sleep before he could examine his conscience. He wondered if similar thoughts were going through Sarah's head, but suspected it was filled with other, more technical concerns, like wind speed, muzzle velocity, and bullet drop. But he realized these thoughts would haunt her too, afterward, when the technical concerns had become irrelevant and all she could remember was the smell of cordite and the sight of blood erupting from the target's chest like a spout of lava. He sincerely doubted anyone was immune to it: not the most cold-blooded assassin or the most fervently religious zealot. It was the common denominator of all killers: the fate of having to watch the slow-motion replay of every life she or he had brought to ruin.

It would come to him, too. He could sense it, like a rheumatic could sense the approaching storm front. There was the isolated muzzle flash here, and the transient whiff of lacerated bowel there, but the trough of low pressure was swirling in, building in intensity. The storm would break, the gale would be unleashed; he just hoped he wouldn't be in the middle of something when it did, like a small boat in unprotected waters trying to weather a typhoon.

He stretched behind the thick bole of a pine and watched as Sarah did one last run-through. He was fascinated by the precision and efficiency with which she fitted the barrel into place, snapped the stock into position, slid the sight over the rail, and screwed the suppressor over the aperture. As she loaded the clip into the magazine and worked the bolt to chamber the first round, he imagined the countless times she had gone through the same routine, lying in cramped quarters to simulate live-fire conditions, so that she could do it reflexively, in the complete absence of direction.

She checked her watch again and disassembled the rifle, stowing the components into her pack in opposite order. When she was done, they crawled back away from their perch, used a couple of pine branches to sweep away any marks they had left in the dirt, and started down the game trail. They hiked down the easier Weitwanderweg, rather than risk a misstep on the precipitous Dopplersteig. The Weitwanderweg was the long way down and around the mountain, more than twice the length of the other trail, which also meant it was less than half as steep, something Marco reminded Sarah of every time she complained about the distance.

"Didn't you hike when you were growing up in Vermont?"

"Sure, I was always out in the woods with my father. In the spring, we walked the riverbeds to gather wild leeks and fiddleheads by the pailful. Come summer, we trekked up to the clear-cuts to pick berries: black raspberries in June, blueberries in July, and blackberries in August, the fattest ones as thick as your thumb. End of summer was mushroom season: yellow and black morels, chanterelles, and hen-of-the-woods."

She stopped for a minute and turned around to splay her hands a foot apart. Even in the dim light of the moon, Marco could see the melancholy expression the memories had drawn upon her face.

"Some of those hens were as big as this, but still tender, cooked up just right in some olive oil and wild leek."

"Sounds idyllic."

"It wasn't. Take my word for it."

"What could be so bad about picking berries?"

"It would have been okay if it were just once or twice, but you have to understand the whole story. We weren't out for a leisurely afternoon; we were picking enough berries to make jam to last us the whole year. It was all right when I was younger, but I had other ideas about how to spend my time as a teenager, and we started butting heads like a couple of bucks."

"No grocery stores in Vermont?"

"Plenty, not that that made any difference to my father, mind you. Twice a year, we would get into the truck and pick up supplies like flour and sugar, but other than that, everything we ate came from the land on which we lived."

"Your father sounds like an interesting person."

She laughed at this, a derisive cackle that echoed off the rocky ground and dissipated into the blackness of the night sky.

"That's putting it mildly. Closest thing to a modern-day Thoreau there ever will be, and that's a fact. He used to quote from *Walden* at town meeting day; drew quite a crowd."

"Did you go to school?"

"I was home-schooled, of course, so that he could control the entire curriculum; I had read the entire works of Ralph Waldo Emerson by the eighth grade."

At a junction in the trail, Marco used his flashlight to consult the trail map, lest they take the wrong spur and end up a long way from their intended destination. Sarah took the opportunity to make sandwiches from the last of the bread and cheese, handing one to Marco.

"When you're a kid, you want to be like everybody else, but instead of Nancy Drew, I read Emerson's essays on the 'infinitude of the private man'; rather than play soccer, I fished and hunted; our vacations were camping trips deep into the woods. We used to go for days at a time with nothing to eat but food we could hunt and gather. When I got older, he encouraged me to go by myself, so that I could be completely alone with nature."

They finished their food, washed it down with what little water remained in the bottles, and resumed the hike. Enough light had gathered by this time for them to see their way without flashlights, and they stowed them away and let the false dawn guide them along the trail, which zigzagged down the steep pitch at the bottom of the mountain.

"I used to think he was crazy. I'm sure my mother had come to that conclusion. He could charm you, hold you in his spell with his shining green eyes, brilliant smile, and smart banter about the primacy of the natural world, but after a while, the spell broke, and you just wanted out. My mom sure did."

It was beginning to get light in earnest by the time they made it back to the bus stop where they had started almost a full day previously. It had been a tedious slog, and Marco was glad to see the end of the trail. They fell onto a bench beneath the bus schedule and leaned against one another for support as they waited for the first bus of the day.

They rode back to Salzburg in silence, watching the vehicle fill up slowly with the other early-morning riders. Marco wondered for a moment what pursuits had brought them to the same intersection of time and space at which he was stopped, but his tired mind couldn't generate enough enthusiasm to sustain this line of thinking, and he went back to just sitting and staring, numbly waiting for the bus ride to end.

They got off at Ferdinand-Hanusch-Platz and plodded back to the Goldener Hirsch. They trudged up the back stairs to avoid the lobby, shed their rucksacks, and collapsed onto the massive bed without changing. Marco fell into a restless sleep full of dreams, during which he relived his frantic dash across St. Peter's Square. It was a different version every time, with the same ending: three bullet holes in the middle of the pope's forehead.

CHAPTER 36

Marco awoke several hours later with Sarah leaning against him. He slipped out of bed, propped a pair of overstuffed pillows behind her back, and left the room with her still asleep. He took the back stairs out and exited onto the Universitätsstrasse, which was crowded with foot traffic from the outdoor market held there every afternoon. Sausages of every shape and color hung from wooden stalls, dozens of different cheeses were displayed in glass cases, and bundles of fresh produce filled baskets on top of horse-drawn wagons. It was an idyllic scene, but Marco had neither the time nor the patience for it; he weaved through the throngs of shoppers in a direct line for the Domplatz and mounted the steps of the cathedral.

The Salzburger Dom had been ravaged by nine fires, imploded by a bomb dropped by a U.S. Air Force B-29, and rebuilt five times since its initial construction by St. Virgil in 774; even so, Marco trod carefully over the heavy stone floor, as if even a small misstep would shake the foundation and send the whole edifice crashing to the ground. It was not the perceived fragility of the building that caused him to walk lightly; rather, it was the fragility inside himself, the feeling that he might break open at any moment and spill his innards all over the floor.

He walked up the central aisle and knelt down in the tenth pew from the back of the church on the right-hand side, as Lucci had instructed him. The cathedral was crowded with tourists, and he watched them with fascination as they milled in every direction. The walls echoed with noise: the shuffling of feet on the stone floor, the clicking of a hundred cameras, the muffled tones of tour guides, and the voice of a young priest in one of the side chapels trying to say mass for the faithful, straining to make his voice heard above the din.

Marco looked up at the mural above, which depicted Christ's passion. He had seen these scenes many times before, in a hundred different churches, but he looked at them differently now, reassured that even Christ had considered laying down the cross and walking away from it.

He closed his eyes and prayed for forgiveness: for the smugness he had always thought was contentment, and for the self-righteousness he had mistaken for belief. He would never confuse these things again. His hour had come in the cabin of Elena's boat that stank of sweat and blood—blood that *he* had spilled. On his knees, head lowered in supplication, he begged for absolution: for the four murders he had committed and for the lust that burned in his heart.

An hour later, he was still praying for forgiveness when the familiar smell of lavender greeted his nostrils. He glanced over without looking up. It was as he had feared: Elena was kneeling next to him, with her head bowed and her hands folded in prayer.

"What are you doing here, Elena?"

"It's good to see you too, Marco."

"I told Lucci to send someone else."

"There was no one else."

Marco craned his neck to look around, making a note of the people sitting in the pews behind him. Other than a middle-aged man wearing a dark wool suit in August, no one attracted his attention.

"What do you have against me?"

"I have nothing against you, Elena, which is why I risked my life to save you. I just don't want to have to do it again, that's all."

Mass ended in the side chapel, and the organ struck up, a thunderous version of Beethoven's "Ode to Joy."

"It is good to see you, Marco."

Marco replied in kind, and he meant it, too. Although he would have preferred Lucci to have sent someone else so that Elena could be with her daughter, there was no denying that her presence made him feel better, like a tonic for a nagging ache.

"Where did you go when you left Rome?"

"Cortina. We're all there: Francesca, Gianna, and my father, staying with Cardinal Scarletti at his villa in the hills above town."

Marco had met Cardinal Scarletti on several occasions and had heard him speak on several others. A particular conference in Venice came to mind: Scarletti had delivered a brilliant oratory on the Avignon Captivity, the period in medieval history in which the Roman Catholic Church had been held hostage in France.

"How are they?"

Elena started to say *good* but left the lie unsaid. Her head dropped, and Marco saw a tear fall from the corner of a dark eye.

"You should be in Cortina with them."

She used the sleeve of her black blouse to wipe her face. "I had to come. A man like Lucci … he can do a lot for my family."

She hadn't come for Marco; she'd come because Lucci had made her an offer she couldn't refuse. He wasn't sure if he was happy about this or disappointed.

"I've made a lot of bad decisions … put my family at risk. Not anymore."

She told him about the apartment in Trastevere, the medical license for her father, the well-paid job for Francesca, and the private school for Gianna.

"What about you?"

"I'm working for him. That's why I'm here. Lucci wanted me to come, to see if I could give you a hand."

She avoided his gaze, finding a spot on the floor to stare at. Marco knew she wasn't telling him everything; he had seen this same maneuver during a hundred confessions in his career, the penitent holding back from confessing all her sins for one reason or another—usually embarrassment or guilt—unable to look at him as she left the critical part out.

"How much do you know?"

Elena leaned in close to whisper in his ear. He could feel the warm dampness of her breath on his neck. "Enough."

He nodded and waited for the "Ode to Joy" to reach a crescendo. "It's on for tonight. The pitons are all in, and the team is climbing the cliff face as soon as it gets dark. The prince is going to the opera and then a late-night dinner at the Peterskeller."

"What do you want me to do?"

"Keep tabs on the prince." Marco reached into his pocket and handed her a piece of paper with his cell number on it. "Text me updates. I need to know when he leaves Salzburg."

"What opera?"

"*Don Giovanni.*"

A group of American tourists clomped past, discussing the beauty of the basilica in loud tones. The man with the dark wool suit was still in the same spot, listening to one of the tapes on the history of the Dom that were available at the back of the church for a small fortune.

"What about you?"

"Didn't Lucci tell you?"

"He didn't. You're not going with them, I hope." There was concern in her big brown eyes and worry tattooed into the olive skin of her face.

"No. I am going to be up top, acting as a spotter for the sniper. We're three hundred meters away from the target."

Her mouth pursed into a thin line of coral lipstick. "Just promise me you'll be careful."

He promised her, but it was an empty promise, like that of a teenager assuring his mother he would be home early from a night on the town. Lucci's final comment to him reverberated in his head: *By whatever means necessary.*

The organ music faded and then quit; his time had run out. He crossed himself as he stood up and exited the church, careful not to look back in her direction.

Marco woke, roused from sleep by the heavy scent of jasmine and the chill settling over his chest. The windows were shuttered, the room was dark, and the only noise he could hear was the drone of the air conditioner, laboring to achieve arctic temperatures. He reached for the covers, but the thick down comforter was pushed to the foot of the bed, where it bound his feet in its twisted length. The linens were gone as well, and he felt around in the dark to retrieve them. His finger brushed against something soft, and he grabbed the corner and tugged. The sheet unraveled, and he rolled over, wrapping it around him as he turned.

But the sheet had not been empty, and its contents spilled out as he pulled, falling over him like a warm blanket. It had been a long time since Marco had shared a bed with a woman, but not so long that he didn't remember the prickly feeling of his skin as it lay against hers, or the brush of soft hair against his face. He assumed he was having an unpleasant dream—if the gentle pressure of heavy breasts against his chest could be interpreted as unpleasant—and focused on letting his mind drift somewhere less perilous. But the dream persisted, and the growing heat in his chest made him question his assumption.

It was the quiet rhythm of her breathing and the warm push of her heaving chest that worried him. Could a dream really be this soft? Could a delusion smell as good as she smelled, as if he were ensconced in a thicket of honeysuckle? He didn't think so, but how else could he explain his predicament? He had taken a vow of celibacy—a vow he didn't want to break again—and any celibate man in his right mind would *never* be lying here wrapped in a silky cocoon with her smell thick in the air like a shroud.

But he remained unconvinced, and he longed either to wake up or to return to his previous nightmares, filled with the satiny sheen of blood and the noxious odor of lacerated bowel. It was true that these visions woke him nightly with his underclothes soaked in sweat and his heart racing, but they were at least familiar, and he had become practiced at ignoring them, like an ogre ignores his hideous reflection or a butcher his bad smell.

But there was no ignoring this, the stirring feeling in his chest and the voice in his head whispering to him that he was on a path he could tread in one direction only—down, in a direct line to Gehenna. He tried to push her away, but when his hands thought they had found her shoulder—which, according to the diocese, was the only appropriate place to touch a woman—his fingers brushed against the warm softness of her breasts and recoiled, as if he had stuck them straight into an electric socket.

His last hope that he was dreaming lost, he decided to change tactics, extending his arms in search of better luck near her midsection. The first expedition was nearly disastrous. His hand touched down on something smooth and firm, and his fingers played over the new surface, trying to read it like Braille. When the mental image of her rounded backside finally entered his head—he was, after all, greatly out of practice—his fingers had been examining the surface for much too long, and he felt her stir in response, exorcising any remaining thoughts that he might still be dreaming. Terror overcame him, and he pulled his hand back. He held his breath for fear of waking her and willed his heart to stop thudding inside his torso like a bass drum. Slowly, inexorably, she fell into a deeper slumber, and he allowed himself to inhale, sucking in a mouthful of warm air, ripe with her scent.

He got out of bed without waking her and waited in the bathroom until his heart rate and breathing had normalized and the stirring in his loins had subsided, then grabbed his phone off the nightstand and went out to the porch. It was just after 9 p.m.; night had fallen in Salzburg, and the lamps were burning, illuminating the thick crowds filling the streets. Dialing the number Lucci had given him, he waited for Pietro to pick up.

"Hello?"

"Pietro?"

"*Sì*. How are you, Marco?"

Marco wasn't even tempted to answer him truthfully; he didn't think Pietro wanted to hear about his fear, his anxiety, or his second thoughts. "I'm good."

"We're leaving for the cliff face soon. Are you ready?"

"Yes." He peered into the room in time to see Sarah getting out of bed. She slipped into the bathroom wearing only a thin shirt that fell to her thighs. "We're preparing now."

"Good. You should leave soon. I want you on that hill above Haus Adler before we get there so you can spot for us. There isn't any cell reception on the face, so I won't be able to contact you until we have reached the top."

"Sounds good. Anything else?"

"One more thing."

Marco waited, watching a group of festivalgoers parade down the street in black tuxedos and ball gowns, speaking loudly in a collage of different languages.

"Do you remember what I told you about bleeding, Marco?"

"Yes."

"What happens? I want to hear you say it."

"All bleeding stops."

CHAPTER 37

The moon dipped behind a lonely cloud, throwing a curtain over the landscape. Abayd checked his watch: it was 9.30, exactly the time he had hoped to begin the assault. Waving two fingers, he watched a band of dark figures creep forward, bent low to the ground. They paused at the edge of the forest, melting behind the last row of thick pines. The large farmhouse loomed ahead, lit up like a lighthouse. Abayd whispered a few words into his collar microphone, and the men began to fan out along the hedgerow that surrounded the house. He waited, watching the windows for any signs of activity as they got into position. When the last of them had checked in, he crawled over to his second-in-command.

"The men are all in position, Abdul. It's your show now, my friend."

Abayd would have loved to lead the attack on their enemies, but Abdul—and all the other bodyguards save Jibril—had served in the Royal Guard regiment. Abayd had not.

"Wait until you hear word the sentry is down, then go."

Abdul nodded and slipped the safety on his Heckler & Koch MP5 into the off position. With its compact design and rapid rate of fire, the fully automatic assault weapon, with built-in noise and flash suppressor, was deadly in urban war situations, which this pastoral scene was about to become.

"And remember, Abdul, we don't want any prisoners. If someone surrenders, shoot him in the head."

Abdul didn't respond, but then again, he didn't need to; he had already been told three times, and Abdul was the sort you only needed to tell once. Abayd had reminded him anyway, because anything was better than the waiting. Although everything had gone smoothly to this point, he was anxious that his luck was going to run out. He was a superstitious man by nature, and he understood that all streaks came to an end. For forty-eight hours, everything had gone according to plan: he had located the Americans without difficulty—although he doubted his real estate agent would be of the same opinion—surveyed the enemy without detection, and moved into position without seeing anyone. Another half-hour or so, and they would be in the clear.

To the best of his knowledge, there were eleven enemy combatants. In normal circumstances, he would have confirmed and re-confirmed the number and bearing of his foes, but these circumstances were anything but normal; the nuclear weapons would be arriving in five hours, and the Americans—or whoever they were—had to be disposed of prior to their arrival.

He did have several things going in his favor, however. The first was the farmhouse; from a defensive standpoint, it left much to be desired. There were four entrances—one to the cellar, two on the first floor, and one on the second at the top of an old wooden staircase that led up from the back of the house—and very few outside lights. There were no cameras or sensors, and no security system of any kind.

The second item in his favor was the plan. What Abayd liked about it was its simplicity. Simple plans meant fewer things to get screwed up; simple plans worked. As soon as the sentry was taken out, four teams of four men would cross the lawn and blow the doors, throw flash grenades inside, and storm the house. There would be no hostages to take, no innocent bystanders to avoid, and no priority targets. Everyone would be cut down; no one would be spared. There was a brutal efficiency about it that stirred him on a base level, and a symmetry that assuaged his guilt. It was exactly what the men in the house planned to do to him; he just happened to be striking first.

All they needed now was word from the man assigned to take out the sentry, and they could move. As if on cue, his earpiece crackled, and the word *clear* spilled into his brain. Abdul turned his head and nodded at him, indicating that he had heard it too. They looked up to the sky in unison, searching for the next cloud. It appeared thirty seconds later, blowing out the moonlight like a candle. The cloud wasn't very big, but it didn't need to be; they didn't have far to go, and Abayd was tired of waiting anyway.

He tapped Abdul on the shoulder and gave him the thumbs-up. He heard Abdul mutter *go* into his microphone and watched four shapes separate from the trees and scurry across the lawn. He pulled his Glock out of its chest harness, hoped to hell he wouldn't need to use it, and knelt down on the grass, waiting for the fireworks to begin.

Pietro circled the cellar one last time, looking for any items his men might have missed in their search. After his second circuit, he was confident there was nothing, and he turned back toward the stairs to the kitchen to check the first floor again. He was restless and slightly agitated—the way he always felt before a mission—and he needed to keep moving. He detoured under the stairs for a minute to check the area where they had stored the weapons and found exactly what he had hoped: nothing. The space was as bare as a pauper's cupboard—they had already moved all the guns to the vans—and he turned to mount the steps.

It was a mouse that saved his life. His foot had just touched down on the first step when he saw a blur along the baseboard to his left. Instinctively he followed, catching up with the little creature in the far corner behind a massive oak bookshelf. Relieved that it had only been a mouse, he wheeled around, ready to head back upstairs. He was still behind the bookshelf when the door leading to the outside world exploded off its hinges and hurtled at him as if whipped by a gale. It smacked into the bookshelf, sending a flurry of paperbacks skyward, and toppled it. Pietro dove out of the way of the falling oak with just a glancing blow to his left thigh, his Beretta already in hand. Loosed from his pocket by the contact, his cell phone skittered away and settled among a pile of romances, memoirs, and thrillers.

He rolled behind a half-wall, shut his eyes tight, and covered his ears. Having practiced and led many such an assault when he'd commanded a platoon in the 4th Alpini Paratroopers, he knew what was coming. The flash-bang detonated, and he started counting: one, two, three … He pivoted around and leveled his gun at the intruders running down the stairs from the outside. He was certain they would be wearing body armor and helmets, so he aimed for their necks. His Beretta recoiled in his hand, firing rapidly in bursts of two, and the bodies tumbled down the stairs, forming a macabre pile at the foot.

He glanced over at the pile of books, decided he didn't have time to look for his cell phone, and ran over to his victims, risking a quick examination with his flashlight. As he had feared, the dead men were Saudis; he recognized all four from the surveillance photos he had pinned to the wall of the living room. Somehow the prince had gotten wind of their assault and attacked first.

He switched off the flashlight and scavenged an assault rifle and four spare clips from the dead men, as the sound of slaughter filtered down from above. The stairs in front of him led to the outside, and he ran up, turning left along the north side of the house. He crouched low under the windows and raced toward the large front porch. The dark outline of the forest beckoned to him as he moved. His mind flirted with thoughts of escape, which he didn't entertain. He was inclined neither by training nor make-up to run out on his teammates; he would try to save them and perish in the attempt if need be. For a millisecond, his thoughts strayed to his confrontation with Alessandro. The man had had a bad feeling about the mission; perhaps, as the others claimed, he did have second sight. Pietro hoped so; he was going to need it to survive.

Brushing these thoughts aside, he vaulted onto the porch and angled for the empty frame where the front door used to hang. He would have loved to stop and look inside before he burst in, but time was not a commodity he had to spare. If his guess was correct, his enemy had employed one of his favorite tactics, something he called the Blitzkrieg, attacking on multiple fronts at the same time using overwhelming force. It meant he had to go in now, blind, if he was going to have any chance at all of saving his men.

He ran inside, letting the short barrel of the assault weapon lead the way. The front door opened into the kitchen, a large room with an old-fashioned stove in one corner and a large wooden table in the other. He saw the three Siracusans still sitting at the table, what was left of their torsos slumped forward against the tabletop. The smell of gunpowder and sweat filled the air. The rustic wooden walls were pockmarked with bullet holes, and blood was splattered over the tiled floor like an abstract painting.

There were no intruders in the room, and he ran toward the hallway that opened up to the living room. Gunfire erupted from above him, covering the sound of his advance. He sliced through the hall and exploded into the room. Two men were standing in the middle of the space, staring off to his right. He shot the first one in the neck with a short burst, cleaving off his head. The second man raised his weapon reflexively, but Pietro cut him down before he could find the trigger. He didn't have time to locate the open area beneath his helmet, so he just opened fire on his chest and toppled him over.

Seeing movement from the dining room to his right, he dove for cover behind a large sofa. He heard the slap of boots on the pine floor and emptied his clip at the noise, showering cotton stuffing into the air. The footfalls stopped, and he heard the satisfying crash of a body hitting the floor. He reloaded, trying to remember where his men had been prior to the attack. The sound of a Beretta came down the stairwell, answering his question.

At least one was still alive—and fighting back.

Abayd heard the sharp crack of a 9mm, and his breath stuck in his throat. None of his men were carrying this caliber of weapon. Not everything had gone to plan, not that he had ever suspected it would. Something about the sound of the shots—the rapid succession of three tight groups of two shots each—told him that the man who had fired them had killed many men before. There was a lethal professionalism, a deadly skill about the sound that was undeniable.

Abayd pushed back from the tree against which he had been standing and set off toward the opposite side of the farmhouse. If his guess was correct, the shots had come from the cellar, which opened on that side of the building.

"Falcon, check in."

No response.

"Falcon!"

Falcon didn't check in. Less than a minute into the operation, Abdul was either off the air or dead, most likely the latter.

"Falcon down." Abayd started across the lawn; there was no point in hiding in the woods any longer. He needed to get to the cellar as fast as he could.

As he rounded the back corner of the dwelling, he saw a shadow slip onto the porch at the front. It was only a glimpse, but he knew it wasn't one of his men. The enemy was entering the house where his men wouldn't expect him. He almost radioed a warning, but if the man had taken Abdul's helmet radio, he would be giving him forewarning.

Abayd remained silent and ran toward the porch. He would follow behind his enemy and take care of the problem himself.

CHAPTER 38

Pietro heard the crash of boots hitting the stairwell; it was time to move. The main staircase to the second floor led up from the hall on the other side of the dining room, and he knew he would never be able to make it up that way with the enemy already mounted there. There was a second staircase, however, spiraling up from the large hearth room at the rear of the house, and he ran down the short corridor to find it.

The hearth room was named for the massive stone fireplace cut into the back wall. Three gigantic stags' heads watched over a cluster of sofas that were littered with the dead bodies of two more of his men, both Palermitani. A single enemy combatant materialized from the door leading from the storeroom, and Pietro greeted him with three shots in the face. The man collapsed onto the pine boards with a thud.

He opened the door to the back staircase, closed it softly behind him, and crept upwards, running through the math in his mind. There had been ten members of his team when the assault began, in addition to himself. He had to assume Carlo, who had been on sentry duty tonight, was the first man down. He added the two in the hearth room and the three in the kitchen: a total of six dead. That left four unaccounted for. He reached the top of the stairs and pushed the door open. The staircase came out in the rear bedroom, which he had been sharing with Alessandro, who was currently lying on the bed in a pool of his own blood. Second sight or not, he was as dead as the others.

Seven down.

He padded across the bedroom and paused in front of the door that let out onto the bottom half of an L-shaped hallway. Unfamiliar voices emanated from around the corner, coming toward him. He flattened himself against the wall and waited.

A weak light ebbed from above, and he saw two shadows advancing in his direction. He waited until he gauged the pair were directly on the other side of the wall, then stepped back and opened fire. A hail of plaster erupted into the air as the ancient wallboard disintegrated in the barrage. The clip emptied at the same time as a small hole opened up in the wall, just below the level of the chair rail, and he saw two bodies writhing on the pine flooring. He yanked his Beretta free and shot the closest one in the back of the neck. The other disappeared out of his narrow field of vision before he could draw a bead.

He dove through the door, biting his tongue as he slammed against the floor, narrowly averting a burst of fire that tore through the wall. His opponent was attempting to crawl around the corner to get out of harm's way; Pietro raised his Beretta and fired twice.

He reloaded the assault rifle, recalling the layout of the second floor. The remainder of the bedrooms and a small upstairs den lay off the main hallway. He remembered that some of the men had been playing cards in the den when the attack had commenced. He turned the corner and ran down the hall. The lifeless body of one of the attackers decorated the otherwise barren corridor. The smell of death, mingled with the stench of sweat, hung in the air like a vapor. The sound of excited voices floated up from below, and he could feel the pulse of another set of boots slamming against the tiled kitchen floor. Blood, sticky and tasting of salt, flowed into his mouth from the gash on his tongue.

He found two more of his men, still warm but lifeless, slumped over the card table in the den. Luca was motionless on the floor, next to a dead Saudi soldier who was oozing blood from a knife wound in his throat. At least Luca had been able to slit someone's throat, even if it wasn't the prince's. He grabbed Luca's Beretta, ejected the clip, and tucked it inside his cargo pocket to save for later.

It was time to go. He relieved the dead Saudi of his last flash-bang, pulled the pin, and lobbed it onto the main staircase as footsteps echoed up from below.

Abayd never saw the flash-bang. His ears buzzed with the concussion, and he was aware of nothing but a wash of white, as if he were staring into the blazing Arabian sun. He lay there for several seconds, inhaling the burnt phosphorus. When the daze cleared, he raised his weapon and fired blindly in the direction of upstairs, succeeding in reducing the opposite wall of the second-floor hallway to a mass of splinters. He wasn't expecting to hit his enemy; he was just trying to keep him on the defensive.

His vision ebbed back, and he saw that the door to the den was open. The ringing in his ears waned, and he could hear the moans of the dying men on the first floor. The second floor was quiet; his target was either running or lying in ambush.

There was only one way to find out.

He got back to his feet and started up the stairs, with the remaining team members behind him. When they stormed the den, they found Sayid sprawled on the floor, unmoving; three of the enemy were there as well, all dead. A glass door let out onto the porch outside. He rammed his finger against the trigger of his weapon, and the door dissolved. He ran through the shattered remnants, ignoring the shards, and his feet landed on the oak planks.

He knew from his surveillance that the porch orbited the second floor, like a rectangular planetary ring, and he motioned for his men to investigate. The lawn stretched out in front of him, but with the cloud cover and the constriction of his pupils, all he could see was the contrast of black on black. In frustration, he pelted the yard with bullets, until he ran out of ammunition, and his finger pressed uselessly against the trigger.

His men returned, shaking their heads, and for the first time, the notion of failure leaked into his head. He did not relish the idea of reporting his lack of success to KiKi.

"Search the house. I will check the woods."

They passed back inside, and he ran the length of the porch, heading toward the stairs. He flew down them, taking three steps at a time, and turned toward the woods where he and his men had massed not fifteen minutes beforehand. He hesitated at the edge of the lawn, uncertain. The chances that he would be successful in his pursuit were small, but he had to try.

Or perhaps it simply had to appear as if he had made a valiant effort. As he slipped into the thicket bordering the forest, an idea germinated in his brain. He unhooked his helmet and tossed it on the ground, then made his way fifty meters into the woods, stopping inside a heavy growth of fir trees. The night was quiet; no twigs snapped underfoot. He let go of the gun, letting it hang loosely from his neck, yanked his blade from the scabbard secured to his calf, and slashed it across the side of his left forearm.

The metal was razor sharp, and it sliced through his sleeve and ripped open the muscle, exposing tendons and yellowy fat. Blood spurted from the wound, and he was overcome with nausea. He vomited violently from the shock, then straightened, switched the knife into his left hand, and repeated the maneuver on the other arm.

Even in the meager light that filtered down through the jumble of branches, he could see that he'd achieved the desired effect. Blood seeped from his arms and smeared his fatigues. He looked like he'd been slaughtering swine with a blunt knife. He dabbed some on his face for good measure, then rammed his knife back into the scabbard.

He lingered to make sure he hadn't drawn any unwelcome attention before making his way back, picking up his helmet where he'd left it. His men were waiting for him in the den, next to the two orderly rows of bodies they had stacked like cordwood against the wall: eleven of his own men in one pile, and ten of his enemies in the other.

Fahwaz saw him limp into the room and rushed over to him. "What happened?"

"I saw the coward running through the woods, and I followed. He ambushed me in a grove of fir trees." He held up his arms for them to see, and the lie slipped out before he had a chance to stop it. "He won't be bothering us again, my brothers."

They pressed him for details, and he gave a brief account of the fictional knife fight, which ended with him slitting the enemy's throat. He finished his tale by describing how he had dragged the dead body under a fallen tree, *where it will fester and rot*, lest they insist on retrieving it for him.

Fahwaz applied a bandage as Abayd called for the vans to pick them up. They heard the engines a few minutes later, followed by the quiet approach of the recovery team. With Abayd directing, the reinforcements removed the dead bodies—of both sides—and piled them into the vehicles. Five minutes after the vans had arrived, the house was empty, with nothing to show for the carnage but large volumes of blood puddled on the floorboards, splashed on the cabinetry, and soaked into the carpets. Abayd personally supervised one last check of the house, blood dripping from his wounds as he went, before he and the five remaining members of the assault team filed into the vans and drove away.

CHAPTER 39

Dr. Khalid al-Sharim surveyed the wounds on his patient's arms, then walked wordlessly to the supply cabinet in his clinic to begin the process of sewing them up. It was a process he had always enjoyed, from his first days as an intern in Riyadh to his required service in the Saudi Royal Army. There was something gratifying about taking a shredded piece of bloody flesh and restoring it to its natural state. It was almost worth being dragged out of bed to do it—it was 11.30 at night—not that he had any choice in the matter.

He selected several items and carried them over to the bench next to the patient: syringes, sterile packages of suture, both absorbable and nylon, and a handful of surgical instruments wrapped in plastic. It would be much easier to have the services of a nurse, but he had been without one for so long he had gotten used to working alone, and he allowed himself the delusion of believing he preferred it this way. He deposited several packaged drapes on the tabletop, along with a large stack of gauze bandages and a bottle of an iodine-based antiseptic.

"How did you say you were wounded?"

"I slipped."

"You must learn to be more careful, Abayd."

"I promise you will never have to fix me up again, Khalid."

Al-Sharim thought about this remark as he looked over the various bottles in his medicine cupboard. There were several types of lidocaine, a handful of narcotic painkillers, and a dozen other medications including injectable anti-emetics, anti-migraine drugs (the prince was a habitual migraineur), and sedatives. He chose a new bottle of two percent lidocaine with epinephrine and returned to the patient.

He had been in the army long enough to recognize self-inflicted wounds when he saw them. In his opinion, there was no doubt about who had sliced open Abayd's arms; the more important question was why. It simply didn't make any sense.

He positioned the patient on the surgical table and mulled it over in his mind. Something smelled like rotten fish, and it wasn't the odor belching out of Abayd's filthy wounds. He rifled through a drawer until he found his magnifiers, slipped them on, then grabbed two sets of surgical gloves and a sterile gown. He was ready, but something nagged at him, and he found a pretense to stall. He walked over to the other side of the room and stood in front of the sink, using the foot pedals to start the hot water. There was something wrong; he could feel it. He had felt it all week, but he was not a man to rely on intuition; he was a doctor, after all, a man of facts and science. He had told himself he was paranoid and tried to ignore the sensation that he was being watched.

He waved his hands in front of the soap dispenser, and a blob of foam spat onto his palms. He lathered slowly, trying to quell a rising tide of panic.

They were on to him. Yes, he was sure of it. It all became clear to him as he scrubbed his hands: the constant companionship of one of the security detail—always with some ridiculous excuse—the loss of his cell phone, and the ridiculous errands he had been asked to do all week, always with a chaperone. He had spent a whole day taking the train to Vienna with Nassir to buy supplies for the clinic, a job he normally assigned to someone else.

He dried his hands and returned to the medicine cabinet. Making sure his tall frame was blocking Abayd's view, he tore the label off a bottle of Versed, a powerful sedative, and replaced it with the label from a reserve bottle of local anesthetic. He deposited the bottle on the bench top, staring coldly at Abayd—they had never liked each other—then went to wash his hands again. When he had finished, he ran his hands through the ultraviolet dryer and donned his gloves and gown.

He slipped his hand inside a sterile bag, picked up the saline, and irrigated the long wound on Abayd's right arm. When he was satisfied that he'd cleared out all the pine needles, soil particles, and leaf fragments, he soaked several gauze pads in antiseptic and began to swab the wound. He knew from experience that this stung quite a bit, but Abayd's square face was neutral. He was a tough son-of-a-bitch.

When he had finished cleaning the wound, he picked up a syringe. He stabbed the fake bottle of anesthetic and withdrew a full three milliliters, then selected a pair of tissue forceps from the surgical tray and used them to lift the wound flap, exposing the deep belly of the muscle. He found what he was looking for near the elbow—a large branch of the antecubital vein—but when he reached for the syringe, Abayd shook his head.

"No drugs."

"I can't stitch you up without the medication."

Abayd wasn't convinced. "I can stand the pain."

Khalid's chest tightened, and sweat beaded up on his forehead, darkening his light blue surgical cap. Suddenly he was sure Abayd was on to him. He wanted to run, but he could plainly see the gun strapped to the bodyguard's chest.

"I wasn't talking about the pain; you can suffer that for all I care. The medication also stops the bleeding so I can see what I am sewing."

He could see the indecision in Abayd's eyes, and he knew it was now or never. Before his patient could object, he inserted the tip of the needle into the vein and depressed the plunger with his thumb.

"I can feel that."

"Give it time. Your arm will be numb in a few seconds."

Khalid counted to ten in his head and grabbed the scalpel by the handle just in case. But there was no need. By the time he got to seven, Abayd's eyes had rolled up, and his body went as limp as a rag doll. Khalid relieved him of his gun, cell phone, and knife, and then refilled the syringe and gave him another three milliliters of the Versed. He was a little unsure if he'd overdosed him, but he didn't care that much either—he just didn't want him to wake up in the next hour. Judging by the flaccid muscle tone and slow, uneven respirations, it was highly unlikely.

A knock on the door gave him a start. "Khalid?"

His heart raced. "I'm operating. What is it?"

"I need to speak with Abayd right now."

He looked around the room in desperation, but he knew there was only one exit from the surgical suite.

"Just a minute."

He grabbed a large drape and spread it over Abayd, so that only his head and arm were visible, then threw his leather coat over the pile of Abayd's things on the countertop, and filled another syringe with Versed. With the needle hidden in his right hand, thumb resting on the plunger, he unlocked the door and opened it a crack. Nassir's head poked in.

"I am right in the middle of something. Can't this wait?"

In reply, Nassir pushed the door open and brushed past him. He stopped in front of the table and bent down to whisper something into Abayd's ear. Khalid stepped toward him and jammed the syringe into his jugular vein, pushing the plunger in as he struck. Nassir's eyes went wide with surprise before he fell heavily to the floor, oozing blood from his neck.

Khalid peered out into the main room of the medical clinic and saw that no one had accompanied Nassir. He stripped off his surgical clothes, donned his jacket, and stuffed Abayd's gun into his waistband at the small of his back. Slipping the wallet and cell phone into his pocket, he closed the door to the surgical suite and locked it. Someone had stolen several bottles of narcotics last year, and Khalid had used the theft as an excuse to change the lock and give himself the only key. He was certain Abayd had acquired a copy, but he was already inside the room, where he would remain until he woke up with a massive hangover.

He sidestepped to the window, back flat to the wall, and peered out. The clinic occupied the south side of the space above the garage; Abayd's office and the CCTV control room consumed the north side, overlooking the turnaround. The second floor had a common staircase, leading up from the rear of the garage to a landing with doors to both offices. The only thing he could see from his current vantage point was the darkness on the other side of the cliff and the lights of Salzburg twinkling in the distance.

He was about to move away from the window when he spotted a tiny red glow below him; one of the bodyguards was standing watch behind the building. His plan had been to take the stairs down to the garage and slip out the back door, hopefully without being noticed. But that was obviously not going to work, with at least one sentry—and possibly several others—boxing him in. He decided to keep his post by the window and wait for the guard to take a break. If an opening didn't present itself shortly, he would try to bluff his way past the sentry. In the likely event that this wasn't successful, he did have Abayd's weapon. He hadn't fired a gun since the early days of his military service, but if push came to shove, he would shoot his way out or die trying.

CHAPTER 40

It was close to midnight by the time Sarah and Marco reached the hill overlooking Haus Adler. They had driven Sarah's car—which, if everything went well, they hoped to use as an escape vehicle—to a trailhead on the north shoulder of the mountain, from where the shooting position they had surveyed the previous night was less than an hour's hike. Unlike the day before, it didn't matter if people found a car left there all night to be suspicious; they would be long gone before anyone thought to connect their car with the imminent attack. *Der Föhn*, the dry wind that warmed the Central European Alps, had sparked up in the afternoon, clearing away any straggling clouds and giving them a clear view of the target. Haus Adler looked much the same as it had twenty-four hours earlier, with one exception. In place of the two sentries who had been patrolling the grounds, a half-dozen had taken their place, all carrying assault rifles. Sarah questioned Marco about the change, but he simply shrugged; she finished assembling her rifle without further comment.

Midnight came; they marked the occasion by installing earpieces and collar microphones. Marco turned on his cell phone and tried to check in with the assault team. "Cobra in position. Copy?"

The only response was from the wind, which blew a little harder, straightening the windsock next to the prince's helipad.

"Alpha, do you copy?"

Alpha did not respond; the only thing Marco could hear was the rush of blood in his ears and the clicking of Sarah's telescopic sight as she adjusted the magnification to her liking.

He checked his diving watch. "They must be behind schedule."

Sarah didn't reply, busying herself erecting a small tripod, on top of which the blades of her wind meter whirred, gauging velocity, direction, and maximum gust.

"Pietro told me there's no cell reception on the face."

Sarah glanced at her phone, where the wind meter's readout was displayed on an application via the Bluetooth connection, and made further adjustments to her sight.

"They have to be almost at the top before we can communicate with them. We'll just have to wait."

He realized she had completely tuned him out, the culmination of a transformation that had begun the moment they left the hotel room. During the drive, she had become increasingly withdrawn—or increasingly focused, perhaps—barely responding to his nervous chatter. The hike across the northern shoulder of the Untersberg had been an extremely quiet affair; other than her complaints about the unnecessary length of the hike they had taken the day before, she had said nothing. And now, stationed three hundred meters above Haus Adler with her right finger on the trigger of her specially modified Sako TRG, she said nothing at all.

Marco started to wonder if the feel of her body next to his had been a dream after all. Or if it hadn't been a dream, perhaps the warmth and the feel of her skin touching his—as if it were being charged by an electric current—had been one-sided. Perhaps she had just been making nice all along to keep their working conditions pleasant, and now that it was almost over, she could just ignore him and do his job.

He took a break from his insecurities and studied the woman he had been getting to know for the last four days. In so many ways, he felt like he knew her well: he knew the things that made her laugh, and he said those things so that he could hear her soft chuckle; he knew the things that would snuff out the sparkle in her jade eyes, and he shied away from those so that he could still see them shimmer like the waters of the Ligurian Sea in the full light of the sun; he knew she was a woman of great faith—in herself but nothing else, particularly not any deity—and this drew him to her like a moon to its planet. But in other ways, he realized he didn't know her at all: he had no idea if she was married or engaged or otherwise involved with another person, or if she ever had been, and he had asked only once, a question she had deflected like a goalkeeper deflects an unwanted strike; he had no idea if she had been brought up with a faith or theology of any kind, other than the transcendentalism her father espoused; and he didn't know why her conscience allowed her to make a living by killing other people, or if it had been beaten out of her by a lifetime of violence and bloodshed.

But while Sarah's conscience was either not present or held somehow in check, Marco's, now that he was here, with a fully loaded gun in a holster on his hip, was operating on overdrive. Whereas it had been possible in the days leading up to today— walking through the rose-scented Mirabell gardens, or hiking up the sunlit slopes of the Untersberg with the smell of pine hanging in the air—to push the smell of blood out of his head, it had come back now with redoubled force. His fingers stank of it, despite the light gloves he wore; his clothes reeked of it, despite being freshly laundered; and his nostrils were inundated by it at all times, the metallic odor of the lives he had extinguished as expediently as an altar boy snuffs out a candle.

Pietro found a slight crack in the rock with his probing fingers, inserted a hand, and pulled himself up and onto a flat slab of stone. He sat for a minute to rest and checked the time. Midnight. He was on schedule.

His practice sessions had paid off. Using the line he had followed every night, he had climbed over one hundred and fifty meters of vertical rock in an hour. He had pushed himself hard to save time, and his shoulders and forearms ached from the effort. But it had been worth the price: he was only fifty meters from the top of the cliff, a distance he could negotiate in another half-hour.

He reached inside a crevasse on the other side of the slab and extracted the waterproof bag he'd hidden there twenty-four hours ago. There were four items inside: a stainless-steel water bottle, from which he drank deeply, two protein bars, and a spare cell phone. He turned the cell on, but there was no signal here; from previous experience, he knew he had to get almost to the top for the signal to be strong enough to text. Having no idea when, or if, his next meal would come, he took a few minutes to eat the energy bars. He finished the water, put the bottle back, and resumed climbing.

The last section would be the most difficult: the face was the steepest at this point, and he had only risked practicing it once, the night before. He checked his heart rate: it was high, driven by the exertion and the adrenaline. He took several deep breaths from the diaphragm, trying to slow his heart rate and lessen the amount of adrenaline surging into his bloodstream. Too much adrenaline created a tendency to hurry, and any rock climber worth his salt knew there was a price to be paid for hurrying. It was usually death, although permanent paralysis and mutilation were also possibilities.

He shrugged these unwelcome thoughts aside and focused on the task. There was a simple truth about rock climbing he found calming: a massive face was scaled one hold at a time. Secure each hold, and you were good. The converse was something he never considered, but it lurked in the recesses of his mind nonetheless: one mistake, and you were fodder for the rocks that waited below with eternal vigilance.

He fell behind schedule quickly, but didn't succumb to panic. He climbed methodically and with purpose, following the route he'd marked previously. Twice he slipped but recovered, and once he sent a loose stone into a freefall. He stopped several times to allow some strength to ebb back into his limbs, and once near the top to eavesdrop, hearing nothing.

He pulled himself over the edge and crawled behind the large rock he had seen on satellite images of the property. When his breath had recovered and the dexterity had returned to his fingers, he grabbed his cell phone and began composing a text to Marco, which he wanted to word carefully. His godfather had taken an enormous risk getting him out of jail, and he wasn't about to turn tail and run at the first sign of difficulty; he just needed Marco to feel the same way.

Marco's phone vibrated on his hip; he had received an incoming text. He put his night-vision binoculars down and snatched up the phone, reading the message twice. When he looked up, Sarah was watching him expectantly.

"Pietro?"

"Yes. His team was ambushed before they left their house. He was the only one who survived."

He tried to gauge her reaction, but her face was inscrutable.

"He made it to the top of the cliff, and he's going into Haus Adler now to get into position in the prince's bedroom before he comes home from Salzburg."

"Any change in plan for us?"

"No."

Marco thumbed a reply as Sarah put her eye behind the scope, where it had been positioned for over thirty minutes. As he sent his message, Cardinal Lucci's warning—*by whatever means necessary*—echoed inside his head. All along, he had feared that his strictly observational role had been a ruse designed by Lucci to ease his conscience; that his destiny was one of violence, and that as a priest, he had no place being here, with a gun in his hand and carnage in his future. The more he tried to push these thoughts aside and concentrate on what he was doing, the more they dominated. Pietro's words reverberated in his skull—*Focus on the moment, on what you are doing … ignore what might happen and what has happened. See only what you are doing in the present moment*—but all he could picture was Gehenna burning around him.

Pietro stowed his phone, readied his Beretta, and dashed toward the house, bemoaning the loss of his silencer. The weaponry had been transferred to the vans before el-Rayad's men had attacked, and he hadn't dared to double back to re-arm. He would have to make do with the Beretta and the extra clip he'd scavenged from Luca. Although he had plenty of firepower, his chief weapon was the element of surprise, and it would be lost the first time his finger whitened on the trigger.

He reached the side of the house and hid in the shadows created by the overhanging eaves. When he was sure he hadn't been spotted, he looked up at the fruit trees trained against the stucco wall, selected the largest one, and began to climb. The tree was a century old, he guessed, but generations of gardeners had pruned it back to a level just below the porch encircling the third story. It wasn't as convenient as a ladder, but it sufficed. He went slowly, trying not to stress the hundred-year-old branches. When he got within arm's reach of his destination, he jumped out toward the bottom of the porch, grabbed the floorboards, and swung up. He landed on his feet and crept to the back corner of the house, where a circular staircase ascended to the porch on the fourth floor. He used a set of lock picks to open the gate and wound his way up.

The fourth floor of Haus Adler was the exclusive domain of the prince. Only a handful of people were allowed to be there, and those only with specific permission. Not even Abayd al-Subail, the head of el-Rayad's personal bodyguard unit, set foot on the fourth floor without the prince to supervise. All of this made Pietro smile as he used a small device to find the contact points on the alarm positioned on the other side of the sliding door. The machine vibrated when it found the right area, and he attached it to the glass. Using a lock pick, he opened the door and stepped into the massive bedroom, where there was little chance anyone would discover him until after he had killed the prince.

Pietro was well aware that the best-laid plans often went awry, and he was not surprised to hear giggling coming from behind the silk drapes covering the prince's four-poster bed.

"KiKi?" a feminine voice called out.

It was one of the prince's concubines—he kept many, in addition to having over a dozen wives—waiting for him to return to earn her keep. A vision of the Caruso woman popped unbidden into his brain. He could still see the horror and fear on her pretty face: horror that he had just killed her husband, fear that he was going to kill her too. He dimmed the lights and strode across the plush carpet.

"You're home early. Couldn't wait to get your hands on me?"

She was right; he couldn't wait to get his hands on her. He saw her shapely outline behind the thin silk hangings and dove through the opening, landing against her and sending her into a tumble.

A burst of giggles erupted from the other side of the bed. "So you want to play rough? Two can play at that game."

She dove back in his direction, arms outstretched in front of her. He easily evaded her and chopped an open palm down against her neck. She went limp instantly. He found some handcuffs in a drawer and secured her hands and feet to the bedposts, then taped her mouth shut with several layers of duct tape. He made sure she was still able to breathe, and then rolled off the bed.

He searched the room in the darkness, looking for the ideal spot to hide. In the end, he chose a large walk-in closet. He carried a desk chair inside, texted Marco that he was in place, and sat in the darkness with the closet door cracked and the Beretta laid across his lap, waiting for the prince to come home.

Marco's phone vibrated: it was Elena, informing him that the prince had just got in his limo and was en route. He had been so absorbed in his thoughts that he had forgotten about her. Speaking as quietly as he could, he filled her in on what had happened.

"What now?"

"I don't know; I'm thinking."

His forehead dripped with sweat despite the cool breeze blowing down from the summit, and his stomach churned as if he were trying to digest a full tray of *Sauerbraten*.

"Where are you now?"

"Just outside the old city."

"You're armed?"

"Yes."

"Drive up here. Pull off the road after you pass the driveway for Haus Adler, close enough but not too close. There are cameras everywhere. Wait there."

"What do you have in mind?"

"Honestly … I have no idea."

CHAPTER 41

Marco ignored the knot in his neck and kept his eyes glued to the binoculars. He could see the lights in the distance, sweeping in his direction. The prince's caravan crested a small hill and appeared beneath him, four vehicles in total. The first was a Mercedes sedan, running some fifty meters ahead of the others. Next in line came the black limousine that he recognized as the prince's Bentley. He was not familiar with its specifications, but Sarah had assured him that the bullets loaded into her gun would scratch its paint, nothing more. It was the third vehicle, a brown UPS van, that took him by surprise.

"Sarah."

"I see it."

He raised the magnification of the binoculars and trained them on the van. The realization came to him quickly. "The nuclear weapons are in that van."

"They're not supposed to be coming until next week."

The caravan approached the garage, and two of the bay doors opened. The lead sedan parked in the turnaround; several men hopped out, swelling the ranks of the armed men standing guard. The Bentley and the van disappeared inside the garage, and a second Mercedes remained in the driveway, blocking the way.

"That's why there are so many guards, when there were only two last night."

"That doesn't mean anything."

"What happened to the assault team? Are you trying to tell me it's a coincidence they were ambushed tonight?"

The garage doors closed. No one entered or exited.

"What are they doing in there, Marco?"

"I suspect the prince has some kind of expert examining the weapons. If I spent millions on something, I'd want to make sure it worked."

"How long is it going to take?"

He had no idea—he was a priest, not an international weapons inspector—but he could guess as well as the next guy, maybe better. "Twenty minutes."

"And then what?"

"The prince is going to go into the house and authorize the money transfer. The delivery men will stay until they get word the payment has been received, then offload the weapons and leave."

"You've got it all figured out, I see."

"Except for the part about how we stop them, yes."

The side door of the garage opened, and the prince's bodyguard filed out. Sarah's finger closed over the trigger. "I think I have a shot."

"They already have the weapons. Killing the prince won't stop them anymore."

"I came here to kill the prince. I don't give a damn about the nuclear weapons."

Her finger started to whiten on the trigger; Marco put his gloved hand over the front end of the scope.

"Move your hand, Marco."

He kept it where it was.

"Move it now."

Neither moved; neither said a word. After a long moment, her finger fell out of the trigger box, and she glared at him. "Why did you do that?"

"I already told you."

Her head moved back to the scope. "What are we going to do now?"

"Leave the prince to Pietro. I'm more concerned about those nuclear weapons."

"What can we do about them?"

An idea germinated in his brain; he wasn't sure from where it had come, but, being a man of God, he supposed it had descended to him from above, borne upon a tongue of flame or on the wings of a dove. Looking around, he saw neither fire nor bird, but the feeling that it was heaven-sent persisted; if nothing else, it made him feel better about the priest he had become and the way he had now chosen to serve God.

"I'm going to steal them."

"How are we supposed to do that?"

He told her his idea. She listened without interruption, never taking her eye off the scope.

"All right, but get going now, Marco. They're not going to hang around forever."

Sarah had two coils of rope on the outside of her backpack; he grabbed one and tucked it into his waistband. "I'm off. Try not to shoot me."

"Don't get in my line of fire."

He promised her he would do his best.

"What's your exit strategy?"

"I don't need one."

"Why not?"

"I'm not expecting to make it out alive."

She mumbled something in response, something that might have ended with *darling*, but it was lost to the whine of *der Föhn*. He wanted to ask her what she had said, but the moment had passed, so he started down the back of the outcrop, grabbing tree limbs to control his descent.

When the pitch flattened, he used a pocket compass to blaze his way east. In short order, he was standing on the edge of the cliff, staring down into the dark abyss. He tied a length of rope to a tree, looped it around his waist and lowered himself over the edge. He dropped slowly, searching for a way to move laterally, and found one right away, a thin ridge running parallel to the face. It would be a feat getting back up—a free climb of ten meters—but the ridge appeared to extend all the way to the garage. If it wasn't too good to be true, it was at least too good to pass up.

His feet found the ledge, and he let go of the rope and started inching his way in the direction of Haus Adler. The going was steady at first, but the ledge narrowed after a few meters, and his pace slowed. As it turned a corner, the width lessened to about the length of his shoe, and his progress stopped. His heart thundered in his chest, and sweat seeped into his eyes, blurring his vision. For a brief second, he was sure he was going to lose his balance and drop two hundred meters through the night air until the craggy floor of the slope below rushed up to meet him. Or, even more likely, he would keep falling until the fires of hell consumed him.

He leaned forward and pressed his body against the cool stone, which felt good on his flushed skin. He let go of his handhold with his right arm and reached into his pocket. His fingers collided with the rosary his mother had given him. He worked the beads and prayed for delivery.

How long he stood there, stuck to the cliff like a fly on tar paper, he didn't know; his watch was on his left wrist, and he wasn't about to give up his hold on the rock to check the time. His fingers slid to the last bead on the rosary, his heart slowed to its normal rate, the streams of sweat ran dry, and his vision cleared. He lifted his right hand, found a crevice in the rock, and resumed sliding his feet along the shelf until he reached his destination, a spot on the cliff face just underneath the garage.

He checked in with Sarah as he gathered his wind.

"You took your sweet time, I see."

"I'm getting paid by the hour. What's happening?"

The situation had not changed. He thought her voice sounded strained, but then again, how could it not be? She was waiting for the opportunity to take a man's life by scattering his brains over the alpine floor.

"Get a move on, Marco; we're running out of time. And be careful."

"Be careful? You're not getting soft on me, are you?"

"Definitely not, darling. I just don't want another mess to clean up."

Up he went, putting a premium on making as little noise as possible, and paused an arm's length from the top to listen. Muffled voices and the sound of a diesel engine idling floated in his direction. He made sure the Beretta was still securely stuffed inside his waistband, switched the safety off, and hauled himself up.

He saw the man immediately, standing guard behind the garage, taking a drag from a cigarette. The glow of the cigarette dimmed, and the guard spotted him and brought his weapon to bear, but Marco was quicker to the trigger. He squeezed his finger twice, and the man slumped to the ground.

He scrambled over the edge. With his feet once more on horizontal ground, he spared a second to look around. The back of the garage, a massive six-door structure with office space above the bays, lay ten meters in front of him. A rear entry was cut into the wall very close to where the dead man lay; the windowless door was slightly ajar. There was no one else visible on the small parcel of land wedged between the back of the building and the edge of the cliff.

Marco pressed himself against the back wall next to the door and risked a glance inside. There were five vehicles parked there: the limo, the UPS van, a Lamborghini Murciélago, and two white vans. He recognized the last two vehicles straightaway; they were part of the large fleet of trucks belonging to the maintenance service of Vatican City. It seemed like an unusual place for Vatican vehicles to be parked, but there was no denying the silver and gold crossed key emblem on the side of the vans, or the license tags, which, like all vehicles belonging to the Vatican City State, began with the prefix SCV.

Six men were standing behind the UPS van, shutting the rear doors. Marco ducked his head out of sight and ran through the numbers: six men inside the garage, and six more standing in front. He supposed there were more inside the main house, but he doubted they would leave the prince's side under any circumstances. The basic framework of a plan began to assemble itself inside his head. If Sarah could manage to take out the men in the driveway, he could probably handle those still inside, especially if their attention was turned elsewhere.

He was going to need more firepower and less conscience, if he was going to be successful. The former he'd have no trouble acquiring. All he had to do was take a few steps toward the cliff and retrieve the dead man's weapon. He had no idea what the make or model was, but the former paratrooper named Pietro—the man who talked about the proper way to kill a person as if it were some kind of engineering project—had demonstrated the use of several similar guns, including the Heckler & Koch MP5s used by the prince's bodyguard, and he was confident he could employ it effectively.

The problem was in the latter half of the equation. He tried vainly to justify it, telling himself that the ends justified the means, that any method was ethical when it came to preventing a nuclear explosion inside Vatican City. He thought about the death toll of such an event: tens of thousands of his innocent countrymen vaporized. He thought about his discussion with Cardinal Lucci, who had told him to use *any means necessary*. And then he thought about holding the gentle gaze of John Paul III, and he knew he couldn't do it. Lucci had chosen the wrong man.

CHAPTER 42

Dr. Khalid al-Sharim rubbed the disbelief from his eyes and stared out the window again; he couldn't be sure, but he thought he'd seen a slight movement in the shadows on the other side of the precipice below him. He focused his gaze on the spot and saw the gauzy form of a man suspended against the rock face, just below the top. At first he thought he must be seeing things, but then there was another movement—an arm reaching up to the edge—and he knew he wasn't. There was only one way to explain why someone would be climbing the cliff in the middle of the night: the Americans were finally making good on their promise to extract him.

He looked back to the spot where the sentry had been holding vigil for the last half-hour and was rewarded with the firefly flash of light indicating another drag from his cigarette. The man on the cliff face must have seen it as well—despite the bad angle—because he chose that moment to burst over the top. The guard reacted slowly and reached for his weapon a second too late. There was a flash of light from the edge of the cliff, and he fell.

An opportunity had opened up for Khalid, but he wasn't sure how to proceed. If he went flying down the steps now, he was sure the American would shoot him before he had the chance to identify himself. No, he would be better off sitting tight for the moment, waiting for things to develop. He watched as the American ran past the dead bodyguard and was lost to sight directly beneath his vantage point. He entertained the idea of opening the window and sticking his head out to see, but caution won out over curiosity, and he left it closed.

An idea occurred to him, and he went back into the surgical suite. He observed with detachment that both men were still alive, but gave them no further consideration. He filled two syringes with Versed, put his surgical garb and magnifiers back on, and walked out with purpose in his stride. The control room was right across the hall from the clinic, and he strode straight in as if he were in a hurry. Waleed was sitting behind the desk, studying the wall of CCTV monitors.

"What are you doing here, Khalid? You're supposed to be operating on Abayd."

"I need another set of hands. Abayd told me to ask you."

"I have to watch the monitors."

"Take it up with Abayd."

"I will."

Waleed brushed past him, and Khalid flipped the cap off one of the syringes and followed. When Waleed slowed at the door, he jabbed the needle roughly into his flank and squirted all three milliliters directly into his right kidney. Waleed whirled around and struck him in the face with his elbow, sending him sprawling. Khalid hit the floor and tried to roll clear, but the other man was too quick and was upon him right away, with his hands on Khalid's throat.

The pressure stopped almost as soon as it had started, and Waleed slumped limply to the floor. Khalid rubbed his neck for a moment, and then used the other syringe to deposit another heavy dose of sedative into Waleed's radial vein. Thirty seconds later, his respirations were slow and irregular, and his muscles had the limp tone of a wet dishrag.

Khalid stood up and walked to the window overlooking the turnaround. The blinds were down, and he pried apart two of the blades to peer out. Six armed men patrolled the area in front of the garage. He had been taking notes on the security arrangements for long enough to know that only two men should be on patrol at this hour, and only one in this specific area.

It was as if the American attack had been anticipated. Somehow—Khalid had no idea how, and he didn't care all that much at the moment—Abayd had been onto him. But there was nothing he could do about that now, and he wasn't a man to dwell on the past. He fished a set of keys out of Waleed's pocket and exited the security office, smiling as he locked the door behind him; there were only two sets of keys to the office, and both of them were now sitting in his pocket.

Pietro didn't have to wait long. He had just finished working out his exit strategy when he felt the vibration of footfalls on the stairs leading up from the floor below. He picked up the Beretta and slowed his breathing, willing himself to be calm. He was almost there; there was no need to rush. The footsteps reached the top of the stairs and then turned in the other direction, toward the office on the opposite side of the floor. He hadn't expected this, and contemplated what to do. The overhead light was switched on, and he heard the prince turning the key to unlock the door to the office. He decided not to delay any longer. Experience had taught him that action was better than reaction. He eased out of his chair, pushed open the closet door, and twisted into shooting position.

There were two men in the dimly lit hallway. Prince el-Rayad was standing in front of the door to the office, pushing it open. A second man was behind him, directly in Pietro's line of fire. But he didn't remain so for very long; grabbing the prince with his powerful arms, he twisted him in front of him. Pietro fired twice, shooting el-Rayad in the neck. Blood spurted over the priceless Persian carpets, and the prince tottered and dropped to the floor. It was all the time the other man needed to slip inside the office and slam the door closed. Pietro fired again, but the door was solid metal, and the bullets ricocheted off and whistled past him.

It pained him to let the other man live—he thought immediately of Roberto Caruso's wife pointing at him in the courthouse—but it was time to go. He pulled the pin on a flash-bang, tossed it down the stairwell, and ran to the far side of the room, exiting via the sliding window as the grenade detonated. He had already tied a climbing rope to the railing; throwing it to the ground below, he vaulted over the top, letting himself freefall for a second before he clamped down on the line to slow his descent. He hit the ground and rolled to break his fall. When he returned to his feet, the Beretta was back in his hand again, but no targets presented themselves.

He heard all hell breaking loose as he ducked behind the large stone marking the land's end. The fifty-meter coil of rope was already secured to the boulder, and he kicked it over the edge. After a last peek from behind the rock, he crawled to the edge on his belly and let himself fall into the abyss.

A gunshot rang out, and Marco froze against the wall. The shot had come from the main house; he was sure of it. He twisted around and peered into the garage in time to see the men inside fleeing. This was his chance. He got up and slipped through the rear door as a chorus of shouts arose from the front. Rifle fire echoed, and he assumed Sarah was creating the ghosts who would haunt her for the next few years.

A stairway led up to the second floor from the corner where he was standing, and he stepped into the alcove to avoid being seen. He heard the pounding of feet on the stairs above and whirled around to face the new threat. A running form appeared around the corner; Marco recognized him right away from the picture Lucci had shown him. It was Dr. Khalid al-Sharim.

*

When Sarah Messier heard the shots from below, she exhaled a breath of relief and tightened her finger on the trigger. The waiting was finally over, and she could get down to the work for which she had been training since she was a little girl. She centered the cross hairs on the first target, fired, and swiveled toward the second target without wasting time to confirm the kill. She acquired the second target and pulled the trigger. The rifle roared again, jamming into her shoulder. She tracked a third man as he ran toward Haus Adler, caught up with him as he skirted the edge of the precipice, and felled him with another round. The man bounced off the ground and rolled over the edge and out of sight.

She lowered the power on her scope to get a better view of the chaos. She expected to see men desperately seeking cover, but was surprised to see a steady stream braving the open ground in between the garage and the main building. The lead man had almost reached the safety of Haus Adler by the time she switched the scope back to full power. She rushed her aim, and the shot went wide, blowing apart a ceramic pot of geraniums on the porch. The target made a frantic scramble for the front door, but Sarah was practiced at moving targets, having felled many a scurrying squirrel with the .22 carbine her father had given her as a young girl, and sent him tumbling to the ground in a heap.

The two men behind him paused for a minute as if they weren't sure where the shots were coming from, allowing her to snap a fresh clip into place and dispatch both of them with clean head shots. She couldn't locate another target with her scope, so she scooped up the binoculars to take a look. It had finally dawned on the enemy to take cover, but at least two of them had chosen the east side of the parked Mercedes, giving her a clear line of fire. She put down the binoculars, located the two men, and killed both as they huddled behind the car.

She grabbed the binoculars again and surveyed the target area. The first Mercedes sedan was still in the turnaround; two dead bodies lay in front of it. No other targets were in sight, so she turned her attention to the area at the bottom of the steep slope Marco had descended. At first, she could see nothing and was just about to put the glasses down again when she spotted movement in the bottom of the field of view. She adjusted the focus and zoomed in. Two men were bent low and running hard, angling toward her position. Her eye moved back to the scope, but they had disappeared into the woods and were lost to sight.

She was going to have company.

Soon.

Streams of conflicting impulses flowed through her head, all unbidden. She was a survivor by nature and through her father's training, and as such, the Volvo sedan beckoned. The spare key to the car was in her pocket, the hike down to it was not long, and the moonlight was sufficient to guide her down the slope. But even as these thoughts materialized in her brain, a second line of thinking came, gaining force quickly. Sarah wasn't sure at what point in time she had become concerned for Marco's welfare, but she had, undeniably so.

She lay still, eye glued to the scope, finger white on the trigger, waiting for the victorious thought to emerge and dictate her actions.

CHAPTER 43

Dr. al-Sharim opened his mouth to speak, but Marco clapped a palm over his face and whispered in his ear in English.

"Do you understand?"

Al-Sharim nodded. Marco removed his hand, pointing upward. "Are there any other men upstairs?"

"Three, but they are all heavily sedated."

Marco gave him a quick summary of their situation. He told him about the UPS van and the trucks with the Vatican insignia. He relayed his theory that the nuclear warheads had not yet been offloaded. "There are two men guarding the van. We have to make sure they don't get in our way."

The doctor reached behind his back and pulled out a handgun, indicating that he was ready to go. Marco flattened himself farther against the wall of the alcove and edged toward the open bay. He could hear the men in front of the garage shouting to each other in a foreign language, presumably trying to figure out who was raining death on them from above. He didn't hear any sound from inside the bay, but he guessed the men who had delivered the bombs were still somewhere in the garage.

The doctor brushed up against his shoulder, and Marco noticed his headgear for the first time: a pair of magnifying glasses with a small mirror attached to the side. He plucked the stem of the mirror off the glasses and positioned it so he could see into the garage. At first, it looked empty, but after a moment he noticed that the two delivery men had gotten back into the vehicle. The engine growled to life, and the bay door crawled upward: either the payment had been received, or the delivery men were splitting without it.

He whispered his plan to the doctor, then counted to three—the fastest three seconds of his life—and rushed into the garage. He ran over to the van, grabbed the door handle, and yanked it open. The driver turned toward him in annoyance, and then in fear as Marco placed the end of the silencer against his throat, similar to the way he pressed candles against the throats of the faithful on the feast of St. Blaise.

The driver held up his hands, but the passenger wasn't as compliant. He twisted quickly and grabbed for the automatic pistol lying next to him on the bench seat, managing to pick it up before Marco pulled the trigger. The bullet severed the driver's brain stem before exiting the base of his neck amid a spurt of flesh, blood, and spinal fluid, hitting the second man in the chest. The passenger dropped the gun and slumped against the door with a jagged divot in his lungs and his partner's innards plastered over his torso.

Marco swiveled and saw the doctor standing guard in front of the open bay door, ready to execute his simple directive: "Shoot anyone you see." He grabbed the driver by the collar and pulled him out of the van, dumping him unceremoniously on the concrete floor. The engine was still idling, and the soft thud of the impact was inaudible. He climbed inside the vehicle and slipped between the two front seats, entering the cargo area. A wall of cardboard boxes plastered with labels and bar codes confronted him. He punched his way through the line and knelt in front of a pair of burnished metal cylinders lying near the back. They were each about a meter and a half long, and half a meter in width, the exact specifications Lucci had given him.

He retraced his steps, satisfied that he hadn't killed two men without purpose. Al-Sharim was still pressed against the front of the garage, standing guard. He motioned to al-Sharim to get in the driver's seat, dragged the dead man out of the passenger's seat, and jumped in. "Sarah."

There was no answer. He adjusted the collar microphone as the doctor took the wheel.

"Sarah."

Still no response.

Marco's tongue felt like he had tried to swallow a handful of sand, and air stuck in his throat. "Sarah?" He could barely get the words out of his mouth. "Sarah, are you there?"

"I'm a little busy. This better be good."

His heart resumed beating; the wind returned to his lungs. "It is. I have the doctor and the weapons. We're going to get out of here in the UPS van. Can you cover us?"

He heard dead air and the crackle of a poor connection.

"Sarah?"

"Are you ready?"

"Yes. As soon as we're gone, get out of there. You have the car keys?"

She didn't respond, but her silence was pregnant with a tension that Marco could not identify.

"Did you hear me?"

"Yes."

"*Yes*, you heard me, or *yes*, you have the key?" He knew neither of them had time to clarify the issue, but he couldn't stop himself from asking.

"It doesn't matter."

"The hell it doesn't."

"This is no time for our first argument, *dolcezza*. On the count of three …"

"Sarah—"

"One …"

"Are you all right?"

There was no response. All he could hear was the idling of the engine and the sound of his heart thumping in his chest.

"It's too late for that, Marco."

The sound of a bullet impacting against rock exploded in his earpiece.

"Sarah!"

"Two …" Her voice was scratchy and thin.

"Wait …"

"Three. Goodbye, Marco."

Sarah centered the cross hairs over the gas tank of the nearest Mercedes and squeezed the trigger, causing a spout of flame to erupt from the side of the vehicle. Aware that the hunters were just beneath her, she slid backward, narrowly escaping several bullets that smashed against the stone upon which her prone form had been resting. The muzzle flashes had been much closer than she had expected, not more than thirty meters away. She knelt behind a large bush and strapped her backpack on tightly. A sniper rifle was no good for this kind of fight, but she had neither the inclination nor the time to break it down and stow it away, so she looped the carrying strap over her shoulder. Bullets ripped through the pine trees above her, creating a shower of needles and pine tar that stuck to her hair like glue.

It was evident that she needed to get off the top of the promontory, so she slid down the rock face, her fingers scraping uselessly against the stone as she tried to grab something to control her descent. She dug her toes in to break her momentum, but the face was uneven and filled with cracks, and she couldn't gain sufficient traction.

A pine tree saved her. Her feet had just bounced off a rocky protuberance, causing her descent to accelerate, when she collided with the top branches of the resilient evergreen growing on a small ledge. Her momentum slowed considerably, and her flailing arms caught a branch stout enough to support her weight. She climbed down to the ledge and tied a length of rope around the base of the tree. After a quick survey of the face, she looped the rope around her waist and started letting herself down. The rope was twenty-five meters in length, and she used every centimeter, rappeling down to where the slope let up enough to allow her to maneuver without it. She worked her way to her right, toward a patch of large pines where she could get lost in the shadows.

She had almost reached the trees when shots rang out, and bullets cratered the stone behind her. Fragments of stone lacerated her legs, and she lost her footing. Her right ankle twisted violently, and she hit the ground and rolled, dropping ten meters before she slammed against the bole of a tree, losing her breath. More shots rang out, but the bullets struck above and to her left as if the hunters hadn't seen her fall.

Air ebbed back into her chest, and she crawled behind the thick trunk of the pine and sat up against it. She unsnapped the Browning from its moorings on her waist, slid off the safety, and set it down on her lap. Using a piece of cloth and several sticks, she fashioned a crude splint to support her swollen and disfigured ankle, then snatched up the Browning again, listening for the telltale signs of approach: the snap of a breaking twig or the slap of a boot against the rocky shelf. But she heard nothing other than the sound of the breeze whistling through the pine boughs and the rush of her own breath as she exhaled.

As luck would have it, she had been prepared for such a contingency for a long time, not by the U.S. Army or the CIA, for whom she had labored for a combined fifteen years, but by her father, the backwoodsman who believed that guns—and knowing how to use them—were the best defense against a corrupt state. Although she hadn't seen or talked to him in years, he was never very far away, especially in situations like this, where his voice whispered into her ear, instructing her how to stay alive.

CHAPTER 44

The sound of an explosion flooded in through the open garage doors, and Marco tapped al-Sharim on the shoulder: ready or not, it was time to go. He opened the window as the doctor backed the van out of the garage, in the event that he needed room to maneuver his gun, and prayed he wouldn't have to use it. The van cleared the confines of the bay, and he saw the burning Mercedes off to the side, as if he was watching a CNN clip of the Gaza Strip. There were no enemy combatants in view, at least none that were going to cause problems. He could see a line of dead bodies extending from the garage to the main house, evidence of Sarah's handiwork.

He heard gunshots echoing down from above, confirming his fears about her safety. A strong urge to go to her aid overcame him, and he moved his hand away from the handle lest it throw the door open of its own accord. He saw several men running out of Haus Adler, gesticulating for him to stop.

Al-Sharim shifted the transmission into drive and eased ahead, trying not to arouse suspicion, but the men began shouting and waving their arms frantically.

"Gun it."

Tires screeched on the asphalt, and Marco's head whipped back against the rest as the doctor floored the gas pedal. He saw the lead man bring his weapon to bear, and he emptied the rest of the clip in his direction, felling him and causing the others to dive for cover. Two men jumped out of the Mercedes parked in the driveway. Marco grabbed al-Sharim's pistol and scattered them with a volley as the doctor drove straight at the car. There was a grinding collision, and the sound of twisting metal and breaking glass. The van ricocheted off the Mercedes and kept going, reaching the track that ran alongside the edge of the precipice. Marco could see the abyss rushing past through the open window. All it would take was a slight miscalculation—or a burst tire—and the van would disappear over the cliff to be swallowed up by the blackness. But the tires maintained their integrity, and al-Sharim made no mistakes. As the road turned to the left and entered the welcoming cover of the forest, Marco heard the staccato sound of gunfire and felt the thud of bullets hammering against the back of the vehicle, but their getaway was unhindered. They negotiated a sharper turn to the left, and he lost sight of Haus Adler in the mirror.

"Is there a man at the gate?"

"Usually not. There is a keypad on the other side, but the bar opens automatically."

"How long does it take?"

"It used to take longer, but the prince is an impatient man, and he put in a hydraulic system that raises the gate in about ten seconds."

"Can they jam it from up there?" Marco remembered seeing the barrier as he had driven past it earlier on the way to the trailhead; it was solid steel anchored in reinforced concrete, capable of stopping the van dead in its tracks, and there was not enough room to drive around it.

"Yes, there is a master switch in the control room, but you need not worry."

Marco got the feeling he was going to like the doctor. "Why not?"

"Because there are only two sets of keys to the security office, and they are both in my pocket."

He breathed out a sigh of relief, but the exhaled air stuck in his windpipe as headlights appeared in the rear-view mirror and the whine of a racing engine poured in through the open window.

"We've got company."

He dialed Elena on his cell phone. She picked up on the first ring. "What's going on?"

He explained his predicament, his words coming in short spurts as he struggled to control his breathing against the rising flood of panic in his chest. Gunshots rang out; bullets shredded the pines trees next to the road.

"Where are you?"

"Just past the gate, like you told me."

"Get to the gate as fast as you can. It takes ten seconds to raise, and the Saudis are right behind us."

Elena ran down the road already brandishing her pistol. The end of the driveway appeared in the darkness ahead of her; she hadn't seen anyone there as she had driven past it, and she didn't see anyone now. As she approached the gate, she could hear the sound of straining engines and gunfire off to her right, but she didn't see the headlights until she had run past. Settling into a good spot behind the bole of a thick pine, she flipped the safety off and held the gun in front of her with both arms extended. All she could see was the driveway snaking away into the night, but from the roar of the nearing vehicles and the flicker of the headlights in the trees, she knew it wasn't going to be long.

"Elena?"

Marco sounded faint and far away despite the excellent reception.

"I'm here, at the end of the driveway."

"They're right behind us."

"Let me worry about them. Just keep driving until you reach the gate."

It was then she realized her mistake. She should have gone much farther down, where the sharp bend in the road would have given her a better shooting angle. Worse than that, Marco was going to have to stop in front of the barrier, giving his pursuers an easy target. She pushed off the tree and started running, as the headlights swept around a turn and came straight at her. Angling to the side of the road, she took a few more steps and went into a head-first dive. She slid to a stop and readied the gun as the vehicles bore down on her.

She heard Marco yelling in her ear, but with the thunder of the engine noise she couldn't decipher what he was saying. Fixing the van in the sight, she slid her finger behind the trigger, pulling with light pressure.

"Marco, on my go, brake hard and steer left."

Engines wailed. Tires screamed against the asphalt.

"What?"

She repeated herself, yelling into her collar microphone. "On my go!"

The clamor of the engines approached a crescendo. The headlights beamed straight at her, blinding her in the glare.

"When?"

"Now."

She tensed for the recoil, but the van didn't waver.

"Now?"

"Now!"

Tires squealed, and the van veered steeply, opening up a direct line of fire to the Mercedes. She pulled the trigger; the gun barked, volleying bullets into the engine of the approaching car. Sparks flew in all directions, metal complained, but the Mercedes came on. The clip emptied; she snapped a new one in place. This time she aimed for the driver's-side tire, blowing it out and sending the sedan into a spin. It skidded into a grove of pines, coming to rest at a ninety-degree angle to the road, about a hundred feet from her position. She sprayed it with bullets, shattering glass, rending metal, and flattening both tires on the passenger side.

The gun fell silent as the ammunition was expended; she loaded the last clip and got up, advancing on the vehicle with her pistol drawn. The rear door opened, and a man tried to get out. She shot him twice in the chest. Arriving at the car, she yanked the front door open. The passenger was slumped in his seat, barely moving; the driver was already dead. She shot them both.

"Elena."

She turned around. Marco was standing beside the van, which was stuck in a patch of mud at the side of the driveway, waving for her to come and help. She ran over and helped him push the vehicle back onto the road; then they both jumped in, and the van accelerated away.

Marco's heart thudded in his chest as the van paused in front of the gate, waiting for it to lift. After an eternal wait of ten seconds, the hydraulic motor raised the steel beam, and they pulled clear. Elena waited for the barrier to descend behind them and used the remaining bullets in her gun to reduce the control mechanism to scraps. Then al-Sharim gunned the engine, and the van swerved onto the Römerstrasse in the direction of Germany.

For the past two weeks, Marco had spent many moments wondering how he would feel when it was all over. And now that the end had arrived, he finally knew the answer: he was angry. As the engine strained to pull the van up the steep gradient upon which the Römerstrasse was built, his anger roiled like a severe case of dysentery. He was angry with everyone and everything, but chiefly with himself. He was angry with Elena for starting the whole sordid affair by entering his confessional, though he was keenly aware that she had never asked him to intervene for her. He was angry with Cardinal Lucci for forcing him into this fool's errand, though it had been Marco himself who had accepted the assignment. He was angry with Sarah for the most egregious of sins—being beautiful and charming—though she had never invited his attentions or begged his eyes to stroll lazily over her shapely form. And he was angry with himself for not going to her aid the moment he realized she was in danger.

As the van crested the hill and approached the trailhead where they had stashed the Volvo earlier, he had an epiphany: the only thing he really cared about was Sarah's welfare.

"I have to go back." He pointed to the parking lot looming ahead. "Pull over here."

Al-Sharim gave him an uncertain look, but turned into the parking area as requested. Marco introduced him to Elena, then activated the navigation system built into the console and punched in an address in Italy. "I've programmed it to take you to my parents' cottage in the Italian Alps. It's a three-hour drive from here; you should be there before first light."

"What do you want me to do?" Elena asked.

"Go with Dr. al-Sharim."

Her face blossomed with protest, but she didn't voice it.

"Get going now, and don't stop for any reason whatsoever. I will come as soon as I can. If I'm not there in twenty-four hours, call Cardinal Lucci."

"What should I tell him?"

"Tell him that Father Venetti is in dire need of his prayers."

CHAPTER 45

The muzzle flashes appeared like orange blooms in the darkness. Sarah ducked instinctively, but the bullets ripped into the felled tree lying in front of her, showering bark everywhere. It was evident her pursuers had finally zeroed in on her position. Just as she had expected, one of the hunters had circled around in the darkness and was now attacking from the slope below. She guessed the other had remained on the hill above her, waiting for his partner to flush her out for an easy shot. She decided to stay put.

Her defensive position was actually reasonably good, even though she had quite literally fallen into it. The thick trunk of the tree against which she was sitting afforded her cover from above, and equally stout trees protected her from both sides. A storm had felled a girthy pine, and its long corpse shielded her from below.

She heard the sound of pounding feet and twisted around, but she couldn't see anything. The running stopped. Shots rang out from above her, smacking into her tree with a heaviness she could feel in her back. She heard more footsteps, this time from the slope beneath her. Her finger remained poised on the trigger, but she didn't shoot, not wanting to give away her position. The next volley came from below, and she could tell by the report that the hunter had moved closer. She guessed the man above would be moving as his partner fired, so she risked a peek up the slope, but saw nothing except the shadows of huge pines.

Gunfire echoed down. They were closing fast, as if they sensed she was dead in the water. Her only chance was to move, but she knew her ankle wouldn't hold her. She had examined it earlier, and even with her limited knowledge she knew it was fractured. A slow crawl would be the best she could manage; they would overtake her in seconds.

"Sarah?"

It was Marco's voice, hissing weakly from her earpiece.

"Marco?"

"Where are you?"

She gave him a basic description of her position.

"Hang on for five minutes. How many are there?"

She told him. "One is above me, and the other is below."

"Keep them busy. I'm almost there."

Marco reached a bend in the trail overlooking a gravelly slope and jumped without looking. He hit the ground, and his legs went out from underneath him, sending him into a feet-first slide. The base of the hill rushed up to meet him, and he regained his footing, using his momentum to traverse the heap of rocks that stretched over to where the promontory began to head upwards at a sharp angle.

Halfway across, he heard the clamor of gunshots, and he adjusted his path across the slag pile. They had come from his right, several hundred meters up the steep incline. He reached the base of the slope and started climbing, angling to the right where the pitch was not as steep. He stopped to catch his breath, lest he give himself away with his gasps for air, and used the opportunity to take the Beretta out of the side pocket of his coat and snap his last clip into place. When his chest was no longer heaving, he resumed climbing at a redoubled pace.

The trees thickened as he went, in both density and girth, and were three times the height of the mangy evergreens that eked out a meager existence on the rocks below. The ground underneath his feet changed as well, taking on a softer texture and a covering of pine needles, dampening the sound of his footfalls to a barely audible slap.

He stopped behind a medium pine and let his pupils adjust. The dense canopy above shuttered the moonlight rather well, and it was much darker here than below. Another burst of gunfire came from somewhere above and to his left, and he started off again in its direction. He smelled the faint odor of gunpowder tainting the pine, and he knew he was close. He went slowly now, keeping one eye out for twigs and the other for men with guns.

He saw the slight sway of a pine bough up ahead in the shadows, perhaps twenty or thirty meters away, and raised his gun. Not wanting to risk killing Sarah, he didn't tighten his finger on the trigger. Moving from one tree to the next, he closed in on the place where he had seen movement, trying to make out a human form, but all he could see was degrees of blackness.

Muzzle flashes pushed back the darkness, and he saw Sarah sitting against a large tree, holding her rifle at the ready. Bullets shredded the trunk above her, showering her with bark and sawdust. The gunman adjusted his aim in the light of his own weapon, lowering the barrel a fraction.

Marco didn't hesitate. He leveled the Beretta and fired, all in one fluid movement, grouping three shots in the man's neck, silhouetted by the muzzle flashes. The gunman toppled over, and the firing stopped, allowing the blackness to return, although only for a second. There was a rush of feet from above, and a second gunman charged toward her position. Marco wheeled but couldn't locate a target. He fired several times at the noise of breaking boughs, but the charge continued unabated.

"Get down!"

His warning was too late; no sooner had he spoken than muzzle flashes once again lit up the night. He returned fire, killing the second gunman, but it was too late. Sarah lay motionless on the ground.

The muzzle flashes faded, the echo of gunshots died away, but Marco remained in place, replaying over and over the film clip of her torso tumbling to the ground. After a time, he fished a Maglite from his pocket and switched it on. He shone the beam at the base of the tree and saw her leather jacket on the ground. He walked over, knelt down, and lifted her up. She was surprisingly light. He propped her up against the tree, and her head wobbled and then fell to the needle-strewn ground.

A sound came from behind him, and he swiveled around, probing the darkness with his flashlight. The beam fell on a downed tree; the noise sounded as if it had come from within. He took a step closer, and watched as Sarah wriggled out from the center of the apparently hollow trunk, wearing only a pair of panties and a bra, both black. She brushed fragments of fungi and decomposing wood pulp from her hair and took a seat on the log. Marco picked up her jacket, which was riddled with bullet holes, then unbuttoned the black, long-sleeved blouse and lifted it off her backpack. He yanked her cap off the round piece of rotting log she'd used for her head and handed it to her.

"I'll take my pants."

He removed the thick branches she'd used for legs, shook out the debris, and handed her the jeans. He noticed she was having difficulty putting weight on her right ankle.

"Are you okay?"

"I broke my ankle."

"I better get a look at that."

He knelt in front of her and examined the ankle, glad to have something to distract him from the fact that he had just killed two men without the slightest hesitation—Pietro would be beaming—and the only thing he felt was relief. He also didn't want to have to look at her right now. He was sure she would be able to read his face like a romance title, so he kept it bent down and hidden from view as he wrapped her fractured ankle in duct tape. When he was done, emotions in check, he handed her the rifle. She broke it down quickly and stowed it away in the rucksack.

"We best be off." He extended his arm, and she grabbed it. They stood up, with Sarah's right arm wrapped around his neck and Marco's right arm hooked around her waist, and started hobbling down the piney slope.

"You shouldn't have come back for me."

"No, probably not."

"So why did you?"

"Leaving didn't feel right."

He steered her around a large pile of moss-covered boulders and filled her in on what had transpired since their last contact, starting with meeting Dr. al-Sharim in the stairwell, and ending with the doctor's departure from the trailhead in the hijacked van, with Elena riding shotgun.

They stumbled down the slope heading west, away from Haus Adler, making reasonable time. After a while, the slope became so steep they had to disentangle and shimmy down on their backsides. Marco went first, making sure Sarah wouldn't fall too far if she slipped, which she did, ending up sprawled awkwardly over his broad shoulders. Their faces brushed as they disentangled, and her lips locked against his. It was only a brief kiss, but when the softness was over, he knew how he felt about her.

"That's for coming back." She kissed him again, longer this time and with a little more urgency; Marco wanted to pull away, to tell her to stop, but he wrapped his arms around her instead. After a moment, they broke apart and continued down the slope, still gripping one another tightly. When they reached the massive slag pile at the foot of the slope, they paused to rest.

"What happened to Pietro?"

"He killed the prince. There was another man as well, but he escaped."

"How do you know that?" she asked.

"Pietro texted me when he got back to the house."

"So that's it, right? The prince is dead, and the weapons are gone."

Marco nodded.

"Good, because I don't ever want to come back here again."

"Come back? We haven't left yet." He helped her up. "And I doubt they're just going to let us walk away."

They staggered across the loose pile of rubble and began climbing the face of the hill. After trying several methods, Marco ended up short-roping her up the slope. She objected at first, but with no ability to dig in with both feet, she couldn't manage any other way.

He was exhausted when they reached the hiking trail just after 4 a.m. They had perhaps another hour and a half of darkness. The trailhead where the car was parked was only two kilometers away. In normal circumstances, it would be a twenty-minute walk, but Marco guessed it would take them at least an hour at their best pace, by which point the parking lot would be crawling with either the prince's bodyguard, all armed to the teeth and lusting for blood, or the Austrian federal police, who were not well known for their sense of humor or leniency. He slid a long arm around Sarah's waist, trying not to notice the smooth firmness of her muscles and the wide curvature of her hips.

"Let's get going."

"Don't we want to go the other way?" She pointed north, in the direction of the path they had taken earlier.

"Not unless you want to find out what the inside of an Austrian prison looks like."

"Then where the hell are we going to go?"

He picked a few strands of grass growing by the side of the trail and tossed them in the air; they swirled south toward the finger of Germany that stuck into Austria. Grabbing his phone from his pocket, he thumbed a text to Pietro and waited for the reply, which came quickly.

"Berchtesgaden, Germany," he said.
"Why on earth are we going there?"
"It's downwind."

CHAPTER 46

Anatoly Gerashchenko pulled his Vektor pistol from its holster on his chest, grabbed the door handle with his other hand, and debated his best course of action one last time. He desperately wanted to know what was going on outside, but he was safe inside the prince's office, which had been surrounded by a ten-centimeter casing of titanium; it was bulletproof, capable of deflecting a rocket-launched grenade, and—with its self-enclosed air conditioner system—impermeable to biological and chemical attack. It was also windowless and completely soundproofed; a war could be going on just outside, and he wouldn't have any idea. The bank of monitors on the wall next to the desk was supposed to be his window into what was happening, but without the prince's fingerprints, he couldn't activate them.

But the waiting was getting to him, and his pride as a former Spetsnaz officer—the only people allowed to carry the Vektor pistol—was taking a beating as he cowered inside the office and allowed others to do the fighting. Worse, he wanted to make sure the nuclear weapons were safe and sound in the garage. His employer wanted those weapons to be deployed against Vatican City; he had been very clear about that, and he wasn't a man who reacted well when things didn't go according to plan. The prince was dead; that was unfortunate, but he had played his part. They would have to find another scapegoat to blame for the nuclear firestorm that would burn Vatican City to the ground, but el-Rayad had at least brought them the weapons.

Gerashchenko twisted the door handle and looked out into the hallway. The prince was gone; only the blood-soaked carpet and the ricochet-riddled walls provided any confirmation of the execution that had taken place less than an hour ago. He padded over to the door leading down to the third floor and peered into the stairway. The walls were scorched, and the air stank of phosphorus, evidence of the recent use of a flash-bang. There was no one in sight. He considered calling out, but if the attackers were still there, he would only be attracting unwanted attention.

He crept down the stairs, peering out into the third floor, which was the residence of the bodyguards. All the doors to the bedrooms were closed, and other than nearly a dozen ashtrays overflowing with cold ash, the living room was empty. Continuing down to the second floor—the bailiwick of the prince's wives and prostitutes, who lived there in oddly peaceful harmony—he found the same situation, other than the ashtrays.

Ibrahim looked up at him as he emerged from the stairwell on the ground floor. The prince's dead body was wrapped in a Persian carpet. Only his head was visible. His normally dark skin was pale and sallow, and his brown eyes were open and staring blindly into the distance. A stream of clotted blood flowed out of his open mouth.

"Where are the others?" Gerashchenko demanded.

"What others?"

"The bodyguard."

Ibrahim shrugged, a scowl adorning his face. Like the other members of the prince's bodyguard, he didn't like the Russian, and he liked taking orders from him even less. "You are looking at it."

Gerashchenko glanced around the room, featuring an open floor plan that incorporated the living room, kitchen, and eating area. It was full of the usual detritus of an armed camp: coffee cups littered the wooden tables, flat-screen TVs blared from the walls, showing a variety of football matches from around the world, and magazines dotted the sofas and overstuffed chairs. But there were no people.

"Where is Abayd?"

"No one has seen him."

"Where was he last?"

"Dr. al-Sharim was stitching him up in the clinic."

Gerashchenko hurried outside with Ibrahim on his heels. Even in the moonlit darkness, he could see the line of bodies running from the porch all the way to the garage, which was lit up like a beacon on the other side of the narrow peninsula. A car smoldered in the driveway; he could smell the acrid fumes of smoking oil and hear the creaking of heated metal. He strode past the bodies without giving them a second look and entered the garage. The van with the weapons was gone.

Cursing loudly, he ran past the trio of BMW motorcycles the prince loved to ride on the mountain roads and hit the stairs at the back of the garage. Hesitating at the top, he waited for Ibrahim to catch up with him.

"Which of these doors is the clinic?"

Two doors and a hallway led away from the foyer in which they were standing. Ibrahim pointed to the one straight ahead. Gerashchenko yanked on the handle; it didn't budge.

"Get a drill, right now."

Ibrahim complied with the order, and Gerashchenko went down the hall to the security office. This door too was locked; he knocked on it, but there was no response. He knocked again, this time pounding with his massive fists, but the result was the same.

Ibrahim was drilling out the lock to the surgical suite when he returned to the foyer. Gerashchenko waited for him to bore all the way through it, filling the air with steel dust and the smell of hot metal, then tried the handle again. The door opened with a smooth swing, and he stepped inside. Abayd was thrashing around on the surgical table; Nassir was prone on the floor, unmoving. They helped

Abayd to a sitting position, and as they waited for him to become more alert, Ibrahim wrapped several bandages around the wounds on his forearms until they could be seen to properly. By the time he had finished, Abayd was awake and demanding something to drink.

"It's about time you woke up."

He eyed Gerashchenko darkly as he gulped at a glass of water. "What happened?"

Ibrahim gave him a quick summary of events.

"KiKi is dead?"

Ibrahim nodded; the scowl on Abayd's face deepened, darkening the circles under his eyes and exacerbating the sharp angles of his face.

"Where are the weapons?"

Ibrahim explained that Dr. al-Sharim and one of the commandos had stolen them.

"And you just waved goodbye as they drove off?"

"Jibril and two others went after them in a Mercedes, but they didn't return. I rode out on one of the motorcycles; all three men are dead, and the gate has been disabled."

"How many men are left?"

"You are looking at them."

Abayd gave him a look that drained the blood from his face.

"You ordered Yasser to dispose of the bodies of the Americans. He took three men with him and hasn't returned yet. Waleed is missing—"

"Waleed? He should be in the security office."

"It's locked, and he isn't answering his phone. Hanza and Brahim left thirty minutes ago to take care of the sniper on the hill above us, and they haven't returned."

"Did you call them?"

Ibrahim nodded.

"They didn't respond?"

He shook his head.

"Did you call the police?"

"No."

"Good. Help me up."

Ibrahim moved over to help, but Gerashchenko pushed him aside and lifted Abayd to his feet as easily as if he were a paper doll. They walked over to the countertop, stepping over the unconscious Nassir, and Abayd searched through his bomber jacket. A series of epithets issued forth from his mouth, echoing in the confined space.

"What is it now?"

"Al-Sharim took my phone."

"The doctor has your phone?"

"Yes, why do you care?"

Gerashchenko produced his own cell phone, thumbing a number of commands. "Because I'm tracking it."

Abayd spit on the floor, nearly hitting Nassir with a wad of tobacco-tinged saliva. "You had no right to do that."

Gerashchenko shrugged indifferently, turning to Ibrahim. "Do you still have the key to the motorcycle?"

Ibrahim dug a key out of his pocket, and Gerashchenko grabbed it and exited the medical suite, taking the stairs down to the garage three steps at a time as Abayd screamed loud curses into the air. He jumped onto the motorcycle Ibrahim had left in the middle of the bay, started it up, and accelerated down the driveway, barking orders into his cell phone as he motored past the burning cars, dead bodies, and large pots of red geraniums, blossoms shining weakly in the growing light.

Abayd and Ibrahim reached the knoll overlooking Haus Adler after a ten-minute climb up the slope; they would have made it in five, but Abayd had to stop and vomit on two occasions. Abayd knelt over Hanza's dead body and saw blood still oozing from the wound in his neck. He put his hand on his friend's arm and noted that the flesh was still warm. It did not take a medical examiner to realize Hanza hadn't been dead for long. He pulled out a detailed map of the area and used his penlight to locate his position on the leeward slope of the small peak that overlooked Haus Adler and trace out the possible escape routes.

The most obvious was a hiking trail that descended from the summit, ending at a trailhead on the Römerstrasse. He had already considered this possibility and dispatched Yasser—who had finally returned from dumping the bodies—to investigate. Yasser had found an empty Volvo sedan parked in the lot and had remained in hiding near the car, but Abayd thought it was unlikely the sniper would return that way. They would have to make for the hiking trail—the topography was such that there was no other way to go—but he guessed they would hike in the opposite direction, toward the summit. There was a confluence of paths there that led in every direction.

He stuffed the map back in his jacket and grabbed his phone, dialing Haddad, the pilot of the prince's helicopter.

"Where are you?" he barked.

"At the airport."

"Is the chopper ready?"

"Yes, on standby."

"Meet me at the top of the Untersberg."

"Why?"

"Just do it."

"It's restricted air space."

"I don't care. Get going now."

"It will take me thirty minutes to get airborne."

"Make it twenty."

It was close to dawn by the time they reached the Weitwanderweg and turned toward the summit, and the darkness was slowly surrendering to the light, a reality with which Abayd was both delighted and unhappy: delighted that the dawn would make his enemies easier to locate, but unhappy that it would bring a host of interlopers to the sunlit slopes.

Abayd didn't like interlopers on any day, and he was in an especially murderous mood today. His arms were sore where his knife had sliced them open, and his head throbbed. He was nauseated and wanted nothing more than to stop and vomit, but there wasn't time for such leisurely pursuits, and he jogged onward with a seasick belly. His legs were weak, and his breath stuck in his throat, but embarrassment and an intense hatred drove him on.

He had never particularly looked forward to killing. In his mind, it was simply part of the job, one that he neither relished nor detested. But now he thirsted for blood with an anticipation that almost frightened him. His whole life had been destroyed. He had failed to protect the prince, the *raison d'être* of his existence, and he would either be sent to jail or buried in a dark hole in the ground; at this moment, he had no preference.

Spurred by hatred, he turned up the hill and redoubled his pace.

CHAPTER 47

Austria 107 wound down the steep slope, hugging the bank of the rushing river on its right-hand side. A road sign claimed they had just passed the village of Unter Lassach, but Elena would have to take its word for it; in the dim light of early morning, all she had seen was a small grouping of houses between the road and the mountains, which lifted steep and rocky into the shreds of the dawn mist. The road continued down the steep valley, twisting and turning in synchrony with the green waters of whatever river ran next to it, bringing them to their next turning point, which, according to the navigation system, was only twenty minutes away, a left onto Austria 100 just past the town at the bottom of the valley.

Elena realized she had drifted too close to the side of the road—and the ten-meter drop into the river. She yanked the wheel, causing the tires to screech against the rutted pavement; the van swerved back onto the carriageway.

"You want me to drive?"

She glared at al-Sharim.

"Keep your eyes on the road, then."

His perfect Arabic reminded Elena of her father, who would be getting up about now, laying down his *sajjāda* in the proper orientation—toward Mecca—and saying his morning prayers. She hoped some of them were for her.

"Almost to our next turn, Elena. Just another twenty minutes."

She braked as a car—the first vehicle they had seen for a long time—turned onto the road from an overlook on the other side.

Her hand shot toward the horn reflexively, but stopped short, arrested by some sort of deeper instinct. She cursed instead, loudly and in Arabic, bringing a smile to al-Sharim's face.

The sweep of headlights came up behind them. Elena glanced into the mirror, seeing two vans in the reflection. She gripped the wheel tighter for a second, but relaxed as they settled a safe distance away, swelling the now slow-moving procession weaving down the valley. Reaching for the coffee they had bought at a gas station in Zell am See, she gulped the last of it, letting its sharp flavor linger on her tongue for a moment before swallowing it down.

"Have you been to Marco's parents' place before?" al-Sharim asked.

"No, but from what he's told me, it's very nice."

The doctor digested this with the last of his coffee, tossing the cup into the back of the van, where it deflected off the stack of boxes and settled next to the lead-lined containers housing the nuclear weapons.

"Marco's father is a retired captain in the Italian navy; they have money."

Elena had started to tell al-Sharim about Marco's family—the mother he was very close to, the father he rarely talked about—when she noticed that the van behind her was accelerating and moving into the other lane.

"This idiot is trying to pass me."

The whine of the van's big engine drowned out the hum of their tires on the road. It came level with them, but then stopped accelerating, trapping them between it and the edge of the road, which fell straight down into the river at this point.

"Elena!"

Al-Sharim was pointing to a sedan in front of them, which was braking hard.

"I see it."

She braked sharply too, to avoid ramming the car, and twisted the wheel, trying to win the narrow gap between the car ahead and the van to her left. But the van accelerated at the last second, getting to the space she wanted before her, and they collided, metal rending in a banshee wail. Tires screamed and then exploded; glass smashed and erupted into the air; both airbags deployed with a loud bang.

The last image that played in her head was that of her daughter, sleeping peacefully in her bed.

Anatoly Gerashchenko sat in the backseat of the second of the two vans that had been waiting for him in Lienz. Following the progress of al-Sharim's cell phone, he had concluded that whoever had stolen the weapons was heading south—likely into Italy—and he had assembled a team of six men and two vans to be ready for him just north of the Italian border. It hadn't been easy, but he had managed, screaming orders into his cell phone as he pushed the motorcycle to its limit on the steep and winding roads. As always, working with good people—people who knew how to follow succinct orders—paid off; as he drove into Lienz, the team had been waiting for him at a pull-off on the outskirts of town, and they had caught up with their target as it negotiated a narrow road that followed a river down a steep valley.

Gerashchenko braced himself as the lead van accelerated into the other lane, trapping the vehicle with the weapons. It slammed on the brakes, causing a cacophony of shrieking tires as all the vans skidded to a halt. Lifting the Vektor out of its chest holster, he waited until his vehicle had stopped completely, then yanked open the door and hopped out, the other men in the van following him. He reached the front of the UPS van and peered inside. The driver, a woman in her thirties, was unconscious; her head sagged against the inflated airbag, and a stream of blood flowed out of her mouth. The passenger airbag had also deployed; in this case, the unconscious form belonged to Dr. al-Sharim.

Gerashchenko ran forward; the sedan was extracting itself from the site of the collision. He inspected the car briefly; the rear left panel was dented, but the tires were intact. He gesticulated in the other direction, and the driver nodded, already heading away with a squeal of rubber. The lead van had sustained more damage, but its tires too were untouched. He leaned in to the open passenger window, locking eyes with the driver.

"Go!"

The van went, belching black diesel smoke. He returned to the UPS van; the occupants were still unconscious. He leveled the Vektor at the driver's head, but didn't pull the trigger as another thought leapt into his head. There was no guard rail on the side of the road; with a little nudge from his van, he could send them into the river, avoiding the unwanted attention a shooting would create.

He jumped into the driver's seat of his own van, waited for his men to get in after loading the weapons, and twisted the wheel sharply. Maneuvering the vehicle to the other side of the UPS van, he inched forward until his front bumper came into contact with the driver's side and stomped on the gas.

His ears ached with the noise of howling tires and grating metal. The acrid smell of burning rubber filled the interior of the van. It didn't move at first, but he kept his foot down and rocked the wheel back and forth to find the best angle. Gaining some traction, it lurched forward, slowly at first, but gaining speed as its big engine screamed in full thrust.

He kept his foot down on the accelerator as long as he dared, lifting it at the last moment to smash down on the brake as the UPS van toppled over the edge. His own vehicle skidded to a halt only a meter from the abyss, but he didn't waste time getting out to confirm the kill. It was almost 6 a.m. by now, and the light was growing; they had been lucky so far, but he wasn't one to press his luck. Shifting into reverse, he backed away from the edge, swinging the van around in the direction of the village at the base of the hill, and set off, nice and slow, like a tourist on a sightseeing trip or a worker getting paid by the hour. The river surged to his right, filling the morning with the placid tones of its coursing down the valley.

It was the water—cold and pure from the melting glacier two thousand meters above them—that snapped Elena out of the fog in which she had been enveloped. Awareness came slowly, creeping into her brain like the slowly dawning day. By the time she was fully conscious, the van was nearly fully flooded; only her head remained above water. She groped around with her right hand, looking for the knife al-Sharim had stolen from the prince's bodyguard. It found her, slicing into her probing finger.

Ignoring the pain from the wound, she grabbed the hilt, using the blade to slice through the seat belts, then stabbing the airbag. The pressure released with a loud hiss, and the level of water in the van sank a little as space opened up. She leaned over, repeating the same process for al-Sharim, who remained knocked out.

She tried the door on her side, but it was hopelessly jammed from the impact of the other van. Taking a deep breath from the now small layer of air remaining inside the vehicle, she wriggled over to the other seat, a maneuver that allowed her to see into the back of the van. The weapons for which she and the others had risked their lives were gone, but there was no time to lament their loss; there was little enough air remaining. Twisting the latch, she pushed the door wide—or tried to, but it stuck early in its swing, giving her only a few centimeters of clearance. She pummeled it with her fists, but her efforts produced nothing more than a few high-pitched creaks, which she felt more than heard, rippling through her chest with a palpable wave.

The air was almost gone when her head hit the ceiling of the van. She gathered what she could in loud whoops, then somersaulted around and kicked at the door with all her strength. The first kick achieved nothing, but the second and third widened the gap some, and she kept at it, desperation lending a feral power to her legs. Her chest tightened, but she didn't stop hammering the door until it was open wide enough for her to slip through.

She rose to the top for more air, but there was none. Flipping around again, she thrust down with short strokes of her arms and squirmed through the opening, tearing a few buttons from her blouse. Safely through, she turned around, grabbed the comatose doctor, and started pulling him out, her lungs screaming at her. He was halfway through when his belly stuck—a consequence of too many heavy Austrian meals—and her arms went numb with the strain. Her lungs suggested she leave him—at least for a breath of air—but she doubted she'd be able to swim back against the current.

With all the energy remaining in her, she tugged one last time, succeeding in freeing him from the van. Now that they were no longer anchored to the heavy vehicle, the surge of water grabbed them, carrying them away in a tumble. They broke the surface downstream; Elena gasped for air, coughing up part of the river as she did so. When her lungs no longer burned from the want of oxygen, she started for the opposite shore, stroking with one arm as she dragged al-Sharim with the other.

The far bank of the river was rocky and steep; she scrambled up, slipping on the slick stones. Gaining a decent purchase, she yanked the doctor out of the water, leaving him supine on the rocks. His dark skin was pale, his lungs didn't heave, and his eyes remained shuttered behind his heavy lids. She pried his mouth open to breathe some air into his starved lungs, wishing she'd listened more carefully the last time she had taken basic life support. Cupping her hands together, she pressed down on his chest, causing a small spurt of water to spill out of his mouth. She continued the compressions as the wail of sirens lifted from the valley below her.

The second wave of compressions achieved the desired effect. She had just finished a particularly stout push, accompanied by a sharp cracking sound, when his eyes opened, and he started coughing up a lungful of water. Rolling him over onto his side, she waited as he sucked in air with gasps loud enough to drown out the roar of the river and the ever louder scream of approaching rescue vehicles.

She helped him to a sitting position, propping him up against a moss-covered rock. It would have been sensible to give him a minute, but she could see the vehicles advancing on them and did not want to be here when they arrived.

"Let's go."

He nodded, but his legs were too weak to stand. She tried to hoist him up, but he was heavy, and her strength was mostly spent. There was only one way out of their predicament, and it was back in the river. She waded in, waist deep at the shoreline, and pulled him with her. He flopped in with a splash of water that cascaded over the rocks.

They eased out into the stream, locked together with out-stretched arms. The river was flatter and slower here for a short way, but not for long. As the vehicles screamed past them, hidden by the high bank, the current picked up speed. Strokes were no longer needed, nor possible for that matter, their free limbs being required for fending off boulders and partially submerged trees.

Down they went, propelled by the spate, to the accompaniment of the splash of the river over the many cascades, the pounding of the water against the banks, and the frolic of the stream as it bounced off the rocks. The journey wasn't long—although it seemed an eternity to the exhausted Elena—and they neared the bottom of the course as daylight came in earnest. Having no wish to wash up in the nearby village, she steered them toward the opposite shore and helped al-Sharim onto the bank.

They rested for as long as they dared and helped each other to stand. A thick grove of evergreens beckoned; they made their way toward it, walking arm in arm to masquerade as lovers, until they reached the welcome cover and collapsed onto the ground.

CHAPTER 48

It was 6 a.m. when Marco and Sarah finally reached the clubhouse of the Alpenverein, and the darkness was stained with the first tinges of light. The clubhouse was a modest but well-kept affair, constructed, like everything else in these parts, of rough-cut pine boards and white stucco. Marco helped Sarah to a seat on a bench that overlooked Salzburg, which twinkled in the early-morning gloom, and walked around to the rear of the building to the shed where the hang-gliders were stored. He removed the padlock with a well-placed shot from his Beretta and swung the doors open. In typical Austrian style, the aircraft were stored away in an organized fashion, with labels identifying the owner and type of each individual glider. He found the training model after a short search and dragged it out onto the grass, then switched on the outdoor lamps.

He hadn't assembled a hang-glider since he'd entered the seminary, but he assumed it was similar to riding a bicycle after a long lay-off. As Sarah elevated her broken ankle on the bench and watched over his shoulder, mouthing the occasional recommendation, he pulled the folded wings out of the canvas bag, extended them, and fixed the battens. He lifted the keel underneath the sail and secured it into position, then found the rigging stored in a zippered pouch and started stringing it up. The tandem model was slightly different from the one he had used before, but with a few tries, he managed to get it right—or at least he hoped he had. As a final step, he attached the flight canopies and double-checked all the joints and wiring.

As the light continued to build, he carried the aircraft the short distance to the top of the runway, then went back to get Sarah before returning to the storage shed. He found what he was looking for right away.

She pointed to his armload of gear. "What's that?"

"Helmets and emergency parachutes."

"Brimming with confidence, I see."

"You're welcome to walk."

The second thoughts didn't commence until Marco had wriggled into the flight canopy underneath Sarah and started the pre-flight checklist. Although it was true he had been a competent pilot, he had never approached the level of expertise required to fly a tandem aircraft, even at the peak of his career. Worse yet, the director of the seminary had turned down his request to continue his hobby when he was a novitiate, citing "unreasonable danger and expense," which meant that he hadn't flown a hang-glider in almost fifteen years.

He was about to share his concerns with Sarah when the first shots rang out. He was so absorbed in his thoughts that he didn't register that they were being fired upon until the bullets began thudding into the ground to their right, spraying dirt into the air. At this point, the risk of flying the hang-glider became less than the risk of trying to outrun the shooter with both Sarah and the aircraft strapped to his back, so he gathered his feet beneath him and started running. It wasn't a textbook take-off, but they became airborne all the same. One second he was pounding down the runway; the next, he was raised up into the air as if the hand of God was holding him by the collar.

He didn't feel like he was being held in the palm of His hand for very long; they whistled past a sharp drop-off, and a downdraft caused the hang-glider to shudder violently and lose altitude. Marco wrestled with the crossbar, trying to get the nose up, but it wouldn't budge. The aircraft started to wobble, and a cold sweat washed over his face.

It was the start of a death spiral. They were going down.

Abayd saw the hang-glider on the top of the knoll, several hundred meters distant, and closed on a dead run. He considered dropping to one knee and firing, but he wasn't that good a shot, and it appeared the pilot hadn't seen them. It would be much better to get closer, especially with only a pistol at his disposal. He approached a slight swale, and the aircraft disappeared from his view. When he crested the dip in the terrain, it was still on the knoll in front of him. The light was dim, but he thought he made out two figures underneath the sail. He smiled crookedly and chugged on, still unobserved.

The smile didn't last. The sound of gunshots erupted from behind him, and he saw the hang-glider rise into position. Ibrahim had given them away, and the glider was going to take off. Realizing that he would lose his line of fire as soon as the aircraft went below the hill, he looked around for a better shooting position. A protuberance arose from the ground to his left, and he ran in that direction. The glider moved down the incline and disappeared from his view, but he realized he would still have a shot if he could get to the peak quickly. He willed his shaky legs to pump up the rocky incline, fueling his surge with a raw hatred. After another few seconds, he threw himself flat on the top, holding his pistol with both hands. Looking right, he saw that the wind was pushing the target hard to port, keeping it within range. He drew a bead on the sail and waited for it to clear the land obstructing his view. He estimated he would have at least three seconds of firing time before the glider disappeared behind a massive outcrop. At a range of only fifty meters and with a clear line of fire, he couldn't possibly miss.

His enemies flew into sight. He fired three quick shots, but misjudged the hang-glider's speed, and the bullets went wide. He swung his arms faster, ignoring the searing pain from his wounds, and caught up with the hurtling aircraft. He waited until he had swiveled past the target, then fired again, leaving his finger down.

But the hang-glider was no longer there. Even as his finger whitened on the trigger, a slipstream grabbed the aircraft and yanked it down, pulling it beneath the lethal hail of bullets.

Marco would never fully understand what had saved them. As a man of faith, he wanted to believe it had been divine intervention, but his feelings of unworthiness made him unsure. One thing, however, was for sure: he had poured out his soul in prayer as the nose of the hang-glider dropped farther, and then a gust of wind had lifted the nose up, and they were floating again. His heart beat so hard he was sure Sarah could feel it as she lay piggybacked on top of him, snuggled into the canopy. Or maybe it was her heartbeat he was feeling.

He shifted his weight, and the glider banked into a long, sweeping turn to the south. He could see the Berchtesgadener Tal stretching out in front of him like a wide green highway. They soared with the wind at their backs, quickly putting the Untersberg behind them, and settled into a serpentine course in the direction of Berchtesgaden.

The hang-glider passed out of view below a ledge, and for a minute Abayd was convinced his enemies had been dashed against the rocks below. But then he saw it again, turning gracefully in a wide arc to the south. He lifted his weapon instinctively, but the glider was well out of range, and he stuffed the weapon into his coat in frustration.

He slid down the outcrop and reached the bottom as Ibrahim approached, huffing and puffing loud enough to wake the dead. Abayd was about to lay into him for firing too soon, but Ibrahim pointed to the eastern sky, where the prince's helicopter could be seen approaching at high speed. In a few minutes, they heard the *whomp-whomp* of the rotors as it came overhead, circling for a place to land.

Abayd waited impatiently as Haddad brought the helicopter down on a flat piece of ground. He ran to the open door with the rotors still chopping the air at a furious pace, dragging Ibrahim by the arm, and moved forward into the cockpit.

"Did you see a hang-glider on your way up?"

Haddad nodded.

"We need to catch up with it."

CHAPTER 49

Pietro sat in an unmarked van in a pull-off just south of Berchtesgaden and hoisted his binoculars to scan the horizon, seeing nothing but the dark silhouette of the Untersberg against the brightening sky. He had been looking at the same thing for the past thirty minutes, ever since he had arrived after picking up one of the vans at the farmhouse and driving over. He was about to put his glasses down when he spied it: an orange and blue dot several kilometers to the north, making its descent into the valley.

He didn't hear the helicopter until moments later, and he followed the sound to see the sleek form of the Sikorsky cresting the ridgeline to his east and taking an intercepting path toward the glider. He threw open the black case lying on the folded-down passenger seat, yanked the metal tube out, and hopped out of the van with the Stinger missile launcher already mounted on his shoulder. He slid his eye behind the optical guidance instrument and located the Sikorsky in the viewfinder. He partially depressed the trigger, and the alarm warbled, then flexed his finger firmly, sending the missile streaking to the target.

Haddad eased the helicopter up and over the ridge, bringing the next valley into view. He saw the hang-glider at once, almost dead ahead, making its landing approach. He didn't bother to inform Abayd, because he could feel the hydraulic door sliding open, and hear the rush of the wind pouring into the cabin, slowing them down. As he turned slightly to the north in an effort to bring them behind the glider, he saw the tiny flash out of the corner of his eye. Haddad recognized a missile launch when he saw one, and he had not graduated with distinction from the naval flight school in Pensacola just by chance. He jabbed the countermeasures button with his finger and steered the Sikorsky into a steep dive as the launcher in the rear of the aircraft began spitting out magnesium flares at a rapid rate, filling the sky with thermal signatures identical to the helicopter's engines. He estimated the time to impact was three seconds, and he counted down in his head.

Three.

The bird continued to dive at the valley below. The pine-covered slopes rushed up to meet them.

Two.

Haddad ejected a dozen flak grenades, which were timed to explode and drape a curtain of shrapnel across the path of the missile.

One.

He leveled out the stick, narrowly avoiding a large church set at the top of a mountain pasture.

Zero.

Marco heard the helicopter before he saw it, as the engine strained to carry it. He looked right. It was still several kilometers away, but closing fast. He pulled the nose of the glider down as hard as he could, mumbling a quick prayer for aid.

The white plume of the missile appeared in front of him and streaked toward the helicopter, reaching out like the hand of God to clear the invader from the skies. The helicopter dove immediately and began ejecting flares, which burned like stars in the murky light. The missile exploded behind him, and he knew it had missed, because he could still hear the *whomp-whomp* of the rotors cutting through the air.

He had gained precious time, however, and the ground was rushing up to meet him. He could feel a warmness covering his body, and he wasn't sure if it was a sign from God or his own body responding to Sarah as the descent forced her against him. A hay field appeared in the distance, and he pulled down on the crossbar with everything he had.

Pietro was not surprised to see the flares erupt from the helicopter. When you were the fifth richest man in the world, your aircraft came with all the bells and whistles. He wasn't worried, though, because Lucci had somehow obtained the latest Stinger missile, a new-generation model with an advanced infrared guidance system that wouldn't be confused by flares. He watched it fly through them and turn toward the diving bird. His mouth dropped when the missile exploded well behind the target, a victim of a flak grenade. The helicopter shook slightly from the concussion, but righted quickly and made a sharp turn toward the glider, which had begun descending in earnest.

Pietro jumped back in the van and gunned the engine, accelerating across the road and onto a tractor path leading to the neatly manicured fields. He let the empty launch tube slide to the floor and grabbed another item from the case, an M-84 semi-automatic grenade launcher. It wasn't the best weapon to bring down a helicopter, but it wasn't bad. The biggest problem was range; without any internal guidance, he needed to be close. He kept his foot down on the gas pedal and swerved onto a flat wooden bridge crossing a small stream. He could see that the glider was still suspended in the air, at least a hundred meters off the ground. The helicopter closed from behind, making up the lost time with a quick spurt and a roar of its engines.

He needed to go faster, but the rough track wouldn't allow greater speed. Through the windshield, he could see the chopper swinging to his right, opening up a firing angle for the men inside the aircraft. The cabin door was already open, and the helicopter was gaining rapidly. In a few more seconds, the hang-glider would be at point blank range, and the men inside would cut Marco and Sarah into ribbons.

Pietro didn't want that to happen. He slammed on the brakes and pulled hard on the wheel, sending the van into a skid. The vehicle slid to a halt, and he grabbed the M4 carbine from its case. Although the range was still much too great for the grenade launcher, the chopper was plenty close enough for the rifle. He kicked the door open and aimed in one swift motion, then pulled the trigger.

Abayd heard the missile explode behind him and concluded that his luck had finally changed. On a night during which everything had gone wrong, a scrap of depleted uranium had intercepted a Stinger missile locked onto the helicopter. It was time to press the attack. He shouted some orders into his headset, and Haddad broke off his evasive maneuvers and resumed tracking the target. As a frequent passenger in a helicopter, Abayd hated Stinger missiles, but he knew it was a single-launch weapon, and he doubted his enemies had a spare. They were far too expensive to carry two.

He saw the glider making a steep descent and screamed at Haddad to go faster. The engines whined in response, making the cacophony in the cabin almost unbearable. The wind whistled through the open cabin door, and the floor vibrated with the strain of the overworked engines. He pulled his pistol out of its holster and watched the glider's advantage shrink. He resisted the temptation of a mid-range shot and waited for the range to be point blank. He had a limited supply of ammunition, and he had to make every shot count.

Bullets struck the undercarriage of the helicopter, and Haddad banked sharply. The glider disappeared. Abayd yelled at the pilot to resume course, but the aircraft continued to swerve away from the target.

"Haddad!"

"We're taking fire, Abayd."

"Go back!"

Haddad didn't reply, but there was no change in direction. Abayd stepped forward into the cockpit and put his gun to the pilot's head. He pressed the barrel firmly into his temple and left it there until the chopper swung back in pursuit of the hang-glider. When it caught up, he removed the gun and shuffled to the window. The glider was only thirty meters to his right. He could see the passenger piggybacked on top of the pilot, and he drew a bead and squeezed the trigger.

Sarah heard the whine of the helicopter's engines and knew it was coming back for the kill. She looked down and saw the ground beneath them, tantalizingly close, but still far enough away to afford the helicopter another pass. Looking back and to her left, she saw it coming on, slicing through the air. Several hundred meters ahead, she spotted the van raising a cloud of dust as it hurtled toward them. Underneath her, she could feel Marco's shoulder muscles straining to hasten their descent. She wished there was something *she* could do, other than lie in the canopy and await her fate.

Marco shifted his weight, and the hang-glider banked evasively, but the chopper was the more agile craft, and it followed easily, shrinking their lead. Sarah took her hands off the crossbar and reached back, managing to free the Browning from its holster and pull it out as the helicopter appeared in her peripheral vision. She switched the gun to her left hand as the aircraft approached from

THE VATICAN CONSPIRACY 315

that side and waited for her moment. In normal circumstances, she was dead on with the Browning from inside fifty meters, but the circumstances were far from normal.

The Sikorsky pulled even with them, and a man appeared in the open doorway, raising his arm into shooting position. Marco adjusted course again, opening up a better angle, and Sarah raised her gun and fired.

The bullet struck Abayd in the shoulder, spinning him around, and his shots went wide. He tried to bring his weapon to bear again, but his arm was useless, and he gave up the attempt.

"Haddad, close the door."

He waited for the door to slide shut, then went forward again, slumping into the co-pilot's seat. "Bring them down."

Haddad hesitated for a second, but then jerked the stick violently to the right, steering the helicopter straight toward the hang-glider.

The van braked to a halt, and Pietro jumped out with the grenade launcher in hand and threw himself to the ground. The glider had gone off course and was just above a stand of pines at the edge of the field; the helicopter was directly behind it and closing swiftly. He put his eye behind the scope and centered the cross hairs on the target, but was unable to do so without aiming at the glider as well.

The distance between the two aircraft narrowed, and he decided he couldn't wait any longer. He squeezed the trigger, and a 40mm grenade was launched at the target. The expanding gases from the first firing pushed the next round into the chamber, and he fired again, and kept firing until the revolving magazine was empty and a series of explosions lit up the dawn like so many strikes of lightning.

*

Marco saw the helicopter coming right at them and knew he wasn't going to land in time. He crossed himself, beseeched the Savior for a merciful judgment, and said a quick prayer for Sarah's eternal soul. He certainly didn't welcome death, but it did have a silver lining: at least he didn't have to have the *I can never see you again because I'm a priest* talk, the one that was already forming in his head like a thunderstorm over the Ligurian Sea.

He heard an explosion from somewhere ahead of him and felt the sail vibrate as if being buffeted by a crosswind. More explosions followed, from above and below. A large gash opened up in the sail, and the glider started to yaw. He could feel himself dropping, as if gravity had rediscovered his true mass. Then the helicopter exploded above him, with a shock wave that ripped away half of the sail. Something large and hard, a piece of the engine, perhaps, struck him on the helmet, and his vision went blurry and then dark. He felt himself descending in a slow spin like refuse flushed down a drain, until his momentum was arrested, and he was left hanging in the air, suspended and teetering between heaven and hell.

And then the arms of the lost souls grabbed him and pulled him down into the netherworld, from where there could be no return.

CHAPTER 50

Pietro Ferraro stood in the doorway of his mother's kitchen. As he'd known she would be, his mother was standing at the stove, with her back toward him, head down, eyes presumably fixed on what she was preparing. From the sharp aroma of capers and the pungent scent of garlic, he guessed she was making caponata, which had always been his favorite dish. He came up to her from behind and hugged her with all his strength, realizing from the vibrations he could feel emanating from her lungs that she was sobbing. Unable to stop his own tears, they cried in synchrony, the quiet heaving of their chests drowned out by the whirring of the ceiling fan overhead.

After a time, Pietro released his mother, dipped his finger into the caponata, and left the kitchen, heading for the porch, where he knew his father would be standing, gazing at Monte Gallo, drinking wine and smoking his favorite cigar. His mother said nothing as he walked out, but he could feel her gaze on him, as heavy on his back as the salty flavor of the caponata was on his tongue.

He passed the pool and approached the porch. The sweet smell of cigar smoke was the first clue that he had been right about his father's location. He turned the corner, hopped onto the teak decking, and walked past the wicker table on which a bottle of limoncello thawed next to two full glasses. Eduardo Ferraro looked exactly the same as the last time Pietro had seen him, the day he had left Pagliarelli in the back of a hearse.

"It's good to see you, Pietro."

Pietro nodded.

"Welcome back."

"I'm afraid I can't stay long."

"Why not? This is your home." Eduardo waved his thick forearm, indicating the stony massif of Monte Gallo to their north and the blue waters of the Bay of Palermo below them.

"Pietro Ferraro is dead."

"Then who are you?"

"I'm not sure, really."

"What will you do?"

Pietro shrugged. "Cardinal Lucci has something for me."

"What is it?"

"I don't know; I came here first."

"Where have you been? That business in Austria ended three weeks ago."

"I had some things to take care of."

Eduardo took another sip of the white wine he drank from noon until midnight every day, and puffed on the cigar.

"What kind of things?"

Pietro shrugged.

"Something to do with your new pal Lucci?"

"He's my godfather."

A Bonelli's eagle soared overhead in the cobalt sky, floating on the thermals that came off the dusty peak of Monte Gallo.

"How long will you be staying?"

"I told you; I can't stay."

"If you're not staying, why did you come?"

"I came to say goodbye."

Eduardo set down his wine and picked up a glass of limoncello, offering it to his son. Pietro made no move to take it.

"I can't."

"Why not?"

"Because I promised Cardinal Lucci I wouldn't."

"I don't care what you promised Lucci."

"I do."

They stood without speaking, listening to the faint sound of the waves breaking against the shore and the whisper of the wind through the umbrella pines.

"Do you know why I want you to drink the limoncello?"

"Yes, I do. It's a rite of passage into the family business. I did it once. I won't do it again."

"It's more than that." Eduardo put the glass down and held up his hands. The thick fingers were bent and knobby; a simple wedding band adorned his left ring finger. "My hands look like this because I dropped out of school to work in the sulfur mines. It was the only way I could earn enough money to eat."

He lowered his hands and used one to grab his wine glass.

"I promised myself I would never allow my children and grandchildren to have to choose between eating and going to school. When I see you drink the limoncello, I know you and your children will never have to make that choice."

The eagle screamed, loud and shrill. In the distance, its mate responded, or perhaps it was just an echo off the limestone bluffs.

"I'll be fine."

"You think so?"

"Yes."

Eduardo scowled, a look that fit his countenance well. "You're too young to understand. When you're old like me, then you'll realize what you passed up."

Pietro turned to go, accidentally bumping into the wicker table as he did so.

"It's never too late to change your mind. I'll always be here for you."

He walked off the porch, taking one last look back at his father. Eduardo was standing in the same spot in which Pietro had found him, staring in the same direction. Behind him, on the table, one of the glasses had tipped over, seeping sweet and sticky liquid into a yellow pool on the tray.

CHAPTER 51

"Mass is ended. Go in peace."

It was a sentiment with which Marco concurred, even if he wasn't sure he would ever find peace again. There were moments, certainly, like now, when all he could hear was the pope's smooth baritone as he said the Eucharistic prayer and all he could smell was the cloying reek of incense, when the harsh report of gunshots and the velvety stink of blood vacated his mind, but they never lasted very long, the vivid memories returning whenever there was nothing else to distract him.

The pope dismissed the small congregation, consisting mainly of maids, gardeners, and other members of the staff at Castel Gandolfo, and stood next to Marco as he watched them file out. When the last of the mass attendees had dipped their fingers into the font of holy water, made a hasty sign of the cross and exited the chapel, he waved for Marco to follow him and strode off. Passing by the large baroque cross Bernini had carved for Pope Alexander VII in 1650, he weaved through an open marble archway made by the same sculptor and stopped in front of the door to his private study, which was the only room in the entire Apostolic Palace in which Marco had not set foot. He opened the door, allowing Marco inside, and then slipped in behind him and closed the door, using the same skeleton key to lock it.

The study was not a large room. It consisted of two long walls adorned by murals and a short wall on the opposite end that was hidden by the bulk of a huge mahogany desk. Tall spires shot upward from the back of the desk, giving it the appearance of a cathedral. The pope gestured for Marco to sit down in the chair in front of it.

"Thanks for coming down from Monterosso, Marco."

"It's good to be here, Holiness."

Marco had seen the pope after returning from Austria, meeting him in a rectory overlooking the city of Florence so that he could tell him what had happened in Salzburg. The pope had listened quietly for the most part, asking only a few questions, most of those relating to Marco's welfare and how Elena was doing. When the invite to Castel Gandolfo had come, Marco had taken it as a sign that the pontiff harbored no hard feelings about him skulking off to Austria behind his back.

"Will you be staying long?"

"Just overnight, I'm afraid."

"Then I will ask you now."

"Ask me what, Holiness?"

The pope paced back and forth in front of a large mural depicting Adam and Eve in the Garden of Eden, a replica of Michelangelo's *Temptation* and *Expulsion* frescoes on the ceiling of the Sistine Chapel, the first depicting Adam and Eve being tempted by the snake with a woman's head—Marco thought she looked a lot like Sarah—and the second picturing them being expelled, ashamed, and in anguish, after eating the forbidden fruit.

"I want you to do something for me."

Marco waited for the pope's request, but he didn't speak, continuing to pace back and forth, back and forth, walking from *Temptation* to *Expulsion* and then *Expulsion* to *Temptation*, the human journey in a microcosm, until at last he stopped in front of the mahogany desk.

"Let me show you something."

Producing another key from the depths of his flowing purple robes, he unlocked the lower right-hand drawer and extracted a document contained in a plastic bag, setting it down on the desk.

"Do you know what this is?"

Marco recognized the lead bulla stamped with the Ring of the Fisherman. "Yes, it's a papal bull."

"Read it, please, aloud."

Marco switched on the desk lamp, which, in contrast to everything else in the study, was modern and functionally designed. He remembered seeing a similar lamp at IKEA. Starting at the top, where the words 'John Paul III' began the document, he read it through, not stopping until he reached the seal at the bottom. In between, with simple and direct wording and in the pope's own cursive, Pope John Paul III declared that birth control and homosexuality were no longer sins, and that women and married persons of either sex would no longer be barred from the priesthood, summarily reversing the Church's long-standing doctrine on these issues.

"What do you think?"

"I'm not sure I know what to say."

The pope grabbed the document, holding it gingerly by the loose end of plastic at the top, and deposited it back in the drawer.

"My reaction was quite the same."

"Your reaction, Holiness?"

"Yes, when I found it on my desk after you saved my life in Vatican City."

"You didn't write this bull?"

The pope removed his white zucchetto, adjusted the chamois liner, and placed it back on top of his tight gray curls. "No, but it is an amazing forgery, don't you think?"

"Yes, I do."

"I fear we have an even greater enemy than the men who brandished guns against us."

He walked over to the far side of the room, gazing at the mural there depicting the Crusaders defending the Holy Land against the Saracens.

"I fear we have an enemy in our midst."

He walked back to the desk and removed several other items from the drawer, dumping a bag of white powder and a stack of pornographic magazines on the desktop.

"If you had not saved my life in Piazza San Pietro, they would have come in here to clean out my study and found these as well." He held Marco in his gaze. "You see, Marco, they didn't want to just kill me; they wanted to discredit me, so that another reformer pope doesn't rise from my ashes."

He returned the items to his drawer, locked it, and put the key back inside his robes.

"It's ironic, because I have considered doing all the things decreed in this fake papal bull, but I held back because of the Curia's extreme resistance to such measures. The Church is weak enough; I'm not sure we would survive it. At best, it would lead to discord that would make the Great Schism seem like a petty squabble."

In 1054, a succession of theological disputes and political differences had led to a break in the communion of what were now the Roman Catholic and Eastern Orthodox churches, which had remained separate since that day.

"I want to unify the Catholic Church, not further divide it. So I have never said anything about these issues. But now I have half a mind to walk down to the Holy Office and just drop that document on Cardinal Garcia's desk."

It was well known that Cardinal Garcia, the chief executive of the Congregation for the Doctrine of the Faith, despised the pope; Marco got the impression that the feeling was mutual.

"Just to see the look on his face might be worth the trouble it would cause."

The pope shuffled over to an armchair the color of burnished bronze, which creaked in protest as he settled into it.

"I'm sorry to burden you, Father Marco, I really am, but I wanted to tell someone about this. And frankly, I'm not sure who else I can trust."

"What about Cardinal Lucci?"

"What about him?"

"You can trust him, can't you?"

The pope leaned back in his chair to consider the question.

"Cardinal Lucci was one of the favorites prior to the last papal conclave, and he made no secret about being disappointed with my election."

"Why did you appoint him to the Secretariat, then?"

"He is an excellent statesman; I will give him that. But that wasn't the reason I gave him the job."

The pope paused, resting his chin on his clasped hands as he searched for the right words.

"I gave him the job because I believe in keeping my friends close, but my enemies closer."

"Is it often that the servant of the servants of God quotes from *The Art of War*?"

"More often than you would think."

He got up and walked over to the desk, using a lighter to fire up the incense burner that sat there. When the sweet aroma of sandalwood had permeated the air, he sat down again.

"But to be fair, Cardinal Lucci has served us all well. And I had started to learn to trust him until …"

"Until?"

"Until I found the items I just showed you."

The pope produced the key he had been using to open the doors and tossed it to Marco.

"There are only three keys to these apartments. I have this one with me at all times; Sister Margarita, the head of the housekeepers, has the second one, and a legion of archangels couldn't take it from her; Cardinal Lucci is in charge of the third."

The smell of sandalwood thickened in the stagnant air. The Apostolic Palace had been retrofitted with air conditioner many years ago, but the pope refused to use it in his study and in many other rooms, despite the clamoring of the palace's curator, who was concerned about the effect of the excessive heat on its many paintings and murals.

"Giampaolo Benedetto is accountable for much of what happened, yes, but he is not solely accountable. He had help from within our ranks, and I want to know from whom. You will be my eyes and my ears."

It seemed like more of an order than a request, but then again, Marco wasn't going to say no, and they both knew it.

"Am I not going back to Monterosso, Holiness?"

"Yes, you are, but I am certain that opportunities will arise in the future, perhaps the very near future. When they do, I want you to be ready."

The pope fixed Marco with his large brown eyes.

"Will you be ready?"

Marco nodded.

"That's good, because the stakes are higher than ever. The enemy has nuclear weapons, and we have to find them before they are used against us. Which brings me to my last question. When you think back to your trip to Salzburg, is there anything that might shed light on the issue of help from within the Holy See?"

It was a question Marco had spent time considering, especially when Father DiPietro, an inveterate conspiracy theorist, had come to visit him at the rectory and insinuated the same thing.

"There was one thing, Holiness."

"Yes?"

"In the garage at Haus Adler, there were two maintenance trucks from the Vatican's fleet."

"Are you sure?"

"Yes, they both had the crossed silver and gold keys emblem, and the tags both started with SCV."

"Did you mention this to Cardinal Lucci?"

"Of course. He said he would look into it."

"He told me the same thing when I asked him if he thought Benedetto had inside help."

"And did he look into it?"

"Not in the two weeks I gave him; he claimed—and with some justification—that he had been busy with other matters. I insisted he delegate the task, and he did, to Cardinal Scarletti, in early August."

The pope got up stiffly and started to pace again, this time with a decidedly unsteady gait. It was common knowledge that he had a badly arthritic hip that he refused to have replaced; he had taken to getting around with the long staff he had brought back from Nigeria.

"Scarletti made some enquiries, or so he said, but he didn't get any further than Lucci in the end. But this business about the maintenance trucks is interesting."

"Why couldn't Benedetto have obtained them for the prince?"

The pope got a chuckle out of this.

"You haven't met Cardinal Kowalcyzk, the head of the Department of Technical Services. He hates Benedetto as much as he hates the devil himself, perhaps more. The last interaction they had was a shouting match several months ago that almost ended up as a boxing match; let me assure you, Kowalcyzk didn't lend a pair of his precious trucks to Benedetto. Those trucks are proof that Benedetto did have help."

Marco inspected the key one last time, as if close scrutiny might discover a clue engraved into the metal, then stood up and walked over to the pope, handing it back.

"I should tell you that Cardinal Lucci is also friendly with Cardinal Kowalcyzk."

Marco stared at the pontiff, but his round face was impassive.

"It doesn't make any sense, Holiness. If Cardinal Lucci wanted to kill you, why did he go to all that trouble to assassinate the prince in Austria?"

"Let's assume for a minute that Lucci is the traitor, that he wants to kill me because he disagrees with everything I have said and done … because he wants to be pope himself … because he believes deep down that I am destroying the Catholic Church to which he has dedicated his life."

Marco felt a chill settle in his spine; perhaps the air conditioner had been switched on?

"As Secretary of State, Lucci worked with Benedetto all the time; he would be aware of the man's hatred of me, and possibly also know about his dire financial situation. Again, as Secretary of State, with full responsibility for our relationship with the Middle East, he would be cognizant of Prince Kamal el-Rayad and his desire to avenge his ancestor and fulfill his destiny to destroy Vatican City."

The pope looked up from the floor and gazed at Marco instead.

"Do you understand what I am saying?"

Marco nodded, understanding very well; he grabbed a tissue from the box on the desk and wiped away the cold sweat from his face.

"I am sure Lucci—or whoever *il traditore* is—did not intend for the prince to actually destroy Vatican City, but when five vanloads of plastic explosives were found in that warehouse, he realized he had made a grave error.

"And that, Marco, explains why the traitor went to all the trouble of killing the prince in Austria."

CHAPTER 52

Vincenzo Lucci had been living inside the walls of Vatican City for over a decade. It was rumored there wasn't one square meter inside the forty-four hectares of grounds that hadn't been trod over by his Sicilian sandals. But it was a rumor without merit—although Lucci had never done anything to put it to rest. In truth, there were several areas he had never visited, most due to happenstance and the vastness of the area inside the ancient walls, but only one he had purposely avoided.

He slipped out of the side door of the Holy Office, where he had been having yet another meeting with Cardinal Garcia, and started working his way up Vatican Hill. The spot he had intentionally never set foot on was an intimate corner of a tiny garden attached to the Ethiopian College, a spot widely regarded as the current pope's favorite place to reflect and pray—which was the sole reason Lucci chose never to go there.

He shivered in the growing breeze that hinted of boxwood and a storm blowing in from the Tyrrhenian Sea, and buttoned his black overcoat as he climbed toward the monument to St. Peter that rose into the gray September sky in front of him. He turned on to the Via dell'Osservatorio and walked past an Australian bunya tree. One of its massive pine cones lay on the cobbled path, and he gave it a swift kick, sending it flying into the air. A gust of wind caught it and sent it tumbling into the gardens of exotic plants adorning the rock that flanked the street. At the top of the road, he stopped in front of the building Pope Pius XI had commissioned to further the ecclesiastical studies of seminarians from Ethiopia. He had nothing against the place, per se, but its special significance to Pope John Paul III repelled him like the statue of the owl repelled the pigeons from roosting on its roof.

He found the Holy Father sitting on a stone bench overlooking the Fontana dei Delfini. The pontiff was leaning forward, resting against the mahogany walking stick he had brought back from his shortened trip to Nigeria. Lucci had seen him on only two occasions since his return; once to tell him of the aborted plot to annihilate Vatican City in a nuclear firestorm, and the other at a formal Curial dinner a few weeks later.

"Your Holiness."

The pope nodded at the seat next to him, and Lucci sat down, disappearing behind the fronds of a banana tree.

"What do you hear from Father Venetti, Eminence? I understand you saw him recently."

Lucci had been expecting this question. It was no secret that the pope was quite fond of the Jesuit priest from Monterosso, and it had been a few weeks since Lucci had arranged for the two of them to meet in Florence.

"I had some business in Milan. On the way back, I stopped in Monterosso to see how he was. I suppose he is well enough."

"Well enough?"

"Yes, considering everything he has been through."

The breeze picked up, carrying with it a line of low gray clouds that scudded over the ancient walls.

"What now, Eminence?"

"Now we carry on like we have for over two thousand years."

"That sounds like something I would say."

"Perhaps you are rubbing off on me, Holiness."

"Let us pray I don't. That isn't the reason I decided to appoint you as Secretary of State. Nor is it the reason I didn't interfere with the deal you made with the Americans."

The air stuck in Lucci's throat, just for a second, but long enough for him to feel it sitting there, like a large hairball in his craw.

"You knew about my deal with the Americans?"

"I am not the doddering old fool you think me."

"How did you find out?"

The pope gave a dismissive wave, then rose and walked over to the large pomegranate tree bordering the walkway. He plucked off one of the dark red fruits and tossed it up and down. "Do you know what happened after the Saracens razed St. Peter's Basilica in 846?"

"Yes, Holiness, I do. Pope Leo IV built walls around the Vatican. I just walked past them on the way up."

"He also made an alliance with the fleets of Naples, Amalfi, and Gaeta to defend Rome from the Saracen fleet massing in Sardinia. The attackers were destroyed off Ostia."

"Aren't you the same person who told me to beware of history?"

"Yes, but I didn't think you were listening." The pope flashed his pearl-colored teeth. "I came up here the day I found out about your plan, and as I walked past those walls, it struck me: if Leo hadn't acted decisively, the whole course of history would have been changed. So I allowed your deal with the Americans to stand, and as a consequence, the basilica stands too, as do we."

He lobbed the fruit into the fountain in front of them, where it bobbed in the flow of water splashing down from above.

"And as in all wars, it is the foot soldiers who pay the biggest price."

"You are referring to Father Venetti, Holiness?"

"The Americans kept the communists out of Brazil, and you and I preserved our precious country, but what became of the man who was actually responsible?"

Lucci considered pretending he didn't know anything about Brazil's presidential election, but it was clear the pope had excellent sources of information. He let the comment go unrefuted, thereby confirming his involvement.

"He has returned to his parish, Holiness. Exactly what he requested."

The pope said nothing, but Lucci could see his disbelief in the purse of his lips and the furrow of his ebony brow. "And the nuclear weapons?"

"Do you remember me telling you I had a lead on Giampaolo Benedetto?"

The pope nodded.

"I believe we are very close to locating him. If we can find him, he may be able to lead us to the weapons."

"I assume you are making plans to apprehend him?"

Lucci nodded.

"I also assume Father Venetti will be a part of these plans?"

"Yes, Holiness, a big part. Do you have a problem with that?"

The pope didn't answer. He clapped Lucci on the shoulder with his huge hand, then started down the gravel path toward the college, using the walking stick to lead the way. Lucci watched him go, and then turned his gaze to the pomegranate, which was still pirouetting gracefully in the current.

CHAPTER 53

The night was unusually warm for September, even for the little village in Crete tucked away high in the mountains that Giampaolo Benedetto was now calling home. He paced back and forth in the lovely courtyard of the rented farmhouse on top of a hill overlooking a valley of grape arbors and olive trees, a glass of his favorite white wine in his hand—several cases of which he had had shipped here months ago—waiting for his satellite phone to ring. Cell reception was excellent in these parts, but Giampaolo had left his cell phone—as well as so many other things—back in Italy, where it could not be used to track him down.

"*Buona sera*, Giampaolo."

"*Buona sera.*"

"I trust you are well."

The electronically modulated voice was devoid of any such sentiment; Giampaolo suspected this was on account of the speaker and not the software.

"Very. You?"

"Not well, not well at all."

"How unfortunate. Hopefully it's nothing serious."

"Of course it's serious. That Nigerian impostor still wears the Ring of the Fisherman."

It was true. Giampaolo had just seen him on television, bragging to all who would listen that he was building a large Muslim community center in Rome, including a clinic that would provide free medical care for immigrants.

"You failed me, Giampaolo."

"On the contrary." Giampaolo took a sip of wine to give himself a second to choose the right words. "I did everything I was asked."

"Everything except for the one thing that mattered, you mean."

"Some things were out of my control."

"Quite a few things seemed to be out of your control. They intended to blow up the basilica? That was not part of the plan."

The voice stopped speaking; in its place, Giampaolo's ear was filled with the bleating of goats and the barking of the dog assigned to herd them.

"St. Peter's Basilica is a priceless treasure. Thank God the terrorists were stopped."

"Now you sound like the Nigerian."

"Please don't ever say that again."

It was a threat, which Giampaolo recognized despite the flat electronic tone and lack of inflection.

"I am afraid I am not going to be able to deliver the final payment of five million euros."

"That was not our arrangement."

"Do you recall telling me that you would not fail?"

"Yes, of course, and I didn't fail."

"Pope John Paul III still breathes. That is failure by my way of looking at it."

Giampaolo tried to remedy the dryness of his mouth with a large swallow of the wine, but his glass was empty. He made his way over to a rustic wooden table hewn out of the trunk of a massive fig tree, on which a bottle of Avignonesi Vin Santo di Montepulciano 1983 rested inside a marble wine cooler, and refilled his glass.

"I am going to give you another chance, however."

He took another sip, letting the subtle tone of apricot seep into his palate.

"I am very concerned that the people with whom you …
contracted will try again."

"Why is this concerning? We want the impostor killed."

The voice fell silent. If possible, the silence was more chilling
than its cold threats.

"Because I don't want them destroying St. Peter's Basilica and
perhaps all of Vatican City in the process."

Another silence. Giampaolo drank more wine.

"I don't want the next pope—and who knows who that will
be?—to celebrate his first mass in a tent erected upon the rubble
of what used to be the greatest monument to God ever created."

A cricket chirped. Another joined in, accompanying the first
in a shrill duet.

"So that means we have to kill him first. Understand?"

"Very well."

"I'll pay you ten million euros."

Another ensemble of crickets struck up from the tamarisk tree
next to the stone barn on the other side of the property.

"Half up front."

"None up front. All upon completion of the job."

The dog barked from the hill below them, causing the crickets
to cease their chorus.

"Agreed?"

"Yes, agreed."

"And one more thing …"

The crickets started back up, discordant and eerie in the night air.

"Yes?"

"I'm not a patient man. Don't fail me again."

CHAPTER 54

Marco heard the slap of feet coming down the aisle and reached for his rosary beads. For a second, he thought it was his last penitent coming back—perhaps she had forgotten one of her husband's sins—but the tread was too light. The door to his left swung open, and a woman sat down on the chair in front of him. Her face was familiar, but he couldn't quite make it out in the murky light of the confessional.

"I heard you were back."

"Elena?"

There was no mistaking that voice. He took a second look at her. Her hair was pulled back into a thick ponytail, and her skin had taken on the healthy sheen of a sun worshipper.

"Cardinal Lucci told me you had moved to Rome."

"He said my family would be better off there."

Judging by her expensive-looking black leather jacket and silk blouse, Lucci had been right.

"You look good, Elena."

"So do you."

It wasn't true, but he thanked her all the same. His cheeks had been sunken and hollow ever since he had spent three days hiding in moldy cellars, dusty hay mows, and unused garages across Germany, waiting for Pietro to get him and Sarah out of the country. Even Signora Grecci's cooking hadn't helped fatten him up, and he was starting to think he would appear malnourished to the end of his days.

"You heard about what happened to me and Dr. al-Sharim?"

He nodded. "Thank God you are both all right. I would never forgive myself if something had happened to you."

"You do remember, Marco, who got you into this in the first place?"

He did remember, with absolute clarity, that fateful afternoon in this very same confessional, recalling even the slightest details: the sheen of her long, dark hair; the sweet smell of her; the warmth that radiated from her body like an oven.

"The nuclear weapons … After everything we did, all that we risked, I feel terrible about it."

"There was nothing you could have done. It wasn't your fault."

Marco smelled the acrid reek of a smoldering Marlboro; the caretaker had come to close up the church. He felt like getting some air. "Want to take a walk?"

She nodded, and they left via the front door leading out to the cobbled piazza. It was cold for September, and the square was empty and dark. Marco threw on the wool peacoat he'd grabbed from the hook in the vestibule and led Elena to the Sentiero Azzurro. They walked side by side along the deserted path, listening to the crash of the breakers below and the rustle of the olive leaves. Something, perhaps the fresh air, sparked his appetite, and they stopped at a trattoria and shared a large bowl of *zuppa di datteri*, a soup made from the local shellfish. Marco washed it down with a carafe of Sciacchetrà; Elena drank only mineral water. She paid the bill, and they took the ferry back to Monterosso.

They disembarked and walked along the darkened quay, past the tied-up umbrellas of closed cafés and a line of abandoned benches.

"What's her name, Marco?"

"Who are you talking about?"

"The woman on your mind."

They skirted a shuttered kiosk and started ascending the stone staircase leading to the village square. "How did you know?"

"A woman knows these things."

He told her about Sarah.

"Do you love her?"

"No, I don't think so, but I think about her all the time."

They walked past the taverna, which was still buzzing with laughter, and turned into the quiet alley in front of his church.

"At night especially."

The alley let out onto the small parking lot next to the rectory, and they stopped in front of Elena's car.

"I need to see her again, to explain …"

"To explain what?"

"Why it could never work between us."

"She doesn't want to hear that. Take it from me."

"I still need to tell her. It's important to me."

A curtain flickered in an upstairs room in the rectory; Marco saw Signora Grecci peering at them from the small slit in the faded fabric.

"There might be a way. I didn't come here just to say hello."

"What are you talking about?"

"Lucci sent me."

The wind picked up, the air turned damp, and a light drizzle fell, slicking the cobbles.

"What does he want?"

"You heard about Giampaolo Benedetto?"

"The Inspector General of the Security Office? The man that conspired with the Saudis?"

"Yes, him. Lucci thinks he may have located him."

"Where?"

"In Crete."

Marco had been to Crete many times, ostensibly to practice the language, but also to stroll the paths that had been laid at the beginning of recorded time, to sip the local wine, and to taste the honey the bees made from the blossoms of the thyme that grew in abundance on the rocky slopes.

"Let me guess; he wants me to find him."

"He wants *us* to find him. I am to bring you there on a boat, and bring you and Benedetto back to Palermo after you've located him. Lucci thinks that finding Benedetto is the key to finding the nuclear weapons."

Marco waited for the pit to open in his stomach, but nothing happened. The pope had already prepared him for this moment.

'Am I not going back to Monterosso, Holiness?'

'Yes, you are, but I am certain that opportunities will arise in the future, perhaps the very near future. When they do, I want you to be ready.'

"We're supposed to leave from Palermo in a few days."

"How does this involve Sarah?"

"Lucci already asked her to help."

The wind lessened, the drizzle ended as quickly as it had started, and a patch of stars appeared on the southern horizon.

"Did she agree?"

"I think so … but I'm not sure."

"Do I have time to think about it?"

"I have to return to Rome in a few hours. I'll stop by before I leave. If you decide to go, have your bag packed." She kissed him on the cheek beneath Signora Grecci's disapproving stare and hopped into her car.

Once her taillights had disappeared behind the café on the other side of the square, Marco jogged down the stone steps leading to the beach. His old boat was gone, but another one had taken its place between the two large rocks that served as a mooring. He clambered aboard, flipped on the search beam bolted to the bow, and headed out to sea. The swell was heavy, but he had a practiced hand, and the boat had a broader keel than his last.

He docked at his usual spot and tied the line to an iron ring bored into the rock. The cove was protected, and the sea was smooth, making it easy for him to climb out with his fishing net in hand. He had inverted the search lamp, and he could see that its luminescence had already attracted a school of anchovies. He looped the cord around his wrist, tossed the net over the fish, and watched as its weighted ends closed over the prey. He pulled the cord taut and hauled the fish out of the water, depositing them in an old pail filled with seawater.

It wasn't long before the gulls found him and gobbled down his catch as fast as he could haul it in. But he didn't mind; at least they were company. When his hands had grown too cold to work the net and his ears had grown weary of the continual arguing, he returned the few remaining anchovies to their home, and boarded the boat to return to his.

About halfway back, he cut the engine, killed the light, and sat with his hands gripping the gunwale as the boat rocked in the growing swell. The pope's words floated to him on the soft night-time breeze: 'You will be my eyes and my ears.' He watched the moonlight scatter over the disquieted waters, and for a moment it was as if he had never gazed into the cold blue eyes of Cardinal Lucci or kissed the warm lips of Sarah Messier. The moment faded, and then passed altogether, and he fired up the motor and started home to pack his bag.

A LETTER FROM PETER

Dear Reader,

I want to say a huge thank you for choosing to read *The Vatican Conspiracy*. If you enjoyed it and want to keep up to date with all my latest releases, just sign up at the following link. Your email address will never be shared, and you can unsubscribe at any time.

www.bookouture.com/peter-hogenkamp

The Vatican Conspiracy is truly a book I have been writing in my head for many years. Its very first origins can be traced to my days at College of the Holy Cross, where I got to know a number of the Jesuit priests. As I interacted with them in their roles as professors, dormitory heads, and mentors, I was so impressed by their intelligence, their thoughtfulness, and most especially their humanity. I'd like to think that Father Marco was born there, on the hill overlooking Worcester, Massachusetts.

After college, I traipsed over to Europe to take a break before going to medical school. I ended up spending three years on the continent, hiking the craggy peaks overlooking Salzburg, wandering the ancient cobbled streets of Rome, and traversing the seaside cliffs of the Cinque Terre. (One thing you should know about me: I like to be in motion.) I remember taking extensive mental notes at the time, convinced I would someday write a book in which these settings would become an integral part.

There's only one more thing I wanted to say about this series, which is that writing the second instalment—which I can't wait for you to read—has been less of an exercise in writing a book and more a way to spend time with people I have gotten to know and come to miss. Marco is never very far from my mind. Even when I am not writing, I find myself wondering if he would like a book I am reading or what his opinion would be about a piece I just watched on the news. I have enjoyed listening to his thoughts again, especially about the unworthiness and doubt he feels as keenly as being pricked by a needle. And I love the courage he always shows by forging ahead in spite of them.

I hope you enjoyed *The Vatican Conspiracy*; if you did, I would be very grateful if you could write a review. I'd love to hear what you think, and it makes such a difference helping new readers to discover one of my books for the first time. And don't forget to tell your friends and family about the book. So many of my favorite books have come to me through good old-fashioned word of mouth.

I love hearing from my readers—you can get in touch on my Facebook page, as well as through Twitter, Goodreads, or my website. If you have a question, ask it; if you have a comment, make it; if you have a complaint, lodge it. Any author will tell you that you have to take the good with the bad. And oftentimes, there's something to learn from the bad. (Though I like the good comments better.☺)

Thanks,
Peter

       peterhogenkampbooks

       @phogenkampVT

       www.peterhogenkampbooks.com

       6884561.Peter_Hogenkamp

ACKNOWLEDGEMENTS

As always, thanks to my wife, Lisa. To say that I couldn't have succeeded without her is putting it mildly. And thanks to my children—Dan, Tom, Abby and Maria—for keeping me grounded and never letting me lose sight of what is important in life: my family. To Hermione, my feisty Cairn Terrier, I say thank you and promise another thousand walks. And thanks to my mother for imbuing me with her resilient nature—the best trait a writer could ever have—and to my late dad, who gifted me his love of writing and finding just the right word.

I am deeply indebted to Ruth Tross for helping me make this book into what it is. Thank you, Ruth, for your wonderful instincts and for your enthusiasm; what a pleasure and a privilege it is to work with you. And thanks to Jane Selley, the copy editor extraordinaire, for your clarity and succinctness. Many thanks also to Jon Appleton for the proofread. To the whole team at Bookouture, especially Peta Nightingale and Alexandra Holmes, I say you are simply brilliant, and I am forever thankful. To Kim Nash and Noelle Holten, the dynamic duo who helped bring *The Vatican Conspiracy* to the known world, thanks for your energy and your patience. The day I became a member of the Bookouture family will always be a landmark in my life.

There are many people who helped me deliver *The Vatican Conspiracy* into the world (and to the publisher prior to submission). In no particular order, thanks to: Thomas Cosgrove, Kirsten Klett, Liz Kracht, Tom Hogenkamp, Conrad Tuerk, Theresa Corsones, Becca Ramos, Beth Higgins, and the late Ed Callahan. To the late Betty Gralton, who gave me an old copy of Alistair MacLean's *Fear Is the Key* when I was a boy, I wish you were alive to see what you started.

I reserve the biggest thanks for you, the reader. If it wasn't for you, I would labor in vain. Nothing is more precious to an author than a reader who has enjoyed their book.

Printed in Great Britain
by Amazon